TEST OF RESOLVE

Also by Peter Murphy

Removal
A Higher Duty

TEST OF RESOLVE

PETER MURPHY

NO EXIT PRESS

First published in 2014 by No Exit Press,
an imprint of Oldcastle Books Ltd,
PO Box 394,
Harpenden, Herts,
AL5 1XJ
noexit.co.uk
@NoExitPress

ISBN
978-1-84344-188-5 (print)
978-1-84344-189-2 (epub)
978-1-84344-190-8 (kindle)
978-1-84344-191-5 (pdf)

2 4 6 8 10 9 7 5 3 1

Typeset by Avocet Typeset, Somerton, Somerset
in 10.9 on 12.5pt Garamond MT
Printed in Great Britain by Clays Ltd, St Ives plc

For more about Crime Fiction go to www.crimetime.co.uk / @crimetimeuk

For
Chris

Acknowledgements

I would like to thank Her Honour Judge Usha Kari for her help with Hindi words and phraseology. I would also like to thank my colleagues of the 'metaphysical faculty' of the law school summer programme which took me to India for the first time: Eileen Kaufman; Louise Harmon; and (sadly, the late) Surya Sinha; and my wife, Chris, who understood far more quickly than I the lack of separation between the mundane and the metaphysical which makes India so extraordinary. Their insight, wisdom, and experience was the foundation of my experience of the country.

The song I came to sing
remains unsung to this day.
I have spent my days in stringing
and in unstringing my instrument.

The time has not come true,
the words have not been rightly set;
only there is the agony
of wishing in my heart…

Rabindranath Tagore, *Waiting*

1

THE VISITOR DID not come often – not more than once every two or three years – but his routine was always the same. He would fly to Houston from Washington DC, having arrived there, Bev's family could only assume, from whichever Indian city he was currently using as his base. He would rent a medium-size car at George Bush Intercontinental Airport, and drive into the city, carefully obeying every speed limit, every stop sign. He would park near the family's home, in the anonymity of a shopping crescent on West Gray, where there was a Starbucks and a Black-Eyed Pea restaurant, and where the short stay of a nondescript rental car would not attract attention. He was always smartly dressed in a western-style suit and tie, the suit a lightweight dark gray, the tie red, worn over a pristine white shirt, his black shoes meticulously shined. He carried a smart black briefcase. All this, also, was for the sake of anonymity, of blending into the background. Bev knew from his previous conversations with him that the Visitor found western dress stifling, oppressive, and would have much preferred to be in the white Kurta pyjamas and sandals he always wore at home. But the Visitor was a man to whom detail was a way of life, because he had sometimes owed his life to the care he took over detail, and he had become an expert in the art of the inconspicuous.

The pattern of his visits never varied. He would first spend up to an hour with Bev's parents. Bev's father, Amit, was a dentist with a successful practice in the affluent River Oaks area of the city, where the family also lived in a discreet detached house guarded by a high fence. The house was not particularly large by affluent Houston standards, but it had every modern convenience, including a heated swimming pool, and was appropriate for a dentist of Amit's standing. Bev's mother, who had long ago adopted the name Marsha, had retired from her position as personal assistant to the president of a bank. The couple had lived in Houston for more than thirty years. Before moving to the United States, they had lived in New Delhi, where both had received a wide, liberal education. Amit had learned his dentistry there, pulling teeth and inserting fillings in hundred degree heat with humidity to match – much like Houston without the air conditioning, he would sometimes joke – and with geckos running up and down the walls. Despite his undoubted skills, he had to re-qualify when he arrived in America in deference to the usual institutional suspicion of foreign qualifications, an annoyance he bore with his usual stoicism.

Bev never knew exactly what passed between the Visitor and his parents. He was always sent to his room until the Visitor was ready to see him. But he knew that money changed hands. He had seen it. As an adventurous 10-year-old he had spied through a keyhole on one such meeting and had seen the Visitor remove from his briefcase wad after wad of crisp green banknotes, which he then handed to his father. Even as a 10-year-old boy, Bev found this odd. He was aware that his father earned a good living as a dentist, and that his mother was also quite capable of commanding a high salary. He did not stay at the door long enough to hear what they were discussing, which he assumed would be related to what the Visitor had to say when his turn came to meet him; but it seemed to Bev that sometimes, from his bedroom upstairs, he could hear his mother crying.

The Visitor was tall and imposing, over six feet in height, with proportionate build. He had a dignified, erect bearing, and thick gray hair, threatening to turn pure white. During his last visit, some two years ago, Bev had judged him to be between sixty and seventy years of age.

The Visitor always began by asking him about his education, on which he seemed to place great store. Through middle school and high school, Bev had to account for his grades, for any lapses in discipline, and for all his extra-curricular activities. As he grew older, there were questions about girlfriends, their names, families, areas of town, studies, ambitions, interests. He was also questioned about the family's Hindu faith. The family worshiped together regularly at a temple on Hillcroft in Houston's Indian district, just a short drive from home.

When the Visitor had last spoken with him, Bev had not found it difficult to reassure him. By that time, his high school grades and activities had taken him to Rice University, where he was majoring in politics with a minor in history. He was working hard and doing well. His love for football was still with him, but was now confined to the role of spectator. He had got away with his lack of size in high school, where he had sometimes come on from the bench as a wide receiver. But his slim frame and light weight ruled out any hope of college football. He now had a steady girlfriend, Shesi, who hailed from a respectable and long-established Indian family. Her father was an importer of rugs, Indian jewelry and other luxuries, and she was learning the business under his tutelage. As his oldest child, she expected to take it over eventually.

No, Bev had insisted, his studies had in no way diminished his religious belief. The truth was, faith and doubt competed every day in his mind; the statues, incense and chants had relaxed the hold they had on him as a child. No, he had insisted, his historical studies had not turned him from his convictions about the correctness of India's political stances; the justice of her opposition to Pakistan; the historical record of the brutality of British Rule. The truth was, he mostly saw not black and white, but many shades of gray; a plague on all their houses, questions of justice and blame seemed to Bev to become easily blurred in the tortuous political webs of the modern world. No, Bev had insisted, his relations with Shesi were chaste and pure. The truth was, they had been sexual partners for over a year, naked and unashamed whenever time permitted, careful in their use of condoms, but joyful in the passion between them. The Visitor took no notes and displayed no reaction to the information Bev gave. But he told him, as he always told him, that he was special;

that he would understand more when he was older; and that he must hold himself in readiness for some great service.

This information disturbed Bev, because he had no conscious understanding of what the Visitor's occasional presence meant, or of what his words signified. It all seemed too grandiose, something set apart from Bev's everyday life; something that invaded his life from another world; something sinister, even; and he had no confidence that he was in any way special. Yet, on another level, there were moments – rare but unmistakable – when he experienced a sudden tantalizing glimpse into the mystery, perhaps a dim memory of words spoken in the distant past. On this level, he almost felt that he knew the truth, and would remember it fully when some future moment came. But the glimpse would vanish as suddenly as it had come in the glare of daily life.

He suspected, of course, that the visits were unusual. None of his friends had ever reported anything similar within their families. But he did not dare ask his friends questions or tell them about the Visitor. He had been instructed from an early age that the visits, and what the Visitor said, were to be mentioned to no one outside the family. It was because Bev was special that the Visitor came, his parents said. No one outside the family would understand. Until recently Bev had followed this instruction faithfully, partly out of respect for his parents, and partly because he was not sure anyone would believe him even if he told them.

But the uncertainty and the sheer weirdness of it all played on his mind and, by the time of the last visit, as he was about to become a college graduate, the need for a second opinion, the need for reassurance, had become overwhelming. A few days after the visit, he had confided in Shesi. He told her after they had made love, which was when they always talked about things. Shesi believed him without hesitation, and quickly offered a decisive reality check. No, it was not a normal situation; no, it did not happen in other families, even Indian families. Was it weird? It was beyond weird, verging on the insane. She suggested a number of courses of action, ranging from coming to live with her family, to taking off to Canada, Australia or, as the evening wore on, anywhere. In a reckless moment, she offered to accompany him, wherever he chose to go. She was pleased that he seemed to like that idea. But these suggestions were not real life, and she did not press them.

That last visit had been almost three years ago. Bev was now in law school. The Visitor had never mentioned a choice of career but his parents, on the other hand, while seeming to leave open the whole range of options, often seemed to lean towards the law or the military. Politics was a third option, perhaps to follow after some success in one of the first two. Bev had no wish to join the military. He was physically very fit and mentally agile, both qualities suitable to an officer, but by temperament he was not aggressive or confrontational, and he had no patience for uniforms or pomp and ceremony. With no other prospects when he graduated from Rice, and with the offer of unconditional financial support through law school, Bev took the plunge. He studied hard, achieved a reasonable score on the LSAT, and was admitted to South Texas College of Law in downtown Houston, not very far from Rice. His political studies had sharpened his understanding of the role of the law in American life, and it seemed to him to be a game he could play well and enjoy. In the back of his mind also was the thought that the law would provide the means for independence. Once independent, he could consign the Visitor to the past. He could have nothing to do with him if he so chose, refuse to see him, tell him to his face to take his weirdness elsewhere. He could opt for a normal life.

The Visitor came on May 25, while he was at home early in the summer vacation at the end of his second year of law school. He was preparing to leave for a summer school program in international criminal law at the University of Cambridge in England. Independence and normality were only a year or two away.

2

'GOOD EVENING,' Conrad Beckers said, facing the camera with the discreet, confidential smile which, over the years, had become almost as much a national institution as the man himself.

'This is a special night for us on the *News Show* on National Public Television, because we have with us the woman at the center of the tumultuous events that have shaken our nation to its core in recent months. A woman who, most Americans believe, saved our system of democracy, indeed our American way of life, for future generations in the face of armed resistance to the rule of law. She has appeared on the *News Show* several times during the intervening period, but always at times of stress, during the rebuilding of our government, when our discussions were dictated by the demands of the moment. Tonight there is an opportunity for a less harried talk. Our guest is the President of the United States, Ellen Trevathan. Madam President, welcome.'

The camera angle widened to show the President sitting to Beckers' left.

Ellen Trevathan was a strikingly handsome woman, over six feet in height, her gray hair short and stylish, her dark blue eyes warm. Most observers thought that she looked every bit of twenty years younger than her age, which was comfortably above the norm for retirement. Much of her popularity derived from the fact that she had not been a career politician. She had started out as a university professor. Her writings on public administration got her noticed, and she soon made the move from a tenured professorship at George Mason University to the first of a number of high-level government jobs. She had a natural gift for dealing with people, a gift which stood her in good stead when Steve Wade asked her to run for the vice presidency on his ticket. Once in the job, she had commanded respect from political colleagues and opponents alike. Wade trusted Ellen, and allowed her an unusual amount of independent action. Taking full advantage of this, she steadily built a reputation in Washington as someone who said little in public, but quietly got things done behind the scenes. Her trademark gray-black suits cut high at the neck, Nehru style, became a familiar sight in the corridors of power. Tonight, she wore the suit over a plain white blouse, and black shoes with a low heel, one discreet silver bracelet partly visible underneath the right sleeve.

'It's my pleasure, Conrad. Good evening to everyone.'

Beckers swiveled his chair around to face her.

'Madam President, I know you have something you would like to say to the American people this evening which has nothing to do with the recent crisis, and we will come to that in just a moment. But first, with your indulgence…'

He swiveled back to face the camera.

'… I would like to remind our viewers of the extraordinary events which brought you to the White House just a few months ago.'

Cut to film. Exterior, day time. Conrad Beckers is standing outside the Russell Senate Office Building. The weather must have been warm; he is wearing a light suit and passers-by are wearing casual tops, shorts and sandals. He faces the camera, microphone in hand.

'It has been barely a year since Ellen Trevathan became President of the United States in the most extraordinary accession in our nation's history. She is, of course, the first woman ever to serve as President. But, for most of her life, she did not seem destined for high office. When she was first elected Vice President on Steve Wade's ticket more than six years ago, very few people would have predicted that she would one day occupy the White House in her own right. Her career in politics had been a short one. Most of her career had been spent in academia, at George Mason University, where she specialized in relations between the states and the federal government. She later held two cabinet posts in which her brief was the environment and energy. She attracted little public attention and, indeed, seemed to thrive on getting things done with minimum fuss and publicity. It was, no doubt, those qualities that recommended her to Steve Wade when he came to choose a running mate. It was a choice which caused surprise in some circles, both within the party and among the public at large. But almost everyone came to agree that the choice was a wise one. She proved to be a competent, if low-key Vice President. She had let it be known within the party that she intended to run for President after Steve Wade's second term of office. But many believe that her nomination would not have been a certainty.'

The camera zoomed in for a close up on Beckers.

'But then, along came Lucia Benoni.'

Cut to film. Interior, day time. The images are of President Steve Wade: working at his desk in the Oval Office; in the White House press room speaking at a press conference; at a White House reception for foreign dignitaries; at Camp David, shaking hands with the Prime Minister of Israel and the President of the Provisional Government of Palestine. Conrad is supplying the voice-over.

'We still await the final report on those terrible events which took place nearly a year ago now. Until that report is released, there is much we do not know. What we do know is that Steve Wade had an affair with a Lebanese woman, Lucia Benoni, and lied about it to the American people, even after Benoni was found murdered, shot in the head, execution-style, in a fashionable Washington apartment. Following reports in the *Washington Post*, it emerged that Wade was sharing Benoni's favors with a Lebanese diplomat, Hamid Marfrela, who was himself murdered in equally mysterious circumstances a short time after Benoni. When evidence emerged of financial links between Marfrela, the President's party, and the Sons of the Land, a white supremacist group based in Oregon, there were fears that the affair with Benoni might have compromised national security. Impeachment proceedings were begun in the Senate, as a result of which Wade was convicted of high crimes and misdemeanors. Steve Wade became the only President in our history to be impeached successfully. Ellen

Trevathan became President by operation of our constitution. Steve Wade was to be removed from office. That was where the story should have ended. But in fact, it was only the beginning…'

The film changes. Exterior, day time, the Russell Senate Building.

'Because as we all know only too well, Steve Wade refused to be removed. A group of high-ranking military officers, led by Marine Corps Commandant Steven Hessler, tried to block Ellen Trevathan's accession to the presidency, and keep Steve Wade in office. With the assistance of former Attorney-General Dick Latham, they invoked a Cold War resolution of the Joint Chiefs of Staff, known as the Williamsburg Doctrine, and Ellen Trevathan was at the center of their attention.'

The film changes again. Exterior, day time. The images are mid-1960's vintage, various shots of cities then behind the Iron Curtain: Belgrade, Prague, Budapest.

'Ellen Trevathan had been a life-long critic of American foreign policy. She was an active opponent of America's foreign wars over many years, from Vietnam to Afghanistan. In her younger days, she attended disarmament conferences and peace rallies, some held in cities behind the Iron Curtain. She wrote articles and position papers condemning American military interventions abroad, including Iraq and Afghanistan, the detentions at Guantanamo Bay, and the practice of extraordinary rendition. Hessler and others claimed to doubt her patriotism and questioned her reliability as Commander-in-Chief, should the use of military force be necessary to defend the United States or its interests abroad. They claimed that the Williamsburg Doctrine, adopted in 1965, in the wake of the assassination of President John F. Kennedy, entitled them to bar Trevathan from the White House on those grounds.'

Exterior, day time, outside the Capitol.

'And it was here, at the heart of our Government, that Hessler marshaled his marines and a crowd of thousands, many of them armed white supremacists, to imprison the United States Senate in its own chamber after the historic vote to impeach Steve Wade was taken.'

Yet another change. Interior, day time, Houston, South Texas College of Law, the student lounge. Video-taped footage of the presidential swearing-in.

'By this time, Ellen Trevathan had removed herself and some influential government figures to Houston for safety reasons, where, as we now know, she took the oath of office in a law school and recruited its dean, Ken Hunt, as her Attorney-General in place of Dick Latham, who was allegedly a moving force behind the conspiracy. It was there also that she made plans with her Vice President, Ted Lazenby, and Secretary of Defense, Raul Gutierrez, to re-take the White House and the Senate, by military means if necessary. Mercifully, that was not necessary. In the most dramatic turn of events of all, Wade was shot dead in the White House by a member of his own detail, secret service agent Linda Samuels. Only after that was President Trevathan able to disperse the crowds and restore order peacefully, bringing an end to what was arguably the most serious crisis in our nation's recent history. Only two reliable witnesses remain of Steve Wade's death. One is Kelly Smith, then Acting Director, now Director, of the FBI. The second is Jeff Morris, a police lieutenant and temporary federal agent, now President Trevathan's Press Secretary. Together, they were attempting to negotiate a settlement on behalf of Ellen Trevathan when Wade was shot by Samuels. Samuels was shot in turn by her colleague, Agent Gary Mills, who is still under psychiatric care in hospital at this time. Steven Hessler and Dick Latham currently face grave criminal charges, including treason. There are doubts, we are told, about Hessler's mental competence to stand trial. Both men deny the charges against them.'

Back to the studio, live.

'Madam President, those were extraordinary times. I know you are glad they are over, as are we all.'

'Yes, indeed.'

'You have made it clear, and I understand why, that you are reluctant to talk too much about them until the final report is released.'

'That's correct, Conrad. I have done everything in my power to expedite the report, and we hope to have it available within the next six weeks to two months.'

'And in any case, Madam President, that is not our main purpose tonight. I know that there is something you want to say to the American people this evening, and the floor is now yours.'

3

THE CAMERA MOVED to Ellen and brought her face to face, alone, with the people.

'Ladies and gentlemen, it was indeed my wish to speak to you this evening. I asked Conrad if he would allow me to be a guest on the *News Show*, and he graciously agreed. I could have chosen to speak to you from the White House. But my subject this evening is not a political one. It is a deeply personal one. This evening, I want to make you aware of something about myself, something I have never willfully concealed, but something I have chosen not to talk about, until now.'

Ellen paused and held her hands together tightly in her lap.

'Tonight I come out to you all – to the people of America – as a lesbian. I have been aware of my sexual orientation from a very young age. I have never been ashamed of my sexuality. But I am a very private person. I have always believed that sexuality is a personal matter, one that should not concern others, even when a person is, as I have been, in the public eye because of his or her career. Before becoming President, I tried my best to live as quietly and unobtrusively as possible, given the positions that I held. And I am grateful that the media respected my privacy and did not find it necessary to confront me. But I do now regret having remained silent, because I understand that, if I had spoken up, it might have made it easier for other lesbians, and for gay men, to offer themselves for public office. I know how hard it has been during our recent history for those in the public eye to come out, because we have in some ways become such an intolerant and divided society. If my coming out this evening contributes in any way to improving that situation, I will be very happy. But I must confess that my reason for speaking out this evening is also much more personal.'

Ellen smiled and extended her left arm. Following, the camera widened its angle to take in the woman seated on the President's left. She was some inches shorter than Ellen, more than fifteen years younger, with a fuller face and longer hair, red, tied at the back, dark brown eyes, wearing a light gray suit over a colorful blouse of brown and orange with flashes of dark and lime green, with high-heeled brown shoes.

'This is my partner, Kay Ryan. I met Kay about seventeen years ago, after her marriage had ended. We fell in love. We have never lived together. Kay has a beautiful daughter, Dani, who is now in law school at Georgetown. I've been privileged to get to know Dani as she has grown up, and I am proud to be her step-mother. Kay and I do now plan to have a home together. We intend in due course to have a ceremony to become civil partners. And tonight I introduce Kay to the American people.'

The camera moved back to include Conrad Beckers in the shot.

'Madam President, this is indeed a momentous occasion. And, Ms Ryan, welcome to the *News Show*. Perhaps I could start with you. If it's not too obvious a question: how do you feel about the President's statement this evening?'

Kay was smiling, but she held her hands with the fingers tightly intertwined.

'I'm really glad that Ellen has chosen to do this. It's something we've talked about over the years, but somehow it never seemed to be the right time. It hasn't been easy with Ellen in such a public position, and especially since she became President, of course. But it's something we have both wanted.'

'Did your daughter, Dani, have anything to say about it?' Beckers asked.

Kay's smile broadened.

'Dani has been goading us to do this for three or four years,' she replied. 'She loves Ellen, and she's an independent young woman with her own views. I know she is watching the show as we speak, and I can almost hear her cheering.'

Beckers laughed.

'That is good to hear,' he said. 'I know that you have your own career, in the law. But could you tell us a little about yourself?'

'That's correct. I'm a partner in the law firm of Mayer Hargreaves Harrison & Ryan here in Washington. We do commercial litigation. My former husband, Dale Harrison, is also a member of the firm. We are still law partners and we remain good friends… and, of course, Dale is Dani's father. They are very close and they spend a lot of time together.'

Kay took a breath.

'I didn't have quite the same experience as Ellen. I grew up in Iowa in a pretty conventional home, and I was pretty conventional myself when I was younger. That involved being a straight-A student, attending Sunday school, being a high school cheerleader, and all that kind of thing. Later it meant getting married and having a child. I don't regret any of that. Without it, I wouldn't have Dani. Dani is the apple of my eye. She is a beautiful and talented young woman. But I was always aware of being attracted to women, and a time came in my life when I had to acknowledge it. I had an affair with a long-time friend. I told Dale about it, and we agreed to part amicably. That affair didn't last, but it was then that I met Ellen. She is my true soulmate.'

'Is this a coming out for you too? How will the other partners in your firm – including your ex-husband – feel about this evening's announcement?'

'They will be very happy for me. We have all been friends for years – it's that kind of firm – and they have known about my sexuality and about my relationship with Ellen for years too. They have always been very accepting.'

Beckers nodded.

'Turning back to you, Madam President, I couldn't help noticing what you said about making a home together for the first time. Where will that home be? Will it be …?'

'In the White House, yes,' Ellen replied immediately. 'That is our intention. The White House is where the President of the United States lives with his family, and now, her family. Kay and Dani are my family. Kay and I will live there. We will also have a home outside the White House, of course, and Dani will be with us in both places whenever she wants to be.'

Beckers chewed thoughtfully on the end of his Mont Blanc pen.

'I guess the question I have is: some people may find that …?'

'I'm sure there are some people who will disapprove, Conrad. I understand that it can sometimes take time for people to adapt to new situations. And, unfortunately, there will always be prejudice, of one kind or another. There were people who muttered about having a black family in the White House when President Obama was elected – and indeed after. I'm sure there will be those who will complain and say hateful things about my family. Frankly, my message to them is: "get over it". There is no place for prejudice in the America I love and whose President I now am.'

'There will be a presidential election in another eighteen months,' Beckers said. 'Do you intend to run?'

Ellen smiled.

'That is a question I have had to put on hold. Since the crisis, my first responsibility has been to hold the government together in the wake of the turbulence we all went through then. We are back on a fairly even keel now, but there is still a lot to do, within the various government departments and within the military. There may well be some parts of our government that are still not entirely reconstructed by the time my present term of office – Steve Wade's unexpired term of office – ends. When I served as President Wade's Vice President, I did intend to seek my party's nomination. But I have to admit that the turmoil has made me think again about what I really want to do. I know I have to make a decision quite soon, and I will. But let me say that, whatever my decision may be, it will have nothing to do with what I have said tonight – except that, of course, I will talk to Kay about it before I decide.'

Beckers smiled, and turned to Kay.

'Would you like the President to run, Ms Ryan?'

She returned the smile.

'I want Ellen to do whatever she wants to do. She knows I will support her, whatever decision she takes.'

'There is still one question that intrigues me, Madam President,' Beckers continued. 'The media in this country, and indeed abroad, are usually not exactly shy about reporting stories, sometimes factual, sometimes mere gossip and rumor, about the private lives of politicians. But I can't recall more than a handful of stories speculating about your sexuality over the years. And they never seemed to last long, or go anywhere. Why do you think that was?'

Ellen shook her head.

'I really don't know, Conrad. Kay and I have asked ourselves the same question many times. We have tried to keep a low profile, as I said before. But even so, there have been times when we felt sure we were about to be outed, and we decided to be honest and make the best of it when it happened. I have to think that the media was so involved with Steve Wade's sex life that mine was uninteresting by comparison. We had issues with stories about Steve throughout my time with him, some real, some probably not, but always out there in public view. And in Steve's case, they were not just stories, they were scandals, so much more interesting than anything I was doing. I guess that must have been the reason. Finally, of course, there was Lucia Benoni.'

Beckers nodded, the pen rolled between his thumb and first finger.

'Would it be fair to say that Steve Wade's departure took away your cover?' he asked with a smile. 'Is that why you chose this evening to come out?'

She returned the smile.

'Yes, I think that's fair. That's part of it.'

'The lack of attention probably wouldn't have lasted much longer?'

'Probably not. And I'm sure it influenced my timing in making the announcement this evening. But whatever the reason, I am grateful to all those journalists – yourself included, Conrad, because I know perfectly well that you knew – who had the kindness to respect my privacy.'

'Madam President, Ms Ryan,' Beckers concluded. 'It has been an honor to have you both on the *News Show* this evening. I hope you will both come back often.'

'I hope so, too,' Ellen replied, smiling.

Beckers turned to face the camera.

'And now to events in the Middle East. The Secretary of State has spent another long day in negotiations in Amman, Jordan.'

4

ELLEN AND KAY had supper with Dani in the White House Residence before watching their programmed recording of the *News Show*. Ellen and Kay were leaning back, side by side, on the sofa.

'What did you think?' Kay asked anxiously, as the credits rolled. 'I don't know. I came across like a complete fool.'

'Nonsense,' Ellen said, taking her hand. 'You were great!'

Dani had been lying on the floor in front of the TV, but now she got to her feet, walked around the back of the sofa, leaned over, and hugged and kissed Ellen and Kay in turn.

'You *were* great, Mom. So were you, Ellen. I am so proud of you both,' she replied, the excitement in her voice obvious. 'Talk about sending a message! You came across so reasonable, so logical, as well as making clear to everyone how much you love each other. I can't see how anyone could argue with what you said, and I can't see how anyone could hold it against you. It's a triumph!'

Kay kissed Dani in return.

'Thank you, sweetheart. But wait until you see some of the headlines tomorrow,' she said. 'We have given the American establishment a major kick in the teeth tonight, and tomorrow they are going to start kicking back.'

'I hope I'm not hearing you say you regret coming out,' Dani replied. 'Because I think it's the best thing you've ever done – apart from having me, obviously.'

Kay reached up her hand to pat Dani's shoulder.

'I have no regrets at all. I would go back to Conrad Beckers' studio right now and do it all again. But I'm still worried about how it will play out. I'm worried that they will be particularly hard on Ellen.'

Dani shrugged impatiently, walked quickly away and stood with her back against the wall by the large table on which the TV stood.

'It would be so unfair for people to criticize Ellen now,' she protested. 'Ellen, you have been such a hero to people since the crisis. I haven't heard a word spoken against you. Everything the press has said has been so positive.'

'That was before I announced on public television that I am a lesbian and that I am going to bring my female lover to live with me in the White House,' Ellen replied, with a grim smile. 'Hero or not, that's not going to sit well with some of those good folks in the heartland. And they will let me know it over the next few days. We have called down a storm on our heads, and there's nothing we can do except batten down the hatches and ride it out. But we knew it would be that way. We did the right thing, and we have to trust that it will work out in the end. "This too shall pass", as the saying goes.'

She stood, walked over to Dani and pulled her into a hug.

'I'm glad you're going to be out of it for a while, Dani. You can read all about it in *The Times* of London, and you can send us emails to let us know what people think about it all in Europe.'

'I almost wish I wasn't going,' Dani replied. 'I feel I should stay in Washington and go through this with you.'

Kay stood, walked over to Dani, and joined in the hug.

'No, this is something Ellen and I have to do,' she said. 'What you have to do is to be on that plane to England at 7.30 on Saturday. You have to take those classes at Cambridge University, learn all about international criminal law, and get those credit hours under your belt.'

'I don't know, Mom. If this is going to be serious…'

'Your Mom is right, Dani,' Ellen said firmly. 'Don't worry. It's going to be bad for a few days. After that, it will settle down. But from now on it will always be part of our lives, so we have to get used to it. We can't let it run our lives. We have to be able to live with it and function with it. The last thing we need is to let it disrupt our plans.'

She smiled.

'Besides, I need an expert in international criminal law. When you get back, I need to talk to you about whether I should try to persuade the Senate to sign up to the International Criminal Court.'

Dani returned the smile.

'Yeah, right. I'm sure you need me to tell you what to do about that,' she said.

'I might,' she said. 'I need to understand why we didn't do it years ago. I'm sure you will make more sense than some of the briefings I've been shown from the State Department. Take some notes for me.'

'I will.'

There was a knock on the door. An agent opened the door and stood just inside the room.

'Sorry to interrupt, Madam President, but the Press Secretary is here.'

Ellen stood and walked towards the door.

'Jeff, come in.'

'Thank you, Madam President.' He nodded. 'Kay, Dani.'

Kay and Dani smiled in response. Jeff Morris was as tall as the President and his bearing was just as assured. During the Benoni investigation and the crisis he had proved himself, both to Ellen and to her Vice President Ted Lazenby, time after time, as a cool head and a capable administrator. During the crisis he had worked alongside Ellen throughout her stay in Houston, leaving only to accompany Kelly Smith to the attempt to negotiate at the White House. He had been there with Kelly when Steve Wade was shot. Once the crisis had been resolved, he had genuinely expected to return quietly to his duties as a lieutenant in the Washington D.C. Police Department. But Ellen had made up her mind to keep him if she could. There were several positions within the administration that might have suited Jeff. The idea of appointing him as her Press Secretary was sheer intuition on Ellen's part. It raised a few eyebrows at first – not least Jeff's. But she had been right about Jeff's coolness, his organizational strength, and his ability to articulate complex issues precisely, yet succinctly. He had been in the role for only one or two months, but the press generally agreed that he had already made it his own. The only overt concessions he had made to it were to sacrifice his wispy moustache and to trade in his preferred sports jacket for a more formal dark gray suit. The dark gray look complemented his salt-and-pepper hair to perfection.

'So what are you hearing?' Ellen asked.

Jeff shook his head.

'It's just as we expected – totally chaotic,' he replied. 'The social networking sites are burning up. We've blindsided the Networks and local TV. They were taken completely by surprise and they haven't been able to gear up for a coherent response. Right now, they are shooting from the hip and completely disorganized. No one's going to be able to make sense of it all tonight. Everyone wants to have their say, and it's going to be some time before it dies down enough for someone to start to analyze the situation objectively. The team will work on it overnight, and we will have some kind of report to you by mid-morning tomorrow. By then, we will also have all the headlines and all the reaction from TV stations across the country, so we should be in a position to evaluate the overall picture a bit more scientifically. I'm still thinking that you need to go ahead with your press conference tomorrow, so that people remember that you are the President, and have your usual work to do, whatever they heard about you tonight.'

Ellen nodded.

'Sounds good, Jeff. Let's meet for coffee and talk about it tomorrow morning. I've had enough for one day. I'm sure you have too. Go on home. Let's get together at about eight.'

Jeff half turned towards the door and stopped.

'If I may, Madam President, whatever the press thinks, and whatever all those people out there think, I think you were great – both of you. I'm proud to be serving under you. Kelly called me a little while ago, and she said to tell you that the same goes for her.'

'Thank you, Jeff,' Ellen smiled. 'Give Kelly my best. I'll see you tomorrow.'

'Good night, Madam President.'

'I need to be going too,' Dani said. 'I still have way too much packing to do. I've put out an unbelievable amount of stuff to take. I can't figure out how to squeeze it all in, and even if I can, I'm not sure I'm going to be under the weight limit.'

Ellen laughed.

'I've been there,' she said. 'You should have seen me when I started going abroad. I couldn't pack a bag to save my life. I was sure I couldn't survive without it all, and I probably never used more than fifty percent of it. How are you getting home?'

'An agent has been assigned to take me home in an unmarked car. I'm supposed to meet him outside. He's probably waiting for me now.'

'Good,' Ellen said. 'And how are you getting to the airport on Saturday?'

'I'm taking her,' Kay said.

Ellen looked concerned.

'I'm not sure that's wise, Kay. The press will be watching. I can arrange transport.'

Kay shook her head.

'No, that's OK. Dale is coming with us. We will use his car, just in case they're waiting for mine. We'll be fine. I have the number to call if there is any trouble.'

'We have to start thinking about things like this more seriously.'

'Not on Saturday,' Kay said firmly. 'I'm a mother. My daughter is going to England for the first time. I want to take her to the airport. I want one more experience of normality, Ellen. Let's think of this as our last purely private trip for a while. OK with you, Dani?'

'I'm cool,' Dani replied. Then she walked over to Ellen, hugged her and held her tight.

'I'm going to miss you, Ellen.'

Ellen kissed her forehead.

'I'm going to miss you too, Dani. Take care of yourself. I love you.'

'I love you too.' She walked across the room to kiss Kay, then turned to leave. She paused at the door. 'You're one of the great Presidents, Ellen. I just know it.'

Before Ellen could reply, she was gone.

* * *

Later, they lay naked together under a single sheet with the overhead fan sending a cool breeze down to play on their bodies, Ellen on her back, Kay resting her head gently on Ellen's breasts.

'This can't be the first time two women have made love in the White House,' Kay said.

'I'm sure it's not,' Ellen replied, grinning. 'I don't know the details of who and when, but if you want, I can have a staff member research it and write us a memo.'

'Not necessary,' Kay smiled. 'I'm just grateful you and I can be together – here, or anywhere else, it doesn't really matter.' She suddenly giggled. 'Still, it is an interesting question, isn't it?'

The giggle was infectious.

'Yes, it is,' Ellen said. 'I may have to have someone check it out, just out of curiosity. Perhaps I can use it with the press as precedent when they give me a hard time about it.'

They lay in silence for some time.

'It's going to be a real storm, isn't it?' Kay asked eventually.

'Yes.'

'Thank God Dani is out of it.'

'Jeff briefed her on handling any press questions in England, right?' Ellen asked. 'She understands what to do?'

'Yes, and she knows our ambassador is keeping a discreet eye open for her, with assistance from the Secret Service and Special Branch in London. I just hope she can put it out of her mind and concentrate on her studies.'

'And on having a good time,' Ellen said sleepily. 'Let's not forget that. That's the best way to take her mind off all this.'

'I just hope they leave her alone,' Kay said, after a long pause.

But Ellen was already asleep.

5

'YOU ARE A sleeper, Bev.'

As the words were spoken, Bev knew instantly. He also knew instantly that he had always known; that the glimpses had been real; and that all that was lacking to bring them into full consciousness was the Visitor's confirmation.

The Visitor sat opposite Bev, across the dining table. He had not asked a single question. Not a word about law school; not a word about grades; not a word about Shesi. Nothing. The omission was so stark, the break in the pattern so radical, that Bev's full attention had immediately been engaged. Something was very different today. Bev's parents had spoken with the Visitor as usual, but then, for the first time in Bev's recollection, and in an almost casual tone, he had asked them to leave the house for an hour or two; take themselves off to Starbucks, have a coffee; keep an eye on his car. His parents complied without a word, his mother's eyes anxiously seeking Bev, his father leading her away by the arm and out through the front door.

'Are you familiar with the term?'

Bev nodded.

'I saw a movie once. The story-line was that the Soviets had planted a young man in America during the Cold War as a small child. He grew up as an American and became an officer in the Navy.'

'Yes. He grew up as an American. To all the world he appeared to be American, an ordinary American young man and nothing more. But he knew his language; he knew his true home and his people. And he knew his destiny. That is the way with sleepers.'

'But how would he know?'

'Sometimes he just knows. But in any case we tell him, or his parents tell him. He must be told – eventually, at the proper time. But not later than the age you are now. This is only fair, because whatever decisions the sleeper takes about his life – about his career, a marriage, children – he must know who he is and what may be expected of him. So it is usual to give him this information at about your age, although in your case there is another reason for doing so.'

Bev held his head in his hands. The Visitor stood, walked around the table and placed his hands on Bev's shoulders.

'Your parents were asked to volunteer to come to America before you were born. We made arrangements for their Green Cards, and later for them to take American citizenship. We paid the expenses of their resettlement, looked after them, provided for them financially until they were secure in their new home. Since then we have continued to supply whatever they might need. We have assisted them with your education, specifically your college and law school tuition fees. And all this is for one reason, and one reason only.'

Bev sat up straight. The Visitor returned to the other side of the table, but remained standing.

'It sometimes happens that there is something we need to have done – in America, in Europe, wherever it may be – which cannot be done by one of us, or that we prefer to have done by someone who is not one of our own. It may be a small thing which can be accomplished with ease and does not affect the sleeper's life at all. On the other hand, it may be something momentous which requires a considerable sacrifice. Often it cannot be done before the sleeper has made his way in the world, established himself in some way, perhaps in military service, the police, the security services, the law, the business world. Often we need someone in a position of responsibility, perhaps even in a position of power. It may take many years before the sleeper can be used.'

The Visitor smiled.

'And sometimes, the time never arrives. Perhaps the sleeper never achieves a suitable position. Perhaps there is simply no service for him to render. In this case, the sleeper lives out his own life.'

Bev looked up.

'Without any demands being made at all?' he asked. 'After you've made all those arrangements, spent all that money? Come on, you must make sure you get something out of him.'

The Visitor smiled again.

'What is asked of a sleeper is always unique to the sleeper. We do not waste sleepers on inappropriate tasks. Therefore, the practice of having sleepers is not always cost-effective,' he replied. 'That is why we do not have many sleepers. We are not like the Soviet Union, Bev. We do not have unlimited resources for such things. We make judgments as best we can. We must try to see events and trends a generation or more before they happen. We make arrangements accordingly. It is not an exact science.'

He looked up.

'In addition, whatever the sleeper does, or does not do, must be voluntary. He has complete freedom of choice. When he is told what is expected of him, he may refuse. He may say to us: "No, I enjoy my life and I prefer to live my life. I have no interest in you or what you propose."'

Bev shook his head.

'Right. Then, what happens to him?'

'Nothing happens to him,' the Visitor replied. 'We have to make a judgment about whether to continue our support, in the hope, perhaps, that some other opportunity for service opens up which the sleeper is prepared to accept; or whether to cut our losses and accept that the project has failed, in which case the sleeper never hears from us again.'

'What? You just leave him alone? There are no consequences?'

'There are consequences in the sleeper's own conscience, of course.'

'That's not what I mean. Are you telling me that you don't do anything about it? I mean, not even get back the money you've paid out?'

'What would you expect us to do?'

'Well, let me see,' Bev replied nervously. 'Perhaps the sleeper might have an accident. He might be run down on the way home from work by a driver who fails to stop. He might receive an exploding package through the mail. His child might disappear from school.'

The Visitor laughed aloud.

'You watch too many movies, Bev. We are not the Soviets.'

'You know where we live,' Bev replied. 'You may not have unlimited resources, but it would not be difficult for you to get back at us, at my family.'

The Visitor seated himself.

'Bev, listen to me,' he said. 'When I say that we are not like the Soviets, I do not speak only of resources. I speak also of our principles, our moral values, our religious precepts. You have been schooled in the Hindu teachings. You are familiar with the law of karma. You must know that if we were to seek any kind of retribution, we would surrender our moral position, and on some level it would come back to haunt us. We would lose our moral claim to make requests of any sleeper. Ours is a just cause, and it must be upheld by just means, or it means nothing.'

Bev looked at the Visitor closely.

'So, if you made a request to me and I were to refuse ...?'

'You would become a lawyer; no doubt you would marry Shesi; you would have children; you would look after your parents; and you would become in all respects a model American citizen.'

'I am the sleeper? Not my parents?'

'Correct. Remember, Bev, a sleeper must appear to be totally natural in his environment. You are a completely American boy ...'

'Even though I go to Temple, and speak Hindi, and ...'

'Yes, despite those things. You are the child of immigrants, but you are not yourself an immigrant. Your whole upbringing, your whole education has been in America. Yes, you are of Indian origin, but America is full of people whose families are from somewhere else. America is the great melting pot. You are American, Bev, in all respects except your soul, and it is because of your soul that we make a request of you.'

Bev stood and banged his fists on the table in frustration.

'My soul? What do you know about my soul? What do you know about me? You show up here for an hour or two every few years and talk about my education, my grades. Then you disappear again. What do you know about what I do the rest of the time, about who I am?'

The Visitor smiled.

'You have not visited Kashmir yet, have you, Bev?'

Bev sat again and looked down at the table.

'No.'

'But your parents have talked to you about their birth place?'

'Yes.'

'It is a place of incomparable beauty,' the Visitor said. 'One day you will see for yourself those majestic snow-covered mountains, the lush valleys, the trees. It is truly a place where the deities themselves may feel at home.'

He paused.

'And your parents have talked to you about what the Muslims have done to Kashmir, what they did to our families?'

'Yes.'

'You have read about the time of India's so-called independence?'

Suddenly, the Visitor became animated, vehement. It was a side of him Bev had never seen, quite different from his usual quiet, logical self. He began to pace up and down as he spoke, waving his arms and, for first time, he raised his voice.

'Our great country did not become independent. It was torn apart. In place of subjugation by England we were made to divide our land, to surrender part of our land to those of the Muslim faith. This should never have been. We would have treated the Muslims fairly. They could have remained in India and prospered, as they had for centuries. But Jinnah had stirred them up. He told them that the government could not protect them, that there would be endless religious wars. But the truth was that Jinnah had too many ambitions, personal ambitions. He wanted his own country. Imagine that, Bev! Imagine the hubris of a man who can think that he can carve his own country out of our mother India! Was it not inevitable that someone would strike him down, or at least send him packing? But no! They failed to stand up to him, every one of them. Nehru failed; Mountbatten failed; even

Gandhi failed – and he paid the price for it.'

The Visitor looked down darkly for a moment.

'So we have Pakistan breathing down our necks,' he resumed. 'And our beloved Kashmir is divided. We have a part of it, which we have to call the Indian state of Jammu and Kashmir. But the Muslims have a great part of it. We have tried to fight, we have tried to negotiate, so far without success. Yet, we will never give up, Bev. It may take years, decades, or centuries. But in time we shall prevail. One day we will bring honor to India and to her deities. One day, the whole of Kashmir will be Indian and Hindu.'

He sat back and placed his arms along the arms of his chair. He made an effort to calm himself.

'It is for this reason that, today, I call on you for a service to your homeland.'

Bev felt his heart racing. He struggled to catch his breath.

'What service?' he whispered. He fought to make his voice work normally. 'You said it yourself, I've never been to Kashmir. All I know is what I've studied and what my parents have told me. And I'm not in a position of power or influence. What can I do, for God's sake? Even if I wanted to.'

'We never ask a service that the sleeper is not capable of rendering,' the Visitor replied. 'Both the nature of the service and the timing of it are most carefully planned.'

He did not seem in a hurry to continue. Bev looked at him in frustration. Eventually he leapt to his feet, put both hands on the table, and leaned over towards the Visitor.

'Well, what is it, for God's sake?' he shouted. 'You tell me you want something. What do you want?'

'I do not know the details.'

'What …?' Bev shouted.

The Visitor stood.

'It is a matter of safety, a matter of security,' he replied. 'Please try to understand, Bev. I am the messenger, nothing more. It is important that I should not know too much. I may be arrested, I may be taken. It is safer that I do not know.'

'Well, then, how …?'

'This is what I am instructed to tell you, Bev,' the Visitor said.

'You are to go to England on Saturday, as planned. You are to attend your summer course at Cambridge, as planned. While you are there, your contact will meet you. Your contact will tell you what is asked of you, and will convey your reply to us.'

Bev shook his head.

'This is unbelievable.' He paused. 'And my parents know about this?'

'They know only that today, I have confirmed to you who you are, and that I am making a request for service,' the Visitor replied. 'They know nothing more, not even that you will have a contact in England. I strongly advise that you tell them no more than they already know. This is for their safety, as well as yours.'

Bev remained silent.

'You need say nothing to me today,' the Visitor said. 'We do not expect any answer until you are fully aware of what is being asked of you.'

'Who is this contact?' Bev asked. 'How will I know him?'

'Her work name is Kali,' the Visitor replied. 'She will make herself known to you at the appropriate time.'

The Visitor smiled as Bev closed his eyes, realising that the reference was not lost on him. Kali was the most feared deity in the Hindu pantheon. Her cult was associated with bloodshed, violent death, and human sacrifice.

'I must go,' the Visitor said. 'Your parents will return soon.'

He turned towards the door, then paused.

'I wish you well, Bev,' he said. 'Whatever you decide. You are a fine young man. And I tell you again, it is your choice.'

He smiled.

'I find it interesting that I have spoken to you of "we" and "us", yet you have not asked me who "we" are.'

Bev looked directly into the Visitor's eyes.

'I know who you are,' he said.

6

TOMMY LANIER, 'BUBBA' to his family, friends, and rapidly growing army of fans, looked around his studio with a satisfied smile. God, he was going to enjoy this morning. In his wildest dreams, he could not have imagined a more perfect opportunity to boost his ratings. The religious and social conservatives who tuned into his show in their tens of thousands every day were going to love this. He was state-wide already. A day or two more of this might even propel him on to the national stage. It wasn't just the hard core conservatives who were upset. Even people who considered themselves moderate, middle of the road, were concerned. Something was going on that was just not right. American family values were at stake, and people wanted answers. Well, they could find them right here on the Bubba Lanier show, on Family of Christ Radio, 88 FM, Dallas, Texas – simple answers, answers for which you only had to appeal to the Bible and the American flag. By the time he got through with Ellen Trevathan, the syndication of his show would be virtually guaranteed and his name would be known in every household in America.

As far as his personal beliefs were concerned, Tommy Lanier was a bit vague on the whole God thing, and the flag was just as much a commercial tool for him as it was for the dealers who sold their pickup trucks from lots along the freeways heading into the city. But Tommy knew how to make the most of both. Dallas had been a step up for Tommy when he joined 88FM about two years before. He hailed from Lake Charles, Louisiana. He was a big man, broad-shouldered, and well-proportioned in his day, though the muscle had run to flab in many areas now and his private penchant for cigars and whiskey had made the once fresh face look old and puffy. He had been a line-backer in high school and had even won a football scholarship to Louisiana State University. But few people thought he had the talent to play professionally, and in any case that possibility disappeared in his senior year when he suffered a serious knee injury. Although he made a good recovery, the injury left him with a slight limp to remind him of what might, possibly, have been.

A college classmate introduced Tommy to radio in Baton Rouge after he had graduated and had no idea what he was going to do next. His first job was behind the scenes, and much of the programming at the station, which featured a combination of music and news shows, bored him. But in his spare time he listened to talk radio, and to Tommy it all seemed so easy. All you had to do was find out what your listeners wanted to hear, and give it to them as clearly and simply as you could, in language they could understand. If your market was the conservative base – and in much of Louisiana a certain type of conservative was the only market that mattered to the sponsors, and therefore to the station – how could you go wrong? America was God's country; the Bible was God's word; the family, consisting of one man, one woman and their children, was God's template for life; the American flag was God's symbol on earth; the American military defended and upheld God's values across the globe. A good radio show reflected these values, and gave callers the chance to do the same. America had enemies, who included atheists, non-Christians, liberals, sexual deviants, immigrants, and indeed foreigners generally, with certain honorable exceptions who shared American values and recognized America's unique position in the world. A good radio show was hard on America's enemies, whoever they might be, and allowed its callers to join in, denouncing and demanding military action against countries they would not be able to find on a map.

He auditioned at a talk station in Baton Rouge, where the station manager recognized his talent immediately. He started by standing in for other hosts during their absences on vacation, but within six months he had his own show, late at night at first, but within another six months in the prime-time morning spot. His reputation and following grew. He moved to Dallas in search of bigger and better things – and also because of Jolene, a black 14-year-old he got careless with one night, who became pregnant as a result. It had cost quite a bit to hush that up, and you never knew when things like that might surface again once he was state-wide in Louisiana. It was just one mistake, it hardly seemed fair really, but all in all Dallas seemed a safer option.

The show was open to callers, whoever they might be. On the other side of the glass wall at the front of the studio, Mike and Karen screened them to get rid of the complete crazies, those who were obviously drunk, totally incoherent, or liable to let loose with profanities on air. Subject to that, the crazier and more extreme the callers were, the better the show was likely to be, and Mike and Karen had a pretty good track record in selecting them. But, just in case, Tommy had a few regulars he could call on. The Rev. Wendell K. Mungo, minister in charge of the Church of the Lamb in Tyler, was a favorite with the rednecks and the white religious audience generally. Pastor Jerome J. Jackson of the Assembly of Brethren in the Vineyard, based in Industry, Texas – wherever that might be – appealed to black listeners with a judicious mix of religion and references to slavery and civil rights. Tommy had little doubt that both would be more than happy to have their say as often as he wished in the coming days, and they would be the first of many. In advance of today's show, Pastor Jackson had supplied him with enough biblical quotes for a years' worth of sermons, all of them proving beyond doubt that Ellen Trevathan's cohabitation with Kay Ryan was an abomination before the Lord and likely to bring the wrath of an angry God down on America in the near future, unless something was done about it. And that was before you added in that they were cohabiting in the White House, the seat of God's authority on earth.

Tommy had begun with a selection of Pastor Jackson's quotes and a general rant about the state of the country before looking up through the glass wall towards Mike and Karen. They were both giving him a thumbs-up. This was not a sign of approval for the show. It was code for having a caller available whom they had vetted and found worthy of putting on air. Tommy returned the sign, meaning, 'OK, put him through'.

'His name is Joe,' Karen whispered into his earpiece.

Tommy flicked the switch.

'OK. I believe we have a caller on the line. Your name is Joe, sir, is that right?'

'Yes, sir.'

'And where do you live, Joe?'

'Right here in Dallas.'

'Well, Joe, what's on your mind today?'

A short silence while Joe comes to terms with the awesome responsibility of speaking his mind to thousands of people he cannot see.

'Well, Bubba, I want to thank you for standing up for us against what's going on in the White House.'

'You're very welcome, Joe. I believe we all have a duty to stand up and be counted when this kind of thing happens.'

'Yes, Sir,' Joe said. 'Bubba, I am a god-fearing man. I grew up here in Texas. I served my country in the Army ...'

'Where did you serve, Joe?'

'I served in Afghanistan, two tours, and of course right here in America.'

'Well, the nation thanks you for your service, Joe. We are all real proud of you.'

'Thank you, sir ... well, as I was saying, I served my country. I pay my taxes. And I have two beautiful daughters ...'

'That's wonderful, Joe,' Tommy interrupted. 'Children are a gift from the Lord. What are their names, and how old are they?'

'Ellie May is twelve, and Lee Ann is ten.'

'That's wonderful.'

'Yes, sir. And I don't understand why my daughters should have to see and hear about what's going on in the White House, and why they should be hearing that it's normal for two women to be living together like this, when God's word says it shouldn't be that way. I don't want them exposed to this kind of thing, Bubba, but it's happening right there in the White House, and it seems that there is nothing we can do about it.'

'Joe,' Tommy replied. 'You are absolutely right. Your beautiful daughters should not have to hear about such godless behavior. They should be able to grow up in their innocence, and they should not have to have that kind of example set for them by those who are supposed to be running this great country.'

'Don't get me wrong, Bubba,' Joe says, in the interests of fairness, 'I didn't have nothing against Miss Trevathan before all this started. She was right to do what she did when President Wade had to be removed from office, and I kind of admired what she did. It's just that now …'

'I understand,' Tommy said.

He had never understood the obsession some journalists had with the idea that you always had to put the opposing point of view. That just watered down the message and suggested you might actually have some sympathy with the liberal nonsense your opponents were peddling. But with experience, he had come to see that it did no harm to make the occasional concession, as long as it was short and was something that was unlikely to offend the fan base.

'President Trevathan is entitled to our thanks for what she did in that crisis, and I have said so many times before on this show. But what's happening now is something else again. God cannot tolerate what's going on now, and neither should we.'

Mike was signaling to him. Tommy nodded, and Joe disappeared from the airwaves. Mike was giving him a thumbs-down. That meant, 'I have someone who disagrees, but it's someone you can take down, and it might be fun'. Tommy smiled. Why not? The show was going well. He was on a roll. Bring it on. He nodded to Mike.

'Joe, thank you for your call. I believe we have another caller on the line. What's your name?'

'My name is Susie, and I'm from Houston.'

'Susie from Houston. It's nice to have you on the show, Susie. What's on your mind today?'

'I think it's terrible what you are saying about the President. This has nothing to do with her being President. It's her private life and she is entitled to her privacy. It's none of our business what she does in private, or who she does it with.'

Tommy winked at Mike and Karen and gave them an appreciative smile.

'Well, Susie, I'm afraid I have to disagree with you about that. The Bible clearly says that women lying together is an abomination unto the Lord, whether they do it in Houston or in the White House. But when they do it in the White House, which is paid for by our taxes, I believe we have every right to be concerned.'

'You're just stirring up hatred and prejudice, Mr Lanier. That's all your show is about.'

'You know, Susie, I should have known when you said you were from Houston. That should have been enough of a clue right there. But then, when you said "hatred" and "prejudice" it became clear to me. You are one of them liberals, and it's people like you who have brought this country to the state it's in today.'

'I am *not* a liberal. I vote Republican, and …'

'Does your husband know you're calling in, expressing these liberal viewpoints?'

'Excuse me? My husband …?'

Mike and Karen were applauding silently from behind the glass wall.

'Yes, your husband. Does he know this is what you get up to while he is out working, supporting your family? I bet he doesn't. In fact, you know what? I bet you don't even have a husband. Are you one of those women who …?'

'How dare you …?' Susie managed, before Karen cut her off on a signal from Tommy.

'I bet she is,' Tommy continued. 'You know what, I just thought of something. I'm going to call her a "friend of Ellen". Hey, how about that, I just made that up. Friends of Ellen. I'm going to use that from now on.'

'Brilliant,' Mike whispered into his earpiece. He and Karen were giving each other five.

'Well, we seem to have lost Susie,' Tommy continued. He looked up again. Karen was signaling. 'But I believe we have an old friend of the show calling in, Pastor Jerome J. Jackson of the Assembly of Brethren in the Vineyard, in Industry, Texas. Pastor, it surely is a privilege to have your wise counsel in these difficult times. We are all grateful that God has anointed you and called you to the great work you are doing. What words do you have to encourage us today?'

'Good morning, Mr Lanier,' Pastor Jackson said. He could never quite bring himself to utter the name 'Bubba'. 'First, let me say that I thank God every day for your show. You stand as a beacon for the people in these times of darkness.'

'Well, thank you, Pastor. I am honored and humbled by those words, coming from a man of God such as yourself. Please, bring us some comfort and encouragement.'

Pastor Jackson stayed on the line for more than half an hour. After that, the phones never stopped ringing. Mike and Karen were overwhelmed. People were calling in their hundreds. Most of them did not get the chance to speak on the show, and were simply thanked and invited to call again on another day. Almost all the callers wanted to jump on the bandwagon, and the most interesting of them, as judged by Mike and Karen, did. There were a handful of women who called in to protest against Tommy's treatment of Susie from Houston, but they were put on hold for long periods before being told that there was no time for them.

By the end of the show, some two hours later, Tommy was flying.

'I am truly grateful,' he said in closing, 'to everyone who has called in today to stand against the wickedness in high places in this country. But I say this. Words are not enough. We must stand together to remove this cancer from our society. I call on all Texans, all Americans, to do whatever they can. Call your congressmen, call your senators. Tell your pastors to speak from their pulpits. Make your voices heard. And if need be, confront the White House itself, confront the demons within the White House. Put an end to this wickedness by any necessary means.'

He sat back contentedly in his chair.

'You have been listening to the Bubba Lanier show on Family of Christ Radio, 88 FM, Dallas, Texas. I'm Bubba. Have a great day, and come on back, y'all.'

7

May 27

'GOVERNOR BETANCOURT ON one, Mr Mason,' Helen announced over the intercom.

John Mason smiled to himself. It was a call he had been expecting – one among many – but an important one nonetheless. Mason was seated at his impressively large desk in his office at the Wilson Foundation. The Foundation was well funded and occupied a spacious suite of offices in a prestigious Washington building. The Wilson Foundation described itself as a 'think tank', and indeed was so. It regularly produced position papers on a variety of issues for the party, both on a state and a national level. Mason's official title was Director of the Foundation. But both the Wilson Foundation and John Mason had a second role, which was less public, but just as important to the party. It played host to the Committee, an informal body of senators, congressmen and party leaders who met from time to time to discuss the kind of strategies and tactics which were not paraded before the media. Mason's role for the Committee was less official. He acted as secretary and convenor, but was also a purveyor of the information on which the Committee's work depended. Much of this information he got from Selvey, a shadowy operative who had offered his services to Mason some years earlier, and whose identity Mason kept hidden from the members of the Committee. Selvey had an astonishing capacity to provide Mason with accurate intelligence on the most delicate subjects. How he did this, Mason did not know and did not care to know.

The Committee had come out of the Steve Wade crisis well,

though it had been a close call. Selvey had unearthed vital information about Steve Wade's affair with Lucia Benoni, which he had discreetly channeled to the *Washington Post's* White House correspondent, Mary Sullivan. The Committee had also leaned heavily on the House Majority leader to institute the successful impeachment proceedings, and had helped to shepherd them to success by gathering sympathy and support in the Senate. That had all gone well. But there were those who suggested that the Committee might also have been involved in bringing many thousands of armed extremists to Washington to help in holding the Senate hostage in its own chamber. As far as John Mason knew, there was no truth in any such suggestion, and he had repeatedly reassured the Committee that there was nothing to worry about. But privately, Mason was not exactly sure what Selvey was capable of. When asked directly about it, Selvey had been quick to insist that a venture on that scale was beyond even his reach, and Mason was inclined to believe him. But the last few months had been nervy ones, especially with the FBI sniffing around in search of conspirators. And only now, with President Trevathan's attention fixed on other matters, did Mason begin to draw breath and think about reaping the rewards.

The rewards were new contacts from some influential individuals who had money to spend and candidates to support, and were interested in enlisting the Foundation's aid. Mason was interested in what they had to say; partly because he believed that it was high time the Wilson Foundation had a higher profile; and partly because he believed that these contacts might be useful to his own career. Hank Betancourt was tangible proof that the Foundation was now showing up on the radar outside Washington. Betancourt was two years into his first term as Governor of Texas, a state which did not always pay much court to the national party, often preferring to set its own agenda. Betancourt was showing signs of reversing that trend. He made no secret of his ambition to win his party's nomination for the next presidential race, and his astute wooing of leading party figures across the country was widely admired. He had impeccable conservative credentials, both socially and economically. He was a man of faith; his wife taught Texas history in a Christian school in Austin. But Betancourt was not by nature abrasive or confrontational, and was known for reaching out to his opponents on bipartisan issues, while never compromising his own views. Moreover, his Bachelor's and Master's degrees from the University of Texas had been well earned, and his keen intellect housed a remarkably detailed grasp of foreign policy – an area in which the party had suffered from much collective ignorance in recent elections. Alex Vonn, the party's leading electoral strategist, and a member of the Committee, was already putting out feelers about running Betancourt's campaign. Mason was not surprised to find him on line one. They had met occasionally at party functions, but most of what Mason knew about Betancourt came from Selvey; Betancourt had survived Selvey's scrutiny thus far almost entirely unscathed, something many politicians had signally failed to do.

'Put him through,' Mason replied.

'John, how are you and all those good folks in Washington this fine day?' Betancourt asked.

Mason winced. He found the false bonhomie and practised drawl of professional Texans grating. Betancourt could draw out the word 'well' over three syllables. But it was part of the style, and it would pass once they got down to business.

'Very well, Governor. How are things with you?'

'Just fine, John; just fine. Family well?'

'Very well, sir, thank you.'

'Good,' Betancourt said, after a pause. 'Good. John, I know you have a busy day, and I will not keep you long. But I have to ask whether you are aware of the President's press conference this morning?'

Mason smiled.

'Yes, Governor, we keep track of all the press conferences here. This one was of particular interest, given that it was her first since the historic announcement.'

'Yes.' Betancourt paused. 'Well, I guess that's the main reason I am calling, John. I was surprised that she was not asked more probing questions about this astonishing announcement of

48

bringing her female lover into the White House. Do we not have people who encourage the press to ask certain questions? Surely we are going to hold her feet to the fire some more over this?'

Mason frowned. He had the transcript on his desk, of course. Helen had produced it, as always, within minutes of the end of the press conference. Betancourt's question was easy enough to answer in itself. But the issue was not so much whether questions could be asked, as whether they *should* be asked. The Committee had not reached a consensus on how to play its hand on the whole question of the President's announcement. It was tempting to unleash the dogs of war, of course, but there was no certainty about how it would play out. Alex Vonn, in particular, was worried that, once the initial conservative outrage subsided, Ellen Trevathan would pick up support from moderates in the party, especially moderate women, if they went after her too hard. He had counseled a period of reflection, and had asked Mason not to be too enthusiastic about any calls for an outright assault.

'Governor, she was asked three questions about it,' Mason replied. 'Two related to what I might call domestic arrangements, including whether Ms Ryan intends to refer to herself as the "First Lady". The third dealt with calls from a number of quarters for her to resign, a suggestion, I think it's fair to say, that she dismissed in strong terms'

There was a silence.

'I am aware of what was asked,' Betancourt said, a little less cordially. 'My question was directed to questions that *should* have been asked. Are we are going to stop playing around and start hammering home our point on this? I think that is what the party expects of us. I was wondering whether the Wilson Foundation and the Committee would take the lead on this. Someone has to, and …'

'You would prefer that we stick our necks out first?' Mason asked.

'I don't see any political risk here,' Betancourt protested. 'I don't see anyone in the party taking her side on this. Even people in her own party are not sure they can go along with it. I think we have a real chance to kick some ass here ahead of the election.'

'Alex Vonn is not sure we ought to move just yet,' Mason replied. 'He is in favor of seeing which way the wind is blowing before we decide on our strategy. There's no rush. This story isn't going away. The new-look First Family is going to be the center of attention for a long time.'

There was another silence.

'John, I understand what Alex is saying. As I'm sure you know, he and I have had certain discussions.'

'Yes, indeed.'

'And I respect his opinions. But … well, I have my finger on the pulse in Texas. And my impression is that this story is going to blow up in the very near future whether we want it to, or not. And when it does, if we are not seen to be taking the lead; if we are not seen to be occupying the moral high ground; if we are seen as conniving to draw a curtain over what is going on out of professional courtesy …'

'Governor, there is no question of that. It's not a matter of whether we take a stand. The only question is how we do it.' Mason permitted himself an invisible smile. 'Besides, no disrespect to the great state of Texas, but it doesn't always reflect national sentiment.'

'Point taken, John. But this is wider than Texas. Did you ever hear of a fella by the name of Bubba Lanier?'

The name sounded familiar, but Mason could not recall specifics.

'Can't say I have.'

'Well, he's one of those radio talk show hosts, out of Dallas. I don't have much truck with those people, if the truth be known. But this fella is burning up the airwaves. He's got a couple of pretty hard-core preachers on board, and he's out to get Trevathan if he can. He has already called for her to resign, but he's interested in more direct action.'

Mason's political antennae signaled danger.

'What sort of action?'

'A campaign of some kind. He hasn't articulated it very well. It's difficult to tell whether he just wants to get people mad at her, organize protests wherever she goes, or whether it might go further and extend to something like impeachment.'

Mason remained silent for some time.

'Governor, I think what you are telling me confirms Alex's view. We have to try to calculate how this might play out for the party in various scenarios.'

'I can't see any down side to it.'

John Mason could. Very clearly.

'Can I talk to Alex and get back to you on this?'

Mason could almost see the smile on the other end of the line.

'Of course, you can, John. Give me a call. Perhaps you and Alex could do a conference call?' He paused. 'Of course, it's possible that this is just a localized Texas thing. But I'm telling you, John, this boy Lanier has quite a way with him. He can be a persuasive fella. I've listened to his show a time or two, and I do believe he could influence some people. I don't think this can be confined to the state of Texas indefinitely.'

Mason nodded.

'I hear you, Governor. I'll be back to you in a day or so.'

'That's mighty friendly of you, John,' Betancourt said, hanging up.

Mason replaced the receiver and drummed his fingers on top of his desk for some time. Then he punched a button on the intercom.

'Yes, Mr Mason?' Helen responded.

'Helen, please get me Senator O'Brien and Alex Vonn. In that order.'

* * *

Mary Sullivan looked up from the mass of paper on her desk and smiled.

'Come back to haunt us after just a week, Harold? Or is it just that you can't keep away?'

She stood, walked around her desk and embraced Harold Philby, kissing him fondly on both cheeks.

'I hope it doesn't feel like I'm haunting you,' Philby replied. 'I had to come in to sign some forms for the Human Resources people, so I thought I would drop by and chat for a moment. How are you settling into your new office?'

'It's weird,' Mary said. 'It doesn't feel like my office. I'm so used to coming here to see you. I can't get used to walking back there and sitting at your desk.'

'*Your* desk now,' Philby pointed out.

'Maybe. I'm the interim editor, while they find your successor. I'm trying not to let myself feel too much at home.'

Philby snorted.

'It's yours if you want it, Mary,' he said confidently. 'They have to look around, of course. That's the name of the game these days. But with your record here, the owners aren't going to look too far.'

Mary waved Philby into a chair and returned to her seat behind the desk.

'I know you recommended me for the position, Harold. It means a lot to me.'

'There was never a question in my mind about it. You led the way during the crisis. The *Washington Post* was out in front and on the right side, and that was your doing.'

'Yours too,' Mary replied. 'You were the editor. You called the shots and let me write my story. A lot of credit goes to you too. And what a story to go out on!'

'Yes,' Philby said. 'I might have retired before, but for that story breaking. I just couldn't bring myself to do it. And things were happening so fast, I'm not sure I could have found a good moment to leave.'

'I'm glad you stayed.'

She looked across the desk, directly into his eyes. Suddenly, she smiled.

'Are you having second thoughts? There's another good story brewing now. I wouldn't blame you if you wanted to reclaim your office and send me out to work.'

'There's always a good story somewhere, Mary,' Philby said, shaking his head. 'If I waited until there was no story to print, I would never go.'

He stood.

'No, the time is right. In addition to which, Becky has everything packed, and we have our flights booked to Portugal next Monday. So that is that. But I have my on-line subscription. I will be reading every word as I sit on my veranda with a glass of white port, watching the sun set over the River Douro.'

Mary stood also.

'How would you handle this, Harold?' she asked.

'You know the answer to that.'

'I would love to hear a word of wisdom on this before you go.'

Philby looked beyond her at his old chair.

'If I learned anything in the years I was here,' he said, 'I learned that it's our job to look at all sides of a question, and try to give the reading public a balanced view. That's a rare thing to find nowadays, and it's going to be a particularly rare thing in this situation. You're going to have a lot of people who think she's the devil incarnate and want her burned at the stake, and you're going to have a lot of people who think she has taken a giant leap forward for civilized humanity and want her to be canonized. And that's the so-called journalists I'm talking about, never mind the great American public. Somewhere in between, you are going to have a few thinking people who say "live and let live", but want to know what it all means for America, for our government. It's the *Post's* job to present all sides of the question and, if you come down at all, to come down on the side you think is right, but in a fair and objective way. It's your job, Mary, to try to revive the lost art of civil discourse and reasoned, courteous disagreement. You won't get much thanks for your troubles, but you will keep a light burning in an intolerant age.'

He held up his hands.

'Be fair to Ellen Trevathan and her family, Mary, and be fair to America. You know that already. Trust your instincts. You're a newspaper woman, and I know you will get it right.'

He turned towards the door. 'Portugal calls.'

Mary moved between Philby and the door to give him a last embrace.

'Don't be surprised if you find me on your veranda one evening in need of a glass of white port.'

'It would be a delight. In the meanwhile, I will be reading your newspaper, the *Washington Post*, with pride.'

He kissed her hand lightly and was gone.

8

May 28

IT WAS JUST before 7 o'clock on Saturday evening at Dulles International Airport, and Dani's American Airlines flight to London was scheduled for takeoff in less than half an hour. Despite Ellen's apprehension, the drive to the airport had been uneventful. The two Secret Service agents who had shadowed Dale Harrison's car, both on the way to the airport and on the return journey, reported no incidents. Dani had a seat in Business Class, next to a window, seat 7A. She had forced her well-stuffed carry-on into the overhead compartment and kicked off her trainers. She stretched out her legs and began to experiment with the screen in front of her seat, which offered her a choice of movies, music and games to keep her entertained during the flight. A flight attendant stopped with a hot face towel and the offer of champagne or orange juice. She chose the orange juice. A few times she glanced at 7B, the aisle seat next to her, and then in front of her to the door of the aircraft. Most of the passengers were on board now and the cabin crew were readying the aircraft for takeoff or assisting passengers having problems with an item of baggage. Seat 7B was supposed to be occupied, and Dani was feeling a little nervous about the fact that it was still empty.

With five minutes to go before the crew closed the door, the person she was expecting suddenly appeared, casually flung her carry-on into the overhead compartment next to Dani's, and took her seat.

'Hi, Dani, I'm Rosa. Sorry to be running a bit late.'

She leaned across and spoke more confidentially.

'There's a lot of paperwork when you bring a loaded firearm on to an aircraft, even for Secret Service agents. They made me cross every "t" and dot every "i". But I promise, I wouldn't have let them take off without me. Nice to meet you.'

Rosa Linda Montalbán was Hispanic, tall and striking, with black hair and dark brown eyes. Her cheekbones were prominent and gave her face an almost sculptured look. She was thirty-two years of age, yet looked little older than Dani. Dani offered her hand.

'You too. I was a bit surprised that I wouldn't meet you until we were on board. They showed me your picture, but …'

'Yes, I know,' Rosa said. 'Protocol. It's to do with not being seen together unnecessarily in public. Don't worry, we will have every chance to get acquainted during the flight. And I will be around every day of your four weeks in Cambridge.'

'You're going to be at my side the whole time?' Dani asked apprehensively. 'How is that not being seen together in public?'

Rosa laughed.

'No. You're not the President. I'm not going to be shadowing you 24/7. I won't be at your side. I will be around, but with any luck you won't notice, at least most of the time.'

A flight attendant stopped at row seven and asked them to bring their seats forward for takeoff.

Rosa touched Dani's hand.

'I tell you what. Why don't we relax for a while, eat dinner, watch a movie, and wait for people around us to start to go to sleep? Then I will fill you in on a few more details.'

Dani nodded her agreement. She had known that, once Ellen and her mother came out, her life would inevitably change. The Director of the Secret Service, Abe Solari, had been briefed in advance and had made discreet preparations to put in place a suitable level of protection for both Kay and Dani. Dani's stay in Cambridge could not be ignored. Both Kay and Dani had asked that any protection should be as unobtrusive as possible, but the details had to be left to the Service. Dani was still not altogether resigned to it. It felt like a restriction placed on her life, an invasion of her privacy, almost as if she were under surveillance. But as the 767 rose effortlessly into the evening sky, leaving Washington behind, there was also a slight feeling of relief that she would not be completely alone.

'My job is to watch from a safe distance,' Rosa said.

The dinner service had ended, and they had watched an indifferent crime movie. Rosa had kept an eye on the other occupants of Business Class by taking a series of short strolls, ostensibly to do some stretching exercises. Some were asleep, others wearing headphones as they used the entertainment system. A few workaholics had laptops and papers open in front of them. She returned to her seat and spoke quietly to Dani about the procedures she had planned, with Solari's approval. She would stay in Downing College where Dani would be based during her summer school program, and where classes would be held. Her cover was that she was a visiting American research student. She would have access to a bicycle and a car, to make sure she could cover distant locations – the library, restaurants, pubs and other places to which Dani might choose to go without much advance warning. She programmed her mobile number into Dani's phone. There was no need for Dani to give her advance warning of movements in Cambridge, but if there was any suggestion of a trip outside the city, to London, for example, she needed to know the day before. Some students were known to be planning weekend trips to Amsterdam, Paris, and Barcelona. Rosa asked for three days notice of any trip of that kind. Rosa's voice suggested the hope that Dani would resist the temptation to go out of the country, but she made it clear that Dani was absolutely free to do whatever she wished.

'You will be able to summon me if you need me, and I will summon you if I need to, and you will catch a glimpse of me from time to time. I will call every morning and evening, just to say "hi", to keep in touch. But I will do my best not to cramp your style. Basically, I want you to carry on as if I'm not there. Go to class, go to the library, go out with friends.'

She smiled.

'Get lucky if you want to. I won't rat on you, but try to make it obvious beforehand so I get a chance to check him out.'

Dani snorted, but could not resist returning the smile.

'Great. That sounds really romantic. In any case, I'm going to England to work, not to pick up men or go off for weekends abroad. You're not going to have to worry about that.'

'I have to worry about everything,' Rosa said, 'I will be receiving daily intel from Special Branch in London, so I'll know if there is anything specific that's concerning them. No one thinks that will be the case, so don't let it bother you. If there is anything that concerns me, you will be the first to know. Just keep your eyes open. If anything happens that you think is strange or unusual, or that bothers you at all, let me know – even if it seems trivial. I won't get upset, however often you call. I will only get upset if something happens and you don't tell me. Above all, remember, everything I'm doing is just by way of precaution. Don't let it affect you. Enjoy Cambridge, have a good time.'

Rosa picked up her purse and took out a small black plastic item.

'When you contact me, use your mobile,' she said. 'But if it's urgent and you can't use your phone, or you don't want to be seen using it, you will have another option. I will give you this device once you have cleared baggage claim at Heathrow. It will fit in your purse or a pocket. It will tell me where you are, and whether you are moving. It has a panic button. If you push that button I will assume that you need me immediately, and that you can't call, for whatever reason. My intention is never to be more than five minutes away.'

Dani nodded slowly.

'Good,' she said. 'I'll do my best to relax and act as if everything is normal.'

Rosa smiled sympathetically.

'You'll get used to it,' she said. 'You will be conscious of the security for a day or two, but once you get into your studies and your social life you will tune it out. After a week or so, it will be so familiar you won't even notice. That's the plan anyway.'

She opened her purse again, took out a folded sheet of paper, and handed it to Dani.

'This is a list of the students on the international criminal law program, names and law schools, thirty-two in all. Twelve are from the States, the others from all over the place, the UK, Canada, Australia, the Netherlands, Italy, Germany, Jordan, South Africa. Do any of these names seem familiar?'

Dani shook her head. 'No, no one I recognize.'

'Have you had any contact with any of these law schools?'

'Contact?'

'Visited them, done other programs with students from the school, had lectures from a professor – anything?'

'No. Not as far as I know.'

Rosa nodded. 'OK. We've given them a preliminary vetting. Nothing came up that concerned us. Just keep me informed if anyone seems to want to spend an abnormal amount of time with you, and we will check them out in more depth.'

'I don't know what you mean by "abnormal",' Dani protested.

'Yes, you do,' Rosa replied, taking a black mask from her purse and pulling it on over her eyes. 'Why don't we get some sleep? When we land, we will make our ways off the aircraft separately and I will see you just after you leave baggage claim. The next time you see me, we will be in Cambridge.'

9

BEV SPENT THE Saturday morning with his parents. At first, little was said between them. The shadow of the Visitor hung heavy over the house. There was so much Bev wanted to ask them. How could they have agreed to move to a new country on the off-chance that a child they had not yet produced might someday be useful to a cause in a land they might never see again? How could they have agreed to conceive and give birth to a child, knowing that the child would be used as a pawn in some political game, like breeding a fighting bull for the ring, or a goat for the sacrifice? How did they feel about him? Were they proud of him? Did they hope he would obey the Visitor's instructions? Did they feel any guilt or remorse? Was there some part of them that hoped he would refuse to be a sleeper, some part of them that wanted a normal life for their son? Who were his parents?

Bev realized, with sadness, that he did not even know the answer to that basic question. The revelation that he was a sleeper – that they had created him to be a sleeper – had destroyed every preconceived idea he had ever had about them. He wondered, with a wry smile, how his high school counselor would have coped with that one. He fully expected his parents to ask him what he was going to do – not that he could have given them any definite answer – but surely they were curious? Even if the Visitor had kept them in the dark about what lay ahead, surely it would only be human nature to try to get some information about this new chapter in Bev's life? But the morning had been passed in small talk, worrying about whether he was forgetting to put something he needed into his case, as if the essentials of daily life could not be obtained in England, if need be. But, then again, he would only be away for four weeks, wouldn't he? In any normal family, the occasion would not call for any special outpouring of grief or sorrow.

But at last, as he stood in his bedroom, his bags packed and ready to leave, they came to him. He sat down on the bed and waited for someone to speak. His mother sat down quietly on the wicker chair at his desk. His father stood just inside the door, looking down at the floor.

'Will you do as they ask?'

'I don't know,' Bev replied.

His father nodded.

'That is a wise answer. Such things do not call for instant decisions.'

Bev pushed himself up from the bed in frustration.

'Maybe. Look, I don't know, OK? I don't even know what they want. Even the Visitor doesn't know. That's what he says, anyway. What if they ask me to do something illegal? What if it's something immoral, something I can't do with a clear conscience? Would you want me to do it anyway? For them?'

'It would be up to you,' his father replied. 'You know that. But remember this, Bev: legality and morality do not exist in a vacuum. What is illegal and what is immoral have to be judged in the context of real situations in the real world.'

'We *are* in the real world,' Bev protested. 'Right here in Houston, Texas. This is where you brought me up. We have laws here, and we have morality – American morality. I don't know who these people are. What if they are criminals? What if they are terrorists?'

His father walked slowly across the room and put a hand on Bev's shoulder.

'You are right, of course, Bev. We brought you up to obey the law and to be a moral young man in the eyes of American society. That is good, as far as it goes. But now you know the truth – that there is a bigger picture; that America is not the world; that your upbringing here has been a means to an end.'

Furiously, Bev seized his father's hand and threw it off his shoulder.

'A means to an end?' he shouted. 'Is that all I am to you …?'

Fighting off Bev's resistance, his father pulled him into an embrace.

'I didn't say that, Bev. *You* are not a means to an end. You are our son, and we love you as much as any parents can love a son. I said that *your upbringing* has been a means to an end. To give you the chance to do something for your homeland, your people …'

'*This* is my homeland,' Bev insisted, pushing his father away. 'It's the only one I know, and the people here are the only people I know.'

'That is not quite true,' his father said quietly. 'I know that you have never been to Kashmir. But you have heard us talk of it. You have heard the stories at the temple. You have heard about the wrongs done to our people, the injustices.'

'There have been injustices on both sides, on all sides.'

His father nodded. 'That is true. All I am saying is that Kashmir, too, has been a part of your life. I understand that it must seem less real to you than Texas, but still, you have learned that it is a part of you.'

'What have I learned?' Bev asked, with a grim smile. 'What have I learned about Kashmir? It's a land a long way away, a land people have fought over for centuries, people who can never agree with each other, people who would rather fight than sit down and work things out…'

'Bev …'

'Well, how many wars have there been over Kashmir just in your lifetimes, Dad, Mom? It's one of those places where the fighting will never stop – like the Balkans, like Ireland. They can have as many ceasefires as they like, declare peace as many times as they like, and nothing changes, they still kill each other. Do you want to sacrifice me for that? Do you want me to sacrifice my children? We don't even live there, for God's sake, and we never will. When will it ever end? Where does it stop? How is this a part of me?'

Bev sat down heavily on the bed, and held his head in his hands. His father sat down next to him, his hands on his knees, looking down. It was some time before he spoke.

'Perhaps the stories you heard at the temple were just stories,' he said eventually. 'Perhaps the history you learned was too remote, too impersonal. Let me try to bring it a bit closer to home for you.'

He placed a hand on Bev's knee.

'Please understand that I say this, not to persuade you, but simply to inform. You are an intelligent and wise young man, and you do not need me to persuade.'

He withdrew the hand, but turned to face Bev.

'You have heard from us about my parents, your grandparents.'

Bev looked up sharply.

'They died when you were young, from an outbreak of cholera.'

'That is what you were told, Bev, yes. It is not the truth. It is true that they died when I was relatively young. But not from cholera.'

Bev suddenly felt cold. He drew his arms around him.

'Your grandparents died in a massacre. As you know, they lived in a small town, not far from Srinagar. It was supposedly a place where those of different faiths could live together. The population was mostly Muslim, but there were some Hindus, including our family; and there were Jains, Buddhists, even Christians, who lived in the area. One day, the Muslims took up weapons; knives, swords, some guns, whatever they could find. They went on a rampage. They killed every Hindu they could find. A few people managed to escape. But your grandparents died on that day, Bev. Some years later, I heard from one of the survivors that they had been hacked to death inside their home.'

Bev looked at his father in horror. He could not speak immediately.

'But why? What caused it? Something must have happened …'

'Yes, no doubt something happened,' his father replied. 'Something always does, doesn't it? You destroyed our mosque. Well, you destroyed our temple. Well, you killed our imam. Perhaps this was a hundred years ago, but people have long memories. And so it goes on. For me, that didn't matter at the time. All I knew was, they had killed my parents. I wanted to do something about it.'

He paused.

'I was young at the time, Bev, but not so young as you were led to believe. I had left home by then. Otherwise, no doubt, I would have been dead also. But I was already far from home pursuing my studies. As you know, my schoolteacher had recognized my aptitude for study. He persuaded my parents to let me leave home to live with the family in Delhi in the hope that I would go to university. In so doing, he not only furthered my education; without knowing it, he saved my life.'

He stood and walked to the window.

'I knew some people in Delhi at the time. One or two of them were members of SK, Svatantra Kashmir.'

'Freedom for Kashmir,' Bev said quietly.

'Yes. I went to them in my grief, in my zeal, to avenge my parents. I offered to do whatever they wished.'

He smiled wanly, looking out of the window into the distance.

'I don't know quite what I expected, whether I thought they would give me a Kalashnikov, or a sword and tell me to go to kill the enemy. I would have done it, or died trying, if they had asked. But they did not. Instead, they pointed out to me that I had the ability to be useful in other ways. I could become professionally qualified. Then I thought, perhaps they would ask me to return to Kashmir to support our people as a doctor or an aid worker. But they did not ask that either.'

'You would have taken up arms?'

'Yes.'

'Would you have been a terrorist?'

Bev's father smiled.

'Define "terrorist",' he replied. 'There is an old saying, Bev, that one man's terrorist is another man's freedom fighter. History is written by the winners, so perhaps a freedom fighter is simply a terrorist who wins. There are many examples in history, are there not? Eamon de Valera; David Ben Gurion; Nelson Mandela. Even Gandhi, in the eyes of some, for all his talk of non-violence. And if you still want to talk about being an American, what about George Washington?'

Bev tried unsuccessfully not to smile.

'I don't know how to answer your question, Bev. At the time, I was consumed by grief and anger. I cannot say what I would have done and what I would not have done. I hope I would have retained my humanity, my decency. But I cannot really say. I was never put to the test. I do not expect you to share these feelings. It was long ago, and they were people you never knew. All you know of them is your heritage in Kashmir. So, of course, you will deal with it in your own way.'

He turned to Bev.

'I knew your mother already at that time. It had been arranged that we would marry. They asked us to come here, with their help. That was their response to my offer of service. We were to move here, Bev, to live here, to have a child, to become American. The rest you know.'

He leaned back against the window frame.

'Perhaps that does not seem very much like a sacrifice compared to fighting in the hills,' he said. 'But knowing that we were to involve you – even before you were born ... I beg you to believe, Bev, that we do feel it is a great sacrifice. And there was another sacrifice we had to make.'

Bev looked up.

'We can never go back, Bev,' his mother said quietly from her chair. 'They told us that quite clearly. We can never go back to Kashmir. We can never see our land again.'

*   *   *

He spent the early afternoon in bed with Shesi. She noticed a special intensity about his love-making, a greater strength and physicality. Bev was always passionate and attentive to her in bed, but on this day he seemed to be unusually strong and insistent. She made a light remark to the effect that he ought to go away more often. He smiled, but Shesi saw in his eyes that he was somehow far away. She tried to connect with him, to match his intensity; she tried to be, for her, unusually seductive, even brazen sexually, and she was pleased that he reacted to her physically. But there was a space between them. Bev, of course, knew exactly what was causing the space, and he was debating in his mind whether or not to tell her. She already knew about the Visitor. It would probably come as no great surprise to her to learn more.

He loved Shesi. He no longer had any doubt about that. If she was to share his life she deserved to know who he was; there could be no code of silence between them as there was at home. But if he told her, she would have questions – and they were questions that he simply could not answer for her yet, because he could not answer them for himself. He might decide to have nothing to do with the Visitor's request for service. The request might be a simple matter that he could attend to without difficulty. Better to wait until he knew more. He did not intend to shut Shesi out. It just made more sense to wait until he got back to Houston before he said anything. She asked him no questions. She drove him to the airport, kissed him lovingly, and promised him a special afternoon when he returned. As she drove away from the drop-off area at Terminal E, looking in her rear-view mirror, she had a clear view of him waving her goodbye.

* * *

As Bev settled into seat 24F on the British Airways Airbus, he suddenly felt tired. With a smile he put it down to his unusual energy in bed with Shesi. He had almost forty minutes to wait until takeoff. He allowed himself to sit back and close his eyes, and gradually the background noise, and the movement of the cabin crew and his fellow passengers faded from his consciousness.

He was walking through the most beautiful landscape he had ever seen. On all sides were high mountains, capped with snow. On the slopes of the mountains were forests, thick with majestic pines, and below the forests, fields of luscious grass and dazzling poppies. He felt, rather than saw, the presence of animals; hares, once a silver fox, and once a tiger. Then suddenly, he was walking through a field in which there had been a battle. The bodies of the dead lay everywhere and vultures descended on them to devour the flesh. But then, just as suddenly, the battlefield was left behind, and he saw villages full of simple people going about their daily lives in peace. Finally, he stood in a vast river valley below the tallest of the mountains, where he was completely alone, and where there was complete silence except for the rushing of the waters of the river. An eagle appeared before him in the sky and pierced him with its eyes. Bev felt no fear of the eagle and tried to return its gaze, but before he could focus on it clearly, the eagle vanished.

Bev awoke feeling refreshed, thinking how welcome it had been to doze off for a few minutes before takeoff. As he stretched out his legs, he realized that he felt hungry, and even the prospect of an Economy Class airline dinner seemed inviting. As he opened his eyes fully, a flight attendant passed Row 24, and ordered him to bring his seat back to upright in preparation for landing at London Heathrow.

10

'WE ARE A bit of a walk from most of the other colleges, here in Downing,' Alfred, the Head Porter, concedes. 'But it's not too bad. Nothing compared to Girton or Churchill, and what have you. If you're stuck out there and you want to come into town, you either buy a bike or take the bus. But from Downing, if you go out through the back gate, you can walk to the Senate House in less than ten minutes. And the good news is, we are right opposite the University Arms Hotel and Parker's Piece, where you can go for a nice bracing walk, and even try your hand at cricket, if you've a mind to.'

The newly-arrived group of summer school students has reported, as instructed, at the Porters' Lodge just inside the main gate. They are still tired from their travels and anxious to get to their rooms. They have had little opportunity to introduce themselves to each other, and a welcoming reception at the Master's Lodge is still to come – with little time to unpack and get ready. But Alfred, as he does with all visitors, insists on pausing outside the Chapel to lecture them on the main features of the College. The college buildings, he points out, are of uniform appearance – a smooth off-white stone. The chapel, the dining hall, and the Master's Lodge feature Doric pillars below a triangular façade; these can be viewed as either a modest homage to the Acropolis or a precocious piece of frippery, according to how you like to think of it. Far be it from Alfred to express a view on that – he has an opinion, of course, but it would be more than his job is worth to give voice to it. Ask the Master when you go to the lodge this evening.

'The college is laid out as a quadrangle, but you will notice that only three sides of the quadrangle have been built on. The fourth side has the lawn and gardens only. Why is this?' Alfred asks rhetorically. 'Well, they say that it was left open because of a lack of funds. The college was founded in1800, thanks to a bequest in the will of Sir George Downing. We don't talk about Sir George too much, you understand. Without going into too many details, he is usually described as an adventurer and entrepreneur, and you can draw your own conclusions from that, if you take my meaning. But don't ask the Master about that, or if you do, don't tell her that Alfred put you up to it. Anyway, be that as it may, Sir George's will was contested and was tied up in Chancery long enough to make a number of lawyers rich and the estate a good deal poorer.' But Alfred can't help thinking it was a good thing, actually. He rather likes the open feeling at the back, much better than being totally enclosed, if he may be forgiven for saying so.

'Now, there is one rule that we do like to have observed,' Alfred concludes. 'The lawns are off limits to everyone except the Fellows. Anyone else has to take the gravel paths. So if you're on your way to hall for breakfast, or the Master's Lodge this evening, please walk around the quadrangle – or find a Fellow to walk with on the grass.'

He pauses, hoping for a little of the sympathetic laughter he sometimes gets from the tourists, but there is none.

'In earlier times the rule was strictly enforced, and anyone caught violating the rule could be fined. We're not likely to do that these days. It's all gone downhill a bit if you ask me – but don't quote me on that, especially to the Master. Just remember that the Fellows still tend to get a bit upset about it, so try to stay off the grass if there's anyone watching.'

The lecture ends abruptly.

Dani looked around the college grounds, and thought briefly that she caught a glimpse of Rosa standing near the back gate. But if so, it was only a glimpse. When she looked again, there was no one in sight. The group of students dispersed slowly as Alfred made his way back to the Porters' Lodge. Dani forced her tired body to drag her bags along the gravel path to T staircase, where she had been assigned her room.

* * *

May 31

Jaap Lammers spoke almost perfect English, his Dutch accent and inflection lending to his words an added degree of interest rather than any difficulty of understanding. He was a young man, still in his mid-thirties, but he had already built a considerable reputation for himself in the field of international criminal law. His home base was Leiden University, but he was invited to teach abroad on a regular basis, and his articles, all written in immaculate English, were read with respect by academics across the world and even at the International Criminal Court at The Hague. This summer, his task was to oversee the international criminal law course at Downing, conducting seminars himself, introducing guest lecturers, guiding his students through the large volume of materials they were expected to read and digest, and awarding each student a grade after setting a written test at the end of their four weeks of study.

Lammers had the wisdom not to expect much from the first seminar. The students were new to the subject; they were still tired, in some cases jet lagged; the weather was warm and humid; and the seminar room on the second floor of H staircase was stuffy. His purpose was mainly to introduce the subject and the materials, to make sure the students knew how to find the library, and to set them an assignment for the first few days. He spoke for only half an hour.

'So, we will begin,' he concluded, 'by trying to answer the question of why it took so long to create an organized system of international criminal prosecutions for genocide, war crimes, and crimes against humanity. Look at why the proposal to prosecute the Kaiser after the First World War came to nothing. Look at why it took so long after Nuremberg – until 1993, in fact – to build on that experience. Look at why it took so long to create the International Criminal Court, which began its work only in 2002. So many political issues. We will discuss all this on Thursday. After this, we will move on to look at the law they created at Nuremberg and what has happened since.'

Lammers glanced across at Dani, who was seated four places down the large conference table to his left.

'And, of course, Miss Ryan, if your step-mother would like my personal opinion about whether the United States should sign and ratify the Treaty of Rome, and become involved in the work of the International Criminal Court, please tell her that it would be my pleasure to visit the White House personally to advise her on that matter.'

There was laughter around the room.

'I'll do that,' Dani replied, smiling.

'All right, that's all for today,' Lammers concluded. 'See you on Thursday. Make sure you make a note of my number and email address in case you need to ask me anything.'

Dani gathered up her papers, put them in the slim light-weight briefcase she had brought for use in Cambridge, and made her way down the stone staircase on to the path. It was lunch time. She walked quickly to her room, dropped off her briefcase, and made her way back along the central pathway of the quadrangle towards the dining hall. Ahead of her she saw one of her fellow students and she quickened her pace to catch up with him.

'Hi, it's Bev, isn't it?'

He stopped and turned towards her. 'Yes.'

She extended her hand. 'I'm Dani Ryan.'

'I know,' Bev replied, smiling and taking her hand. 'Everybody knows who you are.'

She laughed. 'Ah, yes, the price of fame. I wanted to introduce myself to you at the reception last night, but I didn't get the chance. The Master kept me talking for quite a while, then a couple of the Fellows, and after that, it was a free-for-all.'

Including Rosa, hovering on the other side of the room in a black cocktail dress, doing her best to look like a research student and blend in, Dani recalled with a smile. They resumed their walk towards the hall.

'Yes, there was quite a crowd, wasn't there? Between the jet lag and the champagne, I really don't remember who I met or what I said to them. It might have been better if they had left it for a couple of days.'

'It probably would have,' Dani said. 'I guess they were just trying to be hospitable. Anyway, I'm glad to have the chance to say hello now. We have a connection, don't we?'

Bev nodded. 'South Texas College of Law.'

'Where my step-mom took her oath of office.'

'In our student lounge. We have a plaque on the wall to commemorate it. I eat lunch right there five days a week. I wish I could have been around to be part of all that, but they sent us home as soon as our dean knew she was coming.'

'Nothing personal,' Dani smiled. 'I know she is really grateful. She told me she will always remember the school and how kind everyone was. She wants to go back there to visit before too long.'

'I hope she will,' Bev said. 'That would be great. Of course, she also took our dean with her when she left. We had to get ourselves a new one when she made Dean Hunt Attorney-General.'

'Who did you get?' Dani asked, as they climbed the two steps up into the entrance of the hall.

'Professor Salinger. He came from Northwestern. He's a constitutional law expert, so he fits right in where Dean Hunt left off.'

Lunch was served buffet style. The hall was set up in the traditional manner, with long dining tables front to back along its length, the high table at ninety degrees along its width at the top. But the dining hall in Downing is very different from the traditional dark, claustrophobic image of the college dining hall. There are portraits on the walls, but there is a good deal of vivid paint work in bright college colors, giving the hall a remarkably modern and open feel. It was not crowded. A few other students were lunching, as were some of the college staff, but many had chosen to take advantage of the warm weather to take sandwiches outside to the empty fourth side of the quadrangle, or had gone in search of a pub or restaurant with a garden. Dani and Bev built themselves a salad from the buffet, added some bread, and carried their trays to the table nearest the door, where a cool breeze offered welcome relief from the heavy warmth of the early afternoon. Dani poured water for both of them from a bottle on the table.

'Is this your first trip to Europe?' she asked.

'No. I've been to London with my parents several times. Like most Indians, they have an interest in England, but this is my first time in Cambridge. I traveled in Spain and Portugal with a friend for a few weeks in the summer of my senior year. That's it, really. How about you?'

'My mom loves Italy, she cooks great Italian food, so I've spent some time there, and I've been to France with my Dad. But this is my first time in England. I'd hoped to go traveling after the course ends, but now …'

'Security issues?'

'Yes. If I go anywhere on my own, someone has to come with me. And then people are going to complain about the cost to the public. So …'

'That's too bad,' Bev said. 'Do you have someone watching you here? I haven't noticed anyone.'

'I could tell you,' Dani replied with a smile, 'but then I'd have to kill you.'

Bev threw his hands in the air, returning the smile. 'Withdrawn, your honor. I don't want to know.'

'It's all pretty low key,' Dani said. 'I don't think anyone would really mind if I went off somewhere, as long as I let everyone know in good time beforehand. It's just that all this attention is new to me. I haven't got used to it yet.'

'I hear that,' Bev said. 'I think that would take some getting used to. I don't know how I would react to it.'

Dani shrugged. 'It's not like I have any choice. But it could be worse. If you're Ellen Trevathan, you have it 24/7, everywhere you go.'

'I guess so,' Bev said. 'I have been thinking about doing some traveling. I haven't finally decided.' He grinned. 'I don't have any security worries, but I would have to clear it with my girlfriend.'

Dani smiled. 'What's her name? Is she a student too? Could she come traveling with you?'

'Her name is Shesi. Her family has a business importing rugs and stuff from India. They have done pretty well for themselves, and she is in line to take over. So she doesn't get much time off.'

He paused. 'It's going really well, you know. I am going to miss her while I'm here. That's the only downside really.'

'I understand,' Dani said. 'At least that's one complication I don't have this summer.'

She paused and took a breath.

'Listen, do you want to be study partners? I work better when I have someone to prod me and make me get things done. We could go to the library together, talk about assignments, prepare for class. What do you think?'

'Sounds good to me,' Bev replied. 'Why don't we walk over to the library and check it out once we get through with lunch?'

* * *

When she arrived back in room T4 from the library late in the afternoon, Dani kicked off her flip-flops and threw herself back wearily on to the narrow single bed. She had fully intended reading through some of the materials Jaap Lammers had assigned them before thinking about dinner, but she was still suffering from jet lag, and she had been longing to lie down for a rest ever since lunch. She was not sure she could keep her eyes open even if she tried to work. Bev had gone for a walk to acquaint himself better with the city center. They had not made any firm arrangement except to meet at the library again after lunch the following day. Her phone rang.

'Bev Prasad,' Rosa said.

Dani had almost dozed off, and she had to make her mind focus as she brought her head up from the pillow and picked up the phone.

'Bev? What about him?'

'You tell me.'

Dani shook her head. 'What do you mean? Bev is OK. He's a nice guy.'

'I'm sure he is,' Rosa said. 'I'm just checking. You spent quite a lot of time with him today.'

'We're going to be study partners during the program,' Dani replied, suddenly feeling frustrated. 'I suggested it. Is that OK with you?'

'Relax, Dani. Of course it's OK. I just need to be aware. Just to put my mind at ease. Has he said or done anything odd?'

'Odd? No …well… ' Dani hesitated.

'What?'

'Oh it's nothing. He asked if I had someone minding me.'

'Well, you see, that's the kind of thing I need to know.'

Dani sat fully upright.

'No, no, Rosa. You're taking it the wrong way. It wasn't like that. I brought the subject up. We were talking about whether we had any plans to do some traveling after the course. I was trying to tell him about what it's like for me, that I can't just take off on my own. That's all it was.'

'Did you tell him about me?'

'No, of course not.'

'You're sure?'

'Yes, I'm sure.'

There was a silence on the line for a few moments.

'OK,' Rosa said. 'He checks out, anyway – he seems to be a good, hard-working kid from a respectable Indian family in Houston. Nothing negative.'

'Well, thank you,' Dani said, still exasperated. 'And just so you can put your mind further at ease, we are going to be study partners and nothing more. He has a girlfriend in Houston. Her name is Shesi. OK?'

On the other end of the line, Rosa laughed. 'Thank you, Dani. Talk to you soon,' she replied, terminating the call.

With a heavy sigh, Dani threw her phone on to the small armchair next to her bed and laid her head back down on to the pillow. She quickly drifted off, and when she awoke, it was almost time for breakfast.

* * *

The man Rosa had been expecting walked briskly up and sat next to her. She had taken an outside table at a small café near the Drummer Street bus station. It was a warm afternoon and Rosa was wearing a light jacket and a thin green top over khaki slacks.

But her new companion was formally dressed in a dark gray suit and blue tie. He signaled with his hand through the window to the barista to order a coffee.

'Well, imagine seeing you here,' he said. 'I thought you were in London.'

'I had to come up to see some people at college,' she replied.

As a result of this coded exchange, she identified him as Detective Inspector Steve Macmillan of Special Branch. He had identified her as Special Agent Rosa Linda Montalbán, United States Secret Service. They would be meeting at different places in the city on a daily basis. They would be available to each other by phone 24/7. Steve had backup available at short notice, detectives and an armed response unit from the Cambridgeshire police, and one or two intelligence specialists from Special Branch. In a worst-case scenario, a phone call would bring an anti-terrorist unit of the SAS to the scene within an hour. Casually, they both scanned the area around the café. It was quiet in the early evening.

'No new intel,' Steve said, in a conversational tone he might have used to discuss the weather. 'The President and her mother are under siege at home. The press are giving them a hard time. But there's been no chatter about anything unusual, no mention of Dani. My contact at MI5 will let me know if that changes.'

'Good,' Rosa said. 'Nothing to report on my side. Do you have the list of students?'

'Yes. I know your people have been over them. We haven't done any more on that, though we will if any individual seems to be coming into prominence. I did run a check on the lecturer, Jaap Lammers. He does hang out with a few leftie academic types, but you'd expect that, wouldn't you? Nothing to worry about on our radar. Is she spending time with anyone in particular?'

'Her study partner, Bev Prasad. We ran a check on him. He seems to be a solid citizen.'

'No one else?'

'It's too early to say. We will know more in a day or two when social groups start to form and we see patterns forming of who is hanging out with whom. Dani tells me there are plans for groups to go out together in the evenings – pubs, cafés and so on – she will let me know where and when. She's not the nightclub type, so I don't think we have to worry about that.'

'No talk of travel at weekends?'

'Nothing so far.'

They paused as Steve's coffee arrived. He took a sip and smiled broadly.

'In that case, all we have to do is drink our coffee and enjoy this fine English summer weather.'

Rosa returned his smile. 'Don't say that,' she replied. 'I left my umbrella in my room.'

11

June 7

ON LEAVING THE law library, Bev had said goodbye to Dani and begun to walk slowly into the city center. There was a frustrating lack of logic to jet lag, he reflected. He had been in England for over a week. He had thought he was over it. But it had struck again while he was trying to read an article about the war in Bosnia. Outside the fresh air had revived him, but he had no enthusiasm for returning to the library. Nor did he see much point in going back to his room and trying in vain to sleep. Better to force himself to stay awake and have an early night.

He soon found himself in Market Square by Great St Mary's church. A small street market had set up around the church, and he made a leisurely tour of the wooden stalls with their canvas tops, where vendors were displaying an eclectic range of cheap clothing, toys, and office supplies. There was nothing to interest him there. He bought a cold soda from a small convenience store on the square, walked the few yards to King's Parade, and turned right by the Senate House. Following the street, he passed Trinity and St John's, and made his way to Magdalene Bridge. Scudamores, who had been renting punts to students and tourists for more than a hundred years, were taking full advantage of the warm weather. The long, shallow boats were everywhere, leaving and returning to the quay under the bridge, colliding carelessly but harmlessly, their occupants keeping up a hubbub of laughter and conversation. Bev crossed the street and stopped on the bridge, drinking his soda and smiling at the exertions of an inexperienced punter, as he stood on the platform at the rear of the punt, only just managing to push the long pole down to the river bed without falling into the water.

He felt someone push gently past him on the narrow pavement of the bridge. He half turned and had a fleeting image of an Indian girl wearing a red top, jeans, and sandals. Bev suddenly realized that he had had a vague sense of someone shadowing his walk, but he had dismissed the idea as absurd. When he had turned around briefly one or twice, he had noticed nothing untoward.

'Follow me,' she said softly.

She turned left and made her way down to the river by Scudamores, threading her way through the crowd of punters. Bev followed at a short distance, and they stopped together on the edge of the crowd, taking advantage of the security of numbers. Bev looked at her. She was slim, slightly shorter than he, her jet-black hair short, her eyes very dark brown and impenetrable. Facially, she might have been anywhere between eighteen and thirty; her body suggested mid-to-late twenties. But it was her walk, the way she moved, that fascinated Bev. The image that came to him was one of a cat – always perfectly poised, perfectly balanced, seemingly always at ease, yet always ready for decisive action.

'I am Kali,' she said. 'You were told about me. We have to talk.'

* * *

They walked in silence up Magdalene Street to Castle Street. They crossed the street at the traffic lights and turned left on to Northampton Street.

'The ring road,' Kali explained. 'It goes around the city center. Lots of traffic and not so many people walking. Much safer to talk. If you follow the road around, it will bring you back almost to Downing. It's just a longer walk than the way you came.'

They walked together slowly as the traffic ground its way noisily past them.

'The Visitor told you to expect me, of course?'

'Yes.' He paused. 'I didn't see you coming. How did you …?'

She waved the question away.

'The matter in which we require your help is one which must be accomplished soon. Have you decided whether you will fulfil your obligation to your people?'

'I'm not sure I see it that way.'

'Yes, you are,' she said dismissively. 'The only question is whether you will do it. I do not have the luxury of procrastination. If you will not help us, then other plans must be made. What is your decision?'

Bev stopped in his tracks and held her back with an arm across her body.

'You can't seriously expect an answer until you tell me what you want me to do?'

'On the contrary,' she said. 'If the answer is "no", I will tell you nothing more. It will no longer be any of your business.'

Bev shook his head.

'It can't work that way. If I say "yes", and you tell me to shoot the Queen or plant a bomb in the Houses of Parliament, I'm not going to do it. I'm going to change my answer.'

He drew himself up and turned to face her directly.

'In fact, I want to make it clear that I am not going to do anything illegal. If you can't accept that, it's over. You can go your way now, and I will go mine.'

He took a step backwards, away from her, as if to emphasize what he had said.

She smiled thinly. 'The Visitor reported that you had a rather melodramatic tendency,' she said. 'I assure you that we will not ask you to shoot anyone or plant any bombs. What we have in mind is a very simple series of actions, all of which are perfectly lawful, and all of which you can relate truthfully afterwards, should anyone ask you.'

The smile disappeared. 'However, it is also true that we would expect you not to talk about the fact that we asked you to perform these actions. In fact, we would insist on that.'

'The Visitor said there would be no consequences if I said "no".'

'That is not the same thing as saying "yes" and then talking about it. That would unleash forces which neither the Visitor nor I could control.'

Bev turned away, his back to Kali. For some time he stared vacantly into space. His rational nature begged him to end it now. He could walk away. He had burned no bridges. All his options were still open. He could walk back to Magdalene Street; walk back down into the city center; stop for coffee; go back to his room at Downing, work on his class assignment; he could continue his life in an ordinary way, now and forever. He needed to focus on what was real. He was an American. He was going home in a few weeks. He was going to be a lawyer, a husband, a father. Nothing else mattered. Certainly not a religious feud halfway across the world between people he had never met.

But, in his head, he was also hearing his father's words. He was seeing again glimpses of the dream which had occupied his flight to England. And he heard another voice. *'We can never go back, Bev. They told us that quite clearly. We can never go back to Kashmir. We can never see our land again.'*

He turned back slowly towards her.

'What do you want me to do?' he asked.

They resumed their walk, and a full minute passed in silence.

'We need to have a conversation with Dani Ryan,' Kali said.

Bev felt his stomach muscles tighten into a knot. He stopped abruptly and turned to face her.

'What does SK want with Dani Ryan?' he demanded.

Suddenly, she was in his face, rounding on him almost savagely. 'Never say our name in public,' she hissed.

Bev spread his arms out wide. 'There's no one here.'

'Never say it. Never.'

She stared into his eyes with a ferocity which took Bev aback. He said nothing to indicate his assent, but as he spoke, his voice told her that the message had not been lost on him.

'What do you want with her?'

Kali softened her features and backed away slightly, but she remained close.

'I don't know. I just know that we want to talk with her.'

'You don't know?'

'I don't need to know, or I don't need to know yet. It is our rule that no one is given information they do not need, and no one is given information until they need it. What I know is that we need to talk with Dani Ryan.'

Still profoundly shaken, Bev resumed walking slowly. Kali walked close by his side. He did not trust himself to speak. Sensing this, Kali continued.

'We know that she has minders, from the US Secret Service and the British secret services. We don't know who they are, or how many they are.'

'I don't know that either,' Bev pointed out. 'She has to keep that to herself. It has already come up in conversation and it would look way too suspicious if I brought it up again.'

Kali seemed to ignore this remark.

'The point is that we can't approach her directly. It would be far too risky and we would almost certainly fail.'

She allowed some time to pass.

'You, on the other hand, can facilitate an encounter without arousing suspicion. You work together, you socialize together. All we ask is that you arrange for her to be in a certain place at a certain time. We will do the rest.'

Bev was shaking his head.

'It will be a public place,' Kali said. 'She would have no reason not to go there.'

He turned to her.

'Whoever is watching her, I assume they go wherever she goes. I don't know that. But it seems logical. Wherever you approach her, it will attract attention. What are you going to do? Pose as students? They will know you are not part of our group. They know all of us, trust me.'

Kali nodded.

'It is possible that we will fail,' she conceded simply. 'We may have to abandon the plan. That is not your responsibility. We ask only that you facilitate an encounter and allow us the chance to succeed.'

Bev stopped and looked away.

'And all you want to do is talk to her?'

'That is what I have been told.'

'I can't risk any harm coming to her.'

She reached out and touched his arm.

'If we wanted to do her harm, Bev, it would not be difficult. We would not need your help for that. She is walking around in Cambridge in public view all the time. We have people who could …'

She allowed the words to drift away.

They began to walk again, very slowly.

'There is a public house called the Castle Inn, on Castle Street. Just continue up the hill for a short distance from where we turned on to the ring road,' Kali said. 'On Friday you will ask her to join you there for a drink at 6.30. Just the two of you, no one else. At 6.45, you will call her and say that you have been delayed. Think of a good reason, one that will not arouse any suspicion. You may arrive at the pub at 7 o'clock. These times are very precise. There must be no approximations. Everything depends on this. Check your watch carefully beforehand.'

Bev looked closely at her.

'You will have finished your conversation with her by 7 o'clock?'

'I have told you everything I have been told myself,' Kali said. 'Will you do this for us, or not?'

Bev turned away from her again, and looked into the distance. Perhaps it was all harmless. Dani would arrive at the pub on time. They would talk with her. He would arrive shortly afterwards. They would have a drink, then perhaps join some of the other students for dinner. Life would continue. He could tell his parents he had fulfilled his obligation. They would be proud of him. He was one of the lucky ones. His task as a sleeper was simple, and it was legal. On another level, he knew that it might turn out very differently. What if Kali was lying to him? What if they meant Dani harm? At any time in his life before the Visitor came, only two weeks before, that thought would have ended the matter in his mind. He was an American. He lived by American values. He believed in the rule of law. He might pretend to agree to do what Kali asked, but only so that he could tell Dani exactly what danger she was in. She would alert her minders and the plot would be foiled. But the last two weeks had been strange for Bev.

Outwardly, he was unchanged. He had no difficulty in focusing on his studies. His social relations with his fellow-students seemed normal. He talked with his parents, and with Shesi, by phone, and his conversations were typical of any young student abroad. But in his mind, something had shifted. When his father had suggested that his American identity was not the whole truth about him, Bev had dismissed the idea. His parents were good people, but they lived in another world, a world they should have left behind them long ago. Many people had emigrated to America to escape wars, persecution, violence, and injustice. Many had lost relatives. Surely, that was what America was all about? But once you were there, you put the past behind you. You spoke English; you worked for the dollar; and you did your civic duty. Yes, you kept up your customs; you could not forget your language; you went to the temple. But all those things just added to the diversity of America; they enriched America. His parents had done all of those things. But still, the past haunted them. He had always believed that he was a new generation, that he could help them to shape the future, instead of gazing back into a history that could not be changed. He had always believed that he was free of the curse of that history.

That was before the Visitor had told him who he was. That was before the dream during his flight to London. He had felt differently since then. He felt that a part of him was indeed Indian, Kashmiri. He was a part of a people, and a part of their history – whether he wanted to be, or not. Their fight was his fight. Their fight was just because they had been the victims of violence and injustice. Their land had been taken away. Their culture had been torn apart. But it was more personal than that. His grandparents were among the victims His father had been prepared to stand tall, to do what he could for his people, whatever it might be. Now it was his turn.

'*But does this mean it's OK to put Dani at risk, to play games with her life?*' his American conscience demanded to know.

'*You watch too many movies, Bev. We are not the Soviets.*'

'*How do I know you're telling the truth?*'

'*But your grandparents died … I heard from one of the survivors that they had been hacked to death inside their home.*'

'It still doesn't make it right. All that stuff happened years ago, generations ago. Too many people dead; too many villages wiped out. Someone has to say "enough is enough". There has to be a better way of doing it.'

'We can never go back, Bev. They told us that quite clearly. We can never go back to Kashmir. We can never see our land again.'

He turned back to Kali. He had no sense of time, no sense of how long he had been standing with his back to her, battling with himself and his conscience. If it had been a long time, she gave no indication of it, no sign of impatience.

'I will do as you ask,' he said. 'But then, I want you out of my life. You, the Visitor, all of you. For ever.'

12

THE LAW FIRM of Mayer Hargreaves Harrison & Ryan had its offices in a building on Twelfth Street, North West. The building belonged to an older, architecturally more conservative era, but was nonetheless prestigious and exuded success and respectability. The law firm was small compared with other major commercial litigation firms It had been founded by four law school friends as a bold venture within three years of being admitted to the bar. The decision to remain relatively small had been taken right at the outset. It was then, and remained, important in the interests of quality of life and ensuring that the practice of law did not become impersonal.

Three of the four were still name partners. Prostate cancer had claimed Tom Mayer horribly early. It was a huge loss. The firm had weathered the blow, but the grief still lingered. It was resolved that Tom's name would remain on the letterhead as long as the three surviving partners continued in practice. The firm prospered. Inevitably, success brought with it the need to grow to some extent. There were other partners now and, with the associates, the firm numbered sixty lawyers. It was big enough to compete in the marketplace, as long as the firm maintained its reputation for being competent, fast and maneuverable, and for refusing to be slowed down by internal red tape. Dale Harrison and Kay Ryan had married when the firm was young. Neither their marriage nor their subsequent divorce affected their friendship or their effectiveness as law partners.

Kay had been immured in the seventh floor conference room since early in the morning with her paralegal, Catherine, who was working her way through law school at Georgetown. The long table was covered with papers relating to a case brought in by a new client. Brookline Potomac was a new and aggressive engineering firm. It had designed and manufactured a revolutionary piece of equipment intended to simplify and speed up the process of de-icing aircraft in cold weather. Several airlines had bought the technology. But there were some complaints of defects and damage, and the threat of litigation was rumbling on the horizon. Brookline saw Mayer Hargreaves Harrison & Ryan as a law firm in their own image. Like all firms threatened with commercial litigation, they wanted to avoid it if possible. Legal problems that escalated to litigation cost money and got in the way of doing business. They hoped that their lawyers would be able to negotiate a resolution of the dispute, or at least refer the matter to the calmer waters of mediation or arbitration. But if not, they wanted lawyers who would fight as hard and as aggressively as necessary. A first conference was scheduled for the early afternoon with Brookline's president and in-house counsel. Kay thought she understood more or less what the case was about. That was all she needed for a first conference. The client would fill in the blanks over time. Catherine was busily putting papers into folders and labeling them. Many more documents were to follow, but most of them would be stored electronically.

The door opened quietly. Jim Hargreaves peeked into the conference room.

'Kay, do you have a minute?'

Kay hesitated. She wanted to make sure everything was going to be ready before grabbing a quick sandwich to keep her going.

Catherine looked up.

'I've got it, Kay. Angela said she would give me a hand if we ran short of time.'

'Thanks, Cath,' Kay replied.

She walked outside with Jim. Dale Harrison was waiting. Dale led the way to his corner office, ushered them inside and closed the door.

'So, what's up?' Kay asked. 'I've got quite a bit to do before the Brookline conference.'

Jim looked uncomfortable.

'It's about Brookline, Kay,' Dale said. 'They called this morning to postpone the conference.'

Kay was taken aback. She sat down abruptly in the nearest chair, just in front of Dale's desk.

'Postpone? Why didn't someone tell me? Why would they postpone?'

Dale walked to one of the large windows which offered a panoramic view of the street below and gestured to Kay to join him. He pointed to his left.

'You can't see them very well from here,' he said. 'They are close to the main entrance. And, of course, you've been in the conference room on the other side of the building, so you wouldn't have heard anything.'

He opened the window slightly. Kay could hear the sound of voices chanting in unison, indistinct but unmistakable. Leaning slightly out of the window, Kay could see a small crowd standing outside the building's main entrance. Some were holding placards. A solitary police officer was walking up and down slowly behind them in the street.

'There are about thirty of them,' Dale said. 'The placards say things like "Burn in hell" and "Abomination out of the White House". The chants are sending the same kind of message.'

Kay pulled her head back into the office and closed the window.

'Oh, God,' she said quietly.

'Clients have been calling, voicing concerns,' Jim Hargreaves said.

Kay looked up.

'Concerns? What about? Surely they are not worried about getting into the building past a few demonstrators with placards.'

Hargreaves smiled.

'No. I don't think that would deter Bob Seymour or his colleagues at Brookline. They might think that was the fun part.'

He paused.

'What's concerning them is the publicity factor.'

'What?' Kay asked, genuinely puzzled.

'They are sensitive about the publicity their case is going to attract. It's going to be all over the press at certain times. Not all the time, obviously, but from time to time. They are worried that every time the press runs a story about the case, they will find it hard to resist adding a few details about their lead counsel, Kay Ryan. If those details involve constant coverage about demonstrations outside her office and goings on in the White House, they are worried that it may have a detrimental effect on the prospects of settlement or arbitration, or on a jury panel, if it goes to trial.'

'That is ridiculous,' Kay exploded.

'Don't shoot the messenger, Kay,' Jim said.

'We are years away from trial. If it ever goes that far.'

'I know.'

'And the idea that it could affect negotiations is laughable.'

'I agree.'

'This will all be over in a few days. Do you think those people are going to be standing outside a building on Twelfth Street for the rest of their lives? They will find other things to amuse them.'

'We agree with you, Kay,' Dale said. 'But today we have to manage this situation. Brookline is a client with a lot of potential for the firm. We don't want to risk losing them.'

Kay's jaw dropped.

'Losing them?' she gasped. 'Over this?'

Dale shrugged.

'This is their in-house counsel, right?' she said. 'This is not coming from Bob Seymour. It's coming from that asshole Dan Leslie, a lawyer who spends his days poring over documents, who couldn't find his way to the courthouse, much less try a case.'

'Kay …'

'No, Dale. This doesn't make sense.'

Dale placed a hand gently on her arm.

'Kay, this is not about what makes sense. It's about managing the next few days until all the fuss dies down. Once that happens, we go back to business as usual.'

'And in the meantime?' Kay asked.

'In the meantime, I'm going to take over Brookline as lead counsel for a while,' Jim said, quietly but firmly. 'I have the time. This is still confidential until next week, but the Sinclair Booth case is about to settle. The government has made a pretty good offer. Officially, they are still thinking about it, but unofficially, Jerry Booth told me they are going to take it. They just need a few days to get their ducks in a row, before news of the settlement becomes public. So I can give my full attention to Brookline, starting today. I will reschedule the conference for early next week.'

Kay's head sank on to her chest.

'Jim, this is my career. You are allowing these yahoos to fuck with my career – with this law firm.'

'It's just for a few days, Kay. You said it yourself, these things never last long. People like this have a short attention span. Something else will come along to appeal to their sense of outrage. As soon as we can we will re-introduce you to the case. The plan is still for you to be lead counsel. It's your case. I'm just filling in for a short while, and I'm going to make that clear to Bob Seymour.'

'And what about my other clients? Are you going to let them dump me if they are squeamish about my personal life?'

'No. Jaycee is dealing with anyone who calls. You know how good she is at making soothing noises. If anyone is seriously worried, she has instructions to refer them to me. I doubt it will come to that.'

She looked up.

'I would have expected better of you, Jim. You too, Dale. I would have expected better of my partners, my law firm.'

'We are looking after the law firm,' Jim said. 'If you were in our position, you would do the same thing. You know you would. What more do you want of us, Kay?'

She was silent for some time.

'I suppose I wanted you to stand up for me,' she replied quietly. 'The same way you stand up for the clients.'

'I'm sorry, Kay,' Jim replied.

She brought both hands down angrily on the corner of Dale's desk.

'So, what now?'

'We want you to take a few days away from the office,' Jim said. 'Work from home, take a few down days, whatever you like.

Catherine will bring you whatever you need. Once they realize that Elvis has left the building, they will soon figure out that it's a waste of time standing around out there, chanting at nobody.'

She shook her head for some time, choking back the angry responses that were flooding her mind.

'Fine,' she replied eventually. 'I'll walk right out of the front door, right now, so they can all see me leave.'

She walked towards the door.

Jim Hargreaves restrained her, gently but firmly.

'No, you won't, Kay. I will drive you. My car is in the parking garage downstairs. Or, if you want, we could ask the police.'

'No. I'll take my own car,' she said. 'I will drive myself. At least, that way, I can pretend to myself that I still have some control over my life.'

13

GOVERNOR HANK BETANCOURT hung up his phone with a sense of frustration. His conversation with Alex Vonn had not gone the way he had hoped. As John Mason had predicted, Vonn was counseling caution. There were too many unknown factors, he said; too many people nowadays were sympathetic to gay marriage; gays in the military had not brought the United States to its knees; several prominent sportsmen and women had recently come out, apparently without adverse consequences. Opinion polls were not reliable on such a delicate issue.

'We don't want to be on the wrong side of this argument,' Vonn concluded. 'It could hurt us. Let's see which way the wind blows. There will be something we can say about it to our advantage. We just don't know what it is, yet. Be patient. The time will come.'

But, while he understood what Vonn was saying, Betancourt's gut instinct told him that the time to strike was now. It was all very well to wait, but before too long the media spotlight would move on. Before too long Kay Ryan's presence in the White House, and by Ellen Trevathan's side at state functions, would become routine, might even be seen as normal. People might start to wonder what all the fuss had been about. The opportunity would be lost. Vonn was taking the Washington approach, he reasoned. Paint a picture of moderation, of responsibility. Move in an orderly fashion, one safe step at a time. And, in the meanwhile, Betancourt's shot at the White House might fail because he looked a gift horse in the mouth.

'There is a tide in the affairs of men', Betancourt remembered from the Shakespeare of his college days, 'which, taken at the flood, leads on to fortune.' Betancourt had never been one to miss a flood tide. He had come this far by grasping every opportunity as and when it arose. This was not the time to change that successful strategy. It was not the time to vacillate. He looked across his desk to his chief of staff, Rod Christensen, an ambitious young lawyer from Salt Lake City, who had hitched his fortune to Betancourt's rising star.

'So, what do you make of that?'

'He has a point, Governor. It sounds like you're not going to get too much support for an all-out attack right now.'

'I'll get support in Texas.'

'You already have support in Texas,' Christensen pointed out. 'We have been through this before. What you have to do is to appeal to the broader base. The party is looking for a statesman right now, not someone who jumps in without a parachute.'

Betancourt stood and leaned on his desk with both hands.

'I think there's a way to do both,' he said.

'Pray, tell.'

'We need to enlist someone to lead the attack for us – someone to lead the charge. We will be following close behind. We will give it our support. There won't be any doubt where we stand, but we will sound moderate, just like Alex Vonn wants us to. The difference is that we will be nailing Trevathan now. We don't have to risk losing the chance to strike. If Vonn is right, and it goes south for some reason, we're not too close to it, we can back away. But if we score a hit, we can open fire with all guns blazing once the campaign starts. By that time, her defenses will be down.'

Christensen nodded thoughtfully.

'I could see that. But who would we get to be the standard-bearer? That's going to be a very public stance to take. Most people we would be happy to be associated with, by which I mean, people to be taken seriously, might decide that discretion is the better part of valor.'

'I do have someone in mind,' Betancourt smiled.

'Why am I not surprised?' Christensen said. 'Who is it?'

'None less than the great scourge of wrongdoers and warrior of the airwaves.'

Christensen laughed out loud. 'Bubba Lanier? Governor, are you serious?'

'Perfectly. Bubba Lanier is the kind of man who won't back away from a fight, however bloody it may be. Hell, Rod, he's already started without our encouragement. He is calling for Trevathan to resign, every time he's on air. And his shows are reaching a wider audience every day.'

'That costs him nothing. She's not going to resign, and she's not going to get into an argument with Bubba Lanier. He can say whatever he wants. There's no reason for her to care. Besides, do we really want our campaign to be associated with Bubba Lanier?'

'If he's saying the right things, yes. Our association doesn't need to go beyond that. But we can plant an idea in Lanier's mind that he hasn't thought of yet, and we can plant it without attribution to begin with, in case it doesn't work.'

'Oh? And what might that idea be?'

'Taking steps to get rid of Trevathan, rather than just calling on her to resign, which we agree, she is not about to do.'

Christensen looked up. 'Get rid of her? How? She can't be impeached for having a female lover, Governor. It's not a high crime or misdemeanor. You can't even have a recall election in the case of the President. The only way to get rid of her is to vote her out of office at the next election.'

'True,' Betancourt agreed. 'But the people can petition the government for the redress of grievances at any time. Lanier probably feels aggrieved about what's going on in the White House, just as we do. But, instead of just talking about it, he can do something useful.'

'You mean, organize a petition calling on Trevathan to resign?'

'Exactly. Lanier can amuse himself for as long as he likes with that. It will start in Texas, where it will obviously be successful, then it will spread to Oklahoma and Lousiana, likewise successful. From there, it fans out and, we hope, becomes a roller coaster. People all over the country will jump on the bandwagon – cities and towns organizing their own petitions. If it goes viral, we will have the biggest damn petition you ever saw. The beautiful thing is, it can last as long as we want it to. The longer it lasts, the more signatures Lanier collects, the more pressure we put on Trevathan. She can't just ignore Lanier then. She is going to have to use up energy dealing with it. If we keep it up long enough, she's going to run out of steam by the time we start the campaign. If the petition loses momentum too early, we can just pull back.'

Christensen sat back in his chair with a smile. This was why he was in Texas. You just had to hand it to Hank Betancourt. He was better than all those boys in Washington, put together. More brains, more balls.

'I like it,' he said. 'Who shall I use to plant the idea?'

'Have one of our guys call in to the show using an alias,' Betancourt replied. 'And once it's underway, call the station yourself so I can do an interview.'

* * *

After the cabinet meeting ended Ellen had only half an hour to prepare for a cocktail reception honoring leaders of the American Inns of Court, a legal organization devoted to promoting high ethical standards in the profession. Kay had been a member for many years and had recently been elected to the national board of trustees. After the reception, the board members were going to dinner. Ellen had gladly agreed to host the reception, but had chosen not to attend their private dinner outside the White House. Kay had been looking forward to the evening for weeks. Ellen had expected her to be dressed and ready to go. Instead, she found her sitting quietly on the sofa in the living room, still wearing her office suit. She was watching the television news, but had the volume turned right down. Ellen approached cautiously.

'Kay, are you all right?'

Kay looked up slowly.

'They hate us, Ellen.'

Ellen took the remote from her hand and switched the television off.

'Who hates us?'

'The people. Ellen, do you know …?'

Her voice trailed away.

Ellen sat down on the floor at Kay's feet and held her hands.

'Kay, this is not "the people". It's just religious extremists and bigots stirring their followers up. That's all it is.'

Kay leaned forward and put her hands, still in Ellen's, on her lap.

'Ellen, I had to come home from the office. There were people outside with placards, chanting. The placards said we should both burn in hell. I had to cancel a conference with a new client. We might have lost their business already. We may be losing other clients. I left just after lunch.'

Ellen bit her lip.

'God damn it. All right, Kay. I'll call the DC police tomorrow morning. Better still, I'll let Abe Solari deal with it. The Secret Service will know what to do.'

'They are entitled to protest, Ellen,' Kay replied hopelessly. 'If we try to stop them, it will be even worse. Then we will be trampling on their freedom of speech and association. There will be even more protests. And when I was on my way home, I saw that they were protesting right here, outside the White House.'

Her voice trembled.

'It brought back memories of those crowds during the crisis. I got scared.'

Ellen came up on to her knees and put her arms around her.

'The worst thing is knowing how much those people hate us,' Kay continued. 'I know I shouldn't let it affect me. But it feels so personal. So much hate, just because of who we are. This is ridiculous. I'm a lawyer, I fight for people, I'm strong. I shouldn't feel like this. But I do. I just feel so fragile. I keep wanting to cry.'

Ellen kissed her.

'I know,' she said, 'I know. But it's what we expected, Kay. We knew this was coming. It will die down soon. There will be something else for them to get worked up about within a few days. There always is. We just have to ride out the storm.'

She pulled back a little.

'Look, why don't you take a few days away from the office?'

'That decision has been made for me,' Kay replied bitterly. 'Jim and Dale made it clear that I need to stay away until things calm down. It's probably for the best. I can't go into the office in this state. I would be no use to anyone even if I did.'

'Good,' Ellen said, doing her best to adopt a light tone. 'You'll feel better here. So, go get changed. We don't want to keep the American Inns of Court waiting.'

'I don't feel much like it,' Kay said quietly.

'Come on. You always have a good time with those guys,' Ellen smiled. 'And you will be in a crowd, one of several taxis, when you go to dinner. I will have an agent tag along and he will bring you home after dinner.'

She pulled Kay gently to her feet.

'Come on, let's go. I need a glass or two of champagne myself.'

Kay did not move.

'Ellen,' she said. 'You are sure about this, aren't you? It is all going to work out, isn't it?'

Ellen pulled her into a hug, gazing over her shoulder into the distance.

'Yes, I'm sure,' she replied.

14

June 10

ROSA WOULD LATER remember every moment of that Friday as if it were a film, playing non-stop on an endlessly rolling projector in her mind. She told herself, and others told her, that she had done nothing wrong; that her every decision made perfect sense. No one would have done anything differently. But no one else was responsible in the way she was. And when things turned out as they did in this situation, it really didn't matter very much what anyone else thought or said. It was her responsibility to protect Dani Ryan. Hers, not anyone else's. There was no way around that.

The day began with her morning phone call to Dani. They had settled into a routine of a phone call in the early morning and a call last thing at night, with one or two in between, as required, if a schedule changed for any reason.

'Good morning, Dani. So, what's the plan for today?'

'Hi, Mom,' Dani replied, causing Rosa to laugh out loud. 'I'm going to be in class all morning. I have to recite on the jurisdiction of the International Criminal Tribunals for Rwanda and the Former Yugoslavia. After that I will need a long lunch. I will then make my way to the library for a riveting afternoon, beginning my research into the Special Court for Sierra Leone. After that, I will need a drink. As my study partner and I are, strangely, acquiring a taste for this strange English ale, served at room temperature, we plan to try a new pub which comes highly recommended.'

'Time?'

'6.30.'

'Location?'

'The Castle Inn, situated, appropriately enough, on Castle Street.'

'Is that it?'

'Depends on how tired we are. If we go anywhere else, it will probably be to meet up with some of the others for a bite to eat.'

'In which case, you will call me?'

'In which case, I will call you. Can I go to breakfast now?'

'Absolutely, Dani. Have a great day.'

'It's already started,' Dani said.

As she disconnected, Rosa briefly considered whether she should have pressed Dani as to why she and Bev were going to the pub on their own, and why no one else from the group would feature in their plans until later, if at all. But it wasn't the first time they had spent a little time alone together. It was normal, wasn't it? They were bonding as study partners. They had a lot to talk about for class, not to mention needing some downtime for themselves. Bev was all right; he had checked out.

'For God's sake, Rosa, relax. Cut the girl some slack,' she scolded herself.

She called Steve Macmillan, established that there was no new intelligence affecting Dani, and passed on the day's itinerary. Steve acknowledged each detail as he made his notes.

'What are you going to do?' he asked.

'I'll make a pass by the library mid-afternoon,' she replied. 'I will head over to the Castle Inn round about five, just to check it out. If anything bothers me, I will find a place to roost for a while when she and Bev are there. Otherwise I'll make a pass a bit later.'

'Sounds good,' Steve said. 'You'll like the Castle. It's got a hint of Olde England, and they serve an excellent pint of Adnams ale.'

'I have no idea what you just said,' Rosa said, disconnecting.

* * *

Lunch and the library were uneventful. Just before five, Rosa mounted her bicycle outside Downing and threaded her way through town to Castle Street. She wore a light blue top bearing the legend 'Cambridge University' and the University coat of arms, with beige trousers and brown sandals; she would have passed for a research student anywhere. She chained her bicycle to a stand nearby and made her way into the Castle Inn. At the bar, she ordered a large orange juice over ice, and began a slow walk-through.

The pub boasted a large bar on two levels, the bare floors and traditional furnishings giving it a genuine feeling of age. But it also had a beer garden with unsecured access at the rear. The beer garden continued down to another level in the basement. The pub as a whole occupied a large area. Nice place – but easy to infiltrate, and it would probably get crowded in the early evening, Rosa thought, an observation confirmed by one or two touristy questions to the barman. It would be difficult to keep watch without making herself too obvious. She tried sitting in various corners, making her orange juice last, trying to find an optimum place for both observation and a quick escape. At length she bowed to the obvious. The lay-out of the Castle did not lend itself to either. If she came back at 6.30, it would probably be best to take advantage of cover from the crowd. This would allow her to move through the various areas unobtrusively to check for anything suspicious from time to time. At some point, Dani would almost certainly spot her, at which point she would leave, maybe returning, maybe not, depending on time. If Dani signaled dinner, she would follow and, if all seemed in order, she would call it a day. On reflection it seemed better to leave it until some time after 7 o'clock, to let Dani get settled into conversation. That way, she might just manage to sneak in unobserved, or she might just give it a miss altogether.

* * *

Dani arrived at the Castle at 6.30 precisely. That had not been her plan. She had got a bit carried away with the Sierra Leone Court and had not noticed the time until it was after 6 o'clock. She was still dressed in the thin red top, jeans and blue flip-flops she had been wearing all day and, as she had come straight from the library without returning to Downing, she was carrying her briefcase as well as her handbag. She stepped through the door at exactly 6.30, slightly out of breath from her brisk walk. At that exact time, Rosa was in a Costa coffee house on Sidney Sussex Street, drinking a cappuccino. She looked at her watch and decided to leave checking the pub until after 7 o'clock. If necessary, she could be there in two minutes.

On entering the Castle, Dani looked around for Bev. There was no sign of him. It was obviously a big place, she thought, so he might be further inside, or he might be running a few minutes late. He had left the library before her, saying that he had a few errands to run and that he would meet her at the pub. She ordered a half pint of Adnams bitter, and did a brief tour of the Castle. Still no sign of Bev. The pub was filling up, so she grabbed a small table in the main bar and settled down to wait. She scanned the room for Rosa, smiling to herself. They played this game constantly, it seemed, Rosa trying to remain inconspicuous, Dani trying to spot her. Rosa was good, Dani had to admit it. She was sure she had seen her on a few occasions, but it was never more than a glimpse. Sometimes, when they spoke in the morning, Rosa said something that gave the game away, that told Dani she must have seen something. Somehow, she had been at the café where Dani had been the evening before, even though Dani had looked for her in vain. It was frustrating, but it gave Dani confidence.

At 6.40 she looked up to see a young Indian woman standing by her table. Dani had not noticed her before, and was surprised that her approach had been so quiet. The young woman spoke a pitch-perfect southern standard English, with no trace of an Indian accent.

'Hi, you must be Dani?' Kali asked.

Dani was taken aback. Surely no one except Bev – and Rosa – knew that she would be here. Had this woman recognized her? She was, after all, now a public figure – but in a pub in Cambridge? She quickly scanned the room. Silently, 'Rosa, are you here?' No Rosa. 'Calm down,' she told herself. There was no reason to be nervous. She was in a crowded pub, for God's sake.

'Yes. I …'

'I'm really sorry to barge in on you. My name's Kali. I'm a friend of Bev's. I work in London, and I've been trying to come up to Cambridge to see him ever since he arrived. Today is the first chance I've had. He told me he was meeting you here. I hope you don't mind. I stayed with his family on an exchange visit to the States two years ago and we became friends. I haven't seen him since.'

Dani began to relax.

'Oh, right. No, of course I don't mind. Sit down, please. It's just that he didn't mention that you would be joining us.'

Sitting down next to Dani, Kali shook her head.

'I didn't know myself until lunch time. I wasn't sure I could get away. I only spoke to him an hour or so ago when I was already on the train. I tried calling him earlier, but his phone went straight to message.'

'We were in the library,' Dani said.

'Oh, yes, of course. That would explain it.'

'How did you recognize me?' Dani asked, after a pause.

Kali smiled. 'I work for *The Times*, in the graphics department. I see hundreds of photographs every day. There is no one even remotely famous I couldn't pick out of a line up at a thousand paces.'

Dani returned the smile. 'Can I get you a drink?'

Kali glanced at her watch. 'No, thanks. I'll wait for Bev. I'm sure he must be on his way.'

It was 6.45. Dani's phone rang.

'Dani?'

'Yes.'

'It's Bev. I'm really sorry. My parents kept me talking. I'm on my way. I won't be very long. Are you OK there?'

'Yes,' Dani replied. 'I'm fine. As a matter of fact, I'm talking to a friend of yours.'

'Oh?'

'Kali. Ring any bells?'

Dani thought she sensed a slight hesitation before Bev replied. She looked around briefly. Still no Rosa.

'Oh, right. Yeah. Good, she found you OK. Why don't you chat with her for a few minutes and I'll see you soon.'

'You should have told me to expect her.'

'Yeah, I'm sorry. I didn't get her message until after I left the library and then... my parents called... I'll explain when I see you.'

Kali was giving the phone a silly exaggerated wave.

'Kali says "hi"', Dani said.

'Kali says "I need a drink. Don't keep me waiting much longer,"' Kali added.

'And she needs a drink. Don't keep her waiting much longer.'

'I'm on my way,' Bev laughed.

Kali looked at her watch again. This was it. If it worked, she would be a heroine. If it didn't, a lot of planning had been in vain, and a much more dangerous second pass might be necessary. If it went horribly wrong, she might be about to find out how effective her interrogation resistance training had been.

'Dani, I'm gasping for a cigarette. I couldn't smoke on the train, and then I was breaking my neck to get here on time. I shouldn't have bothered rushing, needless to say. Can we go outside for a couple of minutes, so I can smoke? You can bring your drink. I've got a thousand questions to ask you. You don't have to answer, but I can't help being curious about what it's like having the President as your step-mother.'

She produced a pack of Marlboros from the top pocket of her shirt and a lighter from the pocket of her jeans. Dani smiled. Her mother had only recently kicked the habit – she had been an enthusiastic smoker for years. She remembered standing outside so many different places with her for as long as it took to smoke a cigarette.

'Sure,' she said, standing up. 'But I should warn you, it's not nearly as glamorous as you might think.'

Kali led the way through the crowd to the door on Castle Street through which Dani had entered a short time before. They stood just outside the door. Kali lit a cigarette. The large white van approaching the Castle Inn from the direction of the Huntingdon Road had two occupants. The driver was a white man, in his early thirties, his blonde hair long and unkempt, dressed in a grubby T-shirt and equally grubby jeans. His name was Wayne Carter, and he had a varied criminal record for drugs offences, serious assaults and robbery – but nothing on the scale of what he was about to do. The passenger was Indian, about the same age, but neatly turned out in a black shirt with a collar, and black trousers. His work name was Samir, and he had no criminal record at all.

Wayne Carter stopped the van right in front of Dani and Kali. As Samir got out and opened the rear door, Kali quietly dropped her cigarette to the ground. Seemingly without effort, she and Samir lifted Dani bodily into the rear of the van and climbed in after her. Her flip-flops fell from her feet and lay on the pavement. It all happened so quickly that she was completely unable to react in time to attract attention. By the time she had opened her mouth to scream, Samir was holding a pad saturated with chloroform to her mouth, and she soon passed out. Wayne Carter drove down Castle Street without undue haste, and had a piece of luck when the traffic lights turned to green as he arrived at the junction; he was able to turn right on to Northampton Street without either delaying the getaway or taking the risk of running a red light. At the Castle Inn, one or two people saw what had happened, but put it down to students fooling around. No one had even thought of noting the van's registration number. One thoughtful girl handed in Dani's flip-flops to the barman. But the barman was trying to deal with three orders at once, and he tossed the flip-flops carelessly into a corner of the bar, where they lay forgotten until much later.

15

AT 7 O'CLOCK, Bev entered the Castle. He was desperately hoping to see Dani. He was hoping she would say that Kali had had to leave; that she had solicited Dani's help in getting some message about Kashmir to Ellen Trevathan; that Dani had said she would mention it when she got the chance; that they could now have a pleasant pint or two and then grab a bite to eat. He was hoping that life would return to normal. Even if Kali was still with Dani, that would not be so bad. He could go along with whatever story Kali was telling her. But he had a nagging feeling that they had not activated a sleeper for something as insignificant as a message which might, or might not, be delivered.

What kind of conversation did SK intend to have with Dani? That question had plagued his thoughts ever since he had agreed to help her. Kali herself had admitted that she did not know what the conversation was to be about. What if it was something more than a simple conversation? He had spent the past few days deeply troubled. Part of him feared that he had made a terrible mistake. Part of him believed desperately in Kali's assurance that Dani was not to be harmed; and in the Visitor's assurance that they were not like the Soviets. Another part felt the wrong done to his grandparents, to his people, and wanted to help. But Dani had offered him her friendship. He had delivered her to them and, in so doing, he had placed her fate beyond his control.

He bought a pint of Adnams and began a slow walk through the Castle, hoping to find Dani, but feeling in his heart that he was not going to. He stopped abruptly, pint in hand, when he had exhausted the last possibility, the basement extension of the beer garden. A corner table for two became available, and he sat down quickly. There was a seat for her. He called Dani's number on his phone. It rang for some time before her message recording played.

'Hi, Dani, it's Bev. It's a little after 7 o'clock. Where are you guys? Is Kali still with you? I'm in the basement bar. Come and join me, or call me and let me know where you are.'

He left his phone on the table in front of him, and settled down to wait for her to come back to him.

* * *

Rosa entered the Castle at 7.15. For no reason she could define, a cold dread entered her heart. Something was wrong. Nothing that she could put her finger on, but after a few years in the job, you just got a feel for when something was out of place. She quickly maneuvered her way through the crowds in the main bars, her trained eyes taking in every table, every group of drinkers, at a glance. She spotted Bev from outside the basement bar, and stopped abruptly. There was no sign of Dani.

Her professional instincts saved her from an incipient panic. She forced herself to act calmly. 'Move,' she told herself. She was too obvious standing there without a drink. She walked up to the garden bar and returned with a tonic water over ice, good for the stomach. She found a seat across the room from Bev. She noticed his phone on the table and guessed he had been calling Dani. Did he know where she was? The fact that he was still at the Castle meant that he was still expecting her. That was good. But she was still uneasy. She took out her phone and called Dani's number, with the same result as Bev. She left a message asking Dani to call her Aunt Jenny immediately. The name was a code they had developed for when it was urgent that she call. The time limit for an Aunt Jenny call was five minutes, ten tops, if there was a good excuse. After ten minutes, Rosa made another call.

'Steve?'

'Yeah.'

'Listen, it may be nothing, but it's possible we have a problem. Can you meet me?'

Steve Macmillan had just got back to his rented flat in a tree-lined residential area of the city. He had just poured himself a cool drink, which he put down immediately.

'Where are you?'

'The Castle.'

'Ten minutes. Name?'

'Viv.'

'I'll be Jim.'

*　*　*

Steve ambled amiably into the basement bar, looking as though he had just come off the 18th green. He was wearing a golf shirt and slacks, and brandishing a pint he had bought on entering. With practiced bonhomie, he approached Rosa as an old friend, kissing her on both cheeks for public consumption.

'Viv,' he said, a little too loudly. 'It is so great to see you. How are you?'

She squeezed his hand. 'I'm great, Jim. You look good.'

'Can't complain – even though I often do.'

She laughed, and they continued in this vein until they had established their identities as boring professional thirty-somethings, and no one noticed them any more. She inclined her head casually towards Bev. Steve nodded. He had already noticed.

'Where is she?' he asked eventually.

'I don't know. He obviously doesn't know either. He has tried to call her three times since I've been here. I take it he wouldn't be here if he had given up hope of seeing her. But I've tried to call, and she is not answering, even when I send out the urgent signal.'

Steve took a long drink. 'All right. Let's not panic just yet. Let's wait for a while. She may turn up. But if he leaves, we follow him.'

Rosa nodded.

'Did she say anything, anything at all, that may have suggested she might go somewhere else, or might be meeting someone else.'

'No.'

'Sure?'

'Yes, I'm sure. I would have asked her about it. She talked about going for dinner with the other students, but that was later, after the Castle. And if her plans had changed, she would have called me.'

The anxiety returned.

'We can't leave it too long. You know that.'

Steve nodded. 'I know.'

After two more attempts to call Dani in a period of half an hour, an obviously anxious Bev finished his drink and walked quickly towards the entrance. Rosa's own anxiety was about to make her leap to her feet prematurely, but Steve placed a light restraining hand on her knee and held it there until Bev was out of the basement bar.

'OK, you follow him on foot,' he said. 'I've got my car, so I will take the ring road. Call me and let me know where he's headed.'

Rosa nodded and set off in pursuit of Bev. Steve finished his pint appreciatively before walking without apparent haste out of the Castle Inn towards his car, which was parked in St Peter's Street nearby. He had driven slowly along the ring road for two or three minutes when Rosa called.

'He's heading straight back into the city center,' she reported. 'My bet is, he's going back to Downing.'

Steve nodded. 'That would make sense,' he said. 'Let's assume Downing. Call me if he goes anywhere else. I will park at the rear of the College and meet you by the chapel.'

'Roger that,' Rosa replied.

16

ROSA STOPPED AND looked thoughtfully into the window of a book shop as Bev slowed down for a moment, as if hesitating. He had carried straight on at Magdalene Bridge, but now he had stopped in his tracks by the Round Church. If he continued straight on, he would take the shortest route to the main gate of Downing College, via St Andrews Street. If he veered right, he could make for the rear gate via King's Parade. But was there a different option in his mind? Was this a change of plan? Had he spotted her? She had kept a good distance between them, but there was always a risk if he was being vigilant. While appearing to examine the cover of a book in the window display, Rosa kept her eye on him using her peripheral vision. Eventually, whatever question had prompted the hesitation seemed to resolve itself. He resumed his walk at a brisk pace and did not slacken it until he entered Downing College.

Rosa fell back to allow even more space between them. She was exposed in the College grounds, far too visible; and although she had a well-established cover story which easily explained her presence in the College, she preferred to remain inconspicuous, if she could. Bev's room was in Kenney A building, towards the rear gate, which meant that he should have continued straight ahead. But instead, he turned left. Rosa knew at once where he was going. He was on his way to Dani's room, T4. She stopped at the side of the chapel. She saw Steve make his way into the College through the rear gate. No point in following Bev to the room. She hoped to God he would find Dani there. Rosa was now long past the point of caring about any possible romantic entanglement. Indeed, she would welcome it – although it would not prevent

Dani from getting the telling-off of her life for not answering her phone. Steve joined her, and they stepped backwards towards the rear of the chapel. A narrow path for pedestrians and cyclists ran in a semi-circle behind the chapel, and they positioned themselves on the edge of the path, where they could see, without being seen. Less than a minute later they saw Bev make his way back towards them from T staircase. Rosa moved, as if to jump out and confront him. Steve held her back forcefully.

'Not yet,' he whispered. 'Let's see where he goes.'

Bev turned left in front of them and made his way to Kenney A, where he let himself in with his key. Steve released Rosa.

'Right. We know where to find him if we need him,' he said. 'Let's check out her room.'

Rosa nodded her agreement and felt in her purse for a key which would open room T4. They made their way, without undue haste, towards T staircase. It was after 8.30 by now, and there were people walking on the gravel pathways all around the College, leaving the dining hall or their rooms in search of some evening entertainment. Two elderly fellows were making their way along the grass on the vacant fourth side of the quadrangle in the direction of the Master's Lodge.

Steve opened the door to T staircase as if time were no object and he had every right in the world to be there. He held the door open for Rosa. Room T4 was on the right on the ground floor, just inside the main staircase door. Steve leaned against the main door, making sure it stayed shut until Rosa had opened the door to the room. They both went inside. Steve closed and locked the door. Rosa swiftly closed the curtains over the large sash windows. They surveyed the scene in silence. There were books, clothes and shoes on the floor and the bed. One or two drawers were open. But it was just normal student clutter – nothing to suggest an entry or a struggle. Dani's laptop was set up at her desk, surrounded by more books and pages of hand-written notes. There was no sign of her briefcase or of a handbag. There was no sign of Dani. They stood together in silence for some time before Rosa sat down quietly on the bed and held her head in her hands. Steve approached gently and knelt in front of her, taking her hands in his.

'We don't know anything yet,' he said.

'She's gone,' Rosa replied quietly. 'On my watch. I let her go.'

Steve took charge. He understood how Rosa felt all too well. He remembered an informant in Liverpool … But he had to be strong now, and he needed her to be strong. Almost roughly, he pulled her to her feet.

'We can't think that way,' he said. 'We don't know anything yet. There's no reason to panic and start calling everyone just yet.'

He paused.

'On the other hand, just in case, we should probably start one or two balls rolling.'

He took out his mobile. Rosa reacted with alarm.

'Who are you calling?'

He smiled thinly. 'It's all right, I'm not calling the White House. I'm going to call my boss and ask him to circulate Dani's picture to all the ports and airports, with an instruction to detain if seen. I am also going to ask him to contact the Directors of MI5 and MI6, just to put them on standby. That's as far as we will go for now.'

'The word will get out,' Rosa said.

'Possibly,' Steve conceded. 'But we will know if she is gone within a few hours, and if she really is gone, the word has to go out to everyone as soon as possible. We have to raise a hue and cry, to put pressure on whoever has her, and to maximize the chances of finding her. If she has been taken, there are probably people out there who saw something or heard something, and we need to know who those people are.'

He turned his back and she heard him talking quietly, but determinedly. It seemed that his boss – the commander in charge of Special Branch – was, at first, none too pleased to be disturbed in the middle of a dinner party at his home on a Friday evening. But Rosa sensed the mood change as Steve continued to explain the situation. After three or four minutes Steve seemed satisfied and disconnected the call. He turned back towards Rosa.

'Why don't you get into her computer and see if there's anything out of the ordinary there?' he suggested. 'I will take a quick look around the room.'

'Let's be careful,' she replied. 'We may have to get the forensic people in here. We don't want to compromise any evidence.'

Steve nodded. Good, she was functioning again.

'Good thought,' he agreed. 'I will tell the porters not to let the cleaners in until further notice. I asked the boss to have somebody keep the room under surveillance. Hopefully they will be in place within an hour or so.'

Almost an hour later, Rosa closed the laptop in frustration.

'Nothing,' she said, 'but I'll leave it running We may need it again.'

'Nothing?'

'Nothing I can find. We would have to call in an expert to make sure. How about you? Did you find anything?'

He shook his head wearily.

'So, now what?' she asked.

Steve thought for some time.

'My boss pointed out how embarrassed we will all be if we start the alarm bells ringing, including those in the White House, and Dani comes waltzing home on her own after a good night out.'

'I can think of one or two more embarrassing scenarios than that,' Rosa replied grimly.

'Yes. In fairness, so could he. He left it up to me, but he is going to be calling in for updates on a regular basis, and I can't say I blame him. He's the one who's going to be explaining things to the Home Secretary.' He glanced at his watch. 'It's nearly 10.30. I say we give it until midnight. We keep on trying to call her. If we have not contacted her by then, my vote is, we take a stroll over to Kenney A and have an intimate conversation with our young friend Bev Prasad.'

'And if that doesn't help?'

'Then, we panic,' Steve said.

Rosa shook her head vigorously.

'I'm panicking now,' she said, making for the door.

17

STEVE LET HER go. He made sure everything in room T4 appeared as it had when they arrived. He switched off the lights before drawing back the curtains. Finally, he locked the door. By the time he had made his way outside, Rosa was turning the corner by the chapel towards Kenney A. He broke into a trot to catch up with her. She was fumbling in her purse again.

'Do you have a key for every room in Downing?' he asked.

She smiled, despite herself, and nodded. 'It took a special dispensation from the Master,' she replied.

They stopped outside Kenney A.

'Even though you have a key,' Steve said, 'can I suggest that we knock first?'

'It will make more of an impression on him if we just go in,' she replied. 'I want to make sure we have his complete attention.'

She had opened the main door to the building, and they were standing just inside in the hallway, in the dim glow of the subdued night lighting. He placed a hand on her arm.

'Rosa, we have no reason to believe he's involved in anything. In the pub, he seemed concerned about her, and he obviously didn't know where she was. He went to her room to see if she was there. Why don't we treat him as someone who may be able to help us? If we scare him to death, he may go into his shell, or panic, and we may not get anything useful out of him.'

Rosa nodded. 'OK,' she said. 'But if he's not being straight with us, we have to turn up the heat.'

Bev heard the knock and got up instantly to answer the door. He had been expecting someone. He knew that Dani had people watching her. He did not know where she was, or what was happening to her. But he was the last person who should have been in contact with her. Sooner or later, unless she somehow made her own way back, they would realize that she was missing. It was only a matter of time before they came to ask him what he knew. He was lying fully dressed on his bed, the lights in his room burning. Now, here they were. Unless it was…

He ran the last two steps to the door and pulled it open with all his strength.

'Dani, where the …?'

The man and woman pushed the door fully open, entered and closed the door firmly behind them. He retreated back into the room and stood by the side of his bed. He seemed to recognize the woman from somewhere, but he could not have said for certain. He had had a sense of being followed when he left the Castle Inn, but he had stopped once or twice to look around, by Magdalene Bridge and by the Round Church, and he had seen nothing out of the ordinary.

'Good question,' the woman said. 'Where is she, Bev?'

'I don't know.'

'You seemed to be expecting her.'

'No. Not really. I was worried. When I heard the knock on the door I thought it might be her.'

'Why would she come to your room? She has her own room, doesn't she? She could call you, couldn't she, if she wanted to talk?'

'Yes, I guess so.'

'Has she?'

'No.'

'Are you sure about that?'

'Yes. I haven't heard from her.'

'Why don't we make ourselves comfortable,' Steve suggested. 'Let's all have a seat. We have a few questions to ask you.'

Bev sat on the bed. Steve and Rosa took the only two chairs in the small room and turned them to face him.

'First of all, why are you worried about Dani?' Steve asked. 'Is there a reason to be worried?'

'She hasn't come back to college.'

'Which you know, because you checked out her room,' Rosa said.

Bev was taken aback. He looked away.

'Yes.'

'I repeat my question. Why?' Steve said. 'What is there to be worried about?'

'She hasn't come back to college. And I haven't heard from her. We are study partners. We are in touch throughout the day. It's not like her not to call.'

'Maybe she's just out enjoying herself and didn't notice the time?'

Bev shook his head. 'Dani? I don't think so.'

'You know her that well already?'

He hesitated. 'Maybe not. But I can't see her just going off like that.'

'How would you know? Suppose she has a boyfriend, someone she met in Cambridge? Would you know about that?'

'Yes, as a matter of fact, I think I would. We have been spending most of our time together. We don't have much time off from studying. She hasn't been out of my sight long enough to meet someone. Anyway, that's not Dani.'

'Did you have plans to meet her this evening?'

'Yes. We agreed to meet at the Castle Inn at 6.30. I was running late. I didn't get there until about 7 o'clock. I tried calling her, but she didn't answer her phone. It wasn't going straight to message, so I assumed she had it on, but I couldn't contact her.'

'When was the last time you spoke to her?'

Bev hesitated.

'When I left the law library at about 4.30. I came back to college to call my parents and my girlfriend.'

'So, you haven't spoken with her by phone this evening at all?' Rosa asked.

Hesitation again.

'No.'

'You're sure about that?'

'Yes.'

'So if we were to look at your phone, the register of calls made, we wouldn't find …'

Bev made as if to stand, but then settled quickly back down.

'I'm sorry, I'm sorry. Yes, I did speak with her once.'

Rosa and Steve exchanged glances.

'When was that?'

'I'm not sure.6.40, 6.45.'

'Where were you at that time?'

'I was just leaving Downing to go the Castle.'

'Where was she?'

'She said she was at the Castle. Wherever she was, it was pretty noisy. It wasn't easy to hear her.'

'What was said during the call?' Rosa demanded.

'Nothing, really. I said I was running late and I would see her at the Castle in a few minutes. She said she was fine, she had a drink, and she was waiting for me. I got there at about 7 o'clock, but she wasn't there. I had a drink and waited for her, but she never came. I tried calling her again but, as I said, I couldn't reach her. I stayed there – I don't know – forty, forty-five minutes, and then I decided to come back to college to see if she was in her room.'

'Why didn't you tell us about that call before?' Steve asked.

Bev shook his head. 'It slipped my mind, that's all. I'm worried. I'm sorry.'

Steve fixed his gaze on Bev.

'Listen to this question very carefully, Bev,' he said. 'Is there anything, anything at all, you can tell us that might help us find Dani? Anything she may have said about her movements or her plans for this evening? Anything about meeting somebody else – anybody?'

'No. Nothing. After the Castle we were either going to come straight back to college, or hook up with some of the other students. But she didn't mention anything else.'

'So you can't help us at all?' Rosa asked.

Bev looked down. Even now, his American conscience prodded him to tell them the truth. It was a simple matter of his personal morality, his belief in the law. Of course, now, it would cost him dearly. He would have to admit his part in Dani's disappearance. But if that meant finding her, he should do it and take the consequences. There was no guarantee that it would mean finding her. He had no idea where she was. But perhaps the police or the security services had Kali on their radar. Perhaps they could track her down. It was the right thing to do. But… *'You watch too many movies, Bev. We are not the Soviets.'* It could still work out fine. She could walk back into Downing at any moment. They would not have lied to him that much, not his own people. But if it did not work out well, and he said nothing, could he live with himself? *'Your grandparents died in a massacre … I heard from one of the survivors that they had been hacked to death inside their home.'* Long ago. Halfway around the world. People who would rather fight than talk to each other. *'We can never go back, Bev. They told us that quite clearly. We can never go back to Kashmir. We can never see our land again.'*

'I'm sorry,' he said. 'If I knew anything I would tell you. Dani is my friend. I just want to know she is safe.'

Steve saw that Rosa was about to come up out of her chair. He shook his head, and took a card from his jacket pocket.

'If you hear from Dani, or if you receive any information, or if you remember something you haven't told us, you call this number immediately,' he said. 'Understood?'

Bev took the card, standing.

'Yes, of course.'

'And I'm going to need to take your phone.'

Bev looked from Steve to Rosa and back again. For a moment his mind went blank. Was there anything on the phone he hadn't told them about? He didn't think so, but … Steve was holding out his hand.

'No. I can't. I …'

Steve stepped forward. Bev saw that he was not going to take 'no' for an answer.

'I'll return it to you tomorrow,' Steve said, 'unless, of course, there are things we need to investigate further.'

'But my parents might call.'

'We'll take a message,' Steve said. 'Oh, and one last thing. If word leaks out that Dani might be missing before we release the information, I'm going to presume that you are responsible for the leak. Then I'm going to lock you up in the Tower of London. And that will be the last time you see the light of day for a very long time. I have the power to do that. Do you believe me?'

Bev closed his eyes. 'Yes,' he replied quietly. 'I believe you.'

Steve ushered Rosa out of the room and down the staircase of Kenney A before she could protest. By the main door she stood her ground and confronted him.

'He lied to us, Steve,' she said. 'He knows more than he is saying. We need to go back up there and sweat it out of him.'

'I don't think so,' Steve replied. 'I agree with you. He's hiding something. But he's not going to give it up tonight.'

'So what are you suggesting?'

'Let's give him some rope,' Steve said. 'I'll have a tail put on him around the clock, and plant a tracking device in his phone. Let's see where he leads us.'

18

DANI WOKE UP slowly. It was some time before she could open her eyes fully, and a considerable time after that before they would focus properly. She had an awful taste in her mouth, which she could not place, but which reminded her of an antiseptic of some kind. Her head ached, and her shoulders felt as stiff as boards. She could hear nothing. She was in darkness. But there was some dim light. Her eyes began to identify a window or skylight of some kind in the wall opposite her. The next thing she realized was that she was lying on her back on a hard surface. There was a blanket underneath her. She ran her hands over her body. She was fully dressed, but barefoot. She had no idea where she was, or what time it was. Gingerly, she tried to sit up. She encountered resistance from her left wrist. Touching it with her right hand, she felt a metal band with a chain leading from it. The chain had plenty of slack. She could move around to some extent. But her wrist had been chained up. Her left ankle had been chained in the same way. She found the metal band and the chain with the toes of her right foot. She was a prisoner.

She lay back down. Only then did her mind begin to focus. Slowly, her memory began to return. She had been in the Castle Inn. She had been waiting for Bev. But he had not come. There had been a girl, what was her name? Kali. They had gone outside, and then …what? Had they drugged her? She had a vague sensation of being lifted off her feet, and then nothing, until now. They had kidnapped her. But who were they, and what did they want with her?

As her eyes began to penetrate the darkness, she saw the outline of a table and a couple of chairs on the far side of the room. The room itself seemed quite large, though she could not see any other objects in it at all. And only the one window, on the wall to her left. To the left of the wall with the window, she saw the slightest sliver of light on the floor. That must be the main door, she thought. To her right there was a small door, and there were shadows on the wall opposite which suggested another. A sudden thought came to her. She had her phone and the device with the panic button. Desperately, she felt around her on the floor. But there was no handbag, no briefcase. Of course not, she thought. They would have taken them away. It was her first real cognitive thought since leaving the Castle Inn.

To her left, the door opened and someone switched on the lights. The lights were not bright and consisted of two or three wall fittings with cheap white shades. They cast as much shadow as illumination. Dani saw that the floor of the room was uneven, made of large gray stones. She had been right about the lack of furniture. Kali stood before her, holding a tray with water and some food. She placed the tray on the floor at Dani's right hand.

'You should eat something and drink plenty of water, to get the chloroform out of your system,' Kali said. 'There's a toilet and wash basin behind that door to your right. The chains are long enough for you to reach it easily.'

She stepped back. 'You should understand that you are in the middle of nowhere, and no one comes here except us, so don't bother screaming. We disabled your phone and your transponder before we left Cambridge. No one is going to find you.'

She paused. 'Don't try to escape. You will not succeed and, if we find you trying, you will be punished severely. We have no wish to harm you. Providing everything goes well, you will be released unharmed.'

Dani pulled herself up to a sitting position again.

'What do you mean, "everything goes well"? Who are you? What do you want?'

'My colleague, Samir, and I are agents of an organization which seeks to bring justice to a certain part of the world. That's all I can tell you now. We will require you to make a recording, which we will send to your mother and the President, so that they will know you are alive and are being treated well. No doubt the President will then be told of our demands.'

'What if I refuse to make the recording?'

Kali shrugged. 'We could send a finger or a toe instead, so that they can check the DNA,' she replied.

It was at that moment that Dani noticed the black automatic pistol tucked into the side of Kali's jeans. She gave a deep sigh.

'What are your demands?' she asked. 'Do you want money? Is that it? How much money?'

'I don't know what the demands are,' Kali replied.

'What?'

'I don't need to know, therefore, I do not know. I will be told in due course whether our demands have been met or not. If they have, you will be released, as I said.'

There was a silence.

'What happens if the demands are not met?'

'Then I will follow my instructions,' Kali said. 'There is no need to discuss that now. I hope it doesn't happen.'

Dani closed her eyes.

'America does not negotiate with terrorists,' she said, as firmly as she could. 'The President will not give in to your demands, whatever they may be.'

'That's unfortunate,' Kali said. 'I am quite sure that, in those circumstances, my instructions will be to kill you, which I have no wish to do.'

She turned to leave.

'Don't worry,' she added. 'Politicians are good at refusing to negotiate when the lives of strangers are at stake. It's easy to take a principled stand then. When it hits closer to home, they are usually more flexible.'

She walked briskly to the door.

'The dish is a chicken Korma,' she said. 'I hope that's all right. It's quite mild, so it should not upset your stomach after the chloroform. I'll be back to collect your plate in a little while.'

19

STEVE STOPPED JUST outside Kenney A.

'I need to start some more balls rolling,' he said authoritatively. 'I'm going to go back to my flat and set up a conference call.'

Rosa closed her eyes and looked down. It was a moment she had hoped to avoid, one she had dreaded. The situation was about to come out into the open. It would not be long before every officer and agent with any rank or responsibility at all would know what was going on. After that, it would not be long before it was the lead story in every newspaper, and on every news show throughout the world. It would be a story that would run and run; and she would have a lead role – the agent who blew her assignment and lost the President's step-daughter. It was the end for her. But Steve was right. If there was to be any hope of finding Dani, action must be taken now. That meant getting the information out to those who needed to know without any further delay. Her own position, her own feelings, had no relevance. She must simply put herself at their disposal, and fall on her sword, professionally and emotionally, as many times as they demanded of her.

'Who will you speak to?'

'My boss again, to start with. I will ask him to find the directors of MI5 and MI6. Let's hope they haven't gone anywhere too exotic for the weekend. Between them they will have to work out some protocols for who will be doing what: running the search operation; making inquiries in Cambridge; receiving and analyzing information; coordinating – whatever may be involved. Once we've got that started, I'm going to suggest that we wake up your ambassador. We can't risk random calls back to the States. We have to control how the information gets there.'

'What can I do?' she asked dejectedly.

He sensed her mood instantly.

'I need you with me,' Steve replied emphatically. He held both her arms 'Physically and in spirit. You are going to be essential to understanding what has happened and deciding what to do.'

She nodded.

'I want you to be with me at the flat when I make the call. But it's going to take at least an hour to set it up – secure lines, and all that kind of thing. So, in the meanwhile, there are a couple of things you can do.'

She nodded again. 'OK.'

'First, check Dani's room again, just in case our luck has turned. If not, I need you to go to the Porters' Lodge and tell them to wake the Master. Explain to her that her College has just turned into a gigantic crime scene and she is going to have our people crawling all over it, starting in a matter of hours. Also, that she has to keep this absolutely confidential until we say otherwise. Make sure there's no one listening in.'

'Is she secure?'

Steve shrugged. 'I hope so. Her name is Dame Harriet Farmer. She's a retired Court of Appeal judge, so she should be used to dealing with sensitive information. In any case, we don't have a choice. We need her help. Her husband had a stroke a year or two ago and is now an invalid, so he won't be around. But check for a nurse. I don't think any of their children live at the lodge, and there shouldn't be any College servants around at this time of night, so I can't think of any other problems. While you are there, ask her to call the duty porter and make sure no cleaners go anywhere near room T4 until further notice. Then meet me at the flat as soon as you can.'

'Got it,' she said quietly.

He squeezed her arms gently. 'This is not your fault, Rosa,' he said firmly. 'And I'm going to have strong words with anyone who says otherwise.'

'Thank you,' she said.

Her voice lacked conviction, but there was no time for him to say any more. He would have to hope that she held up until the situation was resolved, one way or the other. A final squeeze, then he released her and walked quickly towards the rear gate.

* * *

June 11

The living room of Steve Macmillan's flat looked more like the office of one of the security services. The furniture was utilitarian – two office swivel chairs and three large desks. The only concession to comfort was a brown sofa which had seen better days. Special Branch technicians had installed two secure lines, one of which was attached to a fax machine. Six computer screens were offering information on everything from highly-sensitive police intelligence to weather reports. There was a large map of the United Kingdom on one wall. The locks on the front door of the flat were extremely forbidding, and a special burglar alarm was programmed to activate an alarm at Cambridge Police Station that would bring an armed response unit to the scene at any time, day or night. Rosa had taken possession of the sofa. She had arrived back at Steve's flat just before 2 o'clock. She had reported that there was still no sign of Dani. But Dame Harriet Farmer was very concerned and promised her full cooperation. Rosa had no doubt about her discretion. Rosa had also noticed a plain-clothes officer already on duty outside T staircase. Steve was busy on the phone and acknowledged this information with nods and approving grunts. She wearily kicked off her shoes and lay back on the sofa to wait.

It was almost 4 o'clock in the morning before the conference call could begin. Steve's boss, Gerry McClure, the police commander in charge of the Metropolitan Police's Special Branch, had been easy to find. He was at home helping his wife clear up after their dinner party, and had been expecting a call. He had a secure line in place in his house and was ready to go. Sir Mark Leigh, director of the home security service MI5, was at his country cottage in rural Kent. A hastily diverted high-speed police pursuit car whisked him to his office in Thames House, overlooking Lambeth Bridge in central London, in record time. Dame Heather Watson, director of the Secret Intelligence Service, otherwise known as MI6, presented more of a problem. She and her husband were guests at a weekend house party on the Isle of Wight. But, as good fortune would have it, the carrier HMS Wessex was berthed at Portsmouth for an Open Weekend, and had a number of naval helicopters on board. A call to the First Sea Lord, who happened to be a close friend, got her a lift back across the Solent and to her office at Vauxhall Cross. As the last secure line was connected, and Steve switched to speaker-phone, Rosa stood and walked over to sit beside Steve at his desk.

'I'm sorry to keep you all out of bed at this hour,' Gerry McClure began. 'I'm also sorry that I couldn't tell you more before we were all on secure lines. But you will understand why in a moment. Dani Ryan, President Ellen Trevathan's step-daughter, has been at Downing College, Cambridge, on a summer law school course. She arrived in the UK on Sunday 29 May, and is residing in the College. We have reason to believe that she may be missing. First and foremost, of course, we are concerned for her safety. But in addition, I'm sure you can all imagine, without my spelling it out for you, what her disappearance could mean in terms of nasty work being afoot in the forest.'

No one responded for several seconds.

'Not to mention what it could mean in terms of our relations with the Americans,' Mark Leigh said. 'Have you told the Home Secretary? Surely he ought to know?'

'He will be our next call,' McClure replied, 'followed by the Prime Minister, followed by the American Ambassador. First, I wanted to make sure that we can hit the ground running. I want to make sure the Americans know we are already in top gear. That means complete cooperation and sharing of information between both your services and Special Branch, so that we can have people on the ground with total access to full information without delay. We have to begin a full-scale search operation at first light.'

'How do you know she is missing?' Heather Watson asked. 'When was she last seen?'

'I'll hand over to DI Macmillan for that one,' McClure said.

'Dame Heather, I'm here in Cambridge with Agent Montalbán of the United States Secret Service. Sir Mark, your service is aware of Agent Montalbán. She has been shadowing Dani ever since she left the States a week ago. Agent Montalbán established a protocol for regular telephone contact with Dani, as needed, but at least twice a day. Last contact was at 8 o'clock yesterday morning. Agent Montalbán confirmed Dani's anticipated movements during the day. We know she was in class in Downing all morning, and we know that she was in the Squire Law Library during the afternoon at least until 3 o'clock. She was due to meet an American fellow student called Bev Prasad at a pub at 6.30. She didn't show up. Prasad arrived late, at about 7 o'clock, and Agent Montalbán arrived shortly after that. I joined her a little later. Dani has not called, she is not answering her phone, and she has not returned to College. We have questioned Prasad, and he claims he has no idea where she is. He says he has been trying to call Dani, which is probably true, based on what we saw at the pub. We're not sure we believe him entirely. We have the feeling he was holding something back. But his background is clean. We have his phone, and I have arranged to have him followed, so we will see where that goes.'

'Oh, come on, Inspector,' Heather Watson protested. 'Let's not jump to conclusions too soon. I remember my time as a student at Girton. She's hooked up with some man, had a few drinks, and gone off piste for the evening. She will probably be back in time for breakfast.'

'Excuse me, Ma'am,' Rosa replied. 'I'm Rosa Montalbán, and I have got to know Dani quite well over the past two weeks. She's not the type to do that. She's serious and hard-working. Yes, she likes to get together with the other students, but she always lets me know who she is with and where she is going to be. Always. All right, she whines about the protocol sometimes, but she is very responsible, and she has never missed a call before this afternoon. She knows she can go anywhere she wants as long as I know about it. She had no reason not to call.'

There was a silence.

'I just don't want to tell the Americans that she is missing, only to have her stroll back into Downing an hour later asking what all the fuss is about,' Heather Watson said. 'I would never hear the end of it from the CIA.'

'Believe me, Dame Heather,' Steve said, 'she would not be asking what the fuss is about. She knows what is involved here, and she would be reminded of it by Rosa and myself rather forcefully.'

'She would be grounded for the duration from now on,' Rosa added.

'Better safe than sorry, Heather,' Mark Leigh said. 'The people on the ground generally know best in this kind of situation, and we have to trust them. I can have my duty officer liaise with DI Macmillan and set up protocols for our cooperation. I will get our people moving. We will set up a hotline and transmit any relevant intelligence to Special Branch. And we should issue a port and airports alert.'

'Already done, Sir Mark,' Steve said. 'I'm going to be controlling investigations on the ground in conjunction with the Cambridgeshire Police. The Chief Constable knows someone is missing, but not who it is. I'll tell him that in an hour or two. An hour after that, the search goes nationwide, and all other chief constables are told. With any luck they won't have had time to get her out of the country, but we don't even know that for sure, and she could be a long way from Cambridge by now. The Home Secretary will probably want to call in Scotland Yard to assist. In any case, we will have all the police resources we need. But fresh intel could make all the difference, and your people are the experts on that.'

'All right,' Heather Watson said, 'I will set it up at my end. You'll get whatever we have in the way of foreign intel. My duty officer will be in touch.'

'Thank you,' McClure said.

'I do have one concern, Gerry. I wasn't entirely joking about the CIA. Once you tell the Americans, we will have the Agency all over us. I'm happy to get whatever help I can from them, but they are going to want their people over here on the ground. I want the Home Secretary to talk to the Director and lay down some firm ground rules. If Dani really has gone missing, this is our problem, and we will solve it. We can't have their people charging around Cambridgeshire like Steven Seagal, carrying big guns and scaring the natives.'

'Agreed,' Mark Leigh said. 'Gerry, when you have spoken to the Home Secretary, he should talk to us. Preferably before he speaks to the American ambassador.'

'I'm sure he will want to talk to you both immediately,' McClure said. 'I will arrange to patch him through as soon as he is up to speed.'

He paused for a moment.

'Steve, anything more on your end?'

'Forensic for Dani's room?'

'They have been told. They should be with you by 8 o'clock.'

'I think that's about it for now, sir.'

'All right,' McClure said. 'Stay on the line please Steve, and let's try to raise the Home Secretary. Heather, Mark, would you please remain available? I will call you back as soon as I can.'

20

IT WAS LATE, just after midnight, when Ellen Trevathan arrived back at the White House. She had met a long-standing commitment to attend a fund-raising dinner for some friends who were members of the House of Representatives. She was glad to have the opportunity to repay some of the kindness her colleagues had shown her during the crisis, but it was a long evening, and by the time the speeches had been delivered and the mandatory pleasantries shared, she was very tired.

Worse still, it was not the end of her work day. Jeff Morris was waiting to bring her up to date with the latest installment of a news story which had broken the previous day. Some loud-mouthed radio jock in Dallas had been trying to start a petition to have her removed from office. Ellen had become accustomed to the flow of vitriol from certain sections of the media, which had begun just after she came out. She found it distressing, but was learning to block it out. But Kay was still bitterly distressed, and Ellen was worried.

Ellen was not naturally disposed to take too much interest in whatever someone rejoicing in the name of 'Bubba Lanier' might have to say about her. And the story had appeared to be dying a natural death as fresh news reports competed for the headlines. A religiously conservative congressman in California, who was on record as saying that gays and lesbians had no civil rights, had helped considerably by getting himself caught in bed with a man at the Beverly Wilshire Hotel. But Jeff was concerned about it. He had cornered her before she left for the dinner, and asked for a few minutes when she returned. She suggested that he have supper at the White House with Kay and that he bring his partner, Kelly

Smith, Ellen's newly-appointed director of the FBI. Kelly's brilliance and heroism as assistant director during the crisis had won national acclaim, and many credited her with having played the main role in bringing the conspiracy down. Ellen had not seen much of Kelly recently, but they remained close, and Ellen missed her.

Leaving her evening shoes by the door, Ellen entered, kissed Kay tenderly and gave Kelly a hug. Kay proffered a glass of red wine, which Ellen accepted gratefully. She never permitted herself to drink at official dinners or receptions, and she was more than ready for it. Kay had cooked an informal supper of pasta and salad in the kitchen of the White House Residence.

'How was the fund-raiser?' Kay asked.

Ellen took a seat at the kitchen table and stretched out her legs under the table.

'Oh, you know. When you've seen one fund-raiser, you've seen them all,' she smiled. 'But I'm glad I could do it. One or two of our friends are facing tough races next time round. I see you guys have been enjoying yourselves.'

'We have had a great time,' Kelly said. 'Kay, if you ever get tired of practicing law, you could open an Italian restaurant. I can't remember when I had pasta that good.'

'Amen to that,' Jeff agreed.

Kay was pleased by the accolade. 'I've always thought home-made is best, if you have the time to do it,' she replied. 'It's just finding the time that's the hard part. Usually, anyway. I seem to have quite a bit of time on my hands at the moment.'

Ellen was poised to speak some reassuring words, but Kay spoke first, some concern evident in her face.

'Ellen, Dani hasn't called today.'

'Really? Well, I'm sure she got busy with something – or she's out having a good time.'

'It's not like her,' Kay insisted. 'It's the first time she hasn't called. I hope nothing is wrong.'

She was standing behind Ellen. Ellen reached up behind her chair and took her hand.

'I'm sure she's fine.' She glanced at her watch. 'It's very late in the UK. If we call now, we will wake her up. We'll call her tomorrow morning.'

Kay nodded. 'All right.'

Kelly smiled at Kay. 'If my parents had worried about me not calling every day when I was a student, they would have been institutionalized while I was still a freshman,' she said. 'She is bound to miss a day here and there. I am really impressed that she has called so often. How often did you call home from college, Jeff?'

'That was before they invented phones,' Jeff replied.

Ellen laughed. 'OK, so what have you got for me? What has the good Mr Lanier been up to?'

She turned anxiously towards Kay.

'Kay, if you're not up for this, we could …'

Kay shook her head.

'No, I'm going to hear it some time. Might as well be now.'

Jeff brought a small tape-player to the table from the sideboard, where he had left it during supper. He turned up the volume and pressed the play and rewind button several times. Finding the place he wanted, he stopped the tape.

'The first twenty minutes or so are not particularly interesting. This petition of his has sparked quite a bit of interest in Texas. No surprise there. It has also spread to a number of other states, the more conservative ones, obviously. He goes into numbers of people signing in different areas. But the whole petition is electronic, and you can get the same information from the website, so no point in listening to that. A few worthy citizens call in and say "way to go, Bubba, you're the man", and then …' Jeff pressed play, '… it gets interesting.'

A commercial for Ed's Used Cars of Fort Worth was coming to an end with a blast from *America the Beautiful*.

'I love that song,' Bubba Lanier commented. 'I just love that song to death, y'all. And I will tell you this – I believe that no public event in this country, whether it's a political meeting or a baseball game, is complete unless people sing that song. You know, now that I'm thinking about that, we need to have a conversation about that. So I may get into that topic again on another show. But right now, we have more important things to attend to.'

He coughed, in the hope of gaining added solemnity for what he was about to say.

'We have had many, many people call in to support our petition. But not until today have I been able to say with assurance that your voice, the voice of the American people, is being heard at the highest levels of our government. Today, I can make that proud claim, because our next caller occupies that high level of government. He is a dedicated public servant, and one of the finest sons of Texas. I am proud to welcome him to the show. Ladies and gentlemen, he is none other than the Governor of the great State of Texas, the Honorable Hank Betancourt. Governor, welcome to the show.'

'Well, it's a pleasure, Bubba.'

'Governor, for the benefit of our listeners, can you tell us whether you are calling from the Governor's Mansion? I know many people love those beautiful buildings at our seat of government in Austin, and they can picture just where you are.'

'I surely am, Bubba,' Betancourt replied. 'I am sitting in my office at the Mansion. This is a busy time, and I have much work to do on behalf of the people of Texas. But I wanted to take this time out to say how much I appreciate the fine work you are doing over there at Family of Christ Radio, and particularly to express my support for the petition you are putting together against the wickedness in the White House.'

'Thank you, Governor. We are truly humbled.'

'I want to add that I signed the petition myself this morning, as did the members of my staff. And I will be writing to the governors of other states to suggest that they do likewise.'

'Well, Governor, we thank you, and it emboldens me to believe that, with support from men such as yourself who occupy positions of trust in our country, we may succeed in having Ellen Trevathan removed from the White House.'

'I hope so, Bubba. I thank you for having me on the show. I know it's been just a short conversation but, as I'm sure you understand, my work on behalf of the people of Texas is never done, and I must return to it. I would like to chat longer, but duty calls.'

'Of course, Governor. But if I may be permitted one last question?'

'Shoot.'

'Well, Governor, a lot of people are hoping that you may throw your hat into the ring for the next presidential election. I know you have not made any announcement, but I also know that the people who listen to this show would love to hear that announcement. You would have our full support if you decide to run, Governor, and you would have the support of the State of Texas.'

Betancourt laughed pleasantly.

'Well, thank you, Bubba. I am very flattered by what you have said. I have made no secret of the fact that I am looking into it. You know, there are many things I have to consider before committing myself to such a huge endeavor. A presidential race calls for a great deal of money, as you know, and a great deal of support. I'm not in a position to make that commitment today, but I am working on it, and I can say that the support of people such as yourself will be an important factor in whatever decision I make. And, I promise, you will be one of the first to know when I do decide. Y'all have a good day, now.'

The call from the Governor's Mansion was disconnected abruptly.

'Well, thank you, Governor. Folks, we just had the Governor of Texas live on our show. Doesn't that make you proud? It sure makes me proud. You have been listening to Governor Hank Betancourt on the Bubba Lanier show on Family of Christ Radio, 88 FM, Dallas, Texas. I'm Bubba, and I will be right back after this word from our sponsors.'

Jeff stopped the tape.

'You see why I thought you should hear that?' he asked.

'Yes,' Ellen replied. 'I do.'

She stood and walked, wine glass in hand, to lean against the side of the work area near the sink. She turned and poured herself more wine, placed the bottle on the table for the others, and returned to her leaning.

'Betancourt's been talking about running for quite a while now,' she continued, 'but he's not sure he can. His problem is that he may get along well enough with all those good folks in Texas, but he doesn't play so well in the rest of the country. The party isn't sure they want to take a chance on him for national office. They have been out of the White House for a long time now, and they are serious about taking it back next time. There are other candidates who would offer them a much better chance of doing that. I'm not sure he is electable.'

'That's what they said about George W Bush,' Kay said.

'And they were right,' Ellen replied. 'They should have been right. But Bush had Karl Rove. Betancourt doesn't.'

'He will have Alex Vonn,' Kay said.

Ellen sipped her wine and nodded.

'Yes, and Alex is good. But he is also principled. There are lines he won't cross, even to win an election. I wouldn't mind taking on Betancourt.'

As the others looked at her smiling, she quickly added: 'If I decide to run, I mean. I haven't decided. Neither has Hank. But it's getting close for him. If he doesn't decide soon, he's going to leave it too late to get the support he needs and get on the ballot for the primaries. I'm guessing he will be telling Bubba about his plan to become President in the next couple of weeks.'

'That is the main thing that concerned me, Madam President,' Jeff said. 'The timing of his announcement coincides with the spread of the petition. He gets to start his campaign now, and maybe keep it going for months. It's going to come up at every press conference. I'm worried we will be permanently on the back foot.'

Ellen smiled at Kelly. 'How do you think he's taking to the world of politics?'

Kelly returned the smile. 'I never cease to be amazed.'

'I see your point, Jeff,' Ellen said. 'You're right. This interview is a game changer, and I am going to have to respond. I will start thinking about that tomorrow.' She yawned. 'We have to meet with the staff bright and early tomorrow morning, don't we, to look at the schedule for next week?'

'Yes, Madam President.'

'In that case, why don't you and Kelly stay over? We don't have anyone in the guest rooms. And you've both had a couple of glasses of wine. No point in taking chances driving home.'

Jeff glanced at Kelly, who nodded. He picked up the tape-player.

'I will see you tomorrow morning, Madam President. Kay, thanks again for dinner.'

'Sleep well,' Kay replied.

21

THE PHONE ON Ellen's bedside table rang insistently. She had fallen into a deep sleep, and when she first became aware of the ring, she thought she must be dreaming and turned sleepily on to her other side to shut it out. But it was not a dream, and the ring would not allow her to shut it out. Reluctantly, she rolled back over, reached out a hand, and picked up.

'Yes?'

She looked at her clock radio and made her eyes focus on the subdued red numbers. It said it was 3 o'clock. Her brain kicked into gear. She was not being woken up at that hour for nothing.

'I'm sorry to disturb you, Madam President,' a male voice said. Ellen recognized it as belonging to Sam Davis, currently her night-duty Secret Service agent. 'You have a call on the secure line from our ambassador in London. He would prefer that you take the call in the Oval office, Ma'am. If that's agreeable I will meet you in the corridor.'

Ellen felt her pulse begin to race. She looked across at Kay. She was sleeping peacefully.

'I'll be right there, Sam,' she said.

Quickly, but quietly, she jumped out of bed, took off her nightgown, and pulled on the first clothes she saw, a casual top and jeans she had left on a chair before changing for dinner the previous evening. A pair of sandals lay under the chair. Pulling them towards her and putting them on almost in one movement, she left the bedroom. Sam Davis was waiting for her as she left the residence. They walked in silence to the Oval Office. Despite the hour, lights were burning in the offices around them, and a few figures could be seen bending over computers. The lights were on in the Oval Office also. Hal had asked for the Oval Office. 'There is something he thinks may need to be recorded,' she thought, as she entered. She had a bad feeling about it.

Hal Wilkinson had been appointed ambassador to the Court of St James by President Steve Wade. He and Ellen had not always seen eye to eye, and when Wade was impeached he had immediately offered Ellen his resignation. But he had supported Ellen very publicly during the crisis, and had led the way in persuading his country's other ambassadors around the world to do the same. He also happened to be a very competent ambassador who was well respected by the British Government. Ellen had declined his offer of resignation and asked him to stay on for the remainder of her term.

She picked up. 'Putting you through, Madam President,' Sam said. 'I'm here on the intercom if you need anything.'

'Thank you.'

There was a click.

'I have the President for you, Mr Ambassador,' Sam said. She heard Sam hang up, and Hal Wilkinson's voice came on the line.

'Madam President?'

'Hal.'

A short silence.

'There's no easy way to say this, Madam President,' Wilkinson said. 'I just spoke with the British Home Secretary. The police have reason to believe that Dani Ryan may be missing.'

He paused and heard the sharp intake of breath on the other end of the line.

'She was supposed to meet a friend yesterday evening at about 6.30 British time, so about 1.30, lunch time, in Washington. But she didn't show up, and no one has been able to contact her since.'

Ellen became aware that she was holding the phone so tightly that her fingers were already sore. Her mind seemed to be deserting her. She felt herself going alternately hot and cold. She was trying to speak, but her breath was too rapid, and she could hardly form a word.

'Missing?' she managed eventually.

'The Home Secretary wants you to understand that, at this

stage, it's just an assumption. In the average case, the police wouldn't even be worried for another twenty-four hours, at least. But, of course, in Dani's case they are taking no chances. The police have started a search already, and they have every confidence that the situation will resolve itself. But, obviously, it can't be kept quiet, and in fact the police say the more publicity the better. So you had to be told right away. I'm sorry, Madam President. I'm here for whatever you need.'

Ellen switched to speaker-phone, sat back in her chair and put her hands up to her face. It was the best part of a minute before she spoke.

'I need you to stay on the line, Hal. I'll be back to you in a few minutes.'

'I will, Madam President.'

Ellen punched the button for the intercom.

'Sam?'

'Yes, Ma'am.'

'The press secretary and the director of the Bureau are in one of the guest rooms I'm not sure which one. Could you have someone wake them and ask them to meet me here as soon as they can?'

'Yes, Madam President.'

A practical voice sounded in Ellen's mind for the first time.

'And could you have someone bring some coffee?'

'Consider it done, Madam President.'

Kelly and Jeff were in the Oval Office less than five minutes later. They were sleepy, but concerned that they had been summoned so urgently. The look on Ellen's face was all they needed to know that something was very wrong. Ellen waved them into chairs.

'I have our ambassador in London on the phone,' she said. 'Hal, are you still there?'

'Still here, Madam President.'

'I have my press secretary, Jeff Morris, and the director of the Bureau, Kelly Smith, with me. Hal, would you please tell Kelly and Jeff what you told me a few minutes ago?'

'Yes. I told the President of a conversation I had within the last half hour with the British Home Secretary. It may be that Dani Ryan has gone missing. She didn't show up to meet a fellow student as arranged last evening. She hasn't been in phone contact and she hasn't returned to the College where she is staying. The police have begun a search, which is about to go nationwide, so this will be all over the news any time now. As I told the President, nothing is certain yet. It's early days. It could be a false alarm, but the police are taking no chances. They are working closely with MI5 and MI6 in case any intelligence comes to light. I've got all the contact details to put you in touch with the security services and the police on the ground. We can set that up whenever you are ready.'

Deeply shocked, Kelly and Jeff looked at each other for some time.

Kelly forced her mind to focus. 'Ambassador, do you know who is in charge of the police operation?' she asked.

'Yes.' Wilkinson paused, as if consulting a note. 'Commander Gerry McClure, the head of the Metropolitan Police Special Branch. His man on the ground is a Detective Inspector Steve Macmillan.'

'Thank you. Also, I assume Dani had an agent in place?' Kelly said.

'Agent Rosa Linda Montalbán,' Wilkinson replied. 'She has been working closely with Macmillan ever since Dani arrived in Cambridge.'

'Do we know what she says about this?'

'Not in any detail. But from what I understand, she had a protocol in place that she and Dani would be in touch at least twice a day. Dani had called religiously until yesterday.'

Ellen looked across at Kelly.

'She's been taken,' she said.

'Madam President, it may simply be ...' Wilkinson ventured.

'No. I know Dani too well. If she could call, she would. She's been taken.'

As if regaining her composure, she stood and placed her hands on the table in front of her.

'Hal, I'm going to call you back in about an hour. I'm going to put a crisis team together and set up a situation room here in the White House. In the meanwhile, I want you to send an encrypted email with all the information my team will need to set up communication with Special Branch, the police on the ground, and the British security services. Can you do that for me?'

'It's on the way,' Wilkinson replied, hanging up.

'Kelly, we will meet here again in an hour. This has to be a functioning and effective crisis team. I need the Vice President. I need you as director of the FBI. I need Jeff to deal with the press. I need the directors of the CIA and the Secret Service.'

'Dave Masterson and Abe Solari,' Kelly confirmed. 'What about Attorney-General Hunt? There are bound to be legal issues.'

'Agreed.'

'Madam President, I would also like to suggest bringing in Lisa Carrow as a consultant'

'Who's that?'

'Lisa is in charge of the Bureau's kidnapping and missing persons unit. She's a real pro when it comes to dealing with kidnap situations, negotiations, ransom demands. She could provide some really useful input.'

'Agreed,' Ellen said again.

'What about the Secretary of Defense?' Jeff asked. 'I don't want to be pessimistic, but if it comes to …' His voice trailed off.

Ellen nodded. 'Yes, you're right. General Gutierrez. Kelly, ask the General to talk to Director Solari about setting up the situation room. Between them they can find all the right technical people. We need to have those people made available now. I need Craig, too. Track him down and ask him to be here as soon as he can. He can coordinate for us.'

Craig Diamond was Ellen's chief of staff. He had headed her office when she was Vice President. He was discreet and reliable, and had Ellen's complete trust.

'The Secretary of State?' Kelly asked.

Ellen shook her head. 'I can't take him off the negotiations in the Middle East. But let's make sure we keep him informed'

'I'm on it,' Kelly said on her way out.

Ellen turned to Jeff Morris.

'Jeff, the media is going to be all over this very soon. At some point we will have to make a statement, and after that we will have to provide regular briefings. But I want to make sure I know everything there is to know, and I want to make sure my information is constantly updated.'

'I'll make sure we have the contact details from Ambassador Wilkinson locked in,' Jeff said. 'That should give us access to everything pretty much as it happens.'

He walked towards the door, then turned back.

'I know how difficult this is for you, Madam President. Is there anything else I can do – for you, I mean?'

Ellen smiled. 'No, thank you, Jeff. I have to go break the news to someone else now.'

* * *

Kay was still sleeping soundly when Ellen quietly entered the bedroom. For some minutes, she stood over Kay's sleeping form, listening to the soft, rhythmic breathing, her hands clenched in front of her. Twice, she stretched out a hand with the intention of waking Kay. Twice, she pulled it back. Eventually, she kicked off her sandals, climbed lightly into the middle of the bed. She arranged herself around Kay, the contours of her body following Kay's, touching her lightly. She folded her arms around her lover and joined her hands in front of her. She had done this many times before; at least this way, Kay would wake gently and knowing that she was there.

22

June 12

THE FIRST RAYS of morning light from the high window woke Dani from a light sleep. By the previous evening, her immediate fears had subsided. Whoever these people were, it seemed that they did not believe in violence or ill-treatment for its own sake. In her own way, Kali was trying to make her as comfortable as she could. She had brought a single mattress, with a sheet, a blanket and a pillow. She brought food and a regular supply of fresh water. Dani now felt strong enough to think, to make her mind focus on her situation.

She realized that there was no immediate hope of escaping. There were at least two people keeping watch over her. There might be more. They were armed, and obviously well organized. If she was going to escape, she would have to hope that they made a mistake – or that the police found her. She felt confident that the police knew she was gone. Rosa would have missed her as soon as she failed to call on Friday evening, and she would have raised the alarm. But did the police have any information about what had happened? There was no way to answer that question. But she could try to gather information of her own. She could try to piece together any clues she could find about two vital questions: where she was, and how long she had been gone.

Kali had mentioned chloroform. Dani did not know much about chloroform, but she was pretty sure that its effects were not very long-lasting. She had felt herself recovering from its effects during the period of darkness when she first woke up to find herself a captive. Kali had brought water and told her to drink to flush it out of her system. The probability was that she had woken up in this place on the same night she had been taken, late Friday evening or early Saturday morning. That would mean that it was now Sunday morning. It would also mean that she had not come very far from Cambridge. Dani felt a burst of hope. Perhaps she could devise some questions to put to Kali which seemed innocent, but which might confirm her conclusions. One thing she could do was keep track of time. She had read that captives could lose all sense of time; as a period of captivity became longer, day could turn to night and night to day, unnoticed and unmarked. Unless a record was kept, the mind could simply ignore the passage of time, overcome by boredom or resignation. She needed a way to record the passing of the days.

She scanned the room. Against the wall behind her she saw what looked like a few scraps of paper. She could tear them into small pieces, each piece representing one day. She could begin with all the pieces in one pocket of her jeans, then move one piece from that pocket to the other at the same time each day. First thing in the morning, when she woke up, would be best. She crawled over to where the scraps of paper lay, under a spider's web, screwed up rather than folded, covered with dust and beginning to yellow with age. But when she saw them, Dani's heart missed a beat. This was not just any paper. There were printed words on both sides of each scrap. She was looking at parts of a page torn from a newspaper. She seized the scraps eagerly and started to unfold them. And then she saw it. At the top of one scrap were the letters 'Camb'. The rest of the word had been torn off, and there was no date. But there was no doubt in her mind. The scraps were from a newspaper, and that paper was the *Cambridge News*. She had seen people reading it in the city. The fragments of text, a few words here, a few there, were in newspaper print. Her captors had made a mistake; perhaps a small one, but a mistake nonetheless. She was not far from Cambridge.

She returned to the mattress and placed her scraps of paper securely in her left jeans pocket. She tore one scrap into smaller pieces. She left the 'Camb' scrap intact and transferred it to her right pocket, to signify Sunday. Kali entered with a tray.

'Breakfast,' she announced, setting the tray on the ground. She placed a pad of writing paper beside it. 'And this is your script. Look it over while you eat.'

'My script?'

'You will be making your recording this morning. You don't have to memorize it. You can read it from the pad. But it will be more convincing if you know what you are going to say in advance. And you need to do a good job. Your life may depend on it. I will be back to get you ready in fifteen minutes.'

'What time is it?' Dani asked.

'Quite obviously,' Kali replied, 'it's breakfast time.'

Breakfast was orange juice, scrambled eggs and coffee. After she had eaten, Dani read through the script. It was neatly hand-printed in black ink. The letters were small – feminine, Dani thought: the handwriting suggested Kali rather than Samir.

'My name is Dani Ryan. My mother is Kay Ryan and my step-mother is President Ellen Trevathan. I have not been harmed and I am in good health. Those who hold me have certain demands, which will be communicated to you when you receive this message. If the demands are met, I will be released unharmed. If not, I will be killed.'

As she read the last sentence, her fears returned. She tried to suppress them, and made herself focus on the script. It was formally, even stiffly written. It gave no clue about who her captors were, or what they wanted. The demands were to be sent separately. This recording was not intended as propaganda. There was to be no statement of their case; no denunciation of their enemies; no claim of victory, or even of power; not even a boast about their prowess in snatching the step-daughter of the President of the United States from a busy public street on a busy Friday evening; not even a heart-breaking plea for release: 'Please save me, Mom, I don't want to die.' Just the most basic, unadorned message imaginable. 'I'm OK for now; I will stay OK if you do what they want; otherwise, I'm dead.' The handwriting was Kali's, but she guessed that the language was not. She felt deflated. She had hoped that the text might lend itself to some inflection, some way for her to insert a clue, however vague, about where she was. But she saw no such opportunity in this brusque, prosaic message.

She stared at the wall in front of her and tried to think. No ideas came.

Kali returned. To Dani's surprise, she was carrying a clean top and underwear, which she threw down on to the mattress.

'You're going to have a shower and change,' she said. 'We want you looking your best for your appearance in front of the camera, don't we?'

'How do you expect me to shower, all chained up?' Dani asked. 'I can't even get undressed.'

Kali approached, taking her pistol from her jeans, holding it in her right hand and pointing it at Dani. In her left hand she held a key, which she proffered to Dani.

'Insert this into the small opening on the metal band around your wrist. It will open. Same with your ankle. Then throw the key back to me.'

Kali stepped back. Dani tried the key. It worked with surprising ease. In a second or two she was free. She tossed the key back towards Kali who caught it one-handed with her left hand, still keeping the pistol trained on Dani.

'Over there,' Kali said, pointing with the gun. 'The door on the far wall.'

Dani had noticed the door. She could not reach it chained up, and had no way of knowing where it led. Dani walked to the door and pulled it open to reveal a small, but functional, shower room. It looked like a recent addition to the house. The fittings were contemporary and of a good quality. The floor was tiled, and there were no doors or shower curtain. The shower head was fixed overhead, and the floor drained into a single central drain under the shower head.

For a moment or two, they stood looking at each other. Kali moved her head slightly, as if to say, 'well, don't just stand there; get on with it.' Dani pulled her top over her head and threw it to one side. She undid her belt and let her jeans fall to the floor before kicking them aside. Then she opened her arms and looked at Kali.

'Are you going to watch?'

'Every moment,' Kali replied.

With a shake of her head, Dani undid her bra, tossed it aside, and pulled down her panties. She resisted the impulse to hide her body, and instead faced Kali straight on, her hands on her hips. Kali nodded again and waved the pistol in the direction of the shower. Dani walked ahead, and Kali followed until she was close enough to see fully into the shower room. The warm water felt good. Kali did not hurry her, and she took her time, letting the water run down over her head, her arms outstretched. They had provided a cheap hair shampoo which had no scent, and a basic coal tar soap. In normal circumstances she might have turned her nose up at them, but today she found both comforting. A large gray bath towel, rough and rather ragged, hung from a chrome towel rail screwed loosely into the wall. She seized it and dried herself off. On impulse, she asserted herself again. Instead of wrapping the towel around her, she remained naked and walked boldly towards Kali. Kali retreated softly and quickly with her perfect feline balance, the pistol always pointed directly at Dani.

'Get dressed,' she ordered. 'Then chain yourself back up. You don't need the key to lock the bands. Just insert the clip into the aperture and squeeze it shut.'

Dani did as she was told.

'Thank you for the shower and the clean clothes,' she said. 'I feel better.'

Kali nodded. She had put the pistol back into her jeans and was turning to leave. Dani picked up the notepad from her mattress.

'Can I talk to you about the script?'

'What about it?'

'It doesn't work.'

Kali turned fully back towards her.

'What are you talking about?'

Dani held the notepad up in front of her, and read aloud. *'Those who hold me have certain demands, which will be communicated to you when you receive this message. If the demands are met, I will be released unharmed. If not, I will be killed.'* Is that it? Do you want to end it abruptly like that?'

'Why not?'

'It's too impersonal,' Dani said, 'too mechanical. It needs to have some emotional impact. My mother and step-mother are going to be watching this. They need to feel a connection with me. There's no connection here at all.'

Kali smiled. 'You are an expert on the writing of such notes?'

Dani took a deep breath. It was a long shot, and she might be asking for trouble, but an idea had come to her, and she had to try.

'No. But I am an expert on my parents. And, by the way, both my parents will be watching this, my mother and my father, not just the President. I know what would move them. I know what would make them do everything in their power to secure my release.'

Kali put her hands on her hips. 'I think the note is good as it is.'

'No you don't,' Dani replied. 'These are not your words. And you know I'm right.' She closed her eyes. It was a huge gamble, but now the die was cast.

'I wrote this,' Kali insisted, pointing at the notepad.

'It's in your handwriting, yes,' Dani replied. 'But you didn't compose it. Samir composed this.'

Kali shook her head. Dani knew that Kali's first instinct was to walk away. Who cared exactly what the note said? And why should she listen to her prisoner's views on the subject? And perhaps the text of the note had been lifted word for word from the training manual of whatever organization Kali and Samir belonged to. But Dani had already seen that Kali was not a simple woman – not one to follow her first instincts blindly. And the purpose of the note must surely be to make the maximum impact on her mother and Ellen Trevathan. Kali might well see that she was a better judge of that than Samir.

'Why are you so anxious to help me with the script?' Kali asked.

'You and I have something in common,' Dani replied.

'Oh? And what might that be?'

'We both want this to work, so you don't have to kill me.'

Kali smiled and nodded. She was silent for some time.

'So, what are you suggesting?' she asked.

Dani held the notepad to her chest as if thinking for a few seconds.

'One sentence,' she said. 'I would just add one sentence. It may seem strange to you. It's a sort of joke between my mother and myself. She will recognize it immediately, and it will really make a difference. The sentence is: '*no controversy about that, then*'.

Kali was again silent for some time.

'That doesn't make sense,' she said. 'What does that mean?'

'That's the whole point,' Dani said. 'It doesn't make sense to anyone else. Look, when I was young, my mother was always trying to teach me long words, OK? She's a lawyer. She wanted me to have a good command of the language. So when other people said things like, "*you can say that again*" or "*no doubt about that*", my mother would actually say to me, "*no controversy about that, then*". Then she would ask me what "controversy" meant. It became a joke. We still say it from time to time and laugh about it. That's all it is …'

She allowed her voice to trail away.

'I'm just saying it would have an effect,' she added. 'Take it or leave it. It's up to you.'

Kali looked directly at Dani as if trying to read her mind.

'I will ask Samir,' she said.

Then she turned and left the room.

23

THE FULL CRISIS committee met for the first time at 8 o'clock on Monday morning. It took some time to bring the members together. Secretary of Defense Raul Gutierrez was taking a well-earned week of leave with his family in Florida. Secret Service chief Abe Solari had spoken at a symposium in San Francisco on Friday and had stayed over with friends for the weekend. Lisa Carrow was investigating the disappearance of a fifteen-year-old high school cheerleader in Montana. When they received discreet messages from Washington, they all made their ways to the Capital as quickly as they could. In the meanwhile, a hastily-assembled technical team working under Kelly Smith's direction had made the White House situation room operational. Computers blinked around the room. Dedicated secure phone and fax lines were up and running. Clocks around the walls recorded the time in every time zone around the world. Ellen and Kelly had spoken to Hal Wilkinson and Gerry McClure by phone a number of times, and had received assurances that the search was being pursued as vigorously as possible.

The police had given the story to the media. Dani Ryan was headline news throughout the world. Despite the absence of any evidence, suspects ranging from the Mafia, to terrorists of every hue, to the President herself, to aliens from other galaxies, were already being identified as likely perpetrators. Jeff and his staff were doing their best to monitor the press output, and IT experts sent from the CIA by Dave Masterson were doing their best to analyze the chatter on any number of networking sites. But even leaving aside the lunatic fringe, it was proving impossible to keep up with the sheer volume. The publicity would reduce the kidnappers' options, but it also shone a bright spotlight on the White House and increased the pressure on everyone involved.

Hal Wilkinson and Gerry McClure had been patched through from London on secure lines. The mood in the situation room was tense and anxious.

'If I may bring you up to date, Madam President,' Gerry McClure began. 'As you know, we are pursuing the search on a nationwide basis. There have been no reports from the ports and airports, and at this point we are cautiously optimistic that Dani has not left the country.'

'That's good news,' Ellen said. 'What else?'

Gerry McClure hesitated.

'OK. We have confirmed DI Macmillan's working hypothesis that Dani was taken from a pub in Cambridge called the Castle Inn. That's where she was supposed to meet Bev Prasad on Friday evening. We have some CCTV footage which shows the entrance to the Castle Inn. The quality is not great, but we believe it shows Dani leaving the pub at about 6.50 in company with a dark-skinned young woman. The two of them leave quite quickly, turn left, and disappear from view. Unfortunately, the coverage doesn't continue in that direction. It's only a fleeting glance, and her head is down, but Agent Montalbán is convinced it's Dani. Then we have a white van proceeding down Castle Street past the pub and out of sight. The CCTV is on its way to you now, so you can see for yourselves. Steve Macmillan's officers questioned the bar staff in depth. They also made an appeal on the local TV and radio stations. As a result, a woman came forward to say she had seen Dani at the Castle Inn sometime after 6.30. She saw her walking through the bar in company with a young Indian woman, and she saw them leave the pub together. She didn't see either Dani or the Indian woman come back.'

A silence fell over the room for some moments.

'How reliable is this witness?' Kelly asked. 'Visual identification is hit-and-miss at the best of times.'

'Yes, I know,' McClure said. 'But Steve is an experienced officer, and he thinks it's a good ID. The witness is a post-graduate student in politics and American studies. She had been following the press stories about the President's recent announcement, and she has seen a lot of photos of Dani. We may have had a stroke of luck here. If we could identify the woman who was with her, obviously it would be a huge step forward.'

'So, that's two Indian connections,' Kelly said. 'This student Dani was due to meet, Bev Prasad – he comes from an Indian family, doesn't he?'

'Yes,' McClure answered. 'But there's a risk of putting two and two together and making five. We have many people of Indian ethnic origin in the UK, but we also have many with backgrounds from Pakistan, Bangladesh, and Sri Lanka. To be honest, most people probably couldn't distinguish between them visually. Also, Agent Montalbán checked Bev Prasad out before Dani ever left the United States. He comes from a respectable, well-to-do family in Houston. As far as she could ascertain, there was nothing suspicious about him. Obviously, in the light of this new evidence, we might want to dig a little deeper. But let's not jump to any conclusions just yet.'

'I hear you,' Kelly said. 'But I'm going to take another look at Bev Prasad, just in case. Abe, can we work together on that?'

'Absolutely,' Abe Solari replied. 'I will dig out the records of the inquiries Rosa Montalbán made. We will start from there.'

'There is one other lead,' McClure said. 'Another potential witness called the police hotline. He and some friends were standing outside the Castle Inn at about the time we believe Dani and the Indian woman left. They were all drinking, celebrating the start of the weekend, so they were not paying close attention. But he says that a white van pulled up a bit farther down the street and there was a bit of pushing and shoving going on. He didn't see any more than that. He put it down to students fooling around. The van drove off, and he doesn't remember seeing anyone being left on the street, so he assumed that whoever was involved left together in the van. Obviously, it could well be the same van we caught on the CCTV.'

'Is there a description of the van?' Kelly asked. 'Number, markings?'

'Nothing useful,' McClure replied. 'The CCTV is angled wrong to see even a partial on the plate number, and the witness couldn't give us the make or model. White vans are ten a penny in England, unfortunately. You see them everywhere. No one really notices them. But he says it was a large van, one that could hold several people, and he is fairly sure that it took a right at the next junction. So, we are not sure yet exactly where that takes us, but it means that Steve can expand his inquiries into the surrounding area. He has a lot of manpower available to him, and obviously we are pursuing this as quickly as we can. There is a good chance that something else will open up.'

'Thank you, Gerry,' Ellen Trevathan said. 'Now, what can we do here, in addition to monitoring the situation?'

'Madam President,' Kelly said. 'I would like to get Lisa's thoughts on this.'

'Of course.'

Lisa Carrow was a veteran of more than twelve years of searching for kidnap victims and missing persons. Her experience already told her that this would not be a straightforward case, even if the victim were not the President's step-daughter. With that added factor it was likely to be a nightmare. There was no immediate hope to offer the President. She had been sitting upright in her chair, taking notes on what Gerry McClure had said, deciding what to say to the President, and trying to put out of her mind a fifteen-year-old cheerleader in Montana, who had not yet been found. She put down her pen and clasped her hands in front of her.

'There are only three generalities about any kidnapping,' she said. 'The first is that the first forty-eight hours are crucial. There may be vital leads out there. But, as time goes by, witnesses and evidence can start to disappear. So it's important to pursue any leads as soon as they come in. Commander McClure is obviously on top of that. In this case, because of the high profile, the forty-eight hours may expand into a longer period. We may have more time, but we can't assume that. It's important not to let the grass grow. As I say, I have no concerns about that from what I've heard.'

She looked down at her notes.

'The second thing is that the person or persons who last saw the subject are automatically in the frame unless excluded on a definite basis. They have to be questioned without delay. In most cases, you would start with the immediate family, but that's not relevant here. Bev Prasad is the leading candidate right now, so I would definitely support digging further into his background before he is questioned again. But I also think we have to look at everyone Dani has associated with in Cambridge – other students, her professor, social contacts, college staff, anyone else she may have got to know – however innocuous they may seem.'

'Got it,' Gerry McClure said.

'The third thing,' Lisa said, 'is the most important of all. But there is nothing we can do about it at this precise moment.'

'A ransom demand?' Kelly asked.

'Yes. There is a purpose behind every kidnapping. If you know what the purpose is, you can usually start to make a list of suspects, and sometimes the list turns out to be not very long. In many cases you know exactly who it is as soon as the demand is made. So, then the question becomes where to look, and you may even have clues about that.'

'Once they make contact,' Kelly said.

'Yes. However they communicate, there are risks for the kidnappers. Technology today is very much on our side. We have phone traces, cell site analysis; we can trace electronic communications. If they send letters or other tangible items, there may be fingerprints, or DNA, or other physical evidence.'

'When would you expect a demand?' Ellen asked.

'In this case, I would be very surprised if we don't get one almost immediately. All right, there is always the possibility that this is a random snatching; that they didn't even know who Dani is until they saw her on TV. But that's very unlikely. We have to assume that Dani was targeted specifically, so the kidnappers know exactly what they want. They also know that the police will be using every possible resource to find Dani, and with all the publicity, time is not on their side. It's in their interests to move this along as quickly as possible. My guess is tomorrow at the latest, and quite probably today.'

'Which means that we have to decide now how to respond,' Ellen said. 'Maybe they want money – I would assume, a lot of money.'

Lisa leaned forward against the table and brought her hands up to her face, then back down to the table. She picked up her pen and twirled it between her fingers.

'Ransom demands can sometimes be predictable. For example, some guys try to rob a bank. Someone calls the police. The bank is now surrounded and the robbers have hostages. A negotiator goes in. But there's no real doubt about what they want. They want a free passage out of the bank with the money in exchange for the hostages. But in that situation, there is nothing else they can ask for. Another example: the child of a very wealthy family goes missing; you get a note demanding a few million dollars. All very obvious.'

She replaced the pen on the table.

'But in this case, it may not be so predictable. It might be money but, if so, I would be very surprised.'

'Why?' Ellen asked.

'If all they want is money, there are easier targets,' Lisa replied.

'And wealthier ones,' Ellen added, with a thin smile.

'Yes. Look, these people have chosen to target Dani. There are two things they must be aware of, two things that, for some reason, must seem worthwhile to them. First, they know that they are taking one hell of a risk and they will be aware of the consequences for them if they get caught. Second, they know they are deliberately courting worldwide publicity that is going to run and run. That's a lot to deal with just to make money, even a lot of money. And how would they arrange payment? This would not be a case of: "leave a brown envelope in the trash can outside McDonalds in the mall, and don't bring the police, or else". This would have to be a very complicated series of electronic bank transactions that we would be monitoring every step of the way, and the problems would be almost insurmountable. I doubt that even the most sleazy bank in the world would touch this. No one's going to risk laundering the proceeds of a ransom for the daughter of the President of the United States. You would be calling down

Armageddon on yourself, and on your country.'

'So, we are looking at something political?' Vice President Ted Lazenby spoke for the first time. 'They are going to put pressure on the President to do something, or not do something?'

Lisa nodded slowly. 'That would be my guess.'

'Right,' Ellen said. 'Then we need to anticipate whatever they may demand, and we need to have our response ready. We need to game-play all the options we can foresee, so that we can think through any scenario we may be faced with. Does everyone agree?'

'Excuse me, Madam President,' Lisa said, 'but there is one other thing I feel I must mention. I would not generally say this to a parent unless they ask. But I must tell you that there is never an absolute guarantee of getting the victim back, even if all the kidnappers' demands are met. Sometimes they panic and decide not to leave witnesses. Sometimes they are simply malicious, or take pleasure in doing harm. Sometimes something goes wrong by accident. I don't mean to suggest that such a thing would happen in this case, but ...'

'The stakes are high for them, as well as for us,' Ellen said, nodding. 'I understand.'

Ted Lazenby leaned to his left and had a short, whispered conversation with Attorney-General Ken Hunt. He turned back towards the President.

'Madam President, I really need a short time with you, Dean Hunt and General Gutierrez to address one or two matters of legal concern. Can we have a few minutes now?'

'Legal concern?'

Lazenby looked across the table at Kelly. It was a look she remembered from her time as his personal assistant at the Bureau. It said: 'back me up on this'.

'Madam President, it might be good for us to take a short break,' she said. 'I would like to make a couple of calls to get my people started on a closer look at Bev Prasad and the other American students.'

Ellen hesitated. 'I'm anxious not to waste any time. We really need to move ahead with this.'

'I hope it won't take long,' Lazenby replied. 'But it is important.'

Ellen nodded. 'All right. Everyone take ten and grab some coffee. Start playing with some ideas. Jeff, we still need to hold that press conference before too long. Craig, I need you to be on top of the day-to-day running of the White House while I am focused on this situation. Let's get that organized. We will reconvene here after the break.'

* * *

'How is Kay?' Ted Lazenby asked, when the four were left alone in the room.

Ellen sat down in her chair. Ken Hunt brought her some coffee from the machine and sat to her right. Lazenby and Raul Gutierrez moved to sit opposite them. For the first time, she seemed weary.

'She's sedated and sleeping right now. She was very distressed after I broke the news to her. It was a rough night. I had the doctor prescribe something and I've asked the nurse to check on her at regular intervals. I will need to go to see her myself at some point. She will be OK. Obviously, it's been a shock. Dani's father, Dale Harrison, is with her. I've arranged access to the residence for him for as long as this lasts.'

'And how are you?'

Ellen looked up sharply. The weariness seemed to disappear as suddenly as it had appeared.

'What's that supposed to mean?' she snapped.

'It means that I am asking how you are,' he replied softly.

'My step-daughter has been kidnapped, Ted. How do you think I am?'

Lazenby breathed deeply and leaned forward in his chair.

'I would think you are going out of your mind with worry, just like Kay. Actually, I can't imagine what you're going through.'

'I can cope,' Ellen replied. 'I have to cope. I have to be strong for Kay and for Dani. Whatever I may be going through, I have to put my own feelings on one side until the situation is resolved.'

'Put them on one side? Ellen …'

Ellen was on the verge of saying something, but suddenly choked it back. She put her coffee cup down on the table with a bang and looked directly at Lazenby. There was silence for some time.

'Are you questioning my ability to handle this situation?'

Lazenby did not reply.

Ellen shook her head vigorously and pointed a finger.

'Don't play games with me, Ted. We've known each other too long for that. If you have something to say, come out and say it.'

'What I am questioning,' Lazenby said, 'is whether you should be *trying* to handle this situation.'

'Ellen,' Raul Gutierrez added quietly, 'you are Dani's step-mother, but you are also the President of the United States.'

'Thank you for reminding me of that, Raul,' Ellen replied sharply. 'I hadn't forgotten. What's your point?'

Gutierrez glanced quickly at Lazenby and Hunt.

'My point is that the kidnappers may make a demand that involves your taking some action as President,' he said. 'As Dani's step-mother you would do anything to get her back safely. Any parent would. But what if getting her back safely means doing something that harms the United States? What if you had to choose between Dani and the country?'

'I …,' Ellen began. But she did not complete the thought. Instead she stood and walked to the other end of the room, as if one of the computers had attracted her attention. Eventually, she turned back to face the three men.

'You're personally involved, Ellen,' Ted Lazenby said. 'You have a massive conflict of interest. That might have serious consequences for Dani, or for the country, or for both. And it would tear you apart. You may be the one person who *can't* handle this situation.'

She walked slowly back and resumed her seat. For some time she held her head in her hands.

'Do you realize what you are asking of me?' she murmured.

'Yes,' Lazenby said.

'You are asking me to give up any power I have to get Dani back.'

'We are asking you to trust someone else to take decisions you can't possibly take yourself.'

She looked around at each man in turn.

'What do you want me to do?' she asked eventually.

Lazenby nodded towards Ken Hunt.

'We are suggesting that you execute a declaration under the Twenty-fifth Amendment,' Hunt said, 'to the effect that you are unable to discharge the powers and duties of the office of President. Legally, that means that Ted would take over as Acting President until this particular situation is resolved, and he would assume all the powers and duties of the office. As soon as it is resolved, you would execute a further declaration and resume your duties.'

Ellen stood and looked at Ted Lazenby.

'And you would do whatever you can to bring Dani back?'

'I think that the people of this country, and sane people throughout the world, will give me a lot of leeway to get Dani back safely in this situation.' Lazenby replied. 'But I will do exactly what you would do if you were not personally involved – I will do what is right.'

Ellen turned abruptly and walked towards the door.

'I have to go to Kay,' she said. 'Can you please get everyone back in and start them thinking about various scenarios and options?'

'Ellen ...?' Lazenby began.

'I will think about it,' she replied. 'I have to go to Kay now.'

24

IT WAS ONLY when he picked up the remote and tuned to CNN that Pretorius began to feel really nervous. The assignment itself was routine. There was nothing to distinguish it from hundreds of jobs he had done in the past. There were always a few nerves, of course – particularly if whatever he was carrying was particularly valuable, or he was dealing with people he did not trust. But that was something that came with the job. He took precautions. He never asked too many questions, and he never looked too closely at what he was carrying. One of his many associates would always ensure that he had access to a weapon if he needed one. As a courier, it was his task to make sure that the material he had been entrusted with reached those for whom it was intended, and reached them safely. Pretorius was very good at his job, and that was what kept him out of trouble – and kept his offshore bank balance healthy. As soon as he had talked to his contact, his experience had given him a shrewd idea of what this particular assignment was about. But only now was he beginning to see the whole picture. The step-daughter of the President of the United States? That was out of his league. Pretorius had not signed up for that.

Willem Pretorius had credentials. He was born in 1972 into a prominent Afrikaner family in Potchefstroom. The family claimed some roots among the Voortrekkers, and was descended indirectly from Andries Pretorius, who commanded the Boers against the Zulus at the Battle of Blood River in 1838. Members of his family had died in both Boer wars. Willem's immediate family were moderate people, who supported the National Party and the policy of apartheid more out of a sense of being bound by a burdensome tradition than out of conviction. As a child, Willem was more interested in rugby than politics, and his main interest in apartheid was the dearth of visiting teams from abroad in consequence of the boycott. But his wider family was well represented in the Broederbond, the shadowy Afrikaner political society which was a constant and powerful force in South African Government. And as a student at the University of Pretoria, he discovered that his impeccable Afrikaner credentials attracted him to people with high connections. He was courted by the Broederbond, and made connections in BOSS, the Government's ruthless secret police. His personal conversion to the Afrikaner creed was just a matter of time. A career in the higher echelons of South African Government was within reach. But the writing was already on the wall. Even the National Party was beginning to accept the inevitable. In 1994 came the elections, and the end of apartheid. The world in which Willem Pretorius had grown up had vanished.

After the 1994 elections, Pretorius went abroad. He had little choice. He had committed no crimes, but his name and reputation would not do him any favors until many years of reconciliation and multi-racial politics had transformed South Africa for good. Besides, he remained a loyal Afrikaner, and he knew that he would be a magnet for the many extremists who still dreamed of bringing back the good old days. His contacts started him out in the courier business. Sometimes what he carried was political, sometimes commercial, but almost always it was something that could not be entrusted to any other form of delivery. His efficiency and discretion brought him new clients and took him all over the world. He became a man who could be found when people needed him. He was surprised to find that his Afrikaner background was not held against him at all in his new profession. Indeed, people tended to assume that his background had inculcated the necessary abilities in him, and some of his best clients were the governments of African states.

Pretorius was in his room on the eleventh floor of the Willard Intercontinental Hotel on Pennsylvania Avenue in Washington

DC, a stone's throw from the White House. He had arrived from London only four hours earlier. His contact had asked to meet him in London at very short notice, just two days before. As luck would have it, he had just finished an assignment in Brussels, and the Eurostar train got him to London just in time for the meeting. His contact had instructed him to take the first available flight to Washington, and check into the Willard. He was to call the FBI and deliver the notebook-size laptop personally to the director, Kelly Smith. Pretorius was skeptical about that. It was not that he was unused to making deliveries to law enforcement – indeed it was a fairly common thing for him to do. But he doubted that the Director herself would take the trouble to come to the Willard to meet him. His skepticism vanished after five minutes of watching CNN. And, unfortunately, that was not all. He was to wait at the Willard after making the delivery because it was very likely that his services would be required again for another urgent commission.

He sat down at the desk in his room and contemplated the cold remains of the coffee and sandwiches he had ordered on his arrival. In his mind, he went over his options. He could explore the contents of the laptop himself. He rejected that possibility immediately. He was almost certain that it would have an in-built tracking and activation device, which would give the game away. It would harm his business reputation. But most of all, Pretorius did not want to be involved any more than he already was in what was going on here.

He could simply lose or destroy the laptop. But the results would be the same. Besides, there was something about his contact that told him not to get on the wrong side of whoever these people were. He took out his mobile and confirmed the text from his bank that he had read earlier. The first part of his fee had been received in his numbered account. The balance was due on delivery. And then there might be further fees. Despite a growing feeling that this might not be the most comfortable assignment he had ever accepted, he would carry out his instructions.

Pretorius had often had occasion to lighten a tense meeting with the old saying about not shooting the messenger. Today it seemed particularly apposite. Using the hotel's landline he called the number he had been given which, he had been told, would ring somewhere inside the J. Edgar Hoover Building.

25

KAY WAS SITTING in an armchair, her knees up in front of her face, watching an extended news show on the local NBC affiliate, in which various pundits were cheerfully speculating, without the benefit of evidence or information, about what might have happened to Dani. After a few minutes, she had muted the sound. She was still in her nightgown. She had not been awake for very long, and the after-effects of the sedative she had been given had left her groggy and lethargic. The night nurse had made coffee before leaving; a cup lay, cold and untouched, on the small circular table next to the chair. Dale Harrison was sitting uncomfortably in an armchair across the room. On seeing Ellen enter, he stood and walked over to Kay.

'Kay, Ellen's here,' he said. 'I'm going to go home for a short time and I'll be back in an hour or two.'

Kay nodded silently. He kissed her lightly on the forehead.

'You have my number if you need me,' he said quietly to Ellen.

They touched both hands and exchanged a brief kiss to the cheek.

'Thanks, Dale,' she said.

Ellen stood behind Kay's chair and placed her hands on her shoulders.

'There's no news,' Kay said flatly. 'I expect they would have that "breaking news" tape running if they knew anything, wouldn't they?'

Ellen squeezed the shoulders gently. 'The police have some CCTV footage,' she said, 'and a witness has come forward.'

Kay turned her head sharply. 'CCTV of Dani? Ellen, what does it show? Can I see it?'

'Yes, it's on its way to us from England,' Ellen replied. 'But, Kay, you need to understand, it doesn't tell us very much. All it shows is that Dani left the pub with a young Indian woman. We don't know who this woman was, or where they went.'

Kay slumped back down in her chair.

'But it's a start,' Ellen said. 'It's given the police some leads. They already have a witness who may have seen Dani. We have the lines permanently open to London in the situation room. We will know the minute there is any more information. They are confident that Dani is still in England, and the police are working around the clock. They will find her.'

Kay raised her head slightly. 'Ellen, there are people on TV talking as if Dani is dead, and there are some who are talking about her being ill-treated, tortured. I had to turn the sound off. I couldn't …'

She broke down in tears. Ellen moved her hands down and held her tightly from behind, kissing the top of her head.

'They don't know anything, Kay. They have no information, but they have a show to put out, so they get these so-called experts to invent stories, just to keep people on edge and make them keep watching.'

Ellen seized the remote, which was tucked into the side of the chair by Kay's leg, and turned the TV off.

'Enough,' she said firmly. 'We will be the first to know when there is anything to know. Don't upset yourself watching that crap. I will call down to the kitchen for some breakfast for you.'

'Ellen, what are you guys doing? I mean, I know the British police are searching, but what are *we* doing?'

'We have a full crisis team working. Kelly is updating the Bureau's information on the other students in Dani's program. We have Dani's agent on the ground with the police in England.'

'What about her study partner, Bev?' Kay asked.

'The police are going to interview him again,' Ellen replied.

She hesitated.

'The search is the most important thing right now. There's only so much we can do here until we know what the kidnappers want. The Bureau thinks we will receive a ransom demand very soon.

Once that happens, we will know where we stand. I know it's hard, sweetheart, but we have to believe that we will get Dani back. Whoever took her went to great lengths to do it, so they must have had a reason to do it. They don't want to hurt her.'

Kay reached up and took her hand. 'I know you will do whatever it takes to bring Dani home,' she said.

Ellen kissed her forehead and sat in the armchair opposite Kay. She leaned forward, with her hands clasped in front of her.

'Kay, I need to say something to you, something important. I really do believe that we are going to get Dani back home. But I'm going to have to sit second chair on this. I have to let Ted take the decisions. I will be in there with him every step of the way, I promise you. But he will have the final responsibility.'

Kay's jaw dropped. She stared vacantly at Ellen for a seemingly endless minute.

'I don't understand,' she said. 'You're the President. Why would Ted take the decisions? You just said, we're expecting a ransom demand any moment. Just pay them what they want. Get Dani back. If you want to pursue them later, great, I'll be cheering you on. But don't play games with Dani's life, Ellen. Don't screw around here. Whatever they want, give it to them, for God's sake.'

Ellen took several deep breaths. 'It's not that simple, Kay.'

'It seems perfectly simple to me.'

Ellen reached out an arm, but Kay recoiled, and she withdrew it.

'We don't think they are going to ask for money,' Ellen said. 'It's more likely to be a political demand of some kind. They want me to do something, or not do something, in return for Dani's release.'

'So do it,' Kay said. 'Or don't do it. I don't see the problem.'

'There is a possibility,' Ellen replied, 'that it may be something that, as President, I can't do. It may be something so harmful to the country that no President could agree to it. Until they make the demand, we have no way of knowing. But once we know, we have to react quickly. I have a conflict of interest. Personally, I would do anything and everything to get Dani back. I hope you know that, Kay. But as President, I might not be able to.'

Kay stood abruptly. 'No,' she said, the tears forming again. 'You can't do that, Ellen. You can't abandon Dani like that.'

Ellen stood to join her. 'I'm not abandoning her, Kay. Ted's absolute first priority will be to get Dani back, just as mine is. And I will be by his side as Dani's advocate.'

She sighed.

'Kay, in addition to everything else, can't you see what it would do to me to continue as President while I am trying to get Dani back? I don't think I could handle it. I might lose the ability to take decisions. I'm not sure I could trust my judgment. It might be dangerous for Dani, and for the country.'

She approached Kay and placed both arms around her. Kay did not respond.

'And how could I ever look you in the eye again, if I took a decision and it went wrong? Do you really want to put me in that position? Think about it for a moment.'

Kay pushed Ellen's arms away, but did not retreat. She remained close to Ellen, looking directly into her eyes.

'I want you to get Dani back,' she said, 'using whatever powers you have as President to do it. If you have to send people over to England to sort this out, you can do it. Whatever money it takes, you have the power to spend it. Do whatever it takes. That's what I want.'

'Ted will do whatever I would do.'

'Ted is not Dani's family.'

'That doesn't matter. He's an old friend. The last thing he wants is for anything bad to happen to Dani.'

'If it comes to a difficult choice, he might sacrifice her.'

'If it is possible to bring her back, he will.'

'What he thinks is possible and what you think is possible may be two different things.'

Ellen nodded. 'I think that's what I'm saying, Kay. That's why it has to be his choice.'

Kay could no longer hold back the flood of tears. She turned and ran towards the bedroom. At the living room door, she turned and faced Ellen.

'If Dani is sacrificed because you turned your back on her, I will never speak to you again. I will never forgive you,' she screamed.

Ellen closed her eyes.

'Kay ...,' she began.

But Kay had gone. Ellen managed to make it to the bathroom just in time to throw up into the sink. She ran the cold tap at full force, took in and spat out several mouthfuls of water in quick succession, and then held as much of her head as she could under the powerful stream of water. As she dried her face, she looked at herself in the mirror, and wondered how she would ever get through this.

* * *

It was time to return to the situation room. But Ellen was not sure she felt strong enough to face the crisis committee. She sat quietly in the living room for some minutes, trying to regain her composure. She understood Kay's distress, but she could not give way to it herself. It was something she simply could not afford. Deep in thought, she did not hear the phone until it had rung twice.

'Madam President,' Sam Davis said, 'there's an unscheduled call from the British Prime Minister. The switchboard put it through to the situation room, but they couldn't reach you. May I connect it to you in the residence?'

She sat up in her chair and forced her voice to work.

'Yes, thank you, Sam. Put him through.'

A few seconds later, Sam announced the Prime Minister. Ellen's relationship with Alastair Vaughan had been mixed. Vaughan was an old-school Tory from the heart of the English shires. His manner was patrician. Even his close friends acknowledged that he could seem patronizing, and he was far too conservative for Ellen's taste. But he had never liked Steve Wade, and during the crisis he had thrown his full support behind Ellen, even going so far as to threaten the use of British military might against any state or group that tried to take advantage of the temporary weakness of the United States. It was a favor Ellen had not forgotten.

'Alastair?'

'Ellen, I can't begin to tell you how sorry I am to hear about

Dani. I've spoken to Hal Wilkinson and assured him that we will move heaven and earth to find her, and I wanted to make sure that you heard the same thing from me in person. We are putting everything we have into the search. What can I do?'

'Thank you, Alastair,' Ellen replied. 'I'm sure we will have some requests. We may ask to use your air space for some high-altitude surveillance. But I need to speak with the Secretary of Defense to have a better idea of what we might need. In any case, thank you. It means a lot to know that you are there.'

'Whatever you need,' Vaughan replied.

He paused for some moments.

'Ellen, I don't want to keep you, and I don't want to make the situation more difficult than it already is. But have you any thoughts about what demands the kidnappers may make? You don't have to tell me if you're not ready to. But …'

'We don't know anything yet,' Ellen replied. 'We are assuming that they will make some political demand, but we don't know.'

'That's what I would assume also,' Vaughan agreed.

Again, he was silent. Ellen was disconcerted.

'Alastair, is there something you want to tell me about this?' she asked.

Another silence.

'Ellen, I've discussed this with some of my cabinet colleagues. Briefly, of course. We haven't had time to have a meeting, obviously, but I've spoken with the Home Secretary, among others. We want you to know that we are with you if you need us for anything, and that includes military support if needed. I am confident that the cabinet as a whole will feel the same way. You just have to ask.'

'Thank you,' Ellen said.

'Our only concern …'

'Go on.'

'Our only concern is that both our countries have a long-standing practice of not negotiating with terrorists.'

It was some time before Ellen could reply.

'What exactly are you saying, Alastair?'

'You must understand, Ellen, that we have our own worries

about something like this happening. We have members of the Royal Family appearing in public the whole time, traveling the world. If the idea spread among terrorist groups that the United States or the UK is prepared to negotiate if they hit close enough to home, we feel that we would all be less secure. It would set a precedent.'

Ellen allowed a long time to lapse.

'I see,' she replied eventually.

'I'm sorry, Ellen. I hate to have to bring this up at such a difficult time. But ...'

'There's no need to apologize, Alastair. I appreciate your frankness. Is there anything else?'

'No,' the Prime Minister replied. 'I'm sure there is no need to be pessimistic, Ellen. We have a lot of very able, very experienced people looking for Dani. I have every confidence we will find her.'

26

KELLY HAD JUST made her way back into the situation room when the call came. Ted Lazenby and Ken Hunt had returned some minutes before, and the others were trickling in. There was no sign of the President. Within a few seconds of picking up the call, Kelly put her hand over her phone, and turned to Lazenby.

'It's the Bureau. We may have our ransom demand,' she said.

Ted Lazenby and Ken Hunt stood and approached her.

'No,' they heard Kelly say into the phone. 'This is what you do. Send all available agents to the hotel now. I want at least two agents outside his room, and at least two more in the foyer, at all times, around the clock, starting now. Call Andrew Gardener at Justice and have him prepare a warrant to tap the phone in the room and any phones he may have access to. Be ready to set up a facility for tracing calls in the room. And ask Brian to pick me up at the White House – now. All right. Thank you.'

She turned to Lazenby.

'There's a guy at the Willard who called the Bureau and says he thinks he has our ransom demand,' she said.

'*Thinks* he has?' Lazenby asked.

'He has something that a contact in London told him to deliver to me personally,' Kelly replied. 'He says he didn't know what it was when the contact gave it to him, but since being here and watching TV, he has figured it out.'

'It could be a hoax,' Hunt observed.

'It could be,' Kelly agreed. 'But we can't ignore it. A driver is picking me up. I'll call as soon as I know more.'

* * *

Agents Kim Foxborough and Alan Sentelle were available when Kelly gave the order, and were dispatched immediately to the Willard. When Kelly arrived, they were talking to the duty manager, Ann Sharp, in the foyer. Kelly approached and introduced herself.

'I'm at your disposal, Director,' Ann said. 'What do you need?'

'We don't want to disrupt your operations,' Kelly replied. 'But I am going to need to keep an armed guard outside room 1122, and position several agents here in the foyer. I don't think there is any cause for alarm, and it probably won't be for long, but I can't take any chances. We will be as discreet as we can. If your guests or staff ask questions, please do your best to divert them.'

'I'll say we had a report of someone trying to break into a room, and it's just a precaution,' Ann smiled. 'That's my standard line. It seems to work quite well.'

Kelly returned the smile. 'Thank you.'

She turned to Kim Foxborough. 'Are there reinforcements on the way?'

'We should have at least six more agents here within ten to fifteen minutes, Director. We can arrange more, if needed, but I assumed you would not want too much of a presence unless it becomes necessary.'

'Good,' Kelly said. 'OK. Let's go up and find out what's going on.'

She walked with Agents Foxborough and Sentelle towards the elevators.

'Talk to me on the way,' she said. 'Do we know anything at all?'

'He is using the name Willem Pretorius,' Sentelle replied. 'He has no criminal record in the United States, and no record of prior involvement with the Bureau. We have asked the Agency to let us know if they have anything, but we haven't heard back yet. We have confirmed that someone of that name entered the United States through Dulles yesterday evening on a flight from London Heathrow, using a South African passport. He didn't attract any attention.'

'Well, he has now,' Kelly said, as the elevator began its ascent to the eleventh floor. 'I don't want to wait for back-up. But we are going to assume the worst. Let's have our weapons checked and drawn when we knock on the door. Also, I would prefer no surprises behind the door.'

Kim Foxborough smiled. 'That's Alan's specialty,' she said.

'I never saw a door I couldn't kick open if I had to,' Sentelle said.

Kelly returned the smile and nodded. The elevator quietly stopped and the doors opened. They emerged, looking carefully in both directions, and walked the short distance along the narrow carpeted corridor to room 1122. All three drew their weapons and checked their clips. Sentelle stood in front of the door, with Kim and Kelly a step behind on either side. He knocked loudly on the door three times.

'Willem Pretorius,' he said, loudly but without shouting. 'This is the FBI. Open up.'

He did not have to knock again. Pretorius opened the door within a few seconds. Sentelle saw nothing in his hands, but he was taking no chances. He kicked the door savagely, catching it neatly on the rebound. Pretorius had to jump back smartly to avoid being hit.

'For God's sake,' he said. 'There's no need for all that. I am not armed.'

'Put your hands in the air,' Sentelle said.

When Pretorius complied, Kim Foxborough holstered her weapon and expertly frisked him.

'He's clean,' she said.

'Check the room,' Kelly said to her agents. 'Take a seat, Mr Pretorius.'

The search did not take long. Pretorius traveled light. He was sitting on the sofa behind the coffee table. Kelly sat opposite him. CNN was playing, muted, on the TV set built into the cabinet opposite the bed.

'My name is Kelly Smith,' she said. 'I am the Director of the FBI. I have been told that you may have some information relevant to the disappearance of Dani Ryan that you wish to communicate to me personally. If that is not the case, I suggest you tell me now, because I do not have time to waste, and I am going to run out of patience very fast. Full name?'

'Willem Pretorius.'

'Date of birth?'

'September 18, 1972, Potchefstroom, South Africa.'

'Occupation?'

'I'm a courier.'

'Really? And what exactly do you carry?'

'Whatever people pay me to carry,' Pretorius said defensively. 'As long as it's legal.'

'Of course,' Kelly said.

'I don't do drugs or contraband,' Pretorius insisted.

'What kind of things *do* you do?'

Pretorius raised his hands in the air.

'Things people don't want to entrust to DHL.'

Kelly shook her head.

'All right. I'm already getting a bit bored here. Let's cut to the chase. What do you know about Dani Ryan?'

'Nothing. All I know is, someone approached me in London, and asked me to carry something to Washington DC for delivery to you personally. It's a laptop. He didn't tell me what information it holds, or why you need to have it. But I did get the impression it might contain a demand of some kind.'

'Oh? What made you think that?'

Pretorius shifted uncomfortably in his seat.

'Professional experience,' he replied. 'Then I started watching CNN.'

'What can you tell me about this man?'

'Indian, dark hair, about five six, five-seven, smartly turned out, western-style suit and tie. He was using the name Rajiv.'

'Had you met him before?'

'No. Never.'

'Where did you meet?'

'King's Cross Railway Station. There's a coffee shop in the main concourse.'

'What instructions did he give you, precisely?'

'He told me to book the first flight I could get into Washington Dulles. I was to call the Willard and book myself a room. I was to call the number he gave me, and tell them I was calling about a missing person. I was to tell them I could only hand the laptop to the Director of the FBI personally.'

'And what if I refused to meet with you personally?'

'I was worried about that, but he said it wouldn't be a problem. If I said it was about a missing person, you would come running. I didn't understand until I got here. I do now.'

Kelly thought for some time.

'Who does he work for?'

Pretorius shook his head.

'None of the usual suspects,' he replied.

'Meaning?'

'Meaning, in my line of work, people never give you that information, and you never ask. Not if you want to stay alive and carry on working. But sometimes it's obvious. Look, I can't …'

'I don't care about what you've done in the past,' Kelly interrupted brusquely. 'My only interest is in getting Dani Ryan back.'

'What I meant,' Pretorius said, 'is that we're obviously not talking about any of the Islamic groups. You can also rule out the Balkans, Ireland, and Europe generally, unless it's a really smart cover. When I first saw him, I was thinking Pakistan – their secret service, ISI, or one of the independent groups, maybe even the Taliban. But then I talked to him and watched him. Rajiv is Indian, not Pakistani.'

'You're sure of that?' Kelly asked.

'Absolutely,' Pretorius replied authoritatively. 'I have no idea who he works for. But I will say this: he impressed me as a very serious guy. Whoever he works for, I would not want to cross them.'

Kelly nodded and took a deep breath.

'So, show me what he gave you,' she said.

Pretorius reached for a black carry-on bag on the floor to his right by the side of the sofa. He picked up the bag and extracted a light gray notebook laptop. He handed it to Kelly.

'And you have no idea what is on it?'

Pretorius shook his head. 'I haven't touched it except to take it out to go through Security at the airport.'

Kelly stood.

'Give your phone to Agent Sentelle,' she said.

Pretorius complied.

'You're going to stay put here for a while. You won't be going out, but we will make sure you are looked after. Order your food from Room Service. Nothing from outside the hotel, and no alcohol. Agents Foxborough and Sentelle will stay in the room with you for now. You will have a visit from some technical people in the next hour who will make some adjustments to the phones. Once that is done, you will have agents outside the door 24/7. We may need to speak to you at any time.'

On her way to the door, Kelly took Kim Foxborough aside.

'When he orders food, you take it from the waiter at the door,' she said. 'No one enters the room except our agents. If any of the hotel staff show up wanting to get in, cleaners and so on, tell them to come back later. And make sure your replacements understand what they have to do.'

'Yes, Director.'

'You have my personal number?'

'Yes.'

'Call me if anything happens that bothers you – anything at all.'

'I will, Director.'

Kelly paused with her hand on the door handle and looked back at Pretorius. He was bent over the coffee table, writing what appeared to be a note. He finished it and held it up for Kim Foxborough to take from him.

'You might need this,' he said to Kelly.

'What is it?'

'The user-name and password.'

27

KELLY HAD CALLED ahead and alerted the crisis committee that she was on her way back with the laptop. Two of Dave Masterson's CIA computer experts were standing by to help. They had erected a large screen at the far end of the room. Ellen still occupied her seat at the head of the table. She had only just returned from the residence, and Ted Lazenby had not had time to raise the question of a hand-over of power again before Kelly called to say that she would be back in a matter of minutes. Gingerly, the experts connected the laptop to a mains plug and to the large screen and turned it on. A window appeared asking for the user-name and password. One of the experts typed in the information Pretorius had provided. The window disappeared and a blue screen background appeared with the message:

There are three files on this computer. File one is a video presentation. File two is a set of instructions. File three contains information referred to in file two. To open a file, click on the file number below. To return to this page, press alt, control and delete together.

For some time, the crisis team stared at the screen. No one seemed to want to begin. Eventually, Ted Lazenby signaled to Kelly with a slight inclination of the head in the direction of the experts.

'Thank you, gentlemen. Please wait outside. We will call you when we need you.'

She waited for them to leave.

'File one, Madam President?'

Ellen nodded silently. Kelly clicked on file one. There were gasps around the table as the video began. The quality was remarkable. There was none of the indistinct, grainy film appearance typical of many such videos. Immediately, Lisa Carrow decided it must have been made by someone with professional skills. The backdrop was a series of large, plain gray sheets, which must have been supported by a structure of some kind, but which revealed nothing of that structure or of the wall behind. Dani was seated on a plain wooden chair in front of the backdrop, barefoot, but smartly dressed in her clean top. She looked nervous, but did not show any signs of physical distress. She first looked into the camera, then down to a single sheet of paper she was holding in front of her. She began to read aloud. When she had finished, the video cut to black. It lasted less than thirty seconds.

'My name is Dani Ryan. My mother is Kay Ryan and my step-mother is President Ellen Trevathan. I have not been harmed and I am in good health. Those who hold me have certain demands, which will be communicated to you when you receive this message. If the demands are met, I will be released unharmed. If not, I will be killed. No controversy about that, then.'

No one spoke for some time. Ellen was visibly shaken, and had both hands up to her face. Ted Lazenby took control unassumingly.

'Madam President, do you want to watch it again, or move to the other files?'

Ellen snapped out of her reverie.

'Before we move on, I would like to know what Lisa saw.'

Lisa had done her best to jot down some notes during the video while watching closely. As a result, she could only just read her own handwriting.

'The first thing I noticed about the video itself is its high quality. It's really quite unusual. Someone has put time and effort into this, and I would guess that whoever it was has had some professional training. I will need to see it again, of course, and I would recommend that we let the experts go through it frame by frame and enhance each part of the screen in turn. It's well made. It doesn't give a lot away, but often some details emerge when you slow it down and enhance particular parts.'

Lisa looked at her notes again.

'As far as content goes: obviously, the good news is that Dani is alive, and she looked well physically. She was understandably nervous, but I didn't detect anything else. It seemed to me that she was receiving direction, probably by signs. Did you see the way she looked into the camera before she started to read? They probably coached her to read in that rather flat monotone. So I wouldn't draw any negative conclusions about her psychological state.'

She paused.

'One thing struck me as odd, Madam President. The phrase she used at the end. I wrote it down as: '*no controversy about that, then*'. We can check it again if we need to. The main message had ended with the threat to kill Dani if the instructions are not carried out. Then you have this strange phrase. It's almost like an afterthought, or a post-script. What does it mean? Is it some kind of code or encryption? And if so, why do that? Why not tell us directly?'

'Perhaps it's something they think the President will understand,' Lazenby suggested. 'Madam President, does it mean anything to you?'

'Play the video again,' Ellen said.

Kelly returned to the first page and clicked on file one.

'It means nothing to me,' Ellen said. 'If it's some reference I'm supposed to understand, it's passing me by.'

'Perhaps we will understand more when we know what the instructions are?' Abe Solari suggested.

'Or perhaps this isn't from the kidnappers at all,' Kelly said. 'Perhaps it's from Dani. What if she is trying to send us a message?'

'They wouldn't let her say whatever she wanted,' Lazenby objected. 'They would have told her to read from a script. If she deviated at all, they would delete and start again.'

'Unless they told her to say something with some personal meaning,' Lisa Carrow said. 'That wouldn't be unusual. Kidnappers often do it to tug at the heartstrings a little more – though it is normally something easy to understand, something the family picks up on immediately. That's the whole point.'

Ellen shook her head.

'It's not ringing any bells with me,' she said. She paused and bit her lip. 'I've known Dani for a long time, but it's possible that it's something between her and Kay. We need to get Kay down here.

In any case, she needs to see that Dani is alive.'

She picked up her phone and called through to the agent at the residence.

'They will bring her right down,' she said, hanging up.

'Do you want to go on to the instructions?'

'No,' Ellen said. 'One thing at a time. She will be here in a minute or two.'

'Kelly,' Lazenby said. 'When the analysts have enhanced the video we should make copies of the files and then let them loose on the computer itself. There's a chance they may be able to trace its provenance through the manufacturer.'

'Got it,' Kelly said.

'What did you make of this Pretorius guy?'

'He's a pro,' Kelly said, 'a courier. I'm sure he carries some things he's not supposed to from time to time, but I don't think he knows anything about the kidnapping. He is just the messenger. He is not going anywhere. He will be available whenever we need to speak to him again. The most interesting things he has told us so far are that he met his contact in London; and that the contact is Indian. So, this is our third Indian connection. That can't be a coincidence, and I think we need to pass it on to Commander McClure.'

'Agreed,' Lazenby said.

Kay entered the room quietly. She had hurriedly thrown on jeans and a T-shirt and run a brush through her hair. Her appearance was the last thing on her mind. Dani was alive, at least for now. Her only desire was to see the video for herself. But the absence of make-up and her haggard, distressed countenance told their own story. She watched the video silently, and only when it had been over for half a minute did she cry. Ellen stood behind her chair, her arms around Kay. Kay looked up at her.

'Thank God,' she said softly.

'Yes. Thank God,' Ellen echoed. 'Kay, listen. Did you catch what she said at the end? It was something about a controversy. Did that mean anything to you? The suggestion is that she is trying to send a message of some kind in code, something that only family would know about. But it doesn't register with me. I'm wondering if it's something that goes back a long way, to before you and me. Maybe something you or Dale would know about?'

'I'm sorry,' Kay replied. 'I wasn't really listening. I was too busy just watching Dani.'

'I'll play it again,' Kelly said.

'Kay, think carefully,' Ellen said when the video had played through again. '"*No controversy about that, then*". Does that mean anything to you at all?'

For some time, Kay stared into the distance. Those around her hardly dared to breathe. At last, Kay came back to them and, to their amazement, actually laughed out loud.

'Clever girl,' she said, as if to herself.

'What?' Ellen asked. 'What does it mean?'

Kay looked up.

'It doesn't mean anything,' she said. 'It was the way she said it.'

'What?'

'It was the way she said "*controversy*". She put the stress on the second syllable instead of the first. Dani would never pronounce it like that. No American pronounces it like that. That's the British way of saying it.'

'I say *tomayto*, and you say *tomahto*,' Ted Lazenby said, with a smile.

'She's still in England,' Ken Hunt said.

Ellen hugged Kay and kissed her on the forehead.

'She *is* a clever girl,' Ellen said.

'I want to go back to the residence now,' Kay said, getting to her feet. 'I need to call Dale.' She left without another word.

28

FILE TWO WAS a single page of text with eight numbered paragraphs. At the top of the page was the heading: *Instructions*.

1. *Within forty-eight hours of this file being opened, the information in file three is to be disclosed to the media at a press conference given by President Trevathan.*
2. *The President will inform the media that file three contains our demand in return for the release of Dani Ryan.*
3. *This is not true. The information in file three is to be used to conceal our true demand, which you have not yet received.*
4. *The courier is to return to London from Dulles International Airport and await instructions. We will advise him when the time has arrived for this. He will then be provided with our true demand.*
5. *There must be no attempt to follow the courier. If any such attempt is suspected, Dani Ryan will die immediately.*
6. *Our true demand will be for the eyes of the President only. If she agrees to the demand, she may disclose it only to those who need to know in order for the demand to be carried out. It is to be given the highest secrecy classification, and is to be disclosed to no one else.*
7. *Under no circumstances is the President to hand over her duties to Vice President Lazenby, or anyone else.*
8. *Any failure to comply with these instructions will result in Dani Ryan being killed.*

Once again, there was a long silence. All eyes turned to Lisa Carrow.

'If there was any doubt before,' she said, 'there is none now. These people are highly organized and highly sophisticated. They are extremely dangerous. We have to assume that they are prepared to carry out any threat they make.'

'Let's look at file three,' Ellen said.

Ted Lazenby shook his head. 'We're not through with file two yet,' he said.

* * *

All eyes in the room were on Ellen Trevathan and Ted Lazenby. Ellen was sitting forward in her chair, her hands clasped in front of her, her expression grim.

'That's correct,' she said. 'When we took our break earlier, it was pointed out to me that I have a conflict of interest. I am Dani's step-mother, but I am also the President of the United States. If the kidnappers make a demand which I could not agree to as President, I would be in an impossible position. I agreed with Ted that I should execute a declaration under Article twenty-five and hand over to him for the duration. But now …'

There was a silence.

'But now,' Ken Hunt said, 'you can't do that without breaking condition seven.'

'So what?' Dave Masterson asked. 'We just keep it quiet, between ourselves. How would they ever know?'

'Because an Article twenty-five declaration is not just a matter between the President and the Vice President,' Hunt replied immediately. 'It has to be sent to the Speaker *pro tempore* of the House and the Senate.'

'And that would create one hell of a risk of a leak,' Abe Solari pointed out. 'It's not just the speakers, Ken, it's their staff, their aides, God knows who. In effect it's a public document. All it takes is one blog, one email.'

'It's an unacceptable risk,' Ellen agreed. 'We can't take that chance.'

There was a long silence.

'I don't see the problem,' Masterson said. 'You keep the declaration under wraps for now, and let them know after we get Dani back. No one would criticize you for that. Not in these circumstances.'

'What about that, Ken?' Ted Lazenby asked.

Hunt considered briefly before shaking his head.

'It couldn't work,' he said. 'Technically, every decision you took would be illegal. That would include not only decisions taken with a view to getting Dani back, but any other decisions the President has to take during the same time frame. All right, people are going to be very happy about getting Dani back for a while, and no one is going to ask too many questions at first. But once that wears off and your opponents feel free to attack you again, you would have no place to hide, and the consequences would be too serious to contemplate. In all likelihood, you would both be impeached.'

'So the President has to take the decisions, even though we agree she is in an impossible position?' Lazenby asked.

'I'm sorry, Madam President,' Hunt replied. 'But in the circumstances I can't advise anything else.'

Every eye was on Ellen. She seemed lost in thought.

'Or perhaps it only has to *appear* that I am taking the decisions,' she said eventually.

'What do you mean?' Lazenby asked.

Ellen looked around her.

'I know I can count on the discretion of everyone in this room.'

Those around the table nodded silently.

'What if I were to hand over to Ted without an Article twenty-five, but I continue to be the voice the press and public hear? In other words, I remain in place as President, but I agree to let Ted take all the decisions affecting Dani and not to second-guess him. That way, there is no paperwork and no way for anyone to find out about it.'

She paused.

'Ken, what about that?'

Hunt considered.

'Legally, I don't have a problem with that. Effectively, all that's happening is that you are asking the Vice President for his advice and then accepting that advice.'

Ted Lazenby turned to Ellen.

'But would you do that?' he asked. '*Could* you do it?'

'*Could* I?'

'If I decided that I could not meet the kidnappers' demands, could you go in front of the cameras and tell them that it was *your* decision to risk not bringing Dani back?'

Ellen nodded reflectively.

'To tell you the truth, I'm not sure,' she replied quietly.

She allowed some time to pass.

'So let me ask you all a question: can anyone suggest an alternative? If you can, now is the time to speak up.'

No one spoke.

'In that case,' Ellen said, 'I *have* to do it, don't I?'

She slammed both palms down on to the table.

'So that's it. Ted is now in charge as far as the kidnapping is concerned. I will accept his decisions in this matter without question. And the only people who will know this are those who are presently in this room. The subject is now closed.'

29

FILE THREE WAS short.

In her press conference President Trevathan will say that we are a previously unknown group based in the Middle East, and that in return for the release of Dani Ryan we demand all plans and specifications relating to the new generation of Phoenix unmanned drones. Dani Ryan will be released when our experts have examined the plans and specifications and pronounced them to be genuine. The President may invent such detail as may be necessary to make the demand appear credible.

* * *

When the meeting ended, Ellen walked wearily back to the residence. Kay had not turned the television back on, but she was still sitting in the chair in front of it. Ellen came and knelt in front of her.

'We've received the ransom demand,' she said.

Kay took both Ellen's hands in her own, and held her with her eyes. Resisting a massive urge to break eye contact, Ellen returned the steady gaze.

'They want the plans and specifications for a new generation of drones we are developing.'

'Drones? That's it?' Kay asked. 'No money?'

'No, just the plans.'

Kay shook her head slowly, tightening her grip on Ellen's hands.

'But why … who are these people?'

'Some new group in the Middle East,' Ellen replied. 'We haven't identified them yet. It may be some group that hasn't shown up on the radar before. The CIA is trying to find out more. They haven't given us any instructions for getting the plans to them, so we don't have very much to go on, but we are hoping that something will show up in the chatter. We expect to find out a lot more once they show their hand.'

Kay was silent for a while.

'How did they contact you?'

'They sent an intermediary. The FBI has detained him for questioning, and they are tapping his phone. But so far he seems like a messenger and nothing more. He's not from the Middle East and he doesn't seem to know anything other than that someone asked him to deliver a message.'

'He must know something,' Kay protested. 'If he met them, dealt with them …'

'Not necessarily,' Ellen replied. 'It would be safer for the group to use someone who doesn't know much about them. But if he does know something, believe me, Kelly's people will find out about it. He's not going anywhere for now.'

Kay released Ellen's hands and folded her own in her lap.

'You will give them the plans, won't you, Ellen? I mean, they can't be as important as a human life, and once Dani is safe you can go after this group, and …'

Ellen leaned forward and hugged her.

'Kay, it's going to take some time. We are not even sure yet what plans and specifications there are for this drone. Raul Gutierrez says it's in the early stages of development. He is looking into it at the Pentagon, and he will have to talk to the military procurement officers and probably the defense contractors who are involved with the project. The kidnappers haven't given us a deadline, so they obviously realize that it can't be done overnight. We have to be careful here, because if we miss anything out, or give them the wrong documents, it won't do any good. They say they have experts who will check them, but we have no idea if that's true, or who the experts are. So we need to make very sure we know what we are talking about. Anything less than that will put Dani in danger.'

She paused.

'They have asked that I give a press conference tomorrow

morning, to show them that we have received the demand and that we are taking it seriously.'

Kay put her arms around Ellen and leaned her head on Ellen's shoulder. She began to cry softly.

'I'm not sure I'm going to make it through this,' she whispered. 'There's so much that can go wrong.'

Ellen kissed her.

'I need you to stay strong, Kay,' she replied. 'For me, but mostly for Dani. This is going to be a very difficult time, and I need your support.

She gently lifted Kay's head up to look into her face.

'There's one more thing,' she said. 'I'm staying in charge. Whatever decisions are taken will be mine.'

Kay reached out and hugged her.

'Thank you, Ellen,' she whispered. 'Thank you.'

30

June 15

THE FBI'S HOUSTON field office already knew that the Director needed its help. When Kelly Smith called early in the morning to order a more in-depth look at Bev Prasad, agents Jenny Marshall and Teresa de la Cruz had already been assigned and were hurriedly bringing themselves up to speed. Fortified by coffee and doughnuts, they had been in the office since 5 o'clock that morning, poring over the file that held Rosa Linda Montalbán's initial inquiry into the Prasad family. It contained nothing that would have seemed of particular note to Agent Montalbán. The family was respectable and well-to-do, and was prominent in the Houston Hindu community. Bev was an only child. There were copies of his birth certificate and a summary of his school and college careers, all unremarkable from a criminal point of view. There was mention of a girlfriend, also from a prosperous Hindu family, equally unremarkable. There was no hint of trouble, nothing to call into question the image of a contented, well-adjusted young man. But the Director wanted that image challenged. By the end of her personal briefing there was no doubt about that. As soon as it ended, Agents Marshall and de la Cruz set off for River Oaks.

The field office had kept the Prasad house under observation for the past twenty-four hours and had noted the increasing press presence building outside as Bev's apparent role in the story of Dani Ryan's kidnapping unfolded. At the request of the field office, the Houston Police Department was keeping the reporters and the cameras at a manageable distance. But the Prasads were feeling besieged. Neither had made any attempt to leave the house, and they were not answering their phones. The agents knew this because Kelly had secured a warrant to tap their landline and efforts were underway to listen in to their mobiles. The formidable black metal gates which led into the semi-circular gravel parking area in front of the house were locked. High hedges surrounded the house and protected its privacy, to the frustration of the press photographers and television crews plying their trade on the street in the debilitating heat and humidity of the Houston summer. Jenny Marshall drove slowly up to the gates, opened her window, and pressed the button for the intercom. Ahead of her, to the left of the front door, she saw a shutter being pulled slowly back. A man's face appeared at the window. Jenny held up her FBI badge outside the car window. The man disappeared from view. The agents looked at each other, silently pondering the next move if the siege should not be lifted, but as they were about to speak, the gates swung slowly open, providing access to the house. Jenny inched her Ford Focus forward and parked between the two black E-class Mercedes saloons which stood on either side of the front door.

The man who had appeared at the window opened the door.

'Mr Prasad, I'm Special Agent Marshall, FBI. This is Special Agent de la Cruz. May we come in?'

Prasad nodded and ushered them inside with a nervous glance towards the gates. Outside on the street, one or two of the more aggressive photographers were jostling with a uniformed police officer, trying to establish a position for a long shot into the house. He closed the door firmly. He looked down at the agents' feet.

'It is our custom that shoes are not worn in the house.'

'Of course,' Jenny Marshall replied.

Both agents quickly kicked off their shoes and left them by the door. They followed Prasad along the hallway into the living room, where his wife sat, her face haggard, in an armchair with a burgundy and white floral pattern. Teresa de la Cruz suspected that neither of them had slept in quite a while. She looked around the living room. It was tastefully and expensively furnished, but the furnishings and decoration were exclusively American. There was no hint of India at all, except for the custom of removing shoes. Not even a photograph. For a moment she took the apparently deliberate erasure of the past as significant, perhaps even suspicious. But then she remembered the house in which she herself had grown up. Her family was American, her parents insisted at every opportunity. They spoke English even at home; they owned a Cadillac; they ate hamburgers and fries, and went to high school football games to watch the boys play, while the girls danced and cheered, holding pom-poms Everything about it had been almost obsessively American, with no talk of the old country, no remembrance of El Salvador. But then, her parents had every reason to forget the old country. Was that also true in this house? The suspicion crept back into her mind.

Amit Prasad was inviting them to sit down. They sat side by side on a large sofa, which matched the armchair and was placed opposite it across a light-stained low coffee table.

'When did you last hear from Bev?' Jenny Marshall was asking.

'Be direct,' Kelly Smith had insisted. 'You have to get them out of their comfort zone. And we need a breakthrough, as soon as possible.'

Prasad looked at his wife.

'Oh, it must be two or three days since we heard from him. He does not call every day. You know how it is with young people. Always better things to do than call their parents.'

Jenny shook her head.

'Mr Prasad, I don't have time to waste. Dani Ryan, the President's step-daughter, has been kidnapped. Your son, Bev, is known to be the last person to have seen her before she disappeared. You must be aware of the crowd of journalists camped outside your front door. And you know exactly why we are here. So please don't act as if he is on vacation having a good time. Let me ask you again: when did you last hear from Bev?'

Prasad had been standing by the chair in which his wife was sitting. He began to walk rapidly between the door and the chair, his fingers intertwined.

'You cannot accuse Bev of being involved in this,' he protested vehemently. 'You have no evidence that he has done anything wrong.'

'I am not accusing Bev,' Jenny said. 'Our only concern is to discover any information which may lead to Dani Ryan being found. If you withhold information from us, we are bound to assume the worst. By that, I mean we may have to assume that Bev is somehow involved with Dani's disappearance, and that you and your wife are withholding evidence from us.'

'That is not true.'

'Then help us out.'

'Bev is studying in Cambridge,' Prasad replied, rather too loudly. 'He has gone for the summer to study international criminal law, for which he is to receive academic credit in law school. He never met the President's daughter before this summer. He knows nothing about her.'

'How do you know that?'

'How could he know her?' Prasad spluttered. 'She lives in Washington. She goes to another law school entirely. How could he ..?'

'He told us about meeting her,' Marsha Prasad said unexpectedly, raising her eyes to meet those of the agents for the first time. 'He called one or two evenings after he arrived in Cambridge. He was excited about meeting someone so famous. He liked her. He was pleased that he was to be her study partner. They got on well together.'

Teresa felt Jenny tense and knew she was about to pounce. Briefly, but firmly, she touched Jenny's foot with her own.

'I'm sure it must have been exciting for him,' Teresa said. 'Did he call again? What else did he tell you about her?'

Marsha smiled. 'Yes, he called every night or two. He said that they would go out together, but that Dani was always anxious because she had a Secret Service agent who watched her movements very closely. So they were trying to relax, but finding it very difficult. He said his studies were going well. He liked Cambridge. That was all.'

Teresa leaned forward.

'Mrs Prasad, listen. I am sure you are worried about Bev's situation. But he must have been in touch with you since Friday night. We know that he went to a pub called the Castle Inn to meet

Dani at about 7 o'clock British time that evening – that would be about 1 o'clock, lunch time, here. We also know that she never showed up. Now, if Bev is innocent, he must have been worried to death. I can't believe he would not have called you and told you what was going on. We need to know what he told you.'

Amit Prasad walked slowly past Marsha's armchair and seated himself in an identical one on the other side of a small occasional table.

'He was not able to call that evening,' he said, more quietly. 'He told us later that the British police had taken his phone. It was returned to him the next day, but he assumed that the police would be listening to any calls he made or received. All he told us was that he was expecting Dani to meet him on the Friday evening. He waited until it was obvious that she was not coming, then he returned to his college. He did not know where Dani was, but he was very worried about her. He was also very worried about himself.'

He paused for some time.

'He called us again on Sunday, saying that he was more or less a prisoner, with an officer waiting outside the building if he ventured out of his room. That was the last time. We have not heard from him since then.'

'What did you say to him?' Jenny Marshall asked.

'What could I say?' Prasad replied. 'I told him, if possible, to get a lawyer to advise him. But he did not want to go out. There were police officers all over the college. It was impossible for him.'

'Why would he need a lawyer?' Jenny asked. 'He hasn't been arrested, has he?'

'Not as far as I know,' Prasad replied. 'But he is in a foreign country, and he is under suspicion. Falsely.'

'Before I ask my next question, Mr Prasad,' Jenny continued, 'I want to be up front with you. We have colleagues at the FBI field office who are in the process of obtaining legal orders to go through all your bank accounts, personal and professional, all your domestic accounts, all your credit card receipts, phone records, and all your emails. In the next day or two we will be placing your lives under a microscope. I say this to make it clear that there is no point in doing anything other than tell us the truth.'

Prasad threw up his hands in frustration.

'That's what I'm doing,' he insisted.

'You haven't heard my question yet. Before Bev left to go to England, did he or you have contact with anyone, or did he or you receive money from anyone outside your family?'

'Contact?'

'Yes. Any unexpected visitors, phone calls, emails?'

'None that I can think of. But we don't read his emails.'

Teresa de la Cruz kept her eyes on Marsha. She noted that her head had sunk back down on to her chest.

'What about money?' Jenny asked.

'Just my patients,' Prasad replied. 'They pay their bills as usual. I don't deal with that. My secretary receives the money and makes sure it is all accounted for. You can check with her. I may have received some income from my investments. It will be in my bank statement. I paid all my household bills as usual, my country club membership. I give money to the Temple. Nothing is hidden. You will find it all accounted for.'

'Yes, I'm sure we will,' Teresa said to herself.

She stared quite deliberately at Marsha.

'How long have you lived in the United States?' she asked.

The abrupt change of subject took both the Prasads by surprise. Amit Prasad made a pretense of thinking about it.

'How long have we lived here? Oh, it has been many years. Since before Bev was born. It must be thirty years, at least … yes, I'm sure it must be at least that long.'

'At least thirty,' Marsha agreed.

Teresa smiled and nodded. Her own parents knew the day, the hour, the minute of their departure from El Salvador, and they had been children at the time.

'Which part of India does your family come from?'

They answered together. But he said 'Delhi', while she said 'Kashmir'. Teresa caught the glimpse of pure anger in the look he gave her, and the fear in the look she gave him in return.

'What I mean to say,' Prasad continued, 'is that we were living in Delhi just before we moved to the United States. But it is quite true that the family is from Kashmir originally. For many generations.'

Teresa glanced at Jenny and then stood.

'We will need to speak to you again,' she said. 'Here is my card. If you should hear from Bev again, or if you remember anything else you think you should tell us, please give us a call.'

Prasad stood.

'We will, of course.'

He showed them to the door without ceremony.

'The gates will open for you automatically,' he said, and closed the door abruptly.

'There's something wrong. They know more than they are saying,' Teresa said, once they had pulled away from the Prasad house, with the assistance of the Houston police, through the throng of reporters shouting questions and taking random pictures.

'Yes,' Jenny agreed. 'What do you want to do next?'

'I think we should see the girlfriend,' Teresa said.

31

SHESI BEGAN WITH a feeble protest about work. But the shop, in a fashionable block of Richmond Avenue, with its rich offerings of rugs, artwork and other expensive products of India, was quiet. And Shesi had help. Her younger sister Jyoti was spending part of her summer holidays working at the store for the first time. With some persuasion, Shesi told Jyoti to fetch her if she needed her, and led the way into a back room, where there were several opulent rugs on the floor. This time, the agents did not need to be asked to leave their shoes at the door – the obvious quality of the rugs was reason enough. Shesi walked over to a counter at the back of the room and switched on an electric kettle. She returned and sat down on the largest rug in the center of the room.

Teresa looked her over quickly. The loose top, beige with a design of chocolate brown elephants, was obviously Indian, but it was worn over denim jeans. Shesi wore a great deal of Indian jewelry, a silver necklace with an emerald stone, a number of multi-colored bracelets along the length of her right arm, a silver ankle bracelet above her left foot. She had no nail polish on her fingers or toes, but Teresa detected the fading remains of traditional hand painting on both palms She and Jenny joined Shesi on the rug, sitting in a close circle.

'Have any reporters been bothering you yet?' Teresa asked.

'No,' Shesi replied. 'My parents said I should call if there is any trouble.' Suddenly, she appeared alarmed. 'Do you think they will come here?'

'I am surprised they aren't here already,' Teresa said. 'If they come, tell your father to call HPD, and they will keep them at bay as best they can.'

'Shesi,' Jenny said, 'we need to ask you a few questions about Bev Prasad. Have you heard from him since Dani Ryan went missing?'

Shesi shook her head.

'He called every day until the day she disappeared,' she replied. 'I haven't heard from him since then.'

'Have you tried to contact him?'

'Yes, of course. Several times every day. But his phone goes straight to message and he doesn't return emails. There have been no new posts on his Facebook page for days. He hasn't tried to contact me at all.'

Jenny glanced briefly at Teresa.

'Not even once?' Jenny persisted. 'Not even a text message? Not even to tell you that he was OK, or that the police had spoken to him, or that he was under suspicion?'

'No. I don't understand it. I've been watching it all on TV, and they are saying that Bev was the last person to see Dani before she disappeared. But I haven't read about him being arrested or anything like that.'

'He hasn't been arrested,' Jenny said. 'And he has his phone. So there's no reason why he couldn't get in touch if he wanted to. Unless you know of a reason why he might not be calling you?'

'I don't know of any.'

'Don't you?'

'No.'

'Did the two of you have some kind of argument?'

'No,' Shesi replied firmly. 'Why would we argue? He was in England, I am here, and we were missing each other.'

The kettle boiled. Shesi stood and walked to the counter on which it stood. She selected three colorful mugs, from a selection stored in a roughly hewn wooden rack. She took teabags from a glass jar and placed a bag in each one. She poured water into each, and added some sweetened milk.

'Would you mind moving that small table between us?' she asked.

'I'll get it,' Teresa smiled. Having done so, she walked over to help Shesi with the three mugs.

'It's called chai in India,' Shesi said. 'This is masala chai. You will find it sweet compared to the teas we have in America. But it's genuine Indian. No business is done in India without inviting the customer to take chai.'

'It's delicious,' Teresa said. No shutting the door on the old country here, she thought. But then, they couldn't, could they? Not with the business they were running.

Jenny tasted the chai with approval, then put her mug down on the table.

'Perhaps it was about Dani,' she suggested. 'Perhaps you were jealous of Dani? Perhaps that's why you argued?'

'That's ridiculous,' Shesi replied, with a swift flick of her long black hair. Teresa caught the flash of irritation in the dark eyes.

'Oh? Why? Bev is living the high life in England, visiting pubs and restaurants with the President's daughter, while you are left here working in the family store. I can see where I might get a bit jealous in your situation.'

'He is her study partner,' Shesi said. 'He told me all about her. He likes her. They are friends. There is nothing more than that.'

She swirled her chai around in the mug.

'Besides, we are in love. I think we will be married when he returns.'

'Has he proposed to you?'

'No. But I think he will.'

Teresa finished her chai.

'Shesi,' she said, 'there has to be a reason why Bev has not tried to contact you. If you have not had a quarrel, it must be something else.'

Shesi hesitated. 'Are you sure they have not taken his phone?'

Teresa nodded. 'We are quite sure. To be frank, the British police would want him to have it because …'

'Because they are tapping the phone, reading his messages.'

'Yes. Shesi, please understand. They have to find out if he has any information, if he receives any message, which might give them a clue to where Dani is. It doesn't necessarily mean that they think Bev is involved. But if the kidnappers know that Dani and Bev are friends, we can't rule out the possibility that they might use

Bev to send a message of some kind.'

'OK,' Shesi said.

'The problem is,' Teresa continued, 'that Bev has been in touch with his parents since Dani disappeared. But he hasn't contacted you.'

Shesi looked up sharply. Teresa thought she looked shocked.

'What? Are you sure?'

'We just spoke to his parents,' Teresa replied. She paused. 'And I guess what I'm wondering is: whether Bev knows that there is something that could be said between you and him that might be of interest to the listeners – something that you know about, but his parents don't? Is that possible?'

Shesi put her mug on the table, crossed her legs in front of her and held a foot in each hand, massaging her soles with her thumbs. She did not reply for some time.

'He told me about Dani, but nothing of significance' she said. 'He didn't know Dani before he left to go to England.'

'Perhaps not,' Jenny said. 'But, think, Shesi. Was there anything he mentioned that was out of the ordinary? Anything you found unusual, even if you don't understand why?'

Shesi shook her head.

'Because if there is, you need to tell us. We need to find Dani quickly, Shesi. If we don't, there's every likelihood that she may be killed.'

'I don't know what to tell you,' Shesi replied.

'And if that happens,' Jenny added, 'however bad things may be for Bev now, they can only get worse. For you too, Shesi. If you withhold evidence, you would be committing a criminal offence.'

Abruptly, Shesi pushed herself upwards on to her feet.

'I want you to leave now. I have work I must do.'

'I'm sure your sister can take care of things,' Jenny said.

'Even so … Please…' Shesi entreated.

Reluctantly, the two agents stood.

'Shesi, I want you to think about this very carefully,' Teresa said. 'If Dani dies, or if the President has to do something to get her back that harms the United States, it will have repercussions, not just for you and Bev, but also for India. The stakes are very high here. We are not interested in making things difficult for you and Bev. We just want to get Dani back safely. You may have a clue that will help us, without even knowing it.'

'I wish I could help,' Shesi answered. She had wound her arms tightly around her body, and she was standing with her feet crossed at the ankles, looking down at the rug.

Teresa handed her a card.

'If you think of anything, please call us without delay,' she said. 'We will show ourselves out.'

For some time, the agents sat in the car outside the store, watching Shesi find herself and Jyoti tasks to make them seem busy.

'Now what?' Jenny asked.

'Back to the house,' Teresa said. 'There's going to be a mountain of paperwork arriving, and the Director is expecting a full report early tomorrow morning.'

'I hope she doesn't get her hopes up too much,' Jenny said, pulling the Focus slowly out from the curb.

* * *

By 11 o'clock that evening, Teresa de la Cruz was ready to call it a day. With Jenny Marshall, and several other agents, she had been plowing her way laboriously through the financial history of the Prasad family. All leave had been cancelled, a fresh batch of agents had been called in to take over for the night and, in any case, Teresa was beginning to feel that she was too tired to recognize an important piece of information, even if she found it among the hundreds of pages spread all over the table in the main conference room. She would have to be back by 6 o'clock the following morning for a conference call with the Director. It was time to go home for a few hours of sleep. The night shift would have to press on and hopefully have better luck than she had. Gathering up her disposable coffee cup and plate, she deposited them, together with the remains of her pepperoni pizza, in the trash can. She stood and called across the table to Jenny Marshall, who nodded and raised a hand to say that she too was on the point of going home.

But as she turned to face the door of the conference room, case in hand, a duty agent put her head inside the door.

'Agent de la Cruz, I have two people who want to see you about the Dani Ryan inquiry. A man and a woman, Asian, look like they could be father and daughter. They say it's urgent. I have put them in an interview room on two.'

Teresa felt her pulse quicken. She turned.

'Jen?'

'I'm right with you,' Jenny replied.

Fully energized again, they raced for the elevators.

* * *

The man and the woman stood as they entered the room.

'Agent de la Cruz,' Shesi said, 'this is my father, Danny Gupta.'

Mr Gupta held his hands up to his face, palms together, bowing his head slightly, the *Namaste* gesture, before shaking hands. He seemed very nervous. He wore a western-style shirt and gray slacks with burgundy loafers, but the black jacket was Indian, cut high at the neck.

'Please sit down,' Teresa said. 'How can we help?'

Gupta sat forward on the very edge of his seat.

'My daughter is a good girl,' he said.

'I don't doubt it,' Teresa replied.

'I have always raised her to tell the truth and to respect the law and our way of life.'

Teresa nodded.

'It is just that, when you saw her today, it came as a surprise, a shock even … she did not know what to say for the best. When she returned home, I talked with her. I asked her myself for any information she might have. I tried to make her see how important it is that she should tell you everything. And now I have brought her here. You must understand that she knows nothing about the President's daughter. But there is something she told me. I myself did not know any of this before this evening...'

His voice trailed away. Shesi was looking down at her feet. But abruptly she raised her head.

'Just before he left for England, Bev told me something,' she said.

She hesitated.

'I am sorry I did not tell you before.'

'Tell us now,' Teresa said. 'Take your time.'

Shesi nodded.

'He told me that there was a man who would visit his family.'

'*Visit* them?' Jenny asked.

'Yes,' Shesi replied. 'From India. The family called the man "the Visitor".'

32

'THANK YOU ALL for coming on this difficult morning,' Ellen said.

Jeff Morris sat behind the podium to Ellen's left. He had tried to make himself comfortable, but had failed miserably. His suit and tie felt too tight, his shirt was clinging to his body, and his upper jaw seemed welded to his lower jaw. Since Dani's disappearance he had been so busy monitoring the media and planning the press conference that he had spent little time reflecting on his own feelings. But now that the time had come for the President to face the throng of reporters from across the world, he felt anxious and overwhelmed.

Until now, his press conferences had been, if not yet routine, at least predictable, manageable. When he first took over as Press Secretary, the President had been basking in unprecedented public approval because of her firm stand against Steve Wade during the crisis. Policy matters had so far been mainly uncontroversial. Jeff was grateful for the time this had given him to get used to the job, and to start building relationships within the White House press corps. But today he had no way of predicting what was likely to happen, what their reaction to Ellen would be, what questions would be asked and, critically, how the experienced reporters would respond to the false ransom demand for the plans and specifications for the Phoenix drone – assuming that any such plans and specifications existed – a subject on which General Gutierrez had been worryingly vague. If all went well, the press corps would understand that Ellen could not say very much and they would give her space to work for Dani's release without too much scrutiny. If all did not go well, the story might fall apart immediately, in which case it became useless as a cover story. He preferred not to think about the possible consequences of that. Jeff found himself wondering how much thought the kidnappers had given to how well their proposed cover story would stand up to the incisive minds of some of the world's best reporters.

But Jeff felt some relief that it was happening at what he believed was the right time. He had been one of only a few voices within the crisis committee in favour of delaying the press conference until the ransom demand arrived. To Jeff this made perfect sense. Until the demand was known they had nothing to say that the press did not already know. With nothing new of substance to write about, it would be all too easy for the press to focus on Ellen's personal situation, which could only make things worse. He could see no way of protecting her, and Kay, from the results of that kind of reporting. He understood the committee's desire to make contact with the press, to assure the world – and the kidnappers – that they were doing what was required of them. But Jeff's years with the DC Police Department had left him with a sound instinct when it came to crime, and that instinct told him that these kidnappers were working on a higher level. They did not need to be reassured. But they did need to see results.

Craig Diamond had worked with Jeff closely on the logistics of the press conference, but had not weighed in on the question of timing. Only Ted Lazenby and Lisa Carrow agreed with him consistently – even Kelly had vacillated between the two points of view – but he valued their opinions as seasoned veterans of kidnapping situations. He had often regretted that his predecessor was not available to hold his hand –even to put in a good word for him with the press corps veterans, who had loved her. But Martha Graylor had taken her own life in a quiet corner of the White House during the last hours of the crisis, when the strain of lying for Steve Wade to reporters she respected had risen to a level she could no longer endure. Jeff had felt isolated. But, for good or ill, he was glad that the time had finally arrived.

Ellen had chosen an unusually feminine look, he thought. Instead of the austere high-cut jacket there was a simple dark blue two-piece suit, a plain white blouse underneath, black shoes with heels rather higher than she usually wore during working hours.

Her face was tired, tense, but she seemed composed and fully in control. They had spent almost two hours with Ted Lazenby and Raul Gutierrez earlier in the morning, going over the strategy for the conference – Ellen's short prepared statement, the answers that should be given to the most obvious questions. The plan was to keep it short and to the point. Ellen had walked into the press room briskly and confidently. The atmosphere was sympathetic, the welcoming round of applause sustained and heartfelt. She had smiled as she mounted the podium, and paused to take a drink of water before beginning. Her voice was strong, stronger than she had expected.

'As you all know, my step-daughter, Dani Ryan, was abducted on Friday evening in Cambridge, England, where she has been studying in a summer law school program at the University. I know that you have been kept up to date about the investigation by the British police and other sources, but I'm sure you have been wondering why I have left it so long to say something to you myself.

'Please understand first that Kay and I have had to come to terms with what has happened. It has not been easy, as I hope you can imagine. I am speaking to you today, not just as the President, but as a step-mother, as a member of a family that has been violated, and I have had to deal with the emotional effects of that violation. Dani's father, Dale Harrison, is also affected. Dani and Dale are very close, and of course, he is just as distressed as Kay and I are. Please understand also that for much of the time since Dani disappeared, my advisers and I have known no more than you about the situation. I did not want to make any statement until I had something new to tell you. This morning, I want to bring you up to date with the developments since Friday.'

Ellen paused for more water and looked around. She saw that she had control of her audience. There was not a sound in the crowded room.

'There are things I can't talk about at this time, things that have to be kept confidential in order to keep Dani safe, and there are questions I cannot answer. But this much I can tell you. We do not know where Dani is being held, but we have received evidence that she is alive and has not been harmed. We believe that evidence to be genuine. Yesterday we received a ransom demand.'

Ellen heard and felt the sharp intake of breath around the room as the reporters exchanged glances and made hurried notes.

'The demand came from a group which has not given us a name, but describes itself as based in the Middle East. We know nothing about them beyond that. The demand is that we provide them with the plans and specifications of the new generation of Phoenix drones. Those of you who follow defense matters closely will be aware of the existence of the Phoenix project. The Secretary of Defense, Raul Gutierrez, is looking into the logistics of the demand as we speak, and we will provide a response to it as soon as possible. We will keep you advised of all developments as and when they occur. That is all I have to say at this time, except to ask for your support and understanding for Kay, Dale, and myself. Please allow us some space at this difficult time, and include us in your prayers.'

Conrad Beckers had been sitting several rows from the front of the room, as was his wont, listening intently to what Ellen had said, his trademark Mont Blanc pen playing around his lips when not engaged in writing in the spiral notebook he took everywhere he went. He was not sure whether Ellen would beat a hasty retreat before any questions could be put to her, and he had been ready to implement plan B later in the day, a discreet call to Jeff Morris for any further scraps of information that might be available. But Ellen seemed in control and in no hurry to leave. He stood.

'Madam President, Conrad Beckers. First, I am sure that I speak for all the representatives of the press gathered here today when I express our utter horror and deep sadness about what has happened to Dani. I know that everyone, regardless of politics or personal viewpoints, is praying for her safe return.'

A hearty burst of applause rang through the room.

Ellen bowed her head. 'Thank you, Conrad. Thank you, everyone,' she said quietly.

'Madam President, I assume you have some intelligence about where in the Middle East this group is based?'

'Not at this time,' Ellen replied, a little too quickly.

Beckers paused, the pen tapping his upper lip.

'Following up, Madam President, the reason I ask that question is this. The Middle East is a geographical or political expression for a vast area comprising a number of countries. Some, such as Saudi Arabia and Jordan, are allies of the United States. Others, such as Iran and Lebanon, are not.'

He paused again.

'And of course, Israel falls into a special category. Would it not be important to know, at least in general terms, which part of the forest we are dealing with, before making a decision about how to respond to the demand?'

Ellen shrugged.

'I guess what you're asking is, whether we would be handing the plans to an entity hostile to the United States, or one that would like to get its hands on our technology because of its hostility to others?'

Beckers nodded.

'I have to assume,' Ellen replied, 'that whoever is making this demand is hostile either to the United States or to one or more of our allies, or both. It's possible that it has nothing to do with us other than as a source of information about a weapon, but I don't think we can assume that this group has a benevolent attitude towards America. Having said that, my advisers think it is highly unlikely that this is a state-sponsored act. It is far more likely to be an independent group, which may have its own agenda separate from that of the state in which it is physically based. So I think we have to be wary of thinking that this is all black and white as far as our allies and other states are concerned. It may be much more complicated than that.'

Beckers resumed his seat. Suddenly, the silence that had greeted Ellen's statement gave way to a chorus of voices and a sea of raised hands, as the reporters competed for her attention. She picked out a familiar face from NBC News, one of the network's most senior foreign correspondents.

'Madam President, I'm not sure many of us in the room know very much about a new generation of Phoenix drones. I must confess I thought it was just recently that the first generation was deployed. Can you tell us any more about that? How long has a new generation been on the drawing board, and in what way is it different?'

Ellen took a deliberate sip of water.

'Bill, I am unable to provide any details about that at this time. The Phoenix project is highly classified and, in any case, I can't comment on operational matters. I am consulting with the Secretary of Defense so that I am fully informed before we take any decisions.'

'Madam President, I have been in the Tribal Areas myself, and I have seen the effects of the first generation of the Phoenix drones at first hand.'

Ellen broke in sharply.

'As I said, Bill, I can't comment on operational matters, including whether a Phoenix drone has ever been deployed.'

Bill Merriweather smiled. 'Of course, Madam President. Then, let me just say that, having seen the damage done by whatever weapon I saw used in the Tribal Areas, I can only imagine what the second generation of Phoenix drones may be capable of. No matter who this group may represent, isn't that a lot of military power to put in their hands?'

'As I said,' Ellen replied. 'I have to gather more information. I'm not ready to make any decisions yet.'

By now, reporters were becoming too excited to wait to be asked individually. Questions were being shouted out from all sides. Ellen was amazed how calm she felt. It was, she thought, probably the calm before the storm. The Phoenix drone was a diversion. All that mattered was that she was following the instructions in file three. If the kidnappers were watching, and she was sure they were, they would see that she was doing as she had been told, that there was no need to harm Dani.

'Can you comment on whether the British police are still questioning the other students on Dani's course?' a female reporter asked. Her accent sounded Dutch or Belgian, Ellen thought. 'We know that there was a young man from an Indian family in Houston. Has he been questioned further?'

'I can't talk about details of the investigation at this time,' Ellen repeated.

'Madam President, what evidence was provided to show that Dani is alive?' This time, the questioner was Ed Streeter, a staff journalist working for the *Wall Street Journal*. He was generally not too well disposed towards Ellen, but his tone today was subdued. She glanced over her shoulder at Jeff. He nodded almost imperceptibly.

'We received a video showing Dani alive and well. As I said before, we have every reason to believe it is genuine.'

'Did it yield any leads about where she might be?'

Ellen experienced a momentary flash of anger, which she almost instantly controlled. 'Does he really expect me to answer that on live television?' she asked herself incredulously.

'No, it did not,' she replied.

'Madam President, have the kidnappers given you a deadline for complying with their demands?' The questioner this time was Jeremy Bairstow, the BBC's senior foreign correspondent, an experienced hand and a witty raconteur, a popular guest at receptions on the Washington circuit. He had acted as a conduit with perfect discretion, behind the scenes, between Ellen and the supportive British Government during the crisis, when Steve Wade's control of the White House meant that all normal channels of communication were insecure.

'No, Jeremy, they have not. We think they understand that this is a serious matter, and that we need time to reflect.'

'And perhaps to open negotiations?'

Ellen froze. An unwelcome image of Bairstow's Prime Minister came into her mind. *'Our only concern is that both our countries have a long-standing practice of not negotiating with terrorists.'*

'I can't comment on our eventual reaction to the demand at this time,' she replied.

'We have members of the Royal Family … It would set a precedent.'

Hurriedly, she seized her glass and drank more water.

Unexpectedly, there was a lull in the shouting. A familiar female form in the front row raised a hand. Ellen was surprised to see her at the press conference, having heard of her appointment as Editor.

'Mary Sullivan, *Washington Post*, Madam President. As you know, the United States has long had a policy of not negotiating with terrorists. I think everyone understands that the present situation is quite different from anything that has happened in the past. But do we understand you to say that there may be negotiations in this case?'

Ellen shifted desperately from one foot to the other.

'Mary, I can't discuss any operational details. We have to evaluate the situation and keep it under constant review, then do what is best in the circumstances. I'm sure you understand that certain matters must remain secret at present.'

'Of course, Madam President,' Mary replied. 'I guess what I'm wondering is: how you balance Dani's safety against the possible consequences of giving these people what they are asking for? Given what you must be feeling yourself…?'

Mary allowed her question to drift away. Ellen suddenly stood to attention. She hesitated for a few moments. It was the one question she did not want to answer. She must find a way out, but without drawing too much attention to it. She could not take too long.

'It's a matter of keeping the situation under review as it develops,' she replied. 'But the same is true for the kidnappers. They also have to deal with us. It is not easy for anyone. But I believe that we will find a way to resolve this situation and bring Dani back safely. I'm sorry, but that's all for now.'

A storm of questions broke out, but Ellen ignored them. With a brusque 'good morning and thank you for coming', she turned on her heel and left. Taken by surprise, Jeff forced himself out of his chair and on to the podium.

'Let me add my own thanks to those of the President,' he shouted as loudly as he could above the hubbub. 'We will let you know about the next press conference as soon as we know ourselves.'

He turned and made his escape before anyone could detain him.

Mary Sullivan felt a tap on her shoulder, followed by a note, carefully folded, being pressed into her hand. She looked up and exchanged the briefest of glances with Conrad Beckers, who was moving away from her. She opened the note. 'Lunch, Caucus Room, 12?' the note read, in impeccable Mont Blanc handwriting. She nodded as he left.

33

THE CAUCUS ROOM was Conrad Beckers' home away from home in Washington. It was where he held court. The restaurant is one of those where the Capital's elite gather to be seen, and many of them came to be seen by Conrad Beckers. It was a source of amusement to him that so many senators and congressmen vied with one another for one of the most uncomfortable experiences on the political scene – half an hour with Conrad Beckers in his studio. An appearance on the *News Show* guaranteed a searching cross-examination; guaranteed to expose any ignorance of facts and any weakness of position, and many a promising career had taken a battering in that arena. But still they came. They came to the Caucus Room to meet him, and stood by his table for a moment or two, paying court to him; and he greeted them all with the same formal courtesy, asking after their wives and children, whose names he always seemed to know, and sometimes inquiring as to their availability. And while Beckers was privately amused by them, and while their attention played to his vanity, he had long ago learned never to suggest superiority, never to take them for granted. He was available at the Caucus Room to see and be seen, and it was a good place for it. Besides, he liked the food; the waiters were unfailingly attentive to him; and the restaurant's elegant, clubby atmosphere exactly reflected his personal taste.

When Mary Sullivan arrived, Beckers was already at his favourite discreet corner table, nursing the one glass of champagne he always permitted himself before lunch. He stood as she approached and kissed her lightly on both cheeks. He held her chair as she sat. He raised one hand slightly, which was all that was required to bring a waiter to the table.

'I'm glad you could join me, Mary. What will you have to drink?'

'Sparkling water, please,' she replied.

The waiter nodded and walked briskly away. Mary removed the silk scarf she was wearing around her neck, threaded it through the strap of her handbag, and placed the bag under the table at her feet.

'I was glad to see you this morning,' Beckers said. 'I wasn't sure you were going to grace press conferences in person now that you've ascended to the exalted rank of editor.'

'Old habits,' Mary smiled. 'I was White House correspondent for a long time, you know.'

'Congratulations, Mary. It's well deserved.'

She did not reply, but smiled warmly.

'How is Harold enjoying Portugal, by the way?'

Her smile broadened. 'He seems very happy.'

'I'm sure. In any case, I fully expected to see a new face from the *Post* now that you are in the hot seat.'

The waiter had already returned with her water, which he poured for her before retreating.

'It was one I didn't want to miss.'

'I can quite understand that,' Beckers said. He paused for a sip of champagne. 'And what did you think of it?'

Mary hesitated. 'I'm not sure.'

Beckers nodded. 'My reaction exactly. A thoroughly incomplete and misleading performance. As you say.'

'I didn't say that at all,' Mary insisted.

'Not in so many words, no,' Beckers replied. 'But that's what you meant.'

Mary sipped her water silently.

'It was off on almost every level, wasn't it?' Beckers continued. 'Mysterious group no one knows anything about, a demand that doesn't add up, and no sense of urgency at all. Who's dealing with this, and what is the game plan?'

Mary shrugged.

'She couldn't say too much, could she? She is on a knife-edge. Any false step and Dani Ryan may not come home safely. She has to play her cards close to her chest.'

'Agreed,' Beckers replied. 'But think about it for a moment. She says they have no information about this group. But what kind of group asks for something as sophisticated as the plans for the Phoenix drone? What are they going to do with the plans when they have them, for God's sake? Build themselves a Phoenix drone in their backyard in the glare of every satellite we have up there? This is supposed to be a group no one has ever heard of. Where would they get the engineers, the technology, the materials, to build one of these things?'

'Maybe they are planning to sell the plans on,' Mary suggested.

'Maybe so', Beckers replied. 'But to whom? It would have to be a state actor, wouldn't it, and a major state actor, at that? No one else would have the facilities to even try it. By the time they assembled the materials and people they need, we would be all over them. They couldn't keep it hidden. And then they would have to program and fly the thing. No pun intended, but they would never get it off the ground.'

The waiter returned with their menus. Beckers nodded his thanks.

'The house Caesar salad is fabulous, and they had some great Norwegian salmon yesterday,' he said.

Mary took her reading glasses from her bag, put them on and scanned the menu briefly.

'What you're saying is, why not ask for something realistic – some huge collection of guns, mortars, anti-aircraft missiles, and maybe a million or ten in cash to help them along?'

'Yes,' Beckers replied. 'At least that would make some sense. That would be something they would have some chance of using. They could have it all delivered to some remote spot and make good their escape before they let Dani go. And if they used weapons like that, unlike the Phoenix drone, they would not lead straight back to us.'

'They might still use them against the United States, or against Israel,' Mary pointed out. 'We have troops in harm's way.'

Beckers shook his head. 'But weapons of that sort are not much of a threat against the big powers. They would be more likely to find their way into some regional conflict. The President could easily justify something like that. No one would criticize her for buying Dani's release with a low-level arms deal like that. It's the kind of trading that goes on every day around the world. But plans for a drone, for God's sake? Now you have to worry about Tel Aviv, as well as Washington. I can't see how they could expect any President to agree to that.'

'That's why they have taken Dani,' Mary said. 'That might be the only way to prise the plans loose. But your point is still good. Why ask for the plans for a drone if you have no way to build it or fly it?'

'It certainly puts enormous pressure on the President,' Beckers replied. 'Her critics are not going to worry about details like how useful the plans really are. But I still don't get it. I guess my question is, why put the President in that position, and why take the risk of pulling a stunt like this, unless you're going to make a demand for something useful? Maybe this group is just a front for a rogue state, and maybe they will show themselves in due course, but right now, it's not making sense to me.'

The waiter had returned, notebook and pencil in hand. Beckers nodded to Mary.

'I'll have the pan-seared scallops, and the Caesar as a main,' she said, 'and a glass of Sauvignon Blanc.'

'I'll start with the Caesar and then some of that Norwegian salmon,' Beckers said. 'I know I just had it yesterday, but I'm a creature of habit.'

The waiter smiled. 'Very good, Mr Beckers.'

'Besides,' Beckers continued, once the waiter was at a safe distance, 'I have another objection.'

Mary looked up inquiringly.

'Bill Merriweather raised it with her. As far as anyone knows there is no second generation Phoenix – at least not yet.'

'There was some talk about it when the defense budget was up for discussion,' Mary said. 'Our defense correspondent said some funds were being appropriated for research.'

'I remember that,' Beckers said. 'But it was a long-term project, and it depended on how the first generation played out. I don't recall the first generation being put to the test until recently. Do you?'

'Bill Merriweather claimed he had seen them in use,' Mary replied. 'But even so, it can't be more than the occasional covert op, otherwise we would have heard about it.'

'Exactly,' Beckers said. 'So, is it possible that they are asking for something that doesn't even exist?'

Mary sat back in her seat.

'And, if so, why doesn't the White House just say so and negotiate for something else?'

'Why not indeed,' Beckers said. He paused and leaned across the table confidentially. 'Mary, I know you would have figured all this out for yourself before too long. The reason I wanted to talk to you is that, as I sat there listening to the President this morning, I realised I wanted to make a pact with the Devil, and I want you to be a part of it.'

Mary laughed.

'Now I am intrigued.'

'Mary, this is worse than the White House is saying,' Beckers said forcefully. 'A lot worse. And I think we need to give them some support.'

'Support?'

'I want to work with them, within reason. I want to give them some cover so that they can deal with this without being in the spotlight.'

Mary considered, as she sipped her water.

'How much worse do you think it is?'

'There's no way to say, exactly. But these people, whoever they are, did not kidnap Dani Ryan for peanuts. This is about our country, the United States, Mary, not just about Dani Ryan. We may be in the greatest imaginable danger.'

'That doesn't mean we can just abandon our principles, Conrad. We are journalists.'

'I'm not suggesting abandoning our principles. I'm just suggesting covering for them for a day or two. We are not going to be the only ones questioning the official story. All I'm saying is, let's pretend to buy it for a few days, at least. I can't see this lasting very long. The press has done similar things in the past. '

Mary nodded.

'If you mean, reporting what they say and not looking under the rocks too closely, I have no problem with that. But it has to be an informal understanding, and it can't go on for very long. At some point we have to question the White House about their handling of the situation.'

'Agreed,' Beckers said. 'But let's get Dani back and make the country safe first. If we can.'

The waiter reappeared with their starters, and the conversation ceased, briefly.

'What I don't get,' Mary continued, after a few moments, 'is how the hell Ellen Trevathan is going to cope with this.'

'That's what you asked her just before she left so abruptly,' Conrad said. 'And that may be the most interesting question of all.'

He munched appreciatively on his salad.

'By the way, give my regards to Harold when you speak to him.'

Mary looked up in surprise.

'If I should speak to him, I certainly will,' she replied.

Beckers smiled. 'This Caesar really is delicious. How are your scallops?'

* * *

'I'm not entirely sure what I've just agreed to,' Mary said.

'You've agreed to a sensible period of reflection during which you wait and see,' Harold Philby replied. It was just after dinner in Vila Nova de Gaia, and he was sitting on his balcony with a glass of port, enjoying the river Douro and the lights of the city of Porto on the opposite bank. He had watched the President's press conference, which had been broadcast live throughout the world, and Mary's call came as no surprise. He had made sure to keep his phone by his side.

'After all, you don't know what's really going on. I'm not sure that even the White House knows what's going on. If you did question what the President said, you couldn't put forward any alternative view.'

'There are going to be plenty of people asking questions,' Mary said. 'There are already. Why should we give in to terrorists? Would we do it if it were someone else's daughter? They are questions which should be asked.'

'They are,' Philby agreed. 'And they are not going to go away. There will be plenty of time to ask them. But you don't even know what the questions are at this stage. You don't know what the White House will do. Whatever that is, most of it will be going on behind the scenes. So any comment would be premature. Ask the questions, but don't answer them, would be my approach. And give the President some sympathy. I think I know what you're worried about.'

'Do you?' Mary asked.

'Of course,' he replied. 'You're asking yourself whether, if you support the President, you're in danger of turning the *Post* into a tabloid. You're not. You're not cherry-picking the facts, and you're not following the party line blindly. You're simply doing what the press has always done in times of crisis. You're giving the Government a chance to act in the national interest and reserving the questions for later. I agree with Conrad, and I think you are right to join with him.'

'You had already thought it through, hadn't you, Harold?' Mary asked, smiling.

'Force of habit,' Philby replied, also smiling. 'I don't have enough distance on the job yet, though Portugal is working on it. I still work through how I would approach different issues. I'm sure I will put it behind me eventually. But after so many years, it's not easy. So, while it lasts, you're always welcome to call if you need a second opinion.'

'Thank you, Harold,' she said. 'Conrad sends his regards, by the way.'

'And mine to him,' Harold Philby said.

* * *

Dani sat up sharply as the door opened. Kali was making her way down the staircase. In one hand she held her usual automatic pistol, pointed down; in the other a large clean towel.

'You will shower and wash your hair,' she said. 'You are going to make another video. Samir will bring the script down to you once you are dressed.'

Dani had been trying to snatch a few moments of sleep. She rubbed her eyes and pushed the blanket away.

'Why do you want another one?' she asked. 'What was wrong with the first one?'

'I don't know,' Kali replied. 'I am told only what I need to know. Maybe it didn't work. Maybe this time we need to convince the President just how serious we are.'

34

June 16

THEY ARRIVED JUST a little too late. Word had reached Steve Macmillan about the fresh inquiries into Bev Prasad's background and the growing suspicion of an Indian connection in the kidnapping of Dani Ryan. It was time to talk to Bev again, and this time, in greater depth. But it had taken the Americans some time to coordinate the information. Steve and Rosa Linda Montalbán made their way to Downing without delay, but the officer keeping surveillance on Kenney A reported that Bev had left 20 minutes earlier. The officer's orders were to observe comings and goings, but not follow. Bev was fully aware that he was being watched, and once the tracking device had been placed in his mobile phone, Steve had seen no point in asking for an overt surveillance which was almost bound to be futile. The problem was that Bev had left the phone in his room. Steve and Rosa spotted it immediately when they entered the room to check it out. Nothing else seemed out of place, and there was nothing to suggest that he would not return in due course. But, despite the absence of any concrete evidence, Steve Macmillan had a bad feeling about it. He stood leaning against the wall, scanning each piece of furniture for any clue, however small.

'I think the chicken may have flown the coop,' he said eventually.

'There's been nothing on his phone to cause concern,' Rosa pointed out. 'And your people still have his computer.'

'I know,' Steve replied. 'Even so, I think he may be gone.'

* * *

Bev had used his phone cautiously. When it was returned to him, he assumed that someone was listening to every word of any conversation he might have and was reading any text or email he might send. In any case, he felt little inclination to speak to anyone. Once it became clear beyond doubt that Dani had vanished, he was virtually paralyzed by feelings of guilt and shame. He had allowed Kali to take advantage of him. In his naïveté he had swallowed the story she had told him that all she wanted with Dani was a conversation. More than that, he had swallowed the story he had been told all his life, by his parents, by worshippers at the temple, by the Visitor. Freedom for Kashmir was a righteous cause. Those who pursued it were good people. They were not terrorists. They were not like the Soviets. It was all right to trust them, to help them, to perform on their behalf the service for which you had been conceived, for which your parents had created you, the service which was to define your life.

Except that it wasn't all right. Not when you had grown up in America. Bev felt manipulated, betrayed, used. He could see no way to resist or protest, no way to fight back. He had no idea where Dani Ryan was. Even if he told the police about Kali, how would they ever track her down? He knew nothing about her. He had no address, phone number, email. And if they did track her down, what then? He had contacted his parents briefly, to put an innocent explanation on the record for the benefit of whoever was listening. He read the increasingly worried texts and emails from Shesi. But he could not face the prospect of replying. She would ask too many questions; she would press him too much for answers he could not or was not ready to give. Then his parents sent the texts containing the code.

When he first realized what he was looking at, he was shaken, but somehow, not surprised. It was a measure of how much his world had changed. He had been transported effortlessly to a new world of deception and subterfuge, only to find that his parents lived in it already, and presumably always had. The code had been a childhood game. It was not sophisticated. It depended on a transposition of letters and numbers, and so was not very different from a basic acrostic. But the chances of a westerner deciphering it were minimal, because it was partly composed of Hindi words transcribed into the Latin alphabet. His parents had taught it to him as a child. It was a way of improving his Hindi, an educational parlor game which developed his analytical and linguistic skills at the same time. They would leave messages around the house once or twice a week for him to decode. The messages became more challenging as he got older, and there would be a reward, a dollar bill or a bar of chocolate, for every successful solution. He had accepted all this unquestioningly as an enjoyable part of his education. But now the code had an altogether different purpose. This was no exercise; it was very real. Suddenly, it seemed as if all his training in decoding it had been for this moment. He had recognized the cryptic style of the emails instantly. When the first one came, his first reaction was to smile at the memories it evoked. But by the time he had read the complete message, he was afraid. He knew by now that his parents had been interviewed by the FBI. But where had the coded message come from? From Kali? From the Visitor?

The message frightened him. It was urgent. It left him with no choice. And it propelled him into yet another unknown event, yet another situation he was powerless to control. There was still time to choose. Even now, he could go to the police, tell them what he knew, explain that he had no sympathy with these people or with their methods. He could take his chance with the authorities. But then, he would have to let his parents take their chances with the FBI.

That made his choice for him. On impulse, he left his phone on his desk. He threw a few personal items into a shoulder bag and, with his heart pounding, walked as calmly as he could out of Kenney A towards the main gate. The officer on duty grinned and nodded, just to let him know he was there, that he had not been forgotten. Praying that he appeared to be acting normally, Bev gave him a brief wave. He walked unchallenged out of Downing College.

The assigned meeting point was the bus station, just a short walk from Downing, crossing Regent Street, to the right of the University Arms Hotel, skirting Parker's Piece, turning left on to Parker Street. As he was about to cross from Parker Street to the bus station, the white van pulled slowly away from the curb and stopped right by him. The passenger's side door opened. He saw Kali.

'Get in,' she said.

Bev sat down on the back seat. Kali closed the door and took her seat next to Bev. The driver was an untidy young white man. Kali did not introduce Wayne Carter, but curtly ordered him to drive.

'Turn to face away from me,' she ordered. Bev complied.

In a second or two Kali had tied a blindfold over his eyes, plunging him into darkness.

'It's not possible for you to stay in Cambridge,' she said. 'You will be staying with us for a while.'

35

June 17

'MADAM DIRECTOR, PRETORIUS needs to speak to you,' Agent Alan Sentelle said. 'It's urgent.'

Kelly was at home with Jeff, sharing a few precious moments of rest and a glass of wine after a hard day. It was after 2 o'clock in the morning. The ringing of the phone was unwelcome, but not a surprise.

'They have sent another message,' Pretorius said. 'I am to return to London to receive some new consignment.'

'I'm on my way,' Kelly replied.

* * *

'It's just this one line of text,' Agent Sentelle said, handing Pretorius' phone to Kelly. 'They want him to leave for London from Dulles today.'

They were standing just inside the door to Willem Pretorius' room at the Willard Intercontinental. Pretorius was sitting upright on the bed. Agent Kim Foxborough was seated in an armchair by the desk.

'Any luck tracing it?' Kelly asked.

'Not so far. It's a long shot at best. The phone itself is probably at the bottom of a drain by now. Even if the sim card can be traced to the dealership, it's unlikely we would ever find the purchaser. But we will pass the information to the British police, just in case.'

Kelly walked over to the bed. She looked at Pretorius closely. He had lost something of his outwardly confident, professional manner. Agents Sentelle and Foxborough had alerted her to the change. The tedium of waiting in a hotel room for three days, with no relief from hotel food and two agents keeping constant watch, had taken its toll. Pretorius was growing restless, and any enjoyment he might at first have experienced at his new celebrity status, the honored, all-expenses-paid guest of the United States Government, had faded away. He had fallen off the radar, unable to make contact with his clients, and this was bad for business. In addition, he was still not entirely sure that Kelly Smith believed his truthful account that he was just the courier, and had no information about Dani Ryan's disappearance. In his more disturbed moments he had worried about being interrogated, perhaps even water boarded – who knew what Americans were capable of when their interests were at stake? He had been following the TV coverage of the story, and it did not suggest to him that a happy ending was on the cards any time soon. Like Conrad Beckers, though coming from a different background and experience, Pretorius did not credit the official line about the plans for the Phoenix drone. That was an opinion he intended to keep to himself. But the whole situation was making him very nervous.

'I have no power to compel you to help us, Mr Pretorius,' Kelly said. 'But it seems that these people trust you, and it seems that they want to deliver their messages through you. I know the President would be deeply grateful for your help, as would I. We will pay your usual fee, and we won't ask questions about any payments you may receive from your client. And of course, we will get you a seat on the plane and pay your expenses.'

Pretorius hesitated. 'Look, I'm not sure what I'm getting myself into here. These people are not fooling about. I have no idea where they may take me when I get to London. If they think you are following me, they may decide I'm not worth the risk any more. They might decide it's safer to send you an email instead, and I might end up getting dumped in the River Thames in a bag.'

'We are not going to follow you,' Kelly said. 'We will have a couple of agents at Dulles, and we will put someone on the plane. But they won't be with you. They will not acknowledge you. You won't even know who they are. MI5 will be watching when you arrive in London, but it will be the same with them – just watching, no contact. The kidnappers will have to find some way of contacting you to arrange delivery, but no one will follow you to the venue if it's off the airport. We are thinking of your safety, but it's in our interests also. We don't want to do anything to prevent safe delivery of this message. We can't take the chance of having them call it off.'

Pretorius dropped his head, and nodded slowly.

'And after this…?'

'I have every reason to believe there will be no further communications after this,' Kelly said. 'Once you're back here with the message, and we have verified it, we have no further claim on your time. We will make whatever arrangements we can to help you on your way.'

Pretorius considered the matter just long enough to confirm to himself that his choices were very limited, if indeed there were any at all.

'All right,' he said. 'I will take a taxi to Dulles. Don't follow me.'

'My agents know what they are doing, Mr Pretorius,' Kelly replied. 'Just do your job, and let them do theirs.'

'Easy for you to say,' Pretorius answered, sounding grim. 'It's my ass on the line.'

But then he caught Kim Foxborough's eye and laughed, and everyone in the room joined in.

* * *

Pretorius left the hotel early. This was partly because he had a lifetime's habit of arriving at airports early, and partly because of his relief at finally being released from the claustrophobic atmosphere of his hotel room. During the forty-five minute taxi ride to the airport, he had checked through the back window of the cab regularly. He had detected nothing suspicious. 'But then again,' he reflected, 'at this level you wouldn't expect to, would you?'

When the cab dropped him off at Dulles Airport, it was not yet time to check in for his flight. This allowed him the additional bonus of being able to enjoy a breakfast not supplied by the Willard Intercontinental. He settled happily into a cheerful, bustling airport café with a copy of the *Washington Post*. With a smile he noted that the newspaper was offering yet another day of analysis of the potential hazards of handing over plans for the Phoenix drone. How many times was it possible to beat that topic to death? 'Apparently,' he reflected, 'as many as necessary.' He skipped it in favor of reports from England covering the continuing fruitless search for Dani Ryan. The waitress stopped at his table with a menu, coffee, and iced water and told him she would be back to take his order. When she returned he ordered eggs, bacon, and toast.

'Excuse me, sir. Will you please be so kind as to help me? I am unable to understand.' The voice came from the table to his left. It was female, and had an accent which Pretorius was unable to identify precisely. His suspicions were aroused simply for that reason. He had contacts all over the world and, as a result, he had a wide experience of accents and rarely mistook them. The woman was middle-aged and plainly dressed in dark clothing. She was surrounded by a quantity of papers, including emails containing electronic tickets. His suspicions receded.

'What's the problem?' he asked.

She handed him a selection of the papers.

'I must go to Los Angeles,' she said. 'My sister is living there. She is sending me ticket. I am to fly by the United Airlines. But always I am seeing that I am flying to San Francisco and not Los Angeles. Please help me, where I should go?'

Pretorius smiled. 'No problem,' he replied. 'Let me take a look.'

He examined the emails carefully, and had the answer in a matter of seconds.

'All right, here it is. You are flying to San Francisco on United out of Terminal C. But then, in San Francisco, you pick up a connecting flight to Los Angeles. See …?'

He pointed her to the relevant email. She appeared to study it carefully.

'Ah! So first I must fly to San Francisco, only then to Los Angeles?'

'First you fly to San Francisco, yes. Then you take another plane to Los Angeles. When you get to San Francisco, United will have someone to help you. Ask them to point you to the gate for your flight.'

She took the papers back. 'Now I understand, sir,' she said. 'Thank you.'

She seemed too poised suddenly, too confident. 'I think you understood that before,' Pretorius said to himself.

'Is your sister meeting you at Los Angeles?'

'Yes, she will meet me. Yes.'

'Where are you from?' he asked.

A slight hesitation. 'I am from Iran.'

'No, you're not,' he thought. He wondered whether to pursue it. But before he could decide he became conscious of something leaning against his right leg. How long it had been there he had no idea. He looked down. The object was unfamiliar, and had not been there when he had taken his seat. It was a laptop case. For several seconds he stared at it blankly. Then, slowly, he reached down and picked it up with his right hand. He placed it on his table. Gingerly he pulled back on the zip fastener that opened the main compartment. Inside was a small laptop, identical to the one he had conveyed to Washington on his previous trip. As he looked at it in astonishment, it suddenly dawned on him that he would not be going to London after all. How in God's name had that happened? He looked sharply to his left. The woman had disappeared, taking her papers with her. 'Probably not to Terminal C,' Pretorius muttered to himself. Now what? Somewhere there were agents watching him. This was not in the script. Had they seen what had happened? Would they approach him now? If he left the airport without checking in, they would want to know why. Well, there was nothing he could do about that. He had accomplished his mission unexpectedly early.

Where were they, for God's sake?

The waitress was returning with his breakfast.

36

'THEY BLINDSIDED US,' Kelly Smith admitted ruefully. 'The agents were too busy watching Pretorius talking to the woman at the next table. The restaurant was busy and no one saw exactly how the briefcase was left by his chair, or who left it. We will have the carrying case and the computer itself thoroughly tested, but in all likelihood it will all come back negative, just like the first computer. We will question Pretorius again too, but I don't think he knows anything. These people are very careful. They would have no reason to tell him anything.'

The crisis committee had been summoned as soon as the agents at Dulles Airport reported that the second demand had been received under unexpected circumstances. The agents had driven Pretorius and the laptop back to the Willard Intercontinental at high speed, with a hastily-arranged police escort joining them *en route*, and the laptop had then been transported in the same manner to the White House situation room. Pretorius, despite his outraged protests, had been ordered to remain in his room under the watchful eye of agents Sentelle and Foxborough until further notice.

Dave Masterson smiled thinly. 'You have to hand it to them,' he said. 'It was a nice play. Some of my people at the Agency could learn a thing or two.'

'Let's worry about all that later,' Ellen Trevathan commented. 'I want to see whatever is on this computer and find out what's going on.'

Kelly had already switched the computer on. This time she had decided not to have the CIA's computer experts inside the situation room unless they were needed. There were no technical problems as yet. The window asking for a user-name and password had appeared. Pretorius had not been given new ones, and there was nothing in writing accompanying the laptop. Kelly was working on the assumption that the required details were the same as before. If not, that would be the time to call in the experts. She typed in the details the window required. To her relief, the window disappeared and a blue screen background appeared with a message.

There are four files on this computer. File one is a video presentation. File two provides information about us. File three is a set of instructions. File four contains information referred to in file three. To open a file, click on the file number below. To return to this page, press alt, control and delete together.

'Four files instead of three this time,' Kelly observed, looking down at the notes in her file. 'Madam President, do you want to start with the video?'

Ellen nodded, gripping the table in front of her with both hands.

The set for the second video was the same as the first, a simple backdrop which permitted no conclusions about where or when the video had been made. The quality of the video was again excellent – to Lisa Carrow's experienced eye, work of a professional standard unusual in kidnap cases. Once again, Dani was seated facing the camera. She was well dressed, her hair brushed and combed and pinned up at the back. She was barefoot and wore no make-up, but there was no sign of any mistreatment. She was holding a copy of a newspaper.

'The date today is June 15th.'

Dani held up the newspaper to the camera, which zoomed in. It was a copy of *The Times*, the British newspaper of record. The date of the newspaper, clearly visible on the front page, confirmed what Dani had said. Dani put down the newspaper and picked up a sheet of paper, from which she seemed to read word for word.

'I am well. I have not been mistreated in any way. With this video you will be receiving further instructions. I have been told that, unless these instructions are fully complied with, I will be killed. I believe that those who are holding me are completely committed to their cause. They mean what they say.'

She looked directly at the camera.

'I love you, Mom, Dad. I love you, Ellen. I'm scared, really scared. Please bring me home.'

Abruptly, the scene faded to black. Ellen held her head in her hands for some seconds. She looked across the table to Lisa Carrow questioningly.

'There is no sign of ill treatment. That's good. My first impression is that she is sincere when she says she believes they are going to kill her. When she stopped reading and looked at the camera, it seemed unscripted to me. I would like to see it again at some point.'

'Later,' Ellen said. 'Thank you, Lisa. We have to move on now.'

Kelly returned the computer to the main menu and clicked on file two. At first there was only audio, a male voice. The voice sounded educated, cultured. The accent was Indian.

'I will now tell you who we are, and why we are holding Dani Ryan. We are Svatantra Kashmir, in English, Freedom for Kashmir. Our name is sometimes abbreviated to SK. We are Indian patriots fighting for the liberty of our native region of Kashmir.'

A topographical map of Kashmir appeared on the screen, with bright red lines of demarcation drawn by hand across the west, north-west and north-east areas of the province.

'Kashmir is an integral part of historic India. But it is a divided land. Part of our homeland is controlled by Pakistan, and part by China. The people suffer aggression and violence and are subject to religious and ethnic persecution.'

The map was replaced by several images of the bodies of men, women and children in white Kurta pajamas, or brilliant green or orange saris. The bodies were drenched with blood, the faces of the victims contorted by pain. Smoke was billowing from low brick buildings behind the bodies, which the camera did not define clearly. These were images which would never have appeared on a TV news program. They were well beyond 'some viewers may find these images disturbing'. The reality of death and maiming had been captured with no holding back. The camera moved slowly across the scene, the operator at pains to show as much detail as possible of wounds, missing limbs, of carnage, of debris. On the face of it there was nothing to indicate where or when the images had been recorded, nothing to reveal the identity of the victims or the aggressors. But the reality of the images was not in doubt. It was the record of a massacre of civilians, men, women, and children.

'The international community makes statements deploring the violence, but does nothing. India herself does nothing. That is why Svatantra Kashmir must act. Our name means Freedom for Kashmir. That is our goal. We will not compromise, and we will not stop until our goal has been achieved. The whole of Kashmir will once again be an integral part of India, and will be liberated from all foreign control.'

The voice jumped suddenly from finely modulated to almost screaming. The change was shocking and took everyone in the room aback.

'Svatantra Kashmir!'

The screen went dark, then a message appeared.

You will now go to file three.

File three contained text only, a series of six numbered statements.

1. *You were advised previously that our demand relating to the Phoenix drone on behalf of a middle-eastern group was false, and was for press consumption only. Our true demand is contained in file four.*
2. *The action described in file four must be accomplished successfully within the time frame and under the circumstances specified.*
3. *If the action is completed successfully, Dani Ryan will be released unharmed.*
4. *If the action is not completed successfully, Dani Ryan will die.*
5. *No excuses will be accepted for failure to complete the action successfully.*
6. *If there is any publicity relating to the demand made in file four, Dani Ryan will die.*

Every eye in the room turned towards Ellen Trevathan.

'All right, enough of the bullshit,' Ellen said. 'Let's find out how crazy these people really are.'

'Madam President,' Craig Diamond said, 'I should remind you that the instructions we received previously stipulated that you should watch the file containing the new demand alone. I have a transcript of the first set of files here. It said, '*our true demand will be for the eyes of the President only. If she agrees to the demand, she may disclose it only to those who need to know in order for the demand to be carried out. It is to be given the highest secrecy classification, and is to be disclosed to no one else.*'

Ellen bit her lip. 'I don't think Freedom for Kashmir has any way to find out what we do or don't do here in the situation room. In any case, I am pretty sure I'm going to need you all to deal with this situation, whatever demands they make. Open file four, Kelly.'

Kelly brought up file four. Like file three, it contained text only.

The Prime Minister of India, Anand Mehra, will make an official visit to Kashmir to inspect Indian military positions along the western lines of demarcation on the border with Pakistan between June 22 and 25. During this visit, you will cause the Prime Minister to be assassinated. The assassination will be carried out in such a way as to make it appear the work of the Pakistani Security Service or the Pakistani armed forces. The assassination must be carried out before noon, Indian Standard Time, on June 25.

37

THE COLLECTIVE BREATH of the crisis committee seemed to drain from the room. The committee members slumped in their seats, staring at the screen in disbelief.

'They want us to kill their own prime minister?' Ken Hunt asked quietly, after some time. 'These people *are* crazy.'

Ellen Trevathan took a deep breath and forced herself to sit upright in her chair. Her hands remained tightly clasped on the table in front of her. Ted Lazenby leaned across and whispered into her ear for several seconds. Ellen nodded.

'OK, here's what I want. I want the expert on Kashmir. *The* expert. I want him or her here in the situation room. I want to know who the players are, what the issues are. I want to know everything that can be known about Kashmir. I want to know everything about this group, SK. We must have *some* information about them. I want to know everything about Prime Minister Mehra, in particular his views on Kashmir and his relations with Pakistan. And I want all this yesterday.'

'I'm sure we have some people at the Agency,' Dave Masterson said. 'I'm sure State does too. I'll look into it right away. But the Brits may be the best ones to ask about India, with all the history they have there. It may be wise to ask the Foreign Office also.'

'The Foreign Office is likely to be involved with whatever is going on in Kashmir,' General Raul Gutierrez commented. 'They still like to think that the subcontinent is their sphere of influence. Just bear that in mind. You may not get an entirely neutral view from that quarter.'

'Well, ask whoever you want,' Ellen replied. 'But get me the best person. I want *one* person. We don't have time for a debate between opposing opinions here. If you need to call England, ask Ambassador Wilkinson to facilitate it. If the expert can't come to us, we will do it with conference calls.'

'I'm on it,' Masterson said. 'May I use an office here? Less conspicuous.'

Ellen nodded. 'We are adjourned for now,' she said. 'I need some time with Ted. But I would like everyone to remain available to reconvene at short notice. Make sure your phones are on. Craig, make sure you know where everyone is. And I am sure I don't need to remind you, but out of an abundance of caution I remind you anyway, that there must be no discussion whatsoever of the new demand outside this room, regardless of the circumstances.'

She waited for the nods of assent around the table.

'Jeff, I will need you to bring me up to date about where we are with the press.'

'I'll be ready, Madam President,' Jeff replied. He rose to his feet slowly, picking up his files.

'Kelly, stay for a moment, please.'

'Yes, of course,' Kelly replied.

* * *

Kelly had been sitting by the laptop in case anyone wanted to review the earlier files, half expecting that the President would ask for the video to be brought up or copied for Kay. But she did not. Kelly returned the screen to the main menu. As she stood, she saw Lisa Carrow beckon to her. Lisa had her phone to her ear and Kelly heard her say, 'I'll be there as soon as I can.' As Lisa disconnected the call, Kelly saw the look that crossed her face. Her anger and frustration were impossible to miss. Kelly turned back to the President.

'Madam President, would you give me just a moment?'

Ellen glanced up, then nodded. 'That's fine.'

Kelly walked across to Lisa, put a hand on her shoulder, and led her gently from the situation room.

'Do you need to be somewhere?'

Lisa was looking grimly down at the floor.

'They found my cheerleader in Montana.' The words themselves could have been announcing either good news or bad, but the tone was unambiguous. Her voice was tired, empty and defeated.

Kelly shook her head. 'I'm sorry, Lisa.'

'She was raped and strangled, and buried in a shallow grave in the woods, a few miles outside Billings,' Lisa continued slowly. 'They only found her because some wild animal ...'

She did not complete the sentence. 'I'm sorry, Kelly. I need to ...'

'If you need to be in Montana, I'm sure I can square it with the President,' Kelly said. 'As long as we can reach you if we need you.'

Lisa nodded. 'I need to make sure the evidence gets collected and the scene gets preserved.'

She bit her lip. 'And I need to talk to the parents. It was my case. I can't delegate it. You know how it is ...'

'I do know how it is,' Kelly said. 'Go.'

She could recall times when she had talked to parents herself. It was the very worst thing you ever had to do as an investigator. It made no difference how many cases like that you handled – and Lisa had handled a lot. It was always personal. You could never disengage. She squeezed her shoulder before letting go.

'I'm really sorry, Lisa.'

'She was fifteen,' Lisa said, helplessly. As she turned and walked abruptly away, Kelly saw the tears forming in her eyes.

* * *

Kelly took a moment to compose herself before walking slowly back into the situation room. Only the President and Vice President remained. They were standing together by Ellen's chair, talking quietly.

'Kelly,' Lazenby began, 'the President wants you to go to England. I want to get you over there as quickly as possible, either by civilian or military transport. If we can get you a flight this evening, I want to do it.'

Ellen gestured Kelly and Ted Lazenby to sit, and resumed her own seat.

'I've asked Ted to be your point of contact while you are there.'

'OK,' Kelly replied cautiously. The President's last statement had struck her as odd, although she could not have said exactly why. 'What do you want me to do there that I can't do here?'

'For the first time since Dani disappeared,' Lazenby replied, 'we have a deadline – noon, Indian Standard Time, on June 25th. Indian Standard Time is five and a half hours later than Greenwich Mean Time, but India doesn't do daylight saving, so it's four and a half hours later at the moment. So the deadline is 7.30 in the morning British Summer Time in London, and 2.30 Eastern Daylight Time here in Washington.'

'Why that particular time?' Kelly asked. 'Do we know?'

'I would hazard a guess that that is the time when Prime Minister Mehra is scheduled to return from Kashmir to New Delhi,' Lazenby replied. 'But, be that as it may, it means that we have a limited time frame within which to find Dani. The President and I need to know on a daily basis how quickly the search is proceeding.'

'Gerry McClure's reports …'

'…tell us that they are proceeding as quickly as they can without running the risk of alarming the kidnappers. Yes I know,' Lazenby said. 'But we may have reached a point where we can't avoid taking a few risks. The problem is that we can't tell them that we have a deadline without giving the game away.'

'You're not going to tell anyone over there?' The question was directed to the President, but she did not reply.

'That's one risk we can't take,' Lazenby said brusquely. 'There is no point in telling anyone in England unless we also tell a lot of people in England, and then the cat really is out of the bag. All it takes is one careless word in the hearing of a reporter, and Dani's fate may be sealed. So we have to move things along without disclosing the deadline. That's where you come in.'

Kelly looked up questioningly.

'You and I will speak twice a day,' Lazenby said. 'Morning and evening. I will let you know what's going on here. You will let me know what's going on there. Specifically, I will need your honest, unedited opinion about how much progress they are really making at any given time, and your assessment of the probability of finding Dani within the given time frame.'

Kelly nodded. 'I'll do my best, sir. But …'

'I know it won't be easy, Kelly,' Lazenby conceded. 'You may not have access to all the information you would need to evaluate the situation fully. But you will pick up the mood among the investigators, you know, whether they are confident or getting fatigued or resigned.'

He paused.

'We will need you to be proactive, to keep things moving over there. You will have to create a mood of urgency without telling them why it's urgent. Tell them you're under pressure from us – which you will be – tell them anything, except the real reason for your concern. But see if you can make them pick up the pace. I'll make sure you have a phone that will work over there and a secure number to call me. I'll get them to you before you leave.'

Kelly stood. 'OK,' she said. 'If there's nothing else, I'll run home and pack.'

'Thanks, Kelly,' Ellen said. 'It means a lot to me to know you will be there on the ground. I know Kay will feel the same.'

'I'll do my very best, Madam President,' Kelly replied.

She turned towards the door, then looked back.

'Madam President, I took it upon myself to tell Lisa Carrow that she could go back to Montana. There was a development in her case there that needed her personal attention. We will be able to contact her whenever we need to, and she will come back immediately if we need her.'

'A development?' Ellen asked.

'Yes,' Kelly replied. She bit her lip. She had no desire to explain. Ellen Trevathan was the last person who needed to hear that particular kind of bad news. 'It was something she couldn't delegate.'

Ellen nodded. 'OK,' she said.

Kelly left hurriedly to avoid having to answer any more questions.

38

With Kelly's departure, Ellen Trevathan and Ted Lazenby found themselves alone in the situation room. Kelly had left the laptop in place, but had closed the program. The large white screen which had earlier held the images sent by the kidnappers was blank. A bank of clocks around the wall to their left silently tracked the time in each of the world's time zones. Just as silently, computer screens around the room flashed up images continually, but until the President declared the crisis committee meeting closed, the military personnel and other experts monitoring them would not enter the room to record the information they offered. The silence was unbroken.

The President and Vice President were facing each other across the table.

'I know that you would never order the assassination of a head of state ...' Ellen began.

'Ellen, I don't ...'

'No, Ted, listen, please. I want to say this up front, while I still have the strength,' Ellen persisted. 'I know you wouldn't do it, and I would not ask you to do it. I want to get that discussion out of the way, so that we can move on and focus on helping the investigators to find Dani.'

Lazenby nodded.

'Thank you,' he replied. 'All I was going to say was that I'm not quite ready to have a discussion about this. I need some time on my own to take it in. I need to clear my head. Can we meet again in a couple of hours?'

Ellen smiled.

'Of course. I need to go and see Kay anyway.'

There was a knock at the door.

'Come,' Ellen called out.

Jeff Morris entered the room tentatively, carrying a thick brown envelope under his arm.

'I'm sorry to disturb you, Madam President. I can come back later, but …'

'No, that's all right, Jeff,' Ellen replied. 'We were just about to let the team in to get back to work. What have you got?'

Jeff looked down, as if reluctant to speak. He took a DVD from the envelope.

'I know you have a lot to deal with already,' he said. 'But I think you ought to watch this. I'm going to get a lot of questions about it at the press conference tomorrow. There may even be some demand for you to make an appearance in the next couple of days. I can fight that off if I have to, but you should see this.'

He inserted the DVD into the nearest computer.

'I'm afraid you won't be able to avoid it, in any case. It's all over the web. It's about to go viral.'

Ellen and Ted hurriedly pulled up chairs and seated themselves in front of the computer. Jeff double-clicked on an icon on the screen. Initially the screen went blank, but was then followed by the start of a grainy film. Jeff pulled up a chair beside them.

'He made this himself and posted it on the web via the usual sites,' Jeff said. 'I doubt whether any of the TV stations in Dallas would have run it unedited, but I bet he tried.'

A face appeared on the screen. The face wore a condescending smile which suggested the wearer's belief in his own superiority. It was a smile usually hidden from his audience by the invisibility of sound radio. But today it was on display for the whole world to see. Bubba Lanier was seated at a desk. An array of bound volumes of the Texas law reports behind the desk suggested that the venue was a law office. To his right and slightly behind the desk stood a large American flag on an ornate pole; the state flag of Texas occupied a similar berth to his left; both no doubt specially imported for the occasion. The camera was evidently stationed directly in front of the desk, and the angle and focus did not vary at all throughout the recording. As Jeff Morris had said, this was no professional video, but both the video and audio quality were more than sufficient for its purpose.

'Folks, y'all know me. I'm Bubba Lanier, host of the Bubba Lanier Show on Family of Christ Radio, 88 FM, Dallas, Texas.'

The smile broadened slightly.

'Now, this is my first time on camera, and I just realized today that I don't know how I look on camera. Usually, I'm hidden away in my radio station, and nobody knows what I look like. So I'm a little bit nervous about having all you good folk looking at me. And I just hope I don't look too bad.'

The smile returned to normal.

'But today I have put any nervousness I may feel to one side, because I need to talk with y'all about a very important subject.'

Lanier had been leaning forward on the desk. Now, whether as a result of his own instinct or a gesture from the camera operator, he sat upright in his chair.

'Y'all know what I mean. Ellen Trevathan is the President of the United States. She is supposed to set an example to the American people of Christian virtue and morality. And yet, she lives in your White House in sin with another woman. In the bedrooms of your White House, those two women lie together and practice abominable acts – acts which the word of God declares are worthy of death. In the Book of Romans, the Bible declares that the wages of sin is death. The Book of Leviticus says that for a woman to lie with another woman is an abomination, and that they should be put to death'

He could not resist leaning forward again, as if to increase the intensity, his hands leaning on the desk.

'Now, y'all know that some time ago I called for a petition to be sent to Washington to tell those good folk in our capital that as loyal God-fearing Americans, we will not stand for what's going on in the White House, and to tell them that the situation needs to change. More than a million of your fellow citizens have already signed that petition, and there are more signing every day. I believe that the number will soon rise to two million and more. Many of you are protesting outside the White House and at other places. We are calling for Ellen Trevathan to resign from the office of

President of the United States and leave your White House, taking her whore with her.'

Lanier spread his arms out wide. He paused for effect. His audience already knew what he had said so far. But today Lanier was taking it a step further, and he needed their full attention.

'Unlike some other countries, the United States does not kill people for adultery and other abominations. We leave that to God. But in this instance, God has spoken, and he is in the process of bringing death to these sinners in his own way. When Dani Ryan was kidnapped, I believe God spoke to the President and to Kay Ryan and gave them a final warning. I believe that Dani Ryan's kidnapping and probable death are the judgment of God on Ellen Trevathan and Kay Ryan, a judgment which makes it clear that He will not tolerate such iniquity to exist in this Christian country. It is no more than they deserve, a just and righteous punishment.'

'It seems cruel to Dani Ryan. I acknowledge that. I know nothing about Dani Ryan. It may be that she herself is innocent. It may be that, despite her upbringing, she has not been corrupted; it may be that she rejects relations between women; it may be that she intends to marry and raise children in accordance with God's law. I don't know. But I do know that God's judgments are righteous, and I know that they are hard. And this is not only a judgment against Ellen Trevathan and Kay Ryan. It is also a judgment which threatens to engulf our entire nation. Because, mark my words, if we as a nation ignore God's judgment and permit the situation in the White House to continue, we are all guilty in the eyes of God, and who is to say which of us will be the next to suffer His righteous judgments, and to feel His hand raised in rebuke against us?'

'These are the abominations that led the Lord to destroy Sodom and Gomorrah. Even now, we are being punished. As the price of setting Dani Ryan free, the kidnappers are demanding access to the most sensitive documents dealing with our national security. We will have to give them the means to build and operate terrible weapons, weapons which they can and surely will turn against us. Because of this abomination, Americans will die. The only way out, the only acceptable way to get Dani Ryan back alive, is for the President to repent and resign. Maybe God would relent then. But there's no sign of that from the White House so far.'

Lanier raised his head, to look as directly at the camera as he could.

'This may be America's last chance. Ellen Trevathan is being blackmailed into betraying her country because of the sin she has committed. We need her to resign now, while there is still time. I urge all patriotic Americans to sign the petition. It's easy to do. You can find it at www.trevathanoutnow.org, where you can sign and submit your signature online. This is no time for hesitation. Sign now, and tell your friends and neighbors that they need to sign also. And pass this message on to them.'

The smile broadened again and seemed to cover his entire face.

'Tell them Bubba sent you. Thanks for listening, folks. In fact, thanks for listening *and* watching. I'm Bubba Lanier, host of the Bubba Lanier Show on Family of Christ Radio, 88 FM, Dallas, Texas.'

Jeff Morris ejected the DVD and looked grimly towards the President. Ellen had turned white and was staring fixedly at the computer screen, her hands under her chin.

By way of contrast, Ted Lazenby's face was red and his eyes blazing with anger.

'That self-righteous moron,' he said. 'Who does he think he is? There must be some way to put a stop to this, Ellen. I'll get Ken to look into it.'

Ellen shook her head and shrugged.

'He will hide behind the First Amendment,' she replied quietly. 'People like that always do.'

'In any case, Madam President,' Jeff said, 'I'm afraid that's not quite all.'

He turned to face the President and Vice President.

'This hit the web last night. A producer on *Fox News* picked it up. They wouldn't have touched the original, but once it was in the public domain it became a news story.'

Jeff took another DVD from the envelope and inserted it into the computer.

'My staff copied this earlier today. As this segment begins, they have just played some of Lanier's download.'

In a *Fox News* studio, an anchor was returning her gaze to the camera after whatever she had been watching with the viewing audience had disappeared from her screen.

'Joining us now from Austin, Texas, is Hank Betancourt, the Governor of the State of Texas. The Governor has been a vocal supporter of Bubba Lanier in the past, and has urged Americans to sign the petition calling on President Trevathan to resign. Good morning, Governor.'

The screen split to show Hank Betancourt on the right and the anchor on the left.

'Good morning to you, Julie.'

'Governor, you were watching that segment with us. You have supported Bubba Lanier's campaign for the resignation of President Trevathan. What is your reaction to what you have just seen?'

'Julie, I continue to believe that the President should resign. It's just not right to have that situation going on in the White House, and I believe many Americans, in fact I would go so far as to say most Americans, agree with me on that. I know that in my own State, the great State of Texas, the overwhelming majority of the people agree with me.'

'I understand that, Governor. But do you agree with Lanier when he says that the kidnapping of Dani Ryan is a judgment from God against the President?'

Betancourt hesitated noticeably. Ellen Trevathan and Ted Lazenby saw the look that crossed his face and exchanged glances.

'Julie, you and I have no way of knowing the mind of God. He moves in mysterious ways. On the other hand, it sure is strange that she went missing just a short while after the President announced her intention to live with her female lover in the White House. Now that could be just a coincidence. I don't know, and neither do you, and I think we have to accept that. But that doesn't mean that the President shouldn't resign.'

'So, Governor, you don't rule out that Dani Ryan's kidnapping is the judgment of God? Would that be fair?'

'Can't rule it out,' Betancourt replied.

'Are you saying that the President deserves to have this happen to her family?' Julie persisted.

'Again, that's not for me to judge. The Bible says that such homosexual acts are punishable by death. We don't put people to death for such things in this country. In some countries, like Saudi Arabia and Iran, they do. But, Julie, that's just our opinion. It's God's opinion that matters. Now, whether Mr Lanier is correct in his assessment I don't know. But I am sure that God has charge of this matter, and I believe that everything will work out according to his will.'

Julie's look suggested that she did not necessarily share that belief. Before she could ask her next question, Betancourt continued.

'Just look at the harm the President's actions have caused. The Phoenix drone is one of our most sophisticated weapons, and one of our most sensitive pieces of technology. And now, if Dani Ryan is to be returned alive, we are going to have to place that weapon, that technology, into the hands of terrorists who can't wait to use it against us. It won't just be this particular group. They will probably put it on the internet, or sell it on the black market. Any group that wants it can have it. Mr Lanier is right, Julie. This will cost American lives, and it will set back the war on terror for a generation.'

'And how exactly did the President cause this?' Julie asked. 'By sleeping with Kay Ryan? Is that what you're saying?'

There was a silence. Betancourt seemed reluctant to reply. Julie's patience ran out.

'Finally, Governor, would you like to send any message of sympathy to the President and express your hope that Dani Ryan will return home safely?'

'Julie, like everyone else, I hope that Dani Ryan will return home safely. But I would be failing in my duty if I did not point out the danger in which Dani Ryan, you and I, and every American stands.'

'Governor, thank you for your time,' Julie concluded curtly.

The clip ended.

'Betancourt doesn't know which way to go,' Lazenby said quietly.

'Yes,' Ellen agreed. 'It's a conflict between religious bigotry and basic human decency. I suppose the fact that he acknowledges the conflict is something, at least. That's more than you can say for Bubba Lanier.'

'And, apparently, more than you can say for more than a million of our fellow citizens,' Lazenby added.

Suddenly, Ellen turned to Jeff.

'You said this was about to go viral?'

'Yes, Madam President.'

Ellen stood. 'I really must go to see Kay now. Ted, can we meet in a couple of hours?'

'Of course.'

Ellen glanced once more at the computer screen.

'I'm surprised that Betancourt's people let him do this,' she said, almost to herself. 'Where are they, for God's sake?'

* * *

Hank Betancourt's chief of staff, Rod Christensen, was in Tampa, Florida, for a family wedding. He had taken a few days off, a rare indulgence for him. It felt good to relax. Rod and his wife, Lucy, had little to do that day except to get ready for the rehearsal dinner in the hotel's banqueting chamber that evening. The short break was a welcome respite from the endless pressures in Austin. Lucy was painting her toenails, her feet up on the coffee table, wearing a crisp white robe supplied by the hotel. She was a busy tax attorney, and the trip was just as welcome for her as for Rod. Their relaxation ended abruptly when Peggy, his secretary, called and suggested that he might want to check something out on the web. He rested his iPad on the coffee table and sat down next to Lucy. They watched together in silence. When it ended, he looked at her imploringly.

'Please tell me I didn't just see that,' he pleaded. 'Please tell me it was just a dream.'

'Sorry,' she said. 'It wasn't.'

'Can't I even go away for a couple of days?'

'You can't hold his hand all the time,' Lucy replied. 'If he wants to be President, at some point he's going to have to learn to tie his own shoe laces.'

39

A SENSE OF urgency seized Ellen as she made her way to the residence. So did the feeling that she might be about to throw up, the feeling that had taken her so much by surprise just a day or two before. She felt herself being forced into a corner. She could not tell Kay the truth about what was going on. She could not even play the new video for her with its tell-tale reference to new instructions. And, above all, she could not confide in Kay that Ted Lazenby was now in control, and that because he would not, could not, agree to the assassination of a head of state, Dani would almost certainly be killed unless someone in England found her before noon, Indian Standard Time, on June 25. She quickened her step as she approached the residence. Agent Sam Davis, standing silently outside the door, nodded to her sombrely.

'Hi, Ellen,' Kay called, hearing the door open. 'I'm in the kitchen.'

'I'll be right there,' Ellen called back.

But on the way, the urge to vomit proved too much. This time she was expecting it, and made it to the bathroom in good time. Afterwards she swirled mouthwash around her mouth and threw cold water on her face before resuming her short walk to the kitchen.

When she got to the door, she stopped in surprise. The pajamas and unkempt look had gone. Kay was dressed in a bright orange blouse and beige slacks, with a kitchen pinafore on top. She had fixed her hair and applied make-up. Fresh pasta, vegetables, and salad ingredients were arrayed on the work surface in front of her. Within reach of her hands were a kitchen knife, a glass of red wine, and the bottle from which it had been poured. Kay walked towards Ellen, her hands stretched out. They kissed. Kay returned to the counter, found a glass and poured a glass of wine for Ellen.

'You look like you need this,' she smiled.

Ellen gratefully took a drink.

'I do,' she replied.

She took a step back and studied Kay more carefully. 'Kay you look … I don't know what to say.'

'"Different", I think you were trying to say,' Kay responded with a smile.

She walked towards Ellen once more and took her hand.

'Ellen, I'm sorry for the way I've been behaving since Dani went missing.'

'My God, Kay, you have no cause to say sorry. I know what you're going through.'

'You're going through it with me, Ellen. And in addition to that you are the President of the United States, and you are working to get Dani back. I was thinking about that this morning. I began to see that I must have been making things even harder for you than they already are. Then, I was on the computer, checking for any breaking news from England, and I saw a video. It was that asshole fascist radio show host out of Dallas.'

'Bubba Lanier.' Ellen said.

'Yes.'

'Damn. Did you see Hank Betancourt's contribution as well?'

'Yes. Did you see them?'

'Just now. Jeff showed them to us when the meeting broke up. I'm sorry you had to see that.'

'I'm not,' Kay said defiantly. 'It brought me to my senses.'

'Oh?'

Kay squeezed Ellen's hand.

'Dale was here earlier. He had seen it already. We watched it together. He gave me a great pep talk. He made me realize that I had to snap out of it. Ellen, while you've been working so hard for Dani, I've been sulking like a ten-year-old, sitting around in my pajamas and feeling sorry for myself. That's not going to bring Dani back. Dale reminded me that I'm an adult, I'm a successful trial lawyer, and I need to be there for you while you do what you have to do. And I got so angry watching that crap. Do those losers actually think they can control our lives? Do they really think they have the right to demand your resignation, just because we don't subscribe to whatever medieval claptrap they happen to be peddling? Well, you know what? Fuck them. Fuck them, Ellen. And fuck those bastards who took Dani. I'm in the mood for a fight now. I'm back.'

Ellen laughed out loud. They held each other in a long embrace.

'I knew you would be,' Ellen said.

Kay gently released the embrace and pushed her away, until she held Ellen at arm's length.

'I want to go to England, Ellen,' she said. 'I won't get in the way. But I want to help if I can. If I can't, I want to be there when they find Dani. I want to be there for her.'

Ellen fought back her first instinct to tell Kay that it was a bad idea. Kay needed to do something, she understood that. It had done her no good to sit around in the residence trawling endlessly for news from TV stations and websites. But England was another matter.

'Kay, I can't keep the press away from you there.'

'I can deal with the press,' Kay insisted. 'I just need to be out there. I'm going crazy cooped up here with nothing to do. Abe Solari has made me stay away from Facebook. The Secret Service doesn't even want me sending emails, in case I say something I shouldn't. I understand their concern. But I'm not an idiot, Ellen. I'm not going to say anything stupid.'

'I know that,' Ellen said, 'and that's not what I meant. It's just that they will follow your every move. You will be the news. And the people over there won't want to be distracted by having to protect you.'

'They don't have to protect me,' Kay protested. 'I can look after myself.'

She embraced Ellen again and spoke quietly.

'I'm going, Ellen. I would prefer it to be with your blessing. I would prefer it if you would make the arrangements, so that I can keep it private for as long as possible. But if you don't want to, I'll go under my own steam.'

Ellen kissed her. Her urge to resist evaporated.

'If that's what you want, of course you have my blessing,' she said. 'Kelly is going over on a military flight from Andrews Air Force Base round about 1.30 tomorrow morning. I'll make arrangements for you to travel with her. I'll ask Hal Wilkinson to find you a place to stay. With any luck, you will be there before anyone finds out.'

'Thank you, Ellen. I love you.'

'I love you too.'

Kay looked at her watch. 'There's plenty of time to eat. How does pasta with tomato and fresh basil sound?'

'It sounds great,' Ellen smiled. 'I'll go make a couple of phone calls to get you set up.'

As she walked away towards the study, Ellen admitted to herself that, despite her misgivings, she actually felt relieved that Kay would be away as the situation played itself out. Her absence would lift some of the pressure. It would give her some time and space to maintain her own equilibrium.

'You're all set,' Ellen said, returning to the kitchen.

Water was boiling on the stove, and there was a delicious scent of fresh basil in the air. She picked up the bottle of wine and refilled Kay's glass and her own.

'The car will pick you up at 12.30 to take you to Andrews. Hal will arrange customs clearance and the police will get you to Cambridge. They are putting Kelly up at the University Arms Hotel in Cambridge. They will find you a room there, too.'

'Perfect,' Kay smiled. 'Thank you.'

She drained the water from the pasta, returned the pan to the stove and added the tomato and basil sauce she had prepared from fresh ingredients. She stirred it vigorously, then emptied it quickly on to their two plates. Ellen had cut slices of bread and put out small bowls of olive oil, and was already seated at the table. Kay brought the plates to the table and took her seat.

'What's the latest on the Phoenix plans?' Kay asked.

Ellen swallowed hard.

'General Gutierrez's people are still working on it,' she replied. 'He is making good progress. I know it's taking a while, but ...'

Kay put her fork down.

'Ellen, that's what I see on the network news. I was hoping you might tell me what is actually going on.'

'Kay …'

'Why is it taking so long? The press is asking whether the plans even exist. If they do, why don't you just hand them over, and end this? Everyone knows you could take them out if they ever tried to build a drone.'

'Kay, we've been through all this before. It's not that simple.'

Kay exhaled heavily.

'Look, I understand what Jeff has been saying at the news conferences; that they want to make sure they identify the correct plans.'

'That's correct. The new model is in the early stages of development. They are not even sure there is a complete set of plans and specifications for the new model of the drone. Some aspects of it are still in the planning stage. We may have to include some specs from the existing model. But then we don't know whether it would work. I'm seeing General Gutierrez later. I will get an update then.'

Kay ate a forkful of pasta and looked closely at Ellen.

'Do you have any idea what I would do to you in cross-examination if you were a witness in a case of mine, and you gave me a load of crap like that on the stand?'

Despite her anxiety, Ellen smiled, pleased that Kay's spirit had returned. She reached across the table and took Kay's hand.

'It's the waiting that gets to me, Ellen,' she continued. 'You can at least do things, make decisions. But I can't do anything at all. It's the damned waiting, not knowing anything, that drives me crazy.'

'Kay, there are certain questions I can't answer, certain things I can't share now,' Ellen said gently. 'I promise, when Dani is back safe with us, I will tell you everything. For now, I really need you to trust me when I say I'm doing everything in my power to get her back.'

Kay gazed into Ellen's eyes for some time, then nodded.

'OK,' she said. 'Finish your pasta. I'll get the salad.'

40

TED LAZENBY WAS already in the situation room when Ellen arrived. It was just after midnight. He had a yellow pad in front of him and had filled several pages with notes.

'How is Kay?' he asked.

'Much better,' Ellen replied. 'More like her old self. She's getting herself back on her feet. She's going to England with Kelly – her idea, not mine. She insisted. It's not ideal, but on balance, I think I prefer it to having her sit in the residence, driving herself crazy.'

'You couldn't tell her about the new video, of course.'

'No.'

Ellen seated herself at the table across from Lazenby. He allowed some time to pass before he spoke.

'Ellen, I don't know how fast things are going to unfold, or how many chances we will get to discuss this, so we need to talk now, and we need to talk without holding back.'

'Yes,' she replied quietly.

'This is our opportunity to say whatever we need to say, without any thought that what we say will ever become reality. We need to stare into the abyss and search the very darkest places in the recesses of our minds, places we usually strive to forget about, and we need to speak aloud whatever comes from those places. Just because these things need to be said, just because we can have no secrets from each other now. I need to know exactly what is inside you, and you need to know exactly what is inside me. Because, whatever we choose to do, or not do, now, we are going to have to live with for the rest of our lives.'

She looked at him without replying.

'Before you went to see Kay, you said you would never suggest to me that we should assassinate Mehra.'

'And you said that you would never do it.'

'Yes,' he replied. He paused. 'But there is a part of me that asks the question.'

Ellen looked up.

'It's true,' he continued. 'There is a part of me that weighs Mehra's life against Dani's, and sees that one of them is probably going to die, and asks why, if I have that choice in my hands, I would not save Dani. I can even rationalize it as being in the best interests of the United States.'

'Human beings can rationalize almost anything,' Ellen pointed out. 'How else is it possible for people to commit genocide?'

'I agree,' Lazenby said. 'But we're not talking about genocide here. We are talking about a classic moral dilemma. Two people fall into a river from a canoe. There are strong currents, and they are being swept away. You can save one of the two from drowning, but not both. How do you decide?'

Ellen shook her head.

'You can't decide,' she replied. 'Not on any rational basis. By the time you weighed everything up, decided which of them was more valuable to society or whatever, they would both have been swept away. I think instinct would take over in that situation. You would do what you could without thinking too much about it. That question is fine for students of philosophy, but I don't think it means much in the real world.'

'Then it would not necessarily be wrong to have Mehra killed if it would bring Dani back?' he asked.

She stood and walked slowly to the far end of the table.

'It becomes different once you identify two real people in a real situation, instead of two imaginary characters falling out of a canoe,' she said.

'Dani is much more real to you than Mehra,' he replied. 'It would be an understandable choice.'

'This is not a case about people being swept away in a river, Ted,' she said eventually. 'It's not a matter of saving someone from a natural disaster. It would be a matter of making a deliberate choice to end the life of someone who is not otherwise in danger – at least, not from us.'

She sat down in the nearest chair.

'I had this discussion with Steve Wade once,' she said. 'It began when he first approached me to run as his Vice President. He knew my record. So does everyone now, thanks to what came out during the crisis. You know all about it. I was involved in the peace movement as a student. I went to rallies. I even went behind the Iron Curtain, to Yugoslavia, to support Tito's youth movement for disarmament. I opposed the Vietnam War. I opposed Iraq. I called George W Bush and the rest of that crowd war criminals because of Guantanamo Bay and extraordinary rendition. I was a pacifist earlier in my life, and I suppose I still am, though not so absolutely now. I made it clear to Steve that I would support him in the use of force if America was threatened, as long as it was a real threat, and not some bullshit like an endless generalized "war on terror". But I also told him there were some things I would not be able to support him on. Those things included political assassinations and targeting civilians. And, in fairness to Steve, for the most part, he felt the same way.'

'Our government has always had to do things it would rather not do,' Lazenby pointed out. 'And we have people trained to do those things at our disposal.'

'Yes, and there are cases I would not feel bad about,' Ellen admitted. 'Osama Bin Laden, for example. And I recognize that everything changes when the country is involved in armed conflict. But that's not the case here. We have good relations with India, and Anand Mehra has done nothing to offend us, let alone anything that would justify having him killed. Damn it, Ted, I met the guy when I was Vice President.'

Lazenby stood and walked half the length of the table towards her.

'But you have thought about it, haven't you?'

She smiled.

'Yes, I have thought about it. I was having dinner with Kay earlier, and I thought how wonderful it would be if Dani were there with us. And I saw that one way of getting her back might be …Yes, of course, I've thought about it.'

'But …?'

'But I will not do it,' she said firmly.

'You're sure, absolutely sure?'

'Yes. I recognize that there is a part of me that would do it. But I will not. What about you?'

'I won't do it.'

'Are *you* sure?'

'Yes,' he hesitated, 'I think so.'

Ellen looked up sharply, bit her lip and suppressed the first reply that came into her mind.

'Then there is no disagreement between us, is there? Why have we just had this conversation?'

'Because we have time to discuss it now,' he replied. 'Because, if we were going to do it, we would have to make arrangements without delay. And lastly – and most importantly – because when the chips are down in a few days and the sky is falling on our heads, I don't want there to be any wavering, second thoughts, or lingering doubts. That would be dangerous for everyone, Dani included. Remember, Ellen, you're the one who's going to be making the announcements. You are the one the world is going to be watching. So I needed to have the point settled now, once and for all, if it can be settled.'

Ellen stood.

'Consider it settled,' she said. 'As far as I am concerned. But it's going to be your decision, isn't it? So the real question is whether it's settled in your mind.'

Lazenby did not reply.

'I need to go to see Kay off, and make some calls to England,' she said.

'Ellen, this conversation never took place. You understand that?'

'What conversation?' she replied.

41

THE NAME DAVE Masterson kept coming up with as he inquired about an expert on India was that of James Desai. As it happened, Desai was in Washington. He had been attending a symposium at Georgetown University, and was staying over for two or three days to spend time with old friends who lived in Bethesda. Masterson dispatched an agent to ask him whether he could spare some time for an urgent consultation at the White House. It was framed as a polite request, but Desai understood that it was an invitation he was expected to accept.

James Desai was the Professor of Indian Studies at Oxford University. His personal credentials were impressive. He had taken a first in Oxford's celebrated PPE – Philosophy, Politics and Economics – followed by a Masters in political science at Harvard. He completed his doctoral thesis, on the decline and fall of the British Raj, at Cambridge, before returning to Oxford to take up his first academic position. But his deep knowledge of Indian history was not only academic.

His family had a long and intimate involvement with the inner circles of Indian political life. In the more remote past, they had served for several generations as trusted counsellors to the Maharanas of Udaipur, but Desai's grandfather had forged wider and longer-lasting links. He was a close friend of Jawaharlal Nehru and was with him during the negotiations with Mountbatten which led to Independence. It was this association that gave Desai's father the opportunity to study in Oxford, and to remain in England as a high-ranking officer in the Indian High Commission in London. James was, therefore, educated in England, but his father was wise enough to send him back to spend long holidays in India each year.

He grew up understanding and feeling India, as well as learning about her through study. His many writings about the country were already regarded as essential reading for any serious student.

Ken Hunt had been delegated to ask the few awkward questions that had to be asked when Desai met the crisis committee. With the exception of Lisa Carrow, everyone had returned to the White House as soon as Dave Masterson had announced that Desai was on his way. The CIA chief had briefed them about the expert's qualifications by email and no one was disposed to suggest looking any further. The President seemed happy with the choice, but insisted that some inquiries be made of Professor Desai directly.

'Professor Desai, we really appreciate your willingness to help us in this situation,' Hunt began.

Desai bowed his head slightly and turned towards Ellen Trevathan. 'I am honored to be asked, Madam President.'

Desai was a thin man of medium height, with prematurely silver hair. He was dressed in a double-breasted gray pin-striped suit, a white shirt, his navy blue Balliol tie with the College crest, and perfectly shined black shoes. He was precise in his movements and his darting deep brown eyes gave the impression of missing nothing.

'My name is Ken Hunt. I'm the Attorney-General. You know the President and Vice President. And, of course, you've already met Director Masterson. Let me introduce the others present to you. On Director Masterson's left is Abe Solari, the Director of the Secret Service. Opposite him is General Raul Gutierrez, the Secretary of Defense. At the end of the table opposite the President is her chief of staff, Craig Diamond and. next to Craig, her press secretary, Jeff Morris.'

Desai acknowledged each member of the committee individually with an inclination of his head and firm eye contact.

'Before we begin,' Hunt continued, 'there are one or two matters to discuss. First of all, I believe that Director Masterson has already told you the general nature of the subject on which we wish to consult you. It involves the kidnapping of the President's step-daughter, Dani Ryan.'

'Yes, Madam President.'

'The British Government is very much involved with the investigation, as you know, Professor Desai.'

'Yes, of course. I am aware that the investigators are working on the assumption that Miss Ryan is being held in England.'

'First, I have to ask you whether you have consulted with the British Government at any point about this matter.'

'No,' Desai smiled. 'Somewhat to my surprise, I have to say. No one at the Foreign Office has asked me anything about it at all. I was expecting a call, but it has not come.'

'Why were you expecting a call?' Ted Lazenby asked.

Desai smiled again. 'I have followed the case in the British press, of course. It has not escaped my attention that an Indian woman is thought to have been involved in her abduction. And I believe some suspicion has attached to a young American man of Indian extraction. In those circumstances, it is not difficult to speculate that there may be some Indian involvement in the case. I had expected somebody to take that speculation further.'

'You are a consultant to the British Government on Indian affairs generally, then?' Hunt asked.

'Yes, certainly. The Foreign Office consults me with some regularity,' Desai replied.

'And you must feel, therefore, a certain loyalty to the British Government?'

'I am a British citizen,' Desai said. 'So naturally, I have a loyalty to my government. I also recognize a duty of professional confidentiality. But, please understand, I am not employed by the British Government. I am a university professor. I am quite independent. Indeed, I am consulted by a number of other governments throughout the world from time to time. The Foreign Office is aware of that, and they have never objected to it.'

'Would that include the Government of India?' Hunt asked.

'Yes, indeed,' Desai replied. 'I am also a citizen of India. Although in the case of the Indian Government, I would be consulted about reaction in Britain and other western countries to what India is doing, rather than Indian politics as such.'

He smiled broadly again.

'They have their own experts on that,' he added.

He turned towards Ellen Trevathan.

'Madam President, I know of no reason why I cannot advise you freely in this matter, and I am quite able and willing to give you the same promise of confidentiality I would give to the British Government.'

Hunt looked across the table at Ellen Trevathan, who nodded.

'Thank you, Professor Desai. I don't see any reason not to continue on that basis. Craig, is the computer ready?'

'It is, Madam President.'

'All right, thank you. Professor, what you are about to see has a top secret classification. If you agree to watch, you are agreeing that you will not disclose anything you see, under any circumstances, to anyone – whether in the UK or elsewhere.'

'I understand,' Desai replied. 'I give that undertaking.'

'Thank you,' Ellen said.

She nodded to Craig Diamond, who played all four files in order. Everyone around the table watched in complete silence. Desai leaned forward and seemed to concentrate hard, but displayed no particular reaction.

'Professor Desai, is there any part of that material you need to see again?'

Desai shook his head. 'No, thank you.'

'My first question,' Ellen continued, 'relates to the Kashmir question itself. I'm trying to understand what these people mean when they speak of liberating Kashmir.'

Desai sat up in his chair, and for a few seconds concentrated his gaze on the wall above Ellen's head. He then lowered his head and spoke to her directly.

'Kashmir is a vast subject,' he began. 'It is interesting historically, geographically, economically, politically – in every way. It is a very complex issue, or rather a complex series of issues. It is not something that can be summarized in a few words. It is easy to over-simplify the situation. Actually, that is true of India generally. We have a saying. "Whatever you can say truthfully about India, the opposite is also true." But I understand that you need me to attempt a summary, as time is short.'

'Indeed,' Ellen agreed.

'Well then,' Desai said. 'Kashmir has been the subject of military and political disputes for centuries, perhaps for millennia. But for about a century before Independence it was relatively stable. In 1846 a ruling clan called the Dogras purchased the territory from the British and ruled it as a princely state until Independence. It's important to understand that, just before Independence, Kashmir was more than 75% Muslim in terms of ethnicity, and many people expected that the Dogras would accede to Pakistan when Independence came. That might also have been natural geographically speaking, in view of the proposed borders. But India resisted that idea, and Mountbatten gave India some support.

'So when Independence came, Kashmir was a disputed territory. India, Pakistan, and China all claimed hegemony over large areas of the state. In 1947, India became an independent country, after almost a hundred years of British rule – and that is counting only the governmental rule, the Raj, which followed the great rebellion of 1857. It was closer to two hundred if you count the period of East India Company domination as well. The negotiations for independence were conducted by various Indian nationalist leaders, and by Lord Mountbatten on behalf of the British Government. The negotiations were not conducted in a calm atmosphere.'

Desai looked briefly around the room.

'It is vital to understand that. Instead of exercising leadership and paving the way for an orderly transition to independence, the negotiators on both sides found themselves at the mercy of forces they could not control. The long struggle for independence had created too much instability. The people had lost patience. They were no longer prepared to wait for their leaders to design the perfect blueprint for independence. They wanted independence and they wanted partition, and they wanted them immediately. Not even Gandhi could stem the tide, not even Jinnah, though they were both men of goodwill in their different ways. Partition on a religious basis was already underway. There were already movements of population and acts of religious and nationalist violence. Britain could do nothing. Britain was on the verge of bankruptcy after the War. Ruling India was a luxury she could no longer afford. So the negotiators were not leading. They were following. There was no question of getting ahead of events. They were trying desperately to keep up with them. Mountbatten was obliged to speed up the negotiations and bring the date for independence forward by six months. If he hadn't, the people would have taken it anyway, before any political structure at all was put in place. India might well have descended into anarchy.'

Desai turned to his right.

'Mr Diamond, would you mind bringing up the map of Kashmir they used in file two, please?'

Craig located file two, turned down the sound, and paused when the map appeared.

'One of the projects that had to be rushed was the drawing of boundaries – principally the boundaries between India and Pakistan. But Kashmir was one of a number of areas where boundaries had to be drawn, and drawn quickly. Everyone was squabbling about where they should be drawn. Mountbatten was trying to referee, without much success. If they had had more time, perhaps a greater consensus could have been achieved, and perhaps a more acceptable compromise could have been reached. Who knows?'

'What you're telling us,' Ted Lazenby suggested, 'is that no one was completely happy with the outcome.'

'Exactly,' Desai replied. 'And it didn't last very long. The lines you see on this map are not the boundaries established at the time of Independence. Almost as soon as the ink was dry on the independence documents, India and Pakistan went to war over Kashmir. Pakistan had tried to establish a military presence in anticipation of acquiring the territory, and India sent in forces to drive them out. The war was inconclusive and ended in 1948 with lines of demarcation drawn up by the UN. They went to war again in 1965, and again in 1999. Much the same result, no real progress, UN-negotiated cease-fires. Neither side has ever been able to gain a decisive advantage.'

Desai picked up a baton from the table and walked over to the screen, pointing.

'What you see here is the result of all that. India controls most of the territory of Kashmir. Most of the Indian-controlled territory is now the Indian State of Jammu and Kashmir. But Pakistan controls a very large area in the West and North West, the Northern Areas and Azad Kashmir. It is probably about 80% of the size of the Indian-controlled area. There are also the north-eastern territories, Aksai Chin and the Trans-Karakoram Tract, which are under the control of China. These territories are not insignificant, but far smaller than the Indian and Pakistani areas and, in any case, I sense that they may not have much importance for our discussion today.'

He turned fully towards those seated around the table.

'The most important point to make is that these are not boundaries. They are lines of demarcation, defining areas of control. I'm sure you understand the difference.'

'No one wants or expects them to be permanent,' Ellen Trevathan said. 'They are a temporary compromise, to be revisited when one side or the other feels strong enough to go to war again with some prospect of success.'

Desai nodded.

'Exactly. From time to time efforts are made to reach a long-term political solution, but so far none has been forthcoming. Please remember that Independence, and the atrocities and deportations, the forced relocation of so many people that went with it, is still a recent memory. You are dealing with ethnic and religious differences that run very deep, and have been exacerbated by the events of 1947 and 1948 – not to mention the more recent conflicts.'

There was silence for some time.

'In the light of what you have told us,' Ellen Trevathan asked, 'how do you evaluate the demand for the assassination of Prime Minister Mehra? Why does SK want to kill the Prime Minister of India?'

Desai walked slowly back to his seat.

'Anand Mehra,' he replied, after some thought, 'has not taken a particularly conciliatory approach over Kashmir. He is not a man given to making threats he cannot carry out. But he has taken a fairly hard line, insisting on Indian hegemony at least within the present lines of demarcation, and hinting at more. He has strengthened India's military presence all along the border with Pakistan, both in terms of numbers of troops, and in terms of military installations and weaponry. This has not been lost on Pakistan, obviously. Pakistan has been complaining of provocation, if not actual aggression, and there are those at the UN who are listening sympathetically. But despite this, I do not see him launching a military campaign against Pakistan. Mehra is a realist. He knows that India could lose just as much as she could gain in any such conflict.'

He looked up and contemplated the ceiling. Then he looked down again and posed the question to himself.

'So why would SK make this demand for his assassination?'

He sat forward decisively in his chair.

'It can only be because of the reaction they foresee,' he concluded. 'If Pakistan were to assassinate Anand Mehra while he was inspecting military installations along the line of demarcation, India could only assume that act was tied to the Kashmir question. In any case, it would be an intolerable provocation. India would have to do something. Given the existing atmosphere, SK must have calculated that it would provoke another war between India and Pakistan over Kashmir.'

Desai looked around the table, making eye-contact with every member of the committee.

'I believe that their calculation may very well be correct,' he added.

'So, Mehra is just a pawn in the game?' Ellen asked quietly. 'A martyr for the cause of expanding Indian control of Kashmir?'

'That is my assessment of the facts presented to me,' Desai replied. 'And I'm sure I need not remind you, Madam President, that India and Pakistan are both nuclear powers. The situation would be a very serious one, very serious indeed.'

Dave Masterson raised a hand in Ellen's direction, for permission to speak. She nodded.

'Professor Desai, what can you tell us about this group, SK? We don't seem to have anything much on them at all at the Agency, and that's pretty unusual for the CIA. We have intelligence on just about every terrorist group throughout the world.'

Desai smiled.

'Yes, I'm well aware of that, Director. But I'm not surprised by what you say. I know very little myself, and I'm not aware of anyone who does know much. They are a very shadowy group, obsessive about secrecy. They rarely seek publicity of any kind, and they are not known for claiming credit for any of their actions, with the result that it is hard to attribute any particular actions to them. Their reputation is of a small group of highly-educated men and women, who have in common only an uncompromising commitment to Indian hegemony over the whole of Kashmir, and the domination of the Hindu religion. Even their name is rather odd. "Svatantra" is a Sanskrit word meaning freedom, independence, which is rarely used today. Actually it is archaic. The Hindi word you would use today is "azad", which is the word used in the name of the independent area of Kashmir – Azad Kashmir. It's almost as if they want to hearken back to some remote past time. Their methods are unorthodox also. They seem to shun traditional terrorist activities, such as planting bombs. They are said to prefer strategic operations, sometimes designed to produce results in the future. I believe that they have planted people in various places as sleepers, to be activated as needed. It may well be that the young man Bev Prasad, who seems to have been involved in the kidnapping, is one of these. His family is Kashmiri. It has all the hallmarks of an SK operation.'

'No wonder they are hard to keep track of,' Abe Solari said.

'Yes,' Desai agreed. 'The other reputation they have is rather contradictory. It is said that, once committed to an operation, they are totally ruthless and will use any degree of violence to achieve their goal. Yet, they recruit only agents who abhor violence, people who would never use it unless in the SK cause, and unless it is unavoidable if they are to achieve their aim.'

Ellen took a deep breath.

'I'm sure you understand now, Professor, why we asked you those questions before we began.'

'Of course, Madam President. I can assure you that my lips are sealed. I can assure you of this also. The British Government is not involved in any active way with Kashmir at present. Of course, as a permanent member of the Security Council, the UK would become involved if the region were to flare up again. But there are no mixed motives here. I would know, if there were.'

Ellen stood. She walked over to Professor Desai and took him aside to shake his hand.

'Thank you, Professor.'

'You are welcome, Madam President. I pray for Dani's safe return home.'

He suddenly smiled.

'Don't despair,' he added. 'India is a strange place. Things are rarely what they seem.'

42

THE COMMITTEE HAD taken a recess. Ellen had returned to the residence to confer with Craig Diamond and Jeff Morris about strategies to deal with the media. Ten minutes later, Dave Masterson and Raul Gutierrez made their way back to the situation room, which was exactly what Ted Lazenby had quietly asked of them as they were leaving. The three men sat in a tight group around the corner of the table farthest from the door.

'I have a question to ask,' Lazenby began. 'But I'm not sure who I should be asking; by which I mean I'm not sure whether it is information I should be seeking from the military or the CIA. So I am asking both of you.'

'Go ahead,' Masterson said.

'Before I ask, I need you both to understand that the fact that I am asking for this information does not mean that I propose to take any action on the basis of it.'

Masterson and Gutierrez exchanged glances.

'OK,' Gutierrez said tentatively.

Lazenby took a deep breath.

'Assuming, hypothetically, that the President decided to comply with the demand made by SK, do we have at our disposal a unit capable of taking the necessary action?'

Masterson sat back in his chair. 'Ted …?'

'I said "hypothetically",' Lazenby said.

Masterson stared at Lazenby for some time.

'Hypothetically,' he replied. 'Hypothetically, I would say that to carry out the operation would be a military task. But the Agency could provide essential back-up and intelligence. In reality, it would have to be a joint venture.'

'I agree,' Gutierrez said. 'We have units that could achieve the objective, given appropriate logistical and intelligence support. What I don't know, without asking someone, is whether we have the capability of getting it done by the deadline we've been given. There would be a lot to put in place logistically. I'm just thinking aloud here. Obviously, it's an operation that would call for careful planning. Operatives would probably want to practice the insertion and set-up in similar terrain beforehand, if possible. They would need reliable, detailed maps of the region. They would be operating on foreign soil in a highly sensitive area. There is obvious potential for things to go very wrong. Of course, we would also need the Prime Minister's itinerary in considerable detail.'

'No problem,' Masterson said. 'I could get all that for you by tomorrow, if it were needed – hypothetically speaking, that is.'

'In addition,' Gutierrez continued, 'we would need to find out what weaponry the Pakistani Security Service, or the Pakistani military, uses. There's no time even to think about trying to set up an explosive device, and they probably couldn't get close enough to try that anyway. So I'm guessing we are talking about a sniper using the kind of rifle the Pakistanis might use. And we would need to acquire an appropriate weapon in sufficient time to allow someone to practice with it.'

'I can get that information for you too,' Masterson said. 'Acquiring the weapon may have to be done locally, though it may be of Russian manufacture, in which case we probably have a few lying around somewhere.'

He smiled. 'Actually, if the shot were to be fired from the Pakistani side, there wouldn't be much doubt about who gets blamed, regardless of the weapon used.'

'In that case, Ted,' Gutierrez said, 'it seems the answer to your hypothetical question is "yes", subject to time constraints. I can't give you an answer to that without talking to the appropriate unit leader.'

He paused. 'I need to add that such an operation would be very risky, both militarily and politically.'

Lazenby stood.

'Raul, I want you to bring the unit leader here so that all three of us can ask him the necessary questions together, and answer any questions he may have.'

'Bring him here?' Gutierrez asked.

'Tomorrow,' Lazenby said. 'Can you do that?'

There was silence for several seconds.

'Am I missing something here?' Dave Masterson asked quietly. 'Or are we going a little bit beyond the hypothetical now?'

'It's still hypothetical,' Lazenby replied. 'I'm just asking questions. But if I don't ask tomorrow, I won't have the information I need until it's too late to do anything about it.'

'Ted,' Raul Gutierrez said, 'I'm happy to do as you ask on the basis that you are asking hypothetical questions. But I need you to understand something. Assassinating the prime minister of a friendly state is not on my moral radar. I can't believe it would be on Ellen's. I can't speak for Dave.'

Masterson opened his mouth as if to speak, but remained silent.

Lazenby exhaled heavily.

'What about an operation which results in a failed assassination attempt?' he asked. 'How would that look on your moral radar?'

Gutierrez thought for a moment and smiled.

'You are talking about a staged failure, for public consumption?' he asked.

'I'm talking about an operation carried out exactly as it would be if we were serious about killing Mehra,' Lazenby replied. 'Planned and executed in every detail. But the ultimate result is false and deliberately staged.'

No one spoke for some time.

'It wouldn't be credible,' Masterson said.

'It might,' Gutierrez said, raising a finger. 'It might be. The assassin would only get one chance at this. He would have to take a shot and hope he is on target. Sniping is a difficult art in the most favorable of circumstances. Even if we intended to kill Mehra, there would be no guarantee of success. It's easy to miss at long distance with a sniping rifle, especially if you're not using state-of-the-art weaponry. And remember, it's supposed to be the Pakistanis who are doing it.'

'OK,' Masterson said. 'But what would be the point? SK is threatening to kill Dani unless Mehra actually dies – no excuses accepted.'

Lazenby nodded.

'That's what they are saying,' he conceded. 'But think about it for a moment. It might be enough to cause some kind of reaction if Pakistan were even to attempt to assassinate Mehra – even if they didn't succeed. That alone might be enough to provoke a conflict. That's what SK is looking for. It's possible they might release Dani in those circumstances. Remember what Professor Desai said. They abhor violence and only use it when unavoidable. If they get what they want without killing Mehra, and if it appears that we did our best to comply with their demand, it's harder for them to argue that it's necessary to kill Dani.'

Masterson looked unconvinced.

'It gives us an additional possibility of getting Dani back safely,' Lazenby added. 'I don't see a downside, except for putting some of our people in harm's way, but I doubt they will object to that. It's what they do.'

'What about causing a military conflict between two nuclear powers?' Masterson asked. 'You don't see that as a downside?'

Lazenby shrugged.

'The moment we are sure Dani is safe, the President would get on the phone to New Delhi and Islamabad and explain to them confidentially what had happened. They would have to stand down.'

There was another silence.

'I need to think about this some more,' Gutierrez said. 'But I will find someone for us to talk to tomorrow, and we can think about it overnight.'

He looked directly at Lazenby.

'I assume Ellen doesn't know about this yet?'

'Ellen has enough to worry about,' Lazenby replied. 'Let's see if we can take some of the burden off her shoulders.'

43

THE CAR PULLED up in front of Steve Macmillan's flat. Kelly Smith and Kay Ryan climbed wearily out on to the curb, and thanked the uniformed police sergeant who had driven them to Cambridge from RAF Barkston Heath near Grantham, Lincolnshire, where their military flight from Andrews Air Force Base had landed. Barkston Heath had been selected because it was quiet and unlikely to attract attention, and it had worked. So far, no one outside the investigative team appeared to know that Kelly and Kay were in England. Although that situation could not possibly last, both felt some relief at being given a reprieve from the attentions of the press, if only for long enough for them to adjust to being abroad.

They had been taken first to the University Arms Hotel, where a room had been reserved for each. Kelly's room had been prepared, not only by the hotel, but also by MI5 and Special Branch. Between them they had ensured that she would have access to state-of-the-art communication both with the investigative team and with the White House situation room.

They paused only to shower, change, and attempt to eat some of the continental breakfast rushed to their rooms by the hotel, before undertaking the final, short leg of their journey. A uniformed police constable ushered them into the living room of Steve's flat.

'Madam Director, I'm Steve Macmillan. We've spoken over the phone.'

'Kelly, please.'

'And you must be Kay Ryan.'

'Yes.' Kay shook his hand tightly. 'Thank you for everything you are doing to find Dani. And thank you for allowing me to be here with Kelly. I thought I might have to hide away in my hotel room for the duration.'

Steve smiled.

'Absolutely not. I'm glad to have the chance to show you what we are doing. And you never know, you may spot something we are missing. It's you we have to thank for spotting the message Dani sent on the video. We saved a lot of time once we gave up worrying that she might have been spirited out of the country. So feel free to ask any questions you want, and to give us any insights you may have.'

The door opened again. Steve stretched out an arm to welcome the woman who walked in.

'This is Agent Rosa Linda Montalbán. Rosa – Director Kelly Smith, FBI; and Dani's mother, Kay Ryan.'

They shook hands. Both Kelly and Kay saw at once that Rosa was anxious. Her face was pale and her manner was uncertain. Kay had the impression that she might be about to cry. She decided not to release Rosa's hand immediately after the handshake. With a glance at Kelly, she took the initiative.

'Rosa, let's get this out of the way right now. You were not to blame for what happened. You were doing everything right. You couldn't have foreseen it. It wasn't your fault. I would trust you with Dani again.'

Tears welled up in Rosa's eyes and she felt a lump in her throat.

'Director Solari told me the same thing, Rosa,' Kelly said. 'He wants to make sure you understand that no one is blaming you for this.'

'No one but me,' Rosa smiled thinly through her tears. Then, suddenly, she leaned forward into Kay's arms, and they embraced.

'Thank you,' she whispered.

Steve had fixed a large map of Cambridgeshire and adjoining counties to an easel which stood against the wall to their left.

'Why don't you have a seat,' he said, 'and I'll tell you what's going on with the investigation. There's coffee on the table. Please help yourselves. I'm sure you will be fighting off the jet lag for a day or two.'

Steve picked up a baton as Kelly and Kay poured coffee and took their seats.

'We are operating on two basic assumptions,' he said. 'But we are confident that both are correct. First, we assume that Dani has not been taken out of the country. We base that on the message Dani sent. Second, we assume that she is relatively close to Cambridge. We base that on the assessment made by our experts and by your Lisa Carrow. They all concur that the kidnappers would not have taken her any further than necessary. Taking Dani was a high-risk operation for them. They could not have assumed that they had time to spare once they snatched her. They must have been aware that someone would raise a hue and cry within a short time frame. So, we think that they had a place prepared, not on the doorstep obviously, but not too far away. This place would have to have secure accommodation for Dani, and preferably be a fair distance away from neighbors and busybodies. That suggests to our experts a house in a fairly rural setting within a radius of about 50 miles from the city centre. Lisa also agreed with that assessment, and it accords with the time frame within which the demand was made.'

Steve paused to take a drink from his coffee mug. He immediately made a terrible face and put the mug back down on the table at his side. Kelly grinned.

'Let me freshen that up for you,' she offered, walking to the table and picking up the mug.

'Thanks,' Steve said. 'The only thing worse than bad coffee is cold bad coffee.' He gratefully accepted the hot mug, and continued.

'Unfortunately, even making those two assumptions, we are still left with a lot of territory to cover. Just look at the map. Once you leave Cambridge, you have rural areas all around you, stretching a considerable distance. You can go north west towards Huntingdon; north east towards Ely or a bit more east towards Newmarket; south east towards Saffron Walden or a bit more south towards Bishop's Stortford; or south west towards Royston or Stevenage. You can go beyond those points. It's the same story in every direction. Lots of small villages and towns, surrounded by open countryside. Suitable properties everywhere you look.'

'Like looking for a needle in a haystack,' Kelly commented.

Steve took another drink of coffee.

'There's another problem too. We have a lot of people on the ground, but they have to be careful. All the experts have cautioned us that there's no way to tell how the kidnappers might react if they realize we are getting close. We don't want to provoke that kind of situation. Our ideal solution is that we find them before they know they've been found. We have not been using helicopters and we have been as low key as possible in all our searches. It slows us down, but it gives us a better chance of getting Dani back safely.'

Kelly stood and walked around to lean on the back of her chair.

'Steve, in Washington we're worried that we don't have unlimited time to find Dani. We agree with your experts that the kidnappers may be volatile, and that worries us. We don't want them to lose patience. Is there anything you can do to move the search along a bit more quickly without being too obvious about it? Bring in more people, more satellite surveillance? I don't know. Just something?'

'We already have as much satellite coverage as we need,' Steve replied. 'We can zoom in anywhere we want. We follow up everything we see. If they raise their heads an inch above the parapet, we'll have them. We thought we were on to them last week. We paid a visit to an Indian couple living in a house in Melbourn, just south of the city. The satellite picked them up coming back from the corner shop with what looked like a lot of supplies. We sent in six men from our SAS unit. Scared the living daylights out of them. Turned out they are both pillars of the community. He's a local councillor. It took an hour or more to persuade them not to talk to the press. We're treading on eggshells, Kelly. Any false step could go badly wrong.'

Kelly nodded her understanding.

'If the people in Washington want to move things along,' Steve said, 'perhaps they might show a bit more urgency about handing over the plans they've asked for.'

Kelly bit her lip.

'Just a thought,' Steve said. 'Come on, let's get some fresh air. Kay, if you're up for it, I'd like you to take a quick look around Dani's room in Downing College. We've been over it several times and found nothing. But there may be something you see that we missed.'

'Let's go,' Kay replied.

At the door, Steve allowed Kay to leave the room first. When she was out of earshot, he took Kelly's arm.

'I wasn't trying to be difficult,' he said, apologetically. 'We really are doing all we can.'

'I can see that,' Kelly replied.

'The truth of the matter is,' Steve said, 'we need a break. We need a bit of good luck. That's all. Just one little piece of good luck.'

* * *

The man Barney knew as 'Jason' was an experienced undercover officer based at Cambridge police station. For the past nine months he had been a vital part of *Operation Toytown*, a carefully-planned operation designed to bring down a sophisticated drug importation business. Painstaking investigative work by the serious crime squad had revealed a pattern of large consignments of heroin and cocaine being imported into the country through the docks at Harwich, Felixstowe and Great Yarmouth, as well as through Stansted and Luton airports. The question was: how and by whom? Whatever was going on, it was all very clever. Nothing was showing up in routine searches, and there was a suspicion of significant insider involvement. This, in turn, suggested a well-organized command, and the availability of a lot of money. There was already enough evidence to arrest a number of handlers and distributors and, through them, an even larger number of street dealers. But that would do little to stem the flow of the drugs. The serious crime squad had set its sights on higher targets.

Jason had gradually infiltrated the ring as a buyer with a view to identifying those further up the chain of command. At first he bought fairly modest quantities, consistent with a substantial, but not huge, commercial retail operation. Over a period of time, and as those he dealt with came to accept his legend, he increased the quantities, and put the word out that he was interested in much more, perhaps several kilos of both heroin and cocaine, on a regular basis. Such a suggestion was calculated to bring someone reasonably high up out of the woodwork. Thousands of pounds would be involved in each transaction. It was a reward not to be sniffed at. But it took some time. Jason's contact for the larger purchases was Barney, an amiable enough Jamaican with a record for simple possession, but not yet for supplying. That was about to change. Barney was not higher management material, and Jason had made it clear to him that, when it came to the larger quantities, he would deal only with someone nearer the top. That was not unusual, and indeed was no more than standard business practice. But he was dealing with very cautious people. It was some weeks before Barney came up with an address where larger transactions might be completed – and with the name of Carl Gibson.

When Jason mentioned that name to Detective Inspector Venn, the officer in charge of *Operation Toytown*, they both smiled with satisfaction. Venn immediately began work on an authorization for Jason to purchase one kilo of heroin and one kilo of cocaine, at the address Barney had supplied, within the next few days.

* * *

'I know you don't want to, Madam President,' Jeff Morris said. 'But my strong feeling is that you should make an appearance at the press conference on Monday morning. They want to hear from you. They are not accepting what I'm saying anymore.'

Ellen had given only one press conference since Dani's disappearance, and she was clear in her own mind that it had not ended well. She had walked out abruptly and the experience had turned her stomach inside out. She had asked Jeff to take the conferences until further notice. There was, after all, nothing she could say except the standard thanks to the British authorities and an appeal to anyone who knew anything to come forward.

The story about the Phoenix drone had become the object of

satire; an oblique and rather tasteless reference had been made to it on *Saturday Night Live*. Mary Sullivan and Conrad Beckers were the only reporters who were still offering a serious daily analysis of the story. The *Wall Street Journal* was chomping at the bit, egged on by *The Guardian*, *Le Monde*, and *El Pais* in Europe. In the Middle East, coverage was becoming even blunter. *Al Jazeera* was pouring scorn on the idea that any Muslim state or Islamist group would be interested in the potentially suicidal business of acquiring a drone capable of being used against the United States. The *Times of India* was speculating about the Indian presence in the Dani Ryan story and pointing to the apparent incongruity of a Middle Eastern connection. Jeff had nothing new to offer the press, and it was only a matter of time – and a short time at that – before headlines were written demanding that the people should be told what was really going on. That was not going to happen. The White House still needed time.

'Conrad Beckers came to see me this evening,' Jeff said.

Jeff had come to the residence to give the President his daily update. As both their partners were together in Cambridge, Ellen dispensed with formality and took Jeff into the kitchen for a glass of wine.

Ellen looked up sharply.

'He came here to see you?'

'Yes.'

'Was he alone?'

'Yes. I wasn't sure whether I should see him, but under the circumstances…'

'No, you were right,' Ellen said. 'This is no time for protocol. We have to keep our fingers on the pulse. What did he have to say?'

'He said what I think we already know,' Jeff replied. 'The drone story is as good as dead. It didn't have the legs to carry us all the way through. In a day or two, they are going to be all over us.'

Ellen stood and leaned against the table.

'It's going to have to struggle on for a few days,' Ellen said. 'We don't have an alternative. We can't tell them the truth, and we can't just say, "sorry, we've been lying to you, but we can't tell you what's going on". Can we?'

Jeff shook his head firmly.

'No. That would be the signal for them to bury us with questions and speculation. We would have lost what little control we have of the situation.'

He paused.

'But whatever we say, Madam President, they need to see you. I think if you were to stand up and remind them of the danger to Dani; tell them that there are diplomatic reasons for not going into more detail; tell them you are in charge and you know what has to be done; and say it strongly from a personal point of view, it might just buy us two or three more days. Maybe not from the foreign press – they are already running with alternative theories – but at least from our own press. Not everyone, obviously. There's no holding *Fox News*. The *Journal* is on the edge, but I think we may be able to pull them back. But it's not something I can do, not without at least one appearance by you.'

Ellen bowed her head. She felt the sensation of nausea returning. But she had spoken to Kay earlier. She had sounded strong, and pleased to be doing helpful things in England. Her visit to Dani's room in Downing College had yielded nothing and had upset her, but she had carried on and was ready for anything else they might ask of her. With her anxiety for Kay lessened, Ellen found the nausea and knots in her stomach easier to deal with. She, too, must be ready for whatever they asked of her.

'I'll be there tomorrow morning,' she said.

'Thank you, Madam President,' Jeff said.

'Did Conrad have anything else to say for himself?'

'I really think he's doing his best to be supportive, Madam President,' Jeff replied. 'He didn't have to come. I think he was offering to help with any point of view we might want to put forward.'

He paused to sip his wine.

'He's concerned about the way Betancourt and others are painting this, as a national security story, suggesting that the White House is betraying the country by giving away military secrets.'

Ellen shook her head in frustration.

'That's a load of crap.'

'Yes, it is,' Jeff agreed. 'But there is a market for it among the hard-core conservative and religious types. It doesn't have to make sense as long as it pushes the right buttons. Conrad says Governor Betancourt is going to make a major speech about it within the next few days.'

'Then he's an even bigger fool than I took him for,' Ellen said.

'Yes,' Jeff said. 'But people are listening. It's one more thing we have to deal with as long as the drone story is out there.'

Ellen smiled grimly.

'God, wouldn't you like it if they caught Betancourt in a brothel, snorting coke?' she asked.

Jeff laughed out loud.

'That is one headline I would love to see, Madam President. And I have the impression that Conrad Beckers would enjoy it almost as much as I would.'

44

June 19

THE TIMES AGREED for Kelly's scheduled calls to Ted Lazenby were noon and 11 pm British Summer Time, though if there was any significant breaking news, she would report immediately, regardless of time. Her first call gave him little cause for hope. She repeated the substance of Steve Macmillan's briefing. Lazenby listened in silence.

'Did you suggest any ways for them to speed things up?'

'They don't see any way to do that without giving the game away to the kidnappers,' Kelly replied. 'They've been given some pretty robust advice about that by someone. There's a feeling here that if you spook these kidnappers, they will kill Dani first and ask questions later. I tried to raise the subject, but Macmillan got a bit defensive about it. They do have a lot of people on the ground, sir, I can't fault them for that. But they are dealing with a vast area – and that's assuming they are right about her still being close to Cambridge.'

'All right, Kelly, but you have to keep trying to find ways to increase the pressure on them. Don't let them off the hook. And for God's sake, don't forget the deadline. We will speak later.'

Lazenby looked up at the clocks on the wall of the situation room. He was expecting Raul Gutierrez and Dave Masterson, with a third party, as yet nameless. They were due in five minutes. The President would be preparing for her press conference, and would not come to the situation room until later. He had plenty of time.

They arrived exactly on time. Gutierrez and Masterson were dressed exactly as they had been the day before and both sported visible stubble. Their appearance suggested a long night and a lack of sleep. With them was a man in his thirties, slightly built, casually dressed in an open-necked shirt and jeans, and wearing a black leather jacket. His face seemed to be set in a permanent suggestion of a smile. His eyes were dark and impenetrable and, despite his build, he gave the impression that it would not be advisable to offend him. He was carrying a large shoulder bag. Lazenby poured them coffee and seated them around him at the table.

'This is "Pendulum",' Gutierrez said.

Lazenby nodded. 'Unusual name.'

Pendulum's smile broadened for a moment, then returned to its fixed state. 'I'll have another one, come the next mission, sir,' he replied.

'That's all you need to know,' Gutierrez said to Lazenby. 'He's with special forces, and he is a specialist sniper.'

Gutierrez reached into the shoulder bag, which Pendulum had placed between them on the floor, and took out what looked like a huge mobile phone.

'Anand Mehra's name is "Kestrel". If you send Pendulum out into the field, this is what you will use to communicate. You will be able to find him anywhere with this, unless he disappears a hundred feet or so under rock, and you can probably find him even then. It's a very advanced mobile. Don't ask me. It's all done with satellites. It's classified and very expensive, so make sure you keep it close to hand.'

He smiled at Lazenby.

'By the way, your name is "Moderator".'

'All right, Pendulum' Lazenby said. 'What can you tell me?'

At a nod from Gutierrez, Pendulum stood and reached into the shoulder bag. He produced a large map, which he spread over the table, as the others hurriedly moved their coffee cups to a place of safety. Any small hesitation he had shown in the presence of three such senior officials vanished instantaneously. A natural authority replaced it.

'This is a map of the Indo-Pakistani area in Kashmir, sir,' he said. 'Secretary Gutierrez indicated to me the general nature of the mission. We spent the night at CIA Headquarters, where I was shown this map, and an itinerary for Kestrel's visit to the area. We checked a number of locations on Google Earth to get a better look. I was able to identify a number of camp sites, which is my term for sites from which the operation could be carried out, along his route.'

'Secretary Gutierrez made it very clear, I hope,' Lazenby interrupted, 'that the operation involves Kestrel *not* being shot.'

Pendulum's smile spread across his face.

'Yes, sir. That shouldn't be a problem. Based on what I'm seeing of the terrain, I would be surprised if I can get closer than half a mile to the target. And I'm told I will be using a SVT-40, so even if I wanted to kill him it would be a matter of pure luck – and that's just the weapon, without even thinking about wind and temperature. Give me my M24 and, no problem, Kestrel is history. But with that piece of …'

'The SVT-40 was a Soviet design,' Gutierrez explained. 'It wasn't accurate enough to satisfy their military, so they sold a lot of them off abroad. The Pakistanis bought some of them. They later upgraded to the Dragunov, which was far more successful. God only knows what the Pakistani army did with them all. But we have intelligence that there are still a lot of SVT-40s in use, particularly among tribal and Islamist groups, and probably also within the army. So it's a credible weapon for our purposes, as well, apparently, as ensuring Kestrel's personal safety.'

Pendulum inclined his head to one side and drew his lips together.

'The only thing I do need to point out,' he said, 'is the possibility of an accident. If the shot has to look like a credible attempt on Kestrel's life, I can't miss by a mile, can I? I've got to come pretty close. I can aim with that intention. But at that distance, there's always a chance I could get too close by accident. Or Kestrel could make a sudden move in the wrong direction. Or it could be something as simple as a gust of wind. All I'm saying is, these things happen. Once the bullet leaves the gun, there's nothing I can do. I have no further control.'

'We all understand that,' Gutierrez said.

'All right then. I'm focusing on what I've marked on the map here as camp site four,' Pendulum continued. He pointed the site out to Lazenby. 'It's just here, near where it says Muzaffarabad. That's the only chance I've got, really.'

'Why?' Lazenby asked. 'What's wrong with camp sites one, two and three?'

'No time,' Pendulum replied. 'Not unless you want to provide me with a helicopter to follow him along his route, which would attract far too much attention during an official tour of inspection so close to the border.'

He bent down over the map.

'Look. Camp site four is directly across the border from the last military installation Kestrel visits, according to his itinerary. He arrives at Srinagar by military transport at 09.00 Indian Standard Time, on June 22. That's only three days from now, and in that time I've got to get myself to Islamabad; meet the guide Director Masterson is arranging for me; get myself up country to the camp site; and scout a location for the shoot. Meanwhile, Kestrel is making his way by helicopter and car north along the border for a couple of days to visit three installations. I've marked camp sites one, two and three correspondingly. Then he makes his way back to the installation opposite camp site four. The estimated time for his inspection of that installation is noon on June 25. After that, he hops on a plane and he's back in Delhi in time for afternoon tea.'

'I couldn't follow him all the way up the border without a helicopter, and even if I could, scouting multiple areas takes time. He's not scheduled to spend much time at each base. I can't rely on having him in my sights for very long, unless they are kind enough to lay on a parade for him to review his troops, and I don't think they go in for that at these border posts. By the time I get myself into the area and scout locations, I'll only just make camp site four in time. Even then, there may be conditions I don't anticipate. So…'

Lazenby stood, and paced slowly up and down.

'So, what you are telling me,' he said, 'is that we only get one shot at this – literally.'

'That's right, sir,' Pendulum replied, the smile spreading again. 'It's a good thing you don't want me to kill him. That would be a challenge. But making it look like a bungled attempt should be straightforward – especially if I'm pretending to be a Pakistani irregular with an STV-40. I'll take the shot and get myself back to Islamabad as quick as I can, leaving the weapon at the scene as evidence. As long as I can get a decent location, I should be able to do that for you – barring acts of God, obviously, as I said before.'

'Who is the guide?' Lazenby asked.

'He's one of ours,' Masterson replied. 'He knows the area and speaks the language. Our resident in Islamabad is arranging the weapon. None of that is unusual in Pakistan – it's one of the few advantages of working there. It won't raise any eyebrows. No one knows any details of the operation.'

Lazenby nodded, and continued walking slowly up and down.

'Ted, are we good to go?' Gutierrez asked. 'If so, we can't waste any time. I need to get Pendulum into Islamabad without delay.'

Lazenby stopped pacing.

'We are good to go,' he replied. 'Give us a couple of minutes alone, so I can establish codes and procedures.'

Gutierrez and Masterson hesitated.

'I'm representing the Commander-in-Chief in this matter,' Lazenby said.

Pendulum looked up at him, puzzled. He was a man who understood chains of command and he thought it was a strange thing for Lazenby to say, given that the Commander-in-Chief was in the building. Strictly speaking, the President was the only person without military rank entitled to give him an order. Gutierrez and Masterson left the room. Lazenby picked up the large mobile.

'How long do these things stay charged?' he asked. 'How will you do that out there in the field?'

'Don't worry about that, sir,' Pendulum replied. 'You could start a small motorcycle with one of these batteries. At the rate we are going to be using them, they're good for a week, at least.'

'I will be your only contact,' Lazenby said. 'Call in at your discretion, when you can do so safely. I will have this with me

24/7, and I need to know where you are, and what your operational readiness is, at regular intervals.'

'Yes, sir.'

'I will need to call to give you an operational instruction. I doubt it will be before you are in position at camp site four, but I will certainly do so then. We will work with codes, each code representing a particular operational instruction. The codes will be known only to you and me. The deadline for my activating a code is 11.30, Indian Standard Time, on June 25. We will call that zero hour.'

'Roger that,' Pendulum replied.

Lazenby turned the mobile over in his hand, apparently quite focused on it.

'Code Alpha means, "abort the operation and return to base immediately".'

Pendulum was nodding.

'Roger that, sir,' he said again.

'Code Beta means, "take a shot, but not to kill – the object being to create the impression of a failed attempt at assassination".'

'What's the default code, sir?' Pendulum asked.

'Code Beta,' Lazenby replied. 'If I do not activate a code at or before zero hour, Code Beta applies.'

Pendulum nodded again. 'Roger that, sir.'

He stood up, ready to leave.

'Finally, Code Charlie means take a shot, and use your best efforts to kill Kestrel.'

Pendulum sat back down abruptly.

'Did I hear that correctly, sir?' he asked after some time.

'You did.'

'That's the first time I've heard any mention of that, sir.'

'Does it disturb you – legally or morally?'

Pendulum was silent for some seconds as he again considered the chain of command.

'That's not my department, sir.'

'Would you obey the order if I were to give it?'

'I would need you to tell me whose responsibility it would be, sir. General Gutierrez didn't say anything about that.'

'It would be my responsibility,' Lazenby said. 'And Code Charlie does not leave this room. It does not go to General Gutierrez or anyone else. Are we clear about that?'

'Yes, sir.'

'Let me reassure you, as far as I can. It is not my intention to activate Charlie.'

Pendulum stared at him.

'Then, with all due respect, sir, why do we need Charlie? In my experience, the simpler codes are, the better they work, and the less risk there is of a mistake. If we aren't going to activate Charlie, why do we need Charlie?'

'Because I'm not quite ready to take any of my options off the table,' Lazenby replied. 'I may want to make myself reject Charlie and activate Beta. If there's no Charlie, there's nothing to reject, is there? Call it a test of resolve, if you like. There may come a time when I need to face that test. I'm sure that sounds strange to you. If so, I'm sorry, but this is a complicated situation, and this is the way I need to set it up.'

Pendulum nodded. He was not reassured. The type of commander he was used to, the type of commander he preferred, was the type who gave definite orders and did not second-guess himself. But things were as they were. And the truth was that after his experiences with special forces, there was not much that seemed particularly strange to him anymore.

'In that case, sir, there is one thing you should know.'

'Go on,' Lazenby said.

'I am very good at what I do. I know what I said before. That wasn't exactly the whole truth. It was a bit of professional modesty, because I don't like to boast. None of us do. It's a superstition. In my job, the day you tell a client that the target is as good as dead, that will be the day you miss. But if you were to activate Charlie, I would back myself from five hundred yards, even with a piece-of-crap SVT-40. It's not guaranteed; it never is. But in decent weather conditions, I would back myself. I thought you ought to know that.'

'Thank you,' Lazenby said.

'I'll call in, once I'm in theater,' Pendulum said.

He picked up his bag, folded the map neatly, stowed it away, and was suddenly gone.

45

June 20

JEFF HAD WALKED up to the residence in good time before the press conference. He had nothing new to brief the President about, except that Governor Hank Betancourt had now scheduled his speech supporting the judgment of God theory for a prayer breakfast hosted by the Dallas Association of Christian Businessmen, to be held at the Adolphus Hotel in downtown Dallas in two days time. Bubba Lanier had been invited as a guest. Jeff wanted to make sure that Ellen was still feeling up to facing the press. She had agreed readily enough the previous evening, but he had seen her eyes, and the sudden departure of color from her face. This morning, she seemed calm and composed. She had abandoned the more feminine look she had chosen for her previous conference. The stern dark gray Nehru suit was back, the sharp high collar of the jacket revealing just a little of the pristine plain white blouse underneath, the trousers precisely creased, the low-heeled black shoes shining. With Agent Sam Davis leading the way, they walked in silence to the press room, where the large contingent of reporters had gathered, waiting expectantly.

As she was announced and the reporters stood, Ellen strode boldly to the podium. Jeff thought she still looked pale, but her manner now seemed assured.

'Good morning, and thank you for coming,' she began. 'Once more, Kay, Dale, and I would like to thank everyone who is working so hard to try to resolve the situation, and to make sure that Dani returns home, safe and sound, before too long. We still have reason to believe that Dani is alive and has not been harmed.

Work is still continuing on identifying a complete script for the second generation Phoenix drone, so that a decision can be made about how to respond to the kidnappers' demands. We are making good progress and we expect to have the process complete within a very few days. I would like to assure you that the business of the White House is continuing in every respect. I am monitoring every aspect of our work, even though my main attention, obviously, is on the job of getting Dani home safely. That's all I have to say. I will take a very few questions.'

A chorus of voices erupted, hands waving pencils held high in the air. Ellen picked a familiar face and pointed.

'Daniel.'

The chorus subsided, though not entirely.

'Thank you, Madam President. Dan Stevenson, *Wall Street Journal*. I'm sure you are aware that there is widespread skepticism about the question of the Phoenix drone, and that there is speculation that the kidnappers have made further demands that the White House has not released. Can you comment on that?'

Ellen swallowed hard.

'Dan, the demand for the plans for the Phoenix drone was delivered to us just after Dani was taken. We are fully aware of the interest of the kidnappers, and we are doing our best to work out how we can best reach a solution which will satisfy them, and will bring Dani home. Unfortunately, I can't stop the press from speculating, but I have no further comment to make on that.'

'Following up, Madam President, does that mean that you are in regular communication with the kidnappers?'

'I can't comment on operational details, Dan, you know that. Kathy?'

'Kathy Branahan, CBS News, Madam President. You said that you continue to believe that Dani is alive and well. Certainly, everyone here is glad to hear that.'

A sympathetic round of applause broke out.

'Should we understand that the kidnappers are providing regular updates to you?'

'Again, I can't comment on operational details.'

Further questions were being shouted out. Ellen held up her

hands for silence. It took some time for the noise to subside.

'Look, everyone,' she said quietly. 'I know you have a job to do. I know this is a great news story. But there are two vital things at stake here: the life of Dani Ryan, and our security as a country. It is my job, my duty, to try to preserve both. I'm sure you understand that it is a difficult task. In order to carry it out, a degree of secrecy is necessary. As I said before, and as Jeff has been saying these last few days, there are questions we cannot answer now without jeopardizing both Dani's safety and our national interests. I believe in a vigorous free press, and I believe that my record in public office shows that. It is my policy to give the press as much information as I can. But you must understand that most of my work at present must go on behind the scenes. As soon as it is possible to tell you more, I will. Please, bear with me for just a few more days.'

Ellen paused to allow her words to settle.

'Kathy, did you have a follow-up?'

'Yes, thank you, Madam President. It's a question that's been asked before, but … how can you reconcile your duty as President to protect the national interest with your concern as a step-mother to see your step-daughter return home safe and well?'

Ellen felt the nauseous feeling start to creep up on her. She was conscious that her heart rate and breathing were becoming faster.

'There is no conflict in my mind,' she replied firmly. 'My duty is to protect our national interests. Getting Dani back safely is not inconsistent with that. If I could tell you more, I could explain that better, but I can't. I'm asking the American people to trust me.'

The chorus of voices was becoming ever louder. She gripped the podium tightly. Out of the corner of her eye, she spied Mary Sullivan, who was sitting quietly, not joining in the general hubbub. She had not indicated any interest in asking a question, but Ellen was sure she had quite a few she would like to ask. She would take a chance with her.

'One more, and that's it,' Ellen said. 'Mary?'

Mary rose to her feet. She looked closely at Ellen. She glanced at Conrad Beckers, who was seated to her right.

'Mary Sullivan, *Washington Post*. Madam President, as President, and also as a step-mother, how have you been affected by the demands for your resignation and by the suggestion that Dani's kidnapping is in some manner linked to the fact that you and Dani's mother live together in the White House? Have you considered resigning, and what answer do you give to those who say such things?'

Ellen nodded. She was silent for some time, and the room fell silent with her.

'Mary, before saying anything else, I want to thank you, and many other reporters here today, for your thoughtful and restrained coverage of this question. I am glad that the press is presenting the American people with a more responsible approach to it than they have received from some other quarters. I don't think there is any need for me to name names. There are many things I could say about this, but let me confine myself to just three. First, there is no actual connection between Dani's kidnapping and my relationship with Kay. If there were, that would have become clear once the ransom demand was received.

'Second, I repudiate the kind of primitive superstition that suggests that God would place Dani in harm's way because of my relationship with Kay. That suggestion is not a religious statement. It's a political statement designed to further the political careers of those who make it. It is also a form of hate speech based on my sexual orientation which, in my view, has no place in any civilized society. I'm not trying to stifle debate. If I decide to run at the next election, the voters will have the opportunity to make their opinions known, and I am sure the press will provide a forum for that to be done in the appropriate way before the election.'

She looked slowly across the room.

'Lastly, as a woman and a step-mother, I cannot begin to describe to you my contempt for those who say they are glad that Dani has been taken and may be lost to us. If they intended to hurt Kay and myself, then they have succeeded – they have hurt us very deeply. I won't hide that from you. But they have not brought us down, as they intended. Indeed, dealing with this has made us stronger, and more sure of our love than ever before. This is not the end of this matter. I cannot respond adequately to these people while this crisis is going on, but I will do so when the time is right. For now, I say only that I hold them in the utmost contempt, and I ask the press to continue to hold a mirror up to them, so that people can see who and what they really are.'

Ellen drew herself up to her full height and gripped the podium firmly.

'No, I have not considered resigning, and I will not consider it. Thank you.'

She turned and walked out of the room, leaving the silence unbroken.

46

HELEN SHOWED THE two visitors into John Mason's office, and offered coffee.

'Thank you. Black, no sugar,' Conrad Beckers said.

'Not for me, thanks,' Mary Sullivan said.

Mason shook his head, and Helen left the room quietly.

'This is an unexpected surprise,' he said smiling, waving them into the comfortable armchairs in front of his desk. 'It's not every day I find two such doyens of the press corps in my office at the same time. To what do I owe the pleasure?'

Beckers reached into the inside pocket of his suit jacket for his Mont Blanc pen. He had no immediate intention of taking notes; that might come later, depending on how things went. But he was so used to feeling it in his hand when he spoke that he felt almost felt naked without it.

'We wanted to talk to you about Governor Hank Betancourt,' Beckers replied.

'Oh? What about him?'

'Many informed observers are saying that the Governor is the odds-on favorite for your party's nomination, come the next presidential election,' Beckers said. 'If they are right, it suggests that the Committee has given him its blessing.'

Mason smiled. 'That's very flattering, Conrad. But informed observers say all kinds of things, don't they? That's what makes your show so interesting. Your articles in the *Post*, too, Mary. Where would we be if the pundits could find nothing to disagree about? It's far too early to start making predictions. We're still several months from the start of the primary campaigns.'

'Nonetheless,' Beckers persisted. 'I've learned to read the

entrails during the course of covering presidential elections over many years. One of those entrails is the Wilson Foundation, which is the same thing as saying the Committee.'

'The Committee is simply a group of senators, congressmen and party loyalists, who concern themselves with strategy matters,' Mason said. 'The Wilson Foundation is simply a think tank which provides information services to the Committee, and to the party as a whole.'

Beckers laughed. 'That's rather like saying that the senior lion in the pride is just a cat, isn't it?' he asked. 'I don't know whether you keep statistics on things like this – I bet you do – but did you know that no candidate has secured your party's nomination during the last forty years without the endorsement of the Committee, which in effect means the endorsement of the Wilson Foundation? And coincidentally, John, forty years is also more or less the length of time that the Wilson Foundation has been in existence.'

Mason smiled modestly. 'I believe that is true,' he conceded.

'I also happen to know that Alex Vonn is expecting to run Betancourt's campaign,' Beckers added. 'Alex is a member of the Committee, of course, and it's well known that he is not a man to jump into a campaign without a serious indication that he is backing the right horse.'

Helen reappeared with a cup of coffee and sugar on a small silver tray, which she placed in front of Beckers. He smiled his thanks, and she left, discreetly, soundlessly.

'So, let me come to the point,' Beckers said. 'Governor Betancourt is in danger of stepping over the line. Mary and I agree on that and, given what is at stake – for him and for your party – we felt a sense of obligation to warn you, in the hope that you may take corrective action before it becomes too late.'

Mason sat upright in his chair, and folded his arms across his chest.

'I haven't the faintest idea what you mean,' he said.

'You know exactly what I mean,' Beckers replied. 'But, for the record, I am referring to his vocal support for Bubba Lanier in calling on the President to resign because of her relationship with Kay Ryan, and his support for Lanier's view that the kidnapping and likely murder of Dani Ryan represent the judgment of God against the President.'

Mason tightened his lips.

'Firstly, Conrad, the Wilson Foundation has no control over what Governor Betancourt chooses to say on any particular subject.'

'Control? No.' Beckers replied. 'But the Committee has considerable influence in the matter.'

Mason paused for a second or two.

'And secondly, while you and I may not personally agree with what Lanier says, the expression of his views is protected speech under the First Amendment, and the Wilson Foundation is not in the business of suppressing free speech.'

'Forgive me for saying so, John,' Beckers continued, 'but I have no doubt that the Wilson Foundation is perfectly capable of discouraging free speech if it has the potential to do the party harm. And in this case, believe me, it has the power to do the party considerable harm.'

Mason smiled. 'Really? How do you figure that?'

'It's not complicated, John,' Mary Sullivan broke in. 'Betancourt and Lanier are making a very personal attack on the President while she is trying to rescue Dani Ryan from almost certain death, while at the same time discharging her duties as President. Some people feel that it is an attack on the country, just as much as on the President. If so, it is a deeply unpatriotic thing to do – almost a hint of treason about it, some might say – not to mention the casting off of any last shred of basic human decency. And all for party political gain and personal ambition. It's not a pretty picture, is it?'

Mason placed both hands on his desk and leaned forward. His voice became animated, his usual urbane smoothness temporarily abandoned.

'Unpatriotic?' he replied. 'And this from an administration which is negotiating with terrorists, which is about to hand over military secrets to a terrorist group?' He paused. 'And that's if you believe what they say. I don't. I think the truth is even worse.'

Beckers smiled. 'You don't believe them?'

'No, I don't believe them,' Mason replied firmly. 'And neither do you.'

'Well, perhaps not,' Beckers agreed. 'But consider, just for a moment. If what the administration is saying is true, all they have to do is put together some plans and specifications that basically work, and build in some tracking device, so that if the terrorists do ever try to activate a drone, we can blow them to kingdom come before they can do any harm. Child's play. No risk to national security there, is there?'

Mason sat back in his chair.

'On the other hand,' Beckers continued, 'suppose you are right. Suppose the stakes are even higher. Suppose further that Dani Ryan is murdered, and that some worse harm befalls the country. Suppose both of those things. What are the American people going to say about a candidate – or a party – that supported a vicious personal attack on the President while she was trying to save the country from those outrages? I think Mary put it rather well, don't you?'

'More than a million people seem to agree with Governor Betancourt that the President should resign,' Mason pointed out.

Mary Sullivan smiled. 'Yes, but they're not exactly swing voters, are they? Those are votes you already have in the bank. If you are to have any chance of beating Ellen Trevathan in the next election, you need the swing voters, those who are undecided. They tend not to like putting partisan party politics before the national interest and, for the most part, they seem to dislike personal abuse and negative strategies.'

Mason was silent for some time.

'I don't think they will see Governor Betancourt in that way,' he said.

'Yes, they will,' Mary replied quietly. 'I will make it my personal business to make sure that they do.'

'As will I,' Conrad Beckers confirmed.

John Mason's jaw dropped.

'I don't believe this,' he protested. 'Aren't you forgetting your journalistic ethics here? What about the principle of the press remaining impartial?'

Mary smiled. 'Oh no, John, we haven't forgotten the rules. We're just taking a leaf out of one of our rivals' play book. We have a duty to be impartial and report the news, but that doesn't mean we can't be patriotic at the same time. That is the theory, isn't it?'

'This is outrageous…' Mason spluttered.

'No, it's not,' Beckers answered. 'We will do things absolutely professionally. All views will be fully represented. Your party will have all the air time you want. But we will have a lot of impressive footage of whatever disaster America may sustain to follow you with. That may well include, unfortunately, the funeral or memorial service for Dani Ryan. The editorial coverage will be another matter. That will be distinctly patriotic, and it will raise the question of who put America at risk by undermining the President in our hour of need. If the public were to get the idea that it was your party, that would be a lot for the party to recover from. Editorial coverage is our choice. There's nothing unethical about that.'

Mason brought a hand down forcibly on his desk.

'I cannot believe that you would come here to threaten me,' he said. 'I will take this up with the chair of the Committee, Senator O'Brien.'

'I hope you will,' Beckers replied. 'I have the highest regard for Senator O'Brien. I've interviewed him several times. I can't believe that he would have any truck with someone like Bubba Lanier.'

He paused.

'And I'm not threatening anyone, John, certainly not you. Nor is Mary. We are here to offer you some information. It would be irresponsible of us not to. What use you make of that information, or don't make of it, is up to you.'

He stood. Mary did likewise.

'John,' Beckers said. 'We three have known each other for a long time. You know that Mary and I have no party bias. We call it as we see it, and we put the hard questions to both sides. You know that. We are here because what's happening is wrong. You know that as well as we do and, if you choose to, you can put a stop to it.'

They walked to the door, where Beckers paused and turned around to face Mason.

'And if Joe O'Brien were to say something to distance the party from Lanier on this, I think it would be very well received by the media as a whole,' he added.

* * *

John Mason took some time to calm his rising temper, and then placed what turned out to be a long call to Senator Joe O'Brien. When the conversation ended, he called Helen on the intercom.

'Call the Governor's mansion in Austin and tell them I need to speak to Governor Betancourt urgently,' he said.

It was an hour before Betancourt called back. In the intervening period, Mason trawled the internet for statements Betancourt had made about Bubba Lanier, about the demand for the President's resignation, and for details of what Betancourt proposed to say to the Dallas Association of Christian Businessmen. His anxiety increased with each item he uncovered. Helen, he realized, would already have them all on file, and so would a lot of other people.

'John, what may I do for you this fine day?' Hank Betancourt asked, with his usual grating drawl.

'Governor, I need to talk to you about the speech you're planning to give in Dallas,' Mason said.

'Yes, indeed,' Betancourt replied. 'That speech is going to get a lot of people talking, John. It's going to tell the truth. I believe it will put a lot of pressure on the President – really move us forward.'

'That's why I need to talk to you about it,' Mason said. 'I have just spoken to Senator O'Brien. The Committee does not believe that it is in the party's best interests to support what Lanier is doing on this.'

There was silence for some time.

'But John, this has real traction,' Betancourt protested. 'Do you know how many signatures we have on the petition?'

'I know that, Governor. And it was fine while it was just a general condemnation of what the President and Kay Ryan are doing in the White House. But it's gone a lot further than that now. Lanier appears to be saying that Dani Ryan's kidnapping is a judgment from God, and you have made some statements which could be construed as agreeing with him.'

'What if I have?'

'Governor, what Lanier has said could almost be construed as an incitement to kill Dani Ryan. At the very least, it explicitly condones her kidnapping, and hints that it may even be justifiable, that it may be the will of God. The party can't go on record as subscribing to views such as that. And, frankly, neither can anyone who has a serious ambition to be the party's nominee in the next presidential election.'

Mason heard the intake of breath on the other end of the line.

'Are you saying that, if I go ahead with this speech, the Committee will not endorse me for the nomination?'

'I have said what I intended to say, Governor. I've told you the Committee's view. It's up to you to decide what importance, if any, that has for you. The Committee has not made any decision about endorsement of a candidate. I cannot tell you what to say, nor would the Committee wish to do so. That's up to you. My task is only to place the Committee's opinion on the record.'

Betancourt hesitated.

'John, I have the greatest of respect for the Committee. But I believe they may be a little out of touch with the prevailing public sentiment.'

Mason had had enough. It was already feeling like a long afternoon.

'The sentiment you are referring to is confined to fundamentalist conservatives ...'

'... who represent the backbone of this party ...'

'... in some states where they think it's still 1862, and who do not represent the prevailing sentiment. The Committee understands that you need to appeal to them, and they have no problem with that. But as our nominee, you have to appeal to the American people as a whole. The American people as a whole do not agree that it's all fine and dandy for Dani Ryan to be kidnapped and murdered. In fact, almost every American wants to see her come home safely. The problem is that you are trying to undermine the President during a time of national crisis, while she is trying to get Dani home safely. It's not the Committee that's out of touch with prevailing public opinion, Governor.'

'You have no right to tell me what I can and can't say.' Betancourt had raised his voice now. He was almost shouting. Mason wondered whether any of his staff were in the room with him, listening in. If they were, surely they would drop him a hint of some kind?

'I've already made that clear, Governor. The Committee is not telling you what to say, or what not to say. The Committee has a duty to maximize the party's chances of taking back the White House, and for that purpose we would have to recommend the candidate who has the best chance of appealing to a broad spectrum of voters. I'm sure you remember the price certain of our opponents paid for throwing rocks at George W Bush after 9/11, Governor. We don't want the same thing happening to us, do we?'

There was a long silence, though Mason could hear no whispered conversations, no indication of dissent, on the other end of the line.

'I will be giving my speech in Dallas,' Betancourt said at length. 'After that, I will be speaking to some other people. John, I hate to say this, because I have always had a high regard for you, and there is a place on my staff for you any time you want it. But I have a feeling that this Committee of yours may have outlived its usefulness. Maybe it's a result of spending all your time in Washington and being out of touch with the people across America. But, in any case, we may need to rein it in, and start handing back power to the folks working in the field. I'll be sure to give your best regards to Bubba Lanier.'

He hung up.

* * *

'Get me Selvey,' Mason said brusquely, when Helen answered the intercom.

Even though they had worked closely together for many years, Mason did not know a great deal about Selvey. The Committee knew even less. That was how all concerned preferred it. Selvey enjoyed working for Mason. The money was good, and Mason never asked questions about how he got things done. He had offered his services to Mason and the Wilson Foundation in the interests of financial reward rather than ideology. Selvey was a fixer; he had a fixer's cynical view of life, and was skeptical of ideologies. He suspected, accurately, that he had that much in common with John Mason. Just now, his star was in the ascendant. He had gathered vital evidence to help convict Steve Wade in the impeachment proceedings. In so doing, he had made himself look good to John Mason; he had made John Mason look good to the Committee, and the Committee to the party. Everyone was happy.

But Selvey had another particular role, which was known to John Mason because it was often useful to him. It was this role that mattered to Mason today. Selvey had been a confidential informant of Mary Sullivan for years. They were chalk and cheese in terms of personality and background – Mary came from a wealthy Massachusetts family, Selvey from an alcoholic home in Hell's Kitchen – and they did not get on smoothly. But Mary found his insights into behind-the-scenes political stories invaluable, and was quite happy to overlook the cultural differences to take advantage of them. What Mary did not know was how Selvey came by many of his insights. She did not know of Selvey's connection to the Wilson Foundation. Both he and John Mason had always been careful to conceal it from her.

'There are two people who are causing concern,' Mason said, when Selvey answered the phone.

This was coded language between them.

'How much concern?'

'Serious.'

This also was code.

'Names?'

'Hank Betancourt and Bubba Lanier.'
'Time frame?'
'Rush job. Sorry.'
'Leave it to me, Mr Mason. I'll see what I can do,' Selvey said.

47

June 21

THE ADDRESS BARNEY had given Jason was in Tenison Road, not very far from the train station. 'Cheeky bastards,' he thought, as he walked the final few yards, 'talk about hiding in plain view!' The undercover officer was excited about the prospect of a major arrest, the culmination of many months of painstaking work. But he was also nervous. Barney had seemed genuine about the offer of an introduction. Jason had promised to spend an enormous amount of public money, a sum which ought to reassure even the most cynical of dealers, and his back-up was just around the corner in an unmarked van, just one touch of a key on his mobile away. DI Venn and DS Morgan had briefed all the officers involved in *Operation Toytown* with care earlier in the morning. All foreseeable eventualities were provided for.

But in Jason's field of work, the line between success and disaster was thin and unstable. Paranoia was the normal state of mind for most drug dealers, and paranoia could change the game in a flash. The higher up a dealer was in the chain of supply, the greater his level of paranoia. When you dealt with a player like Carl Gibson, you could expect to negotiate your way through any number of levels, and each negotiation involved infinite care. He was grateful for the cover bought by the expenditure of earlier public funds – Jason sometimes wondered what the average member of the public would say if he knew how much of his taxes found its way into the pockets of drug dealers in the course of any given year – and as he rang the bell, he hoped that cover would be enough to last one more day.

The house had two main storeys and a basement. In its heyday it might have been a single family residence, but that day had passed and the building had long been divided into separate flats, no doubt mainly for student occupation. Like much student accommodation in Cambridge, the whole building was showing signs of benign neglect. The paint was beginning to flake, the woodwork in the windows was beginning to crumble in places, and no one had tended the small area of grass and flowerbeds outside the basement windows for a considerable time. The basement was where Jason had his appointment.

He walked briskly down the three steps that led from the street to the basement door and rang the bell. He wondered, in a disinterested professional way, who had the lease on the basement flat. No one who knew what was going on, that was for sure, no one who could be linked to Carl Gibson or his immediate associates; probably a graduate student short of funds who could be relied on, in exchange for some ready cash, to make himself scarce when the flat was needed for business, and could be relied on not to ask any questions. After the arrests he would be interviewed, would pronounce himself shocked at the abuse of his hospitality, and would in all likelihood be released with a warning, once DI Venn advised the Crown Prosecution Service that his prosecution would not be in the public interest, given his presumed level of involvement and the doubtful prospect of conviction. So it went in Jason's field of work.

Jason knew the man who opened the door as Charlie. In the course of *Operation Toytown* he had bought drugs from Charlie with his public funds on many occasions, one or two wraps of heroin and cocaine at first, to gain his confidence, then ever-increasing quantities leading to the serious commercial deal on the table today, which had, it seemed, finally brought him to the personal attention of Carl Gibson. Jason submitted without protest to the routine frisk. The hallway before him seemed to lead directly to the kitchen. To his right was a door leading into the combined living room and bedroom of the small flat. Another man was leaning against the wall. The name this man used was André. André was no street dealer. Jason had seen him at a distance from time to time, keeping an eye on things as the street dealers worked, but it was to police intelligence that Jason owed what he knew about André; Hungarian by origin, he had led a life of serious crime in several European countries. He had served time in France and the Netherlands, but for relatively short periods, and for offences less serious than those of which he had often been suspected. His current role was thought to be chief of operations for Carl Gibson.

André gestured Jason to enter, and followed him into the room. Whoever had the basement lease had allowed his living room to become a wreck. The bed was unmade. Unwashed cups and glasses lay on the floor, together with discarded items of clothing and unopened correspondence. Only one battered lamp supplemented the limited natural light from the low windows. On the cheap wooden coffee table were two glass ashtrays overflowing with cigarette ends. Also in evidence were a set of electronic scales and several small plastic bags containing a white powder.

'You have the money?' André asked. His accent was harsh and guttural. Charlie had followed him into the room and closed the door.

'I have it.'

'I don't see it,' André said.

'My associate has it,' Jason replied calmly. 'Do you have the stuff?'

André nodded vaguely in the direction of the kitchen.

'Can I see it?'

'As soon as I see the money.'

Jason smiled, shaking his head. Moving slowly, he took a pack of Marlboros from the inside pocket of his leather jacket, and offered them around. André accepted and Jason offered him a light before lighting his own. Charlie declined.

'Those things will kill you,' he said, with a nervous laugh.

Jason nodded. 'Well, we all have to go eventually, don't we, Charlie?'

He turned back from Charlie.

'You're André, right?'

'So?'

'Nothing, nice to meet you,' Jason said, extending his hand. André took it reluctantly. 'They say you're Carl's main guy.'

'People say a lot of things,' André replied cautiously.

'So, where's Carl?'

'*I'm* here.'

'I can see that, André. I asked where Carl is.'

'I handle the deals for Carl.'

'Not today,' Jason replied definitively. 'The deal today is, with the quantity we are talking about, I'm supposed to deal directly with Carl. You understand, I'm representing some serious people. These people are putting up serious money here, and they intend to put up more serious money in the future, assuming that they receive the level of service they require. So it's nothing personal, but my instructions are to deal with Carl.'

'What the fuck?' André asked petulantly. 'You give me the money, I give you the stuff, what the fuck do you care who you deal with?'

'No,' Jason said. 'From what I hear, the difference is that Carl doesn't fuck around when it comes to business. That's what I hear, and that's all that interests me.'

'So who's fucking around?' André demanded.

'Anyone who thinks I am going to walk in here on my own with the price of a kilo of white and a kilo of brown, and hand it over without seeing the goods. I'm not some fucking amateur, André. Show me some respect.'

'The goods are here,' André insisted.

'Good. So show me. Give me a taste.'

André hesitated. 'Where did you say the money was?'

'I didn't. What I said was, my associate has it. He's parked nearby. He can be here in less than two minutes. All I have to do is call him and say I have seen the stuff and tasted it, we've confirmed the weight, and it's all OK. Now, where's Carl?'

Suddenly, Jason heard a new voice.

'All right, all right, keep your hair on. Don't give André the hump, there's a good lad. Everything's under control innit?'

The voice, with its pronounced cockney accent, belonged to a middle-aged man with thinning dark brown hair, dressed in a chequered light and dark brown suit and a bright yellow tie. He had entered quietly through the door leading into the kitchen. He had obviously been listening, weighing the situation up, just outside the living room.

'Give me one of whatever you're smoking.'

Jason shook a cigarette loose, allowed Carl Gibson to take it, and lit it for him. He surveyed Gibson as he lit another cigarette for himself. The tone of Gibson's voice was light, but there was no mistaking the serious intent. Gibson had left the sound of Bow Bells behind him many years before, and now presented himself as a respectable businessman based in Peterborough. His children were being privately educated. Both he and his wife had expensive tastes when it came to their house, cars and jewellery.

This ostentation was the only weakness in his running of a sophisticated international business specializing in the importation of Class A drugs. There had been rumors about him for several years, but it was only when the Drugs Squad's forensic accountant was satisfied that the Gibsons' expenditure could not be accounted for by their Scandinavian furniture business that the case against Carl Gibson had begun to come together. And even now, it hung by a thread. Gibson was careful to mix only in the best of circles. None of the dealers knew of his existence. Even his closest associates saw him only when strictly necessary, and none of them saw the whole picture. Only the biggest deals, the most important clients, could expect his personal attention. It had taken DI Venn a long time and much persuasion to procure the money necessary to put Jason in the position of an important client, but now, perhaps, they were about to learn how Carl Gibson was bringing in and distributing Class A drugs along with his Scandinavian furniture.

Gibson drew deeply on the cigarette.

'So, you're Jason, then? I've heard a lot about you. And thanks for not using the old line about wanting to deal with the organ grinder, not the monkey. We get that a lot. It really pisses André off, doesn't it, André?'

André had retreated silently to the wall behind the bed.

'I'm not here to piss anyone off,' Jason replied.

Carl nodded. 'No, I can see that. They're all wankers, anyway. You're not a wanker, obviously, Jason. But you never know, do you? I have to rely on André to let me know what I'm dealing with. I don't get involved in the day-to-day stuff much anymore, you understand. All I want to know, Jason, is what sort of market I can expect from your people. What sort of quantity are we looking at, and how often?'

'My people can dispose of at least two kilos of each roughly every six to eight weeks,' Jason replied. 'As long as we can rely on the quality. The money's not a problem as long as the quality is OK, and we can rely on regular delivery your end. And while I'm on that subject, I'm not exactly overjoyed with this place. I would prefer somewhere a bit more discreet, given the quantities we are talking about.'

Gibson nodded. 'Yeah, you've got a point,' he conceded. 'Not to mention that it's a bloody slum,' he added, looking around. 'I don't know how people can live like this. I'll get somewhere better for next time. Might even lay on coffee and biscuits.'

He looked carefully at Jason, and eventually turned to André.

'He's all right,' Gibson said. 'Bring the stuff in.'

He turned back to Jason.

'You don't mind getting the money here at the same time, do you, Jason? I'm sure we trust each other now. Is that all right?'

'No problem, Carl,' Jason said.

He took out his mobile and punched a key.

'My associate will be here in no time at all.'

48

'THE TIME IS 8.30 am on June 22. We are in interview room A at Cambridge Police Station. Those present are myself, DI Venn, and DS Morgan of the regional serious crime squad; Mr Carl Gibson, who is being interviewed; and Mr Ken Chamberlain, Mr Gibson's solicitor.'

Detective Inspector Arnold Venn paused for a deep draught of his latte. It had been a long night and he had managed to snatch only a few brief moments of sleep as suspects arrived at Cambridge Police Station. He wanted to be sure that his fatigue did not lead to any mistakes. At the same time, he was elated. *Operation Toytown* was a spectacular success. In addition to Carl Gibson, his officers had arrested a number of other high-ranking members of a massive importation and distribution ring based in Cambridge and Peterborough. They would all be interviewed throughout the day. Large quantities of heroin and cocaine had been seized at Gibson's warehouses. Some foreign contacts appeared to have slipped through the net and fled the country. But a sizeable collection of documents abandoned in haste would identify them, and would probably explain how Gibson had imported Class A drugs into the United Kingdom under cover of his furniture business, and who had helped him to do it. Interpol would be on the lookout for the foreign contacts, and his own officers would round up a large number of smaller players – street dealers and local organisers – at their leisure over the next few days. Jason's evidence of so many undercover deals would be more than enough to convict them. But Venn was going to start at the top.

'Mr Gibson, you are still under caution, as you were when you were arrested. I will remind you of the terms of the caution. You are not obliged to say anything, but it may harm your defence if you do not mention, when questioned, something which you later rely on in court. Anything you do say may be given in evidence. Would you like me to explain that in more detail?'

'That's not necessary,' Ken Chamberlain replied.

'All right, thank you.'

'Mr Gibson understands the caution. I can also confirm that he and I have had the opportunity of a private consultation. On my advice, Mr Gibson will answer "no comment" to all questions put to him at this time. This is a highly complicated case, and so far we only have a vague outline of the allegations. Once we see the evidence, we may respond in more detail at a later time.'

Venn nodded. 'Thank you for making that clear, Mr Chamberlain. Nonetheless, I will put certain questions to Mr Gibson in line with the disclosure I have provided to you this morning, which I suggest is considerably more than a vague outline. First of all, Mr Gibson, you were arrested at an address in Cambridge yesterday afternoon in the company of two individuals who have significant criminal records. Also found at that address were four brown paper packages enclosed in cellophane, which we believe to contain a total of one kilo of heroin and one kilo of cocaine, as well as two sets of electronic scales, supplies of cellophane wrapping and a large sum in cash. Can you explain your presence on those premises at that time?'

'No comment.'

'Are the drugs yours?'

'No comment.'

'Is the money yours?'

'No comment.'

'While you were on the premises, you entered into an agreement to sell the drugs to an individual known to you as Jason, is that correct?'

'No comment.'

DI Venn sat back in his chair and put his papers down on the desk. He already had at least two hours' worth of questions to put to Gibson and, as the papers which had been seized revealed further details, the number of questions could only grow. There was no rush. Gibson was going to be charged with importing Class A drugs and he was going to be remanded in custody, a fact to which he and his solicitor were already resigned. But Venn's instinct told him that a quicker breakthrough might be possible. Gibson's 'no comments' sounded definite enough, but Venn thought he detected a wish to be cooperative, to say something more, perhaps to offer something. It might be in Gibson's best interests as well as those of the police. Solicitors meant well, but they sometimes got in the way. Silence was not always the suspect's best option. Sometimes it was better to speak out while there was a chance.

'Mr Gibson, I know that Mr Chamberlain, with his experience, has fully advised you of the sentence you are likely to receive for offences of importation of Class A drugs. I also know he will have advised you of the discount the courts give for early pleas of guilty.'

Chamberlain raised his hand. 'There's no need to go into all that, Inspector. Whatever I may have said to Mr Gibson, and whatever he may have said to me, is privileged. You're not entitled to ask about that. I have already told you …'

'I understand, Mr Chamberlain. I don't intend to go into privileged matters. My point is that Mr Gibson might also benefit if he were to be of assistance to police in other ways.'

Gibson looked across at his solicitor meaningfully.

'Such as …?' Chamberlain asked.

Venn shrugged, then glanced at DS Morgan, who looked on impassively.

'Various things come to mind. In no particular order, we believe that there are substantial quantities of Class A drugs which we have not yet recovered. If we were able to take these drugs out of the chain of supply, that would be of importance to us. There are various individuals still at liberty who we believe to be involved in this matter. We would like to arrest these individuals, if we can find out who they are and where they are. Some of them may have gone abroad. And we would like information about the methods used to import the drugs, so that we can be on the lookout for those methods in future. In some ways, that would be the most valuable assistance you could give, Mr Gibson, and I know you could give it if you chose to. As Mr Chamberlain knows, the courts give substantial discounts for assistance of that kind to police, in addition to any credit for an early plea. So, what about it, Mr Gibson? Once others start talking to us, and I guarantee they will, it may be too late.'

'As I said before, Inspector …' Chamberlain began. But Gibson interrupted.

'Hang on a minute. Not so fast. I think I would like to speak to my solicitor again.'

Venn nodded.

'All right,' he said, for the benefit of the tape recording. 'It is now 8.38 am I am suspending the interview so that Mr Gibson may confer further with his solicitor. I will stop the tape now. Please let us know when you are ready to resume.'

'Do you really think he's going to give us something, sir?' Morgan asked. They had taken Gibson and his solicitor to a nearby conference room, then walked out into the hallway and waited until the doors were closed .

'Possibly,' Venn replied. 'Gibson is a shrewd character. Must be, to have got away with his business on this scale for so long. He knows he's going down for at least fifteen years, in all probability. Chamberlain has been around the block a few times too. He's told him what the score is. I wouldn't be surprised if he starts clutching at a few straws.'

While he finished his coffee, Venn made a few calls on his mobile, receiving encouraging word about the progress of the mop-up operation. As he was about to place another call, Chamberlain emerged alone from the conference room. He looked shaken. Venn signalled to Morgan to join them.

'I think you had better come into the conference room, Inspector,' Chamberlain said.

Venn shook his head. 'With all due respect, you know better than that, sir. Any interview must take place in the interview room so that it can be recorded. Otherwise the judge may not allow any of it in. I'm not allowed …'

'We can put something on tape later,' Chamberlain insisted. 'Mr Gibson wishes to say something to you in private. He has told me what it is, and I suggest that you do as I ask, and do so without delay.'

Venn and Morgan exchanged glances.

'All right, sir,' Venn replied. 'If you have no objection. But it had better be good, or I am going to resume the interview immediately.'

Gibson was seated on the far side of the table. Chamberlain sat beside him. Venn and Morgan took the seats opposite.

'All right then, Mr Gibson,' Venn said. 'Let's have it. What have you got to say to us?'

Gibson took a deep breath.

'What would it be worth if I could give you something that might help you find that American girl?'

The officers gaped at him, speechless, for some moments.

'What? You mean …?'

'Yeah, the one that's been missing, the President's daughter. What if I could help you find her? What discount would I get for that?'

Venn stared at him.

'I can tell you what you'll get if you fuck us around with something like that, mate, and it won't be a discount, believe you me.'

'I'm not …'

'I'll start with wasting police time. After that …'

'I'm not fucking around with you. I know something. I can't guarantee a result, but I know something and, I'm telling you, it's worth your while to take a look at it.'

He smiled unpleasantly.

'Bit of a feather in the old cap if you were the one to find her, Guv, and no mistake. You'd be a regular hero, wouldn't you?'

Venn's first instinct was to reach across the table and strangle the man. But Gibson had him. He could not take the chance of ignoring possible information about Dani Ryan. Every police officer in England was on the lookout for her. There was only one thing to do. He turned to Morgan.

'Get Special Branch here,' he said. 'Quick as you can.'

He turned back to Gibson.

'Fuck with Special Branch and see what happens, mate,' he said. 'By the time they're finished with you, you'll be praying to do fifteen for importing Class A.'

49

'THEY DIDN'T WARN you to expect this?' Murchie asked. 'What were they thinking, for God's sake?'

Pendulum took a deep breath, placed his backpack and the long carrying case on the ground, and squatted on his haunches.

'They weren't thinking,' he replied. 'It was all arranged too quickly. No time to worry about the details.'

They had just arrived on a thickly-wooded hillside above campsite four. The Indian military installation that Anand Mehra was scheduled to inspect on the following morning was clearly visible through the trees, some three-quarters of a mile distant. But so, somewhat closer, was a Pakistani Army command point, from which guards could keep constant surveillance on the Indian forces and be prepared for any confrontation at a moment's notice.

Pendulum had flown to Islamabad under diplomatic cover. Murchie had met him at the airport, and had conducted him up-country using back roads and cross-country hikes – uncomfortable but safe. Murchie had brought with him green camouflage uniform for both of them, and a Soviet-made STV-40 sniper's rifle in a green camouflage carrying case. Murchie's family was from South Carolina. His parents had lived in Pakistan for some years, working as teachers. They moonlighted as Christian missionaries, holding services and evangelical meetings and distributing Bibles. When those activities became too dangerous, they packed up and went back home to South Carolina. But Murchie, by then a 19-year-old natural entrepreneur, decided to stay. The gospel message had not quite taken with him. Even at that tender age, he had made the acquaintance of some shady characters who had introduced him to lucrative activities – such as smuggling drugs, arms, and sometimes people across the porous Indo-Pakistani border. He knew the country intimately, and he knew how to avoid attracting the attention of the ubiquitous police and military presence in the densely-forested mountainous border area. But he was playing a dangerous game, and his luck could run out at any moment. Before it did, he came to the attention of the CIA's Islamabad resident, who knew a potentially valuable asset when he saw one, and put Murchie on the payroll, on condition that he kept out of trouble with the police. Since then, Murchie had more than proved his worth in the area of intelligence and, occasionally, local covert operations.

Murchie was used to having to deal with the mess caused when those higher up failed to plan things as carefully as they should. It was frustrating, but you just had to carry on and make the best of it. You had to make adjustments on the ground, often without too much time to think it through. That was what had happened now. Locally, everyone knew that the Indian and Pakistani forces matched each other across the border, every installation or post faced by a presence directly opposite on the other side of the border. All visible on Google Earth, if you knew what to look for. Someone should have seen it, or asked for advice. But that was too much to ask for. Murchie understood Pendulum's frustration completely. But just in case, Pendulum was spelling it out for him.

'I wanted to be at least two hundred yards further downhill,' he was saying. 'From there I would have a decent shot. But now, I'll have to find a position closer to the ridge. It's well over half a mile, and there's a bit of a breeze blowing – not to mention all those trees.'

'You're worried about the Pakistanis giving chase as soon as they hear a shot?' Murchie asked.

Pendulum nodded.

'The boys down there are not your problem,' Murchie said. 'Look at that terrain. It would take them an hour or more to get here on foot. Besides, they are going to be too busy returning fire across the border once the Indians figure out what's happening and start to react.'

He shook his head.

'No. Your problem is that the boys down there are going to call for reinforcements as soon as it goes up. You're going to have troops arriving on the main road just above us, and you're going to have helicopters all over the place. We have to be on the other side of the main road before they arrive. That doesn't give us much time. Think of how we got here, and remember we are going back uphill.'

Pendulum thought for some time.

'So, I'm figuring that my position has to be no more than a hundred yards down from the ridge.' he said eventually.

'Even that's cutting it fine,' Murchie replied. 'But with a little luck, if we really push it, we ought to make it. Response times in this sector are not what they could be.'

'How fit are you?' Pendulum asked.

'I've been running over these hills most of my life,' Murchie grinned. 'And I'm used to the altitude. You'll get tired before I do.'

Pendulum thought again.

'It makes the shot next to impossible,' he said. 'I'm not even guaranteed a straight shot; there are too many trees.'

Murchie smiled.

'It's just as well they don't actually expect you to kill anyone, then, isn't it?'

Pendulum looked thoughtfully down through the trees at the Indian installation.

'Yes,' he replied. 'Isn't it?'

50

'I ASKED YOU a question,' Bev insisted.

He was speaking as loudly as he could without actually shouting. At first he had been ambivalent about his incarceration in the bedroom. The lack of freedom to move around was unpleasant, but he had accepted that it might be a necessary alternative to a police cell where he would be at the mercy of Special Branch. He realized all too well how precarious his position was, how easily he could be implicated in Dani's kidnapping. But, on the other hand, how would that change once the situation was resolved? Where would he go from here? What would he do? He was seated on the sofa in the main living room before being returned to the bedroom after lunch. The curtains, as always, were drawn, and no lights were burning. Kali and Samir were seated on the hard wooden chairs opposite him, their weapons not drawn, but obvious.

'And I told you I wasn't going to answer,' Samir replied.

'We are not allowed to talk about operational matters, Bev,' Kali added. 'It's not secure. Everything will become clear in a few days. Please be patient until then.'

'All I am asking is, what is going on?'

'You read the newspapers. You know what's going on,' Kali replied.

'What? That nonsense about wanting plans for a drone? What does Svatantra Kashmir really want …?'

'I told you not to use that name.'

'What in God's name does SK want with a drone? Do you think you can drive Pakistan out of Kashmir with drones? Not to mention the Chinese?'

'That's not our concern.'

'Nobody believes that story any more.'

'That's not our concern.'

'Even the *Wall Street Journal* doesn't believe it any more. The BBC says …'

Samir stood.

'Enough,' he said to Kali. 'I have better things to do than listen to him.'

'Bev,' Kali said, 'things are not always what they seem. Our job is to follow the orders we have been given. Others are responsible for the strategy. Again, I tell you, in a very few days all will be clear.'

'What if it's something they can't do?' Bev demanded.

'What?'

'What if it's something no President could possibly agree to do. It can't be the plans. I mean, they would give you the plans to get Dani back.'

'Oh, really?'

'Of course. Why not? They could write some fault into them that would make the plans useless, but it would take you six months to find the problem, if you found it at all. SK probably doesn't have anyone capable of reading them, in any case. They would give them to you in a heartbeat. If that was really the deal.'

He extended the forefinger of his right hand towards Kali.

'But that's not the deal, is it?'

She spread her hands wide.

'I don't know. That's the truth, Bev.'

'What do you think?'

'I don't think.'

Bev stood up. 'Well, I *do* think. And what I think is that your people have given the Americans a demand they can't possibly meet, and when they say no, you're going to kill Dani. That's what I think.'

Samir sneered. 'Is that the best you can do with your famous western education? That it's all about Dani Ryan? Why don't you see it from the other side? Why don't you ask yourself about Kashmir, what Kashmir needs? She needs her freedom, and that is why we are doing this.'

'Dani Ryan is a human being, and she needs to live.'

'So do the thousands of our people the Pakistanis kill.'

Bev moved towards Samir and they stood face to face. 'I helped you to get close to her because you told me no harm would come to her.'

Kali also stood and approached, standing not quite between them but very close.

'It was I who told you that, Bev, and that was my intention and my desire. It still is. But circumstances may change.'

'I would never have done this if I had thought …'

'Then you are not worthy of being Kashmiri,' Samir said.

Now Kali did step between them, gently but firmly, pushing them apart.

'We abhor violence, Bev,' she said quietly, 'those of us who work in this cause. We are chosen partly for that reason. That is why we are sometimes called upon to exercise violence. Only those who hate violence can be trusted to exercise it, because we do so only when it is necessary, and we do it with regret.'

Bev flung himself back down on to the sofa.

'I have heard that crap all my life,' he shouted. 'And you know what, that's all it is, a bunch of crap. What the hell does it matter whether you regret killing someone if you kill them anyway?'

'It makes all the difference in the world,' Kali replied. 'Only in that way do you kill as a warrior, and only then is your intention pure, and your karma pure. Only then will you be reborn with honor. If I have to kill Dani Ryan I will do so gently and, as far as I can, with love. I hoped you would understand this, Bev.'

'Well, I don't,' Bev said. 'And I won't let this happen.'

Samir smiled. 'Oh, really? And how exactly do you plan to prevent it? Not by killing myself or Kali, I hope. We need to live too.'

Kali was not fast enough to stop Bev as he hurled himself at Samir. Samir was almost thrown off balance, but Bev had launched himself from a seated position, and he lacked the momentum to take Samir down. Samir pushed him away, drew his automatic, and struck Bev violently in the face with the butt. Bev fell to his knees, his hands up to his face. Blood was flowing from a gash on his cheek. Kali went to the kitchen and returned with a wet towel. She knelt, took Bev's hand from his cheek and began to wipe the blood away.

'He goes downstairs with her now,' Samir said to Kali. 'We can't risk having him up here any longer. We can't trust him. They can amuse themselves discussing what the demand is.'

Kali nodded. 'I think he would prefer it in any case,' she said quietly.

51

WHEN THE CALL came, Kelly and Steve broke off a conference with the Home Secretary and the Director of MI6. They rushed to Steve Macmillan's car and, with the aid of the flashing blue light to force their way through the traffic, were being briefed by DI Venn at Cambridge Police Station within fifteen minutes. The Home Secretary was not pleased by the abrupt end to the call. He had spent an hour on the phone with Vice President Ted Lazenby earlier in the morning, and had listened at some length to a lecture on the need to find Dani Ryan before the American Government was obliged to surrender the plans and specifications for the second generation of Phoenix drones. Lazenby had seemed rather vague about the deadline for surrendering the plans, but the Home Secretary was left in little doubt that the time was fast approaching. He would have much preferred to stay on the phone and press Macmillan further about what he and the officers under his command were doing, but Macmillan made it clear, respectfully but firmly, that he needed to leave.

They walked into the conference room with DI Venn and found seats. DS Morgan had remained in the room throughout with Gibson and Chamberlain, and uniformed officers had brought in several extra chairs, making the small room rather too crowded for comfort.

'This is Carl Gibson, and this is his solicitor, Mr Chamberlain,' Venn said. 'I'll let you introduce yourselves.'

'Mr Gibson, I'm DI Steve Macmillan of Special Branch. With me I have Kelly Smith, the Director of the United States Federal Bureau of Investigation, and Agent Rosa Linda Montalbán of the United States Secret Service.'

Gibson sniggered unpleasantly.

'I'm duly impressed,' he said.

Macmillan pointed a finger towards his face.

'Lose the attitude,' he replied. 'I won't say that again. You may be a big-time drug dealer, Mr Gibson, but I assure you, you are well out of your depth here. Please try to understand that you are dealing with people who have serious responsibilities and very little time to spare, and who have the power to fuck with your life in ways you can't even imagine. So I'm going to ask you to tell us whatever you have to tell us quickly, but precisely. Mr Chamberlain, you may remain or leave, as you wish. But if you choose to remain, you will remain silent unless asked a question. You will also either have to sign a declaration under the Official Secrets Act regarding the secrecy of this meeting, or be kept in custody once it ends, pending the resolution of the present crisis.'

Chamberlain looked up sharply.

'I don't think you have the power ...'

'Yes, actually I do have the power, and I have the express support of the Home Secretary in using it. Whether I *should* have that much power we can debate later in calmer circumstances, and when we do, I may even agree with you. But I don't have time for that today. What's your decision?'

Chamberlain took a deep breath. 'I'll sign the form,' he replied.

'Good. Now then, Mr Gibson, what have you got to tell us?'

Gibson had shrunk back in his chair, intimidated by the array of officialdom suddenly interested in listening to him. But he had not forgotten the opportunity that good fortune had placed before him; and he saw that he had to seize it now, while it remained available.

'What's my discount going to be?' he demanded sullenly.

'If you tell us the truth,' Steve Macmillan replied, 'and if the information you provide gives us a chance of rescuing Dani Ryan, the discount you get will make your head spin. This is the chance of a lifetime – if you're telling the truth. Don't screw it up.'

'I'll need something in writing,' Gibson insisted, 'to show the judge.'

'You will have it,' Macmillan promised. 'Everyone present has heard me say that, including your solicitor. And whatever you tell us is off the record as far as the drugs charges are concerned. I've confirmed that with DI Venn.'

Venn nodded his agreement.

'So, there you have it, Mr Gibson,' Macmillan said. 'Start talking.'

Gibson looked slowly around the room, then down at the table, and finally pulled himself forward in his chair.

'My associates employ a number of individuals to help them distribute the product,' he said. 'I try to tell them to hire reliable people. But you know what it's like. You can't get good help these days, can you? Most of them are not all that bright, and many of them don't have their heads on straight because they use too much of the product themselves. Most of them have been in trouble with you lot. God only knows what they get up to when they're not working for us. Anyway, there's this one guy, local lad, late twenties, one of André's boys …'

'Name?' Steve Macmillan asked.

'Carter, Wayne Carter.'

He nodded to DS Morgan, who stood, took out his mobile and, moving to the door, began to speak in quiet tones, half turned away from the others.

'Go on.'

'Well, Wayne's not too bright, poor lad – a couple of wraps short of a kilo, if you take my meaning. But he's reliable; that is to say, he shows up for work on a regular basis and, even when he's had a few jars the night before, he's not messed up. He's a decent driver, and he's got a bit of form for GBH, so André finds him useful.'

'All right, get to the point.'

'So, a few days ago, André comes to my place in Peterborough to pick up a consignment for London. He's brought Wayne with him, because he's had a bit of aggro with the client in the past over the money. I've met Wayne a few times by now, so I'm OK with him. But it's been a busy day, and by the time they get to me it's getting a bit late for a London run. I prefer to do those in the day time, less conspicuous.'

'And the point …?'

'I'm getting there, I'm getting there. So, with it being so late, André and Wayne decide to bed down in the garage and get an early start. We have a few drinks during the evening, just to be sociable, and Wayne has one or two more than is good for him. He starts talking about this girl being kidnapped and how it was all down to him. At first, we didn't know what he was talking about, did we? To be honest, I thought he was trying to impress me with what a big bad man he was, you know, Wayne Carter playing in the major league. André and I were taking the piss out of him and telling him he was full of shit, but he wouldn't shut up about it. And finally, it was André who worked out what he was talking about. André says to him, "you're talking about the American girl, the one who's on the TV, aren't you?" Wayne didn't deny it.'

Gibson smiled.

'So now, we're all over him, aren't we? "Oh yeah, Wayne, you tosser, you're just the person they would need for that job, incha?" But he still won't give it up, will he? He was the driver, he says, they needed someone who knew his way around the area. And then he pulls out a stack of bills. "Look at that", he says. "Didn't get that doing twenty-quid deals on the street, did I?"'

Steve Macmillan leaned forward. 'I'm betting you're a man who can read a stack of bills, Mr Gibson' he said. 'How much was it?'

'A lot,' Gibson replied, non-committally.

'Not good enough. Try harder.'

'Three or four grand, easily. Could have been five. Way above Wayne's pay grade, let's put it that way.'

'It could have been legitimate income.'

Gibson snorted. 'Wayne Carter, legitimate income? Don't make me laugh. Wayne wouldn't know a legitimate income if it bit him on the arse. I made a joke out of it, didn't I? I said, "André, what the fuck are you doing? You're paying this guy too much." But André wasn't laughing, and neither was I once I stopped to think about it. We were starting to believe him, and we didn't need that kind of stuff going on around us, believe you me. Bad for business, I reckoned. If the Old Bill came sniffing around Wayne because of that, I could be in all sorts of trouble.'

'Did you ask him any more questions about it?' Macmillan asked.

'One or two, but he didn't want to talk very much. He seemed to sober up a bit when we started asking questions. He said they were not the kind of people to mess with. He could get in trouble if he said anything.'

'Did he say anything at all?'

Gibson looked up directly at Macmillan. 'Yeah,' he said. 'He told us the people who hired him were Indian, a man and a woman. He said they told him where to drive to in Cambridge to pick the girl up. That's all he would say. Then he buggered off and went to sleep. I told André to keep an eye on him. I didn't want to believe him at first. But I think I do now.'

'Why?'

'It's the money, innit?' Gibson said. 'Whoever paid him that much wasn't from around here. That's serious money round here, and no one who knows Wayne Carter is going to hire him for a job that pays four grand.'

He laughed. 'Fucking wanker. He'd have more chance of playing for Manchester United.'

Macmillan turned questioningly towards DS Morgan, who was still in conversation and lifted a finger, which clearly meant: 'give me a moment'.

'You wouldn't happen to know where we might find Wayne Carter, would you, Mr Gibson?'

Gibson smiled.

'Well, if you lot haven't nicked him last night, I would imagine he is probably at home drinking away his ill-gotten gains. I don't know the address, but it's in Swavesey. He's got a bird there he's shacked up with. I think they've got a kid, about a year old. That's what André says, anyway.'

52

SAMIR MARCHED BEV briskly at gunpoint across the living room, through the kitchen, and down the steep flight of stairs that led to the basement. Kali followed, her weapon also drawn, her movements ostensibly casual, but precise and focused.

The basement was dimly lit. Dani had been trying to sleep, without much success. She was restless and anxious. Her system of transferring small pieces of paper from pocket to pocket had kept her aware of how long she had been in captivity. But, as each day went by, she had become less confident of being rescued. She knew that she was not far from Cambridge. The police must be searching the area systematically, and it sometimes seemed maddeningly frustrating that no one had found her. Perhaps they had even come to the building, she thought sometimes, and Kali had talked them round, overcome any suspicions they may have had. That wasn't hard to imagine. Perhaps there were just too many buildings to search. Unless the police had some kind of lead, how would they ever find this one? Worst of all, she had no idea how much time she had left before any rescue would come too late.

When the door was thrown open and she heard the hurried footsteps on the stairs, she rolled over quickly, and with some alarm. When she saw Bev, her jaw dropped; she sat up in disbelief. Samir virtually pushed Bev down the last two stairs and across the floor, where he came to rest, sprawled next to Dani. As Kali gave him cover, Samir swiftly added manacles to Bev's wrist and ankle and to the chain that held Dani. He stood and began to walk away.

'We'll leave you two love birds alone. I'm sure you have a lot to talk about,' he sneered.

The door banged shut and they were gone. Bev slowly dragged his body across the floor until he could lean against the wall. He closed his eyes.

Dani was in shock. For some time, she could only stare at Bev, trying to make sense of what was happening. He did not seem to be in any hurry to enlighten her. Eventually, she reached out a hand and touched his arm.

'Bev, what are you doing here? What's going on?'

He kept his eyes closed, and did not reply. After some time, she repeated the question. This time, he did open his eyes, and she saw that they were filled with tears.

'Bev, ...'

'I'm sorry, Dani. I am so sorry. I had no idea.'

She stared at him blankly. 'Bev, what are you talking about?'

He lifted his head and looked at her directly.

'This is all my fault,' he whispered.

'What?'

'I led them to you. I told Kali you would be in the Castle at 6.30 that Friday. I betrayed you.'

It took Dani some time to digest what Bev had said. It made no sense to her. She shook her head.

'I don't believe you.'

'It's true.'

She brought both her fists down hard on to the mattress beneath her.

'I don't believe you.' She was almost shouting. 'What are you telling me? You're with them? You're a terrorist? I don't believe it. I spent time with you. I got to know you. My Secret Service agent checked you out before we even left the States. This is too ridiculous. This is bullshit.'

Her voice had risen in pitch and she was speaking very fast. She stopped abruptly. 'Why? Why would you do that? It doesn't make sense. I don't believe it.'

She leaned back against the wall and buried her head in her hands. Bev gave her some time.

'I'm not a terrorist,' he said. 'I had no idea they were going to kidnap you. I would never have agreed to that.'

She raised her head and threw her arms out to her sides.

'Then, how is it your fault?'

'Kali said they wanted to talk to you,' he replied. 'That was all. They were going to see you at 6.30 to talk.'

'To talk? What about?'

'She didn't say. I thought they probably wanted to pass on some message through you to President Trevathan, something political. She said I should ask you to be at the Castle at 6.30, and I could come at 7 o'clock. She said they would have finished speaking to you by then, and that would be it. I swear to you, Dani, I had no idea what their plan was. I went to the Castle at 7 o'clock and waited. When you didn't show up I was worried. I walked around and looked for you. Eventually I went back to Downing and checked your room. I thought you might have missed me and gone straight back. I was getting frantic by then.'

He sighed deeply. 'Then the police came to see me, and I knew it had all gone wrong. I'm sorry. I would give anything to be able to turn back the clock, do it differently, warn you, not let this happen...'

They were silent for some time. Then she touched his arm again.

'It's not your fault,' she said. 'If they wanted to know where I was going to be, all they had to do was follow me. I was wandering around Cambridge on my own most of the time. My agent said it wasn't possible to shadow me 24/7 – not without making my life unbearable. Even my step-mother says they can't guarantee to protect her against every eventuality. If someone is prepared to trade their life for hers, that's it. She didn't want me to have my every move tracked in England, and I wouldn't have wanted that either. Kali seems like a very resourceful and intelligent woman. She would have got to me somehow, even without you.'

'I made it a lot easier for them,' Bev said quietly. 'You trusted me. I would love to be able to think it made no difference, but it did.'

'It was a small thing compared to what she did,' Dani said. 'I forgive you.'

Bev bowed his head. 'Thank you,' he whispered, barely audible. Dani sat up straight.

'But I still don't understand, Bev. How do you know Kali, how did you come to be involved with her. I mean, who is Kali? Who is Samir? What do they want?.'

Bev took a deep breath.

'Kali and Samir are members of a group called Svatantra Kashmir, SK for short. That's their Hindi name. It means *Freedom for Kashmir*. They are dedicated to freeing Kashmir from Pakistani and Chinese interference, and making the whole of the territory of Kashmir subject to Indian control and under the domination of Hinduism. They are very secretive. No one really knows who they are, where they are based, or what their resources are. But they have the reputation of being efficient and ruthless. That's what I thought they wanted to talk to you about, getting some kind of political message to the President about Kashmir.'

Dani put a hand over her mouth for a moment.

'And what do you think now?'

'Now, I think they have made some kind of demand to the President as a condition of your release. We are waiting to see what she will do about it.'

Dani shook her head. 'But what demand? I haven't had any access to information since I've been here. I'm completely in the dark. What is the demand? Do you know?'

'Officially,' Bev replied, 'the demand is that the United States hand them the plans and specifications for a new generation of unmanned drones called Phoenix drones. The White House has been saying for almost a week now that they're looking into it.'

Dani stared at him vacantly. 'Looking into it?' she breathed.

Bev reached out and took her hand.

'That's what the White House keeps saying,' Bev said. 'But I don't think that's the real demand, Dani. I don't think that's what's going on. And neither do the media, except for one or two sources that are trying to provide the President with cover. If that were the real demand, the President would have agreed to it right away. Those plans are of no use to SK. Even if they had them, they wouldn't know what to do with them.'

'But why would the White House put out the word about a false demand?' Dani asked.

'Obviously, to conceal the real demand.'

'And what would that be?'

Bev shrugged. 'That's anyone's guess. But I would be surprised if it didn't have something to do with Kashmir. That's the only thing SK cares about. And it may be something the President can't do, or doesn't want to do. Maybe that's what they are really looking into at the White House.'

Dani released Bev's hand and closed her eyes for a while. Abruptly she changed the subject.

'What are the media saying about Ellen Trevathan, about my mother? Have you heard anything?'

'Nothing about your mother directly, that I've seen,' Bev replied. 'They've kept her out of sight. The President has only given one press conference that I know of. Everyone says she is holding up well, but …'

'She will be going crazy,' Dani whispered, 'my Mom and Dad too.'

'Yeah, I think everyone is assuming that, but no one is asking too many questions about what is actually going on in the White House. Oh, and she and your mother are getting it in the neck from this redneck preacher, Lanier, an ultra-right-wing religious nutcase talk radio host in Dallas. According to Lanier, God's wrath is about to descend on America because of your mother and the President living in sin in the White House, and your kidnapping is God's judgment, the first of many we can expect, apparently. He is organizing a petition demanding that the President resign. So far he's persuaded close to two million of his fellow nutcases to sign it.'

Dani buried her head in her hands again, and cried softly.

'My Mom will go crazy,' she said. 'She won't make it.'

'You're staying strong, Dani,' he replied gently. 'I bet your Mom will, too. She just wants to see you again.'

There was a long silence.

'I didn't answer your question, did I?' Bev asked.

She looked up and shook her head. He ran his hands through his hair.

'My family is Kashmiri. They came to the States before I was born. They were sent by SK. My grandparents died in a religious massacre carried out by some Muslims in their village near Srinagar. I only found that out just before I left to come here. Until now, my parents had always fed me a story about a cholera epidemic. But the truth is, they were murdered. My father is an intelligent man, but in his grief he was an easy target for SK. That's the way it has always been in Kashmir, violence followed by revenge, people against people, religion against religion. My father is a dentist, an educated man, a cultured man. But even he couldn't break the pattern, or didn't want to. He was perfect for what SK wanted. They wanted to plant a family in the States for future use. He and my mother were perfect, totally above suspicion. They helped my parents to get their Green Cards, and they supported them financially, settled them in Houston, where there's a large Indian community.'

'Future use?' Dani asked incredulously.

'That refers to me, mainly, even though I wasn't even born at the time. I'm the asset they really wanted. I'm Indian, ethnically speaking, I speak some Hindi, I go to the temple with my parents. But the world sees an all-American boy. The world sees a boy who went to college, who got into law school. In the future, maybe I would get into politics, or business, or even just practice law. I might make some money, or get into a position of power. Maybe then, I could be of more use to Kashmir than a hundred guys shooting over the border on the ground. I'm an investment.'

Dani nodded. 'I understand.'

'The deal is,' Bev continued, 'that one day they can ask you for a service – something to repay the financial investment they have made, the comfortable life they have provided. You can refuse to do it – that's the funny thing – and, if you do, they go away and don't bother you any more. But then again, you can't refuse. I don't know how to explain it...'

'I understand,' Dani said again.

'You never know what it's going to be until they ask. It may be something easy – give some money, use some influence – something you can do without interrupting your life too much. Or it might be something that costs you your life.'

'So they asked you to help them get to me?' Dani asked quietly.
Bev took some time to reply.

'I didn't know I was their asset until just before I left to come
to Cambridge. When they explained, they told me that I would
receive a request for service while I was here. I had no idea what it
would be, Dani, I swear. They don't tell you anything you don't
need to know, nothing at all. I was given instructions to meet Kali,
and even then she didn't tell me what was really going on. Just that
I was to arrange to meet you at the Castle, and be late showing up,
so they would have time to speak to you.'

Dani nodded. 'And then you would be off the hook?'

Bev laughed bitterly. 'Off the hook, service complete, yes. I
would be free to return home, practice law, make money, marry
Shesi, have kids, live the American dream. All for one small
service.' The tears returned to his eyes. 'All for betraying you.'

'What does it mean to you, Bev?' she asked suddenly. 'Kashmir.
All right, your parents chose this path for you before you were
born, but …'

He shook his head.

'You have no idea, Dani. It was there every day of my life,' he
replied. 'I would go to the temple, I would listen to my parents
talking over dinner, I would read the books they gave me. It was
never overt, though; they would never try to indoctrinate me in so
many words. They would talk about Kashmir, but not about using
violence to liberate it. They would teach me to love Hinduism, but
not to hate Islam. But it was like a constant drip, an unspoken
conversation that never took place. And then there was this guy –
we called him the Visitor – who would show up from India every
couple of years, just to make sure we were still on message. And
the message got through – how our people had suffered; what we
stood for as a family; what I was expected to stand for.'

'It was a subtle indoctrination' she said.

'Yes. But, for all that, I kept telling myself that I would break
the cycle. Kashmir was a long way away. I'd never been there. I
might never go there. It had nothing to do with me, not in any real
way, you know? I told myself I was growing up as an American.
Kashmir was just a headline on the evening news, something

happening to other people. And I read about other kids who had opted out – Bosnian kids, Irish kids – who said, "no, enough, no more, not me". And they managed it. So why shouldn't I?'

He paused.

'I really thought I had put my parents' past behind me.'

'But you couldn't. Not entirely.'

'No. In the end, you can't entirely. It's in your DNA. And however much you pretend otherwise, it will find you out one day.'

'So, there's some part of you that supports what Kali is doing?' she asked.

The question appeared to take Bev's breath away. He struggled in vain for words. She took his hand.

'I'm not blaming you, Bev,' she said gently. 'The way you were raised, how could it be otherwise?'

'I was so sure I wouldn't compromise what I believe,' he said finally. 'In my mind, I drew a line in the sand. If there was something I could do to help them that didn't involve violence, I would do it. But I would draw the line at violence. I would not become a terrorist. That's what I promised myself, swore to myself. And now …'

'You haven't become a terrorist,' she said, still in a gentle tone.

Bev raised his arm with the chain that held both of them.

'But look at us. What do you call this?' he asked, a note of despair in his voice.

'Foolishness,' she replied eventually. 'That's what I call this. But it's not your fault. It started long before you and I were born. It will go on long after we die. And we are both victims of it.'

'I'm going to make this right, Dani,' he said suddenly. 'You are walking out of here unharmed.'

She shook her head and smiled sadly.

'Don't feel badly about it,' she said.

53

June 23

'SO, THIS IS Swavesey,' DS Morgan began, using his baton to point to the spot on the giant map of Cambridgeshire he had hung on a large screen up against the wall of the hastily-improvised situation room. Doug Morgan was a local lad, born and bred in the fen country around Ely, and he knew the area like the back of his hand.

As soon as Carl Gibson had given up the name of Wayne Carter he had made a series of phone calls and, within a few minutes, he had obtained Carter's address, registration information about his white van, and details of his criminal record for serious assaults, drug dealing, and the occasional burglary. A short time later he also had the layout of the small bungalow which Wayne Carter rented from month to month from one Michael Bowler, ostensibly a respectable racehorse trainer at nearby Newmarket but, according to police intelligence, also a lower-level associate of Carl Gibson. Morgan made a mental note to have Bowler brought in for a chat at a later date, but today he had no time for routine drug squad inquiries. He was overseeing the fitting out of the situation room in the bowels of Cambridge Police Station and, at the same time, briefing the team on the local geography and what, according to local records, they could expect to find within Wayne Carter's place of abode. As he spoke, officers he had never seen before were quietly carrying in computer and telephone equipment, which would soon give the situation room the capacity to communicate with agencies around the world.

The team included a sixteen-strong unit of the terrorist

squadron of the 22nd Special Air Service, the SAS, the cream of Britain's élite special forces; fourteen men and two women, highly trained in covert operations and hostage rescue situations. The unit was under the command of Captain Simon Walker-Jones, a fresh-faced but serious young officer, who enjoyed the absolute respect of his troopers. The unit had been on standby as part of the search team ever since it had become clear that Dani was still in the United Kingdom.

At the insistence of the Secretary of State for Defence, the search team as a whole was technically under the joint command of Captain Walker-Jones and DI Macmillan, but they were also required to consult with the Director of the FBI, Kelly Smith, as representative of the United States Government. This was an awkward political arrangement, which the Secretary of State felt had been forced on him. He had been caught up in refereeing a dispute over chain of command, not only between his own military and civilian authorities, but also between his own military and the Americans. The Americans had, none too subtly, expressed a preference for importing members of their own special forces to take a combat role if necessary, and had further suggested that any British forces would then operate under their command.

Seething, he had approached the Prime Minister to inform him of this suggestion. Alastair Vaughan had looked up briefly from his desk. 'Ellen Trevathan knows better than that,' he said. 'Tell them to fuck off – in the nicest possible way, of course. See if you can keep them happy without having them getting in the way.' Since then, the Secretary of State had fended off senior American military officers on a regular basis, until, eventually, he complained to Vice President Lazenby that the constant demands were interfering with the search for Dani.

At that point, the compromise of consultation was reached. As experienced professionals, Walker-Jones and Macmillan had taken it all in their stride. They had immediately established a protocol. Macmillan would command all police operations, and would decide on the timing of any military action to be taken, but would consult with Walker-Jones before taking his decision. But once a military operation began, Walker-Jones would be in sole command until the operation was concluded. Kelly had reassured them that, while she might have suggestions to make, she would not get in their way. As a further conciliatory gesture to the Americans, Macmillan had asked Rosa Linda Montalbán to join the search team. He had imposed a total ban on anyone divulging the information they had received from Gibson, who was being kept in custody, in isolation, until further notice.

'Swavesey is about nine miles north-west of Cambridge,' Morgan continued, pointing on the map with a long baton. 'and about three miles south-east of St Ives. Carter's bungalow is here, on the outskirts of town, between Boxworth End Farm and Thorpe's Farm. If you turn off the A14 here, at Boxworth End, you come right to it. This is the preferred approach. The road takes you straight to the house without going into town. If you approach from the other direction, you have to drive right through town. Swavesey is a fairly quiet little town, with a population of less than 3000. Depending on the time of day, you would be fairly conspicuous in anything other than nondescript vehicles. And even then, typical small town, you know, people notice ...'

Captain Walker-Jones nodded.

'I agree,' he said, glancing at Steve Macmillan.

'The main concern,' Macmillan said, 'assuming that Carter is our man, is that if Dani is not at that property, she might be somewhere not too far away. I doubt that Carter would offer his own place to keep her in, but we can't risk having the entire town of Swavesey talking about us.'

DS Morgan now had the layout of the Carter bungalow up on the screen, using the overhead projector.

'It doesn't look big enough to hold someone in,' Kelly observed. 'It looks like only two rooms, one to the right of the front door, maybe the living room, then one to the left down the corridor a little way, could be the bedroom. The area to the rear of the living room is probably the kitchen. I don't see any out-buildings. You would need a bigger place for a hostage if you're going to be holding her for some time. Steve, couldn't we get a thermal reading on the property? We know there should be three people in there – Carter, his girlfriend, and their child. Unless it has a basement, which isn't shown on the plan, that should tell us whether Dani is likely to be there.'

Steve Macmillan bit his lip. 'That would mean either flying a helicopter over the property, or taking the risk of getting someone close enough in on foot. There's no cover, and it's set back at least thirty feet from the road with large windows in the front.'

'The nearest houses are a good couple of hundred yards away,' Morgan pointed out.

'Even so, too much of a risk,' Walker-Jones said. 'If they get any inkling at all about us being there, it's all over. In any case, our entry strategy doesn't change. If Dani's there, we have to go in quick enough and hard enough to prevent any harm from coming to her. If she's not there, we still have to neutralize Carter before he can even make a phone call. That's all it would take to tip somebody off. Obviously, there is a risk that we may attract some attention. But we have no real choice here.'

'In that case,' Macmillan replied, 'my vote would be, we approach from the A14 in the early hours.'

'Agreed,' Walker-Jones said. 'Can we keep the house under observation between now and then?'

'I have unmarked cars driving by every fifteen minutes, without stopping,' Morgan said. 'So far, there is no sign of activity, no coming or going at all. Carter's van is parked in the driveway and hasn't moved.'

'What kind of van?' Macmillan asked.

'Honda, white, beaten up,' Morgan replied, 'I've got someone working on getting the vehicle's history.'

'It could be the vehicle used to snatch Dani,' Kelly said.

'Could be,' Macmillan agreed. 'I've asked for a tap on any landline there may be at the bungalow, but I'm hearing that there may not be one. We're checking for a mobile for Wayne.'

'I recommend entry at about 03.30,' Walker-Jones said. 'Typically, people are deeply asleep at that hour, defences are down and, if the intel about Carter's drinking is accurate, we should be able to overcome resistance before he realizes what is happening.'

'Agreed,' Steve Macmillan said.

'Don't forget they have a very young child,' Kelly cautioned. 'That tends to disrupt normal sleep patterns.'

'It does indeed,' Doug Morgan smiled knowingly.

'Knowing what we do about Wayne Carter,' Macmillan responded, 'I would put money on the girlfriend being the one to get up and sort the baby. But we will keep an eye out. The unit will notice if there are lights on, and we will re-assess if we have to.'

'I'm going to need some time with my people and the house plans, to draw up a detailed plan for entry,' Walker-Jones said. 'After that, we will eat, and rest for a while. Let's plan on leaving at 02.30.'

The meeting ended.

* * *

Kelly took a deep breath. Time was fast running out. Her deadline was only two days away, and it was weighing on her mind. Her morning call to Ted Lazenby had revealed a state of rising anxiety, even resignation, within the White House. The Phoenix drone story was unraveling quickly, and the true deadline they faced was looming. Until the team had been given the name of Wayne Carter she had felt herself slipping into the same state of resignation. The prospect of finding Dani in time seemed hopeless, so far away. But now, something had shifted. They had a chance, and the chance was real. Somehow, she had to meet the deadline, and she hoped to meet it with time to spare.

There was still a lot that could go wrong. All that was needed for disaster to strike was a last-minute change of plan in Srinagar, for someone to decide to get Anand Mehra home to Delhi an hour or two earlier than originally scheduled. On such details their chance of rescuing Dani depended. Ted Lazenby had insisted that no one should be told about the kidnappers' real demand. But they were running out of time. She had to find a way to convey a sense of greater urgency. Quietly she asked Steve Macmillan and Simon Walker-Jones to meet with her privately in the Chief Superintendent's office.

'There's something I need to tell you,' she said. 'This is just between the three of us. It can't go any further. But we need to find Dani before 07.30 on June 25 – that's two days from now. We have less than 48 hours.'

Both men were taken aback.

'Because …?' Steve asked.

Kelly bit her lip, then looked directly into his eyes.

'I can't tell you that, I'm afraid.'

Simon Walker-Jones put his hands on his hips.

'Are you telling me for the first time that we have a deadline? Now?'

'Yes. I'm sorry, Simon. It's something …'

Walker-Jones shook his head vigorously 'I don't like having to make operational decisions for non-operational reasons. I especially don't want to do so on the basis of whatever navel-gazing is still going on in Washington about whether to hand over a few diagrams to some band of rag-tag criminals. We are about to embark on a very dangerous operation, Kelly. I'm putting lives at risk here, including your hostage's life. Deadlines change everything in a rescue situation. I've been given no official briefing about a deadline. Are you telling me that position has now changed?'

'I need you to understand,' Kelly said. 'I am not providing any official briefing. I'm just telling you I need the operation to be complete before 07.30 on June 25. Ideally, I would like it completed significantly before that time. I can't tell you what to do in terms of conducting the operation, Simon. It's your call. I can't tell you why. But that's what I need. I hope you will understand that I wouldn't ask this of you unless I had a good reason.'

Walker-Jones shook his head.

'There are deadlines, and there are deadlines,' he said. 'We get deadlines all the time. Sometimes the deadline is real. But often, after the dust has settled, it turns out that it wasn't so much a deadline as somebody's idea that it would be nice to have things resolved quickly. Any deadline changes the calculations. It changes the methods of carrying out the operation, and it changes the degree of risk that is acceptable.'

'He has a point, Kelly,' Steve agreed. 'I understand that you may not be able to tell us everything, but can you at least give us some hint of how serious the deadline is? Could it change? What is at stake if we don't meet the deadline?'

Kelly turned her back on them for a moment, leaned on the Chief Superintendent's imposing wooden desk, and closed her eyes. She turned back.

'You did not hear this from me,' she said quietly.

'Agreed,' Steve said.

Walker-Jones nodded.

'The story about the plans for the Phoenix drone is just that – a story,' she said. 'It is a cover for the kidnappers' real demand. I can't tell you what that is. Believe me, I just can't. What I will tell you is that it is something that no President of the United States could agree to. If the President does not comply with the demand – or we don't find Dani – by 07.30 two days from now, Dani is dead. And we have no reason to think that will change. That's the reality of it.'

Both men were silent for some time.

'It would have been nice to know that earlier,' Steve said. 'We have been working closely together. There should have been some trust.'

'There is,' Kelly replied. 'Steve, if you knew what was going on here, and if you were in my position, you would have done the same as I have.'

'That's not what I'm talking about. You are asking us to …'

Simon Walker-Smith held up his hand.

'Enough talk,' he said. 'There is nothing more to say. We have a deadline. Let's get this done.'

54

June 24

THE LEAD VEHICLE, a nondescript black van with impenetrable tinted windows, pulled up on the side of Boxworth End Road, on the outskirts of Swavesey, just before 03.00. The driver, Staff Sergeant Jim Hendricks, glanced across to the front passenger seat, and saw Captain Walker-Jones give the slightest of nods. Instantly, Hendricks killed the engine and switched off the lights. In his rear-view mirror, he saw the second van come to rest a few yards behind, and dim its lights. The SAS unit was split between the two vehicles.

Also in the lead vehicle was DS Morgan, whom DI Venn had released to be seconded to Special Branch for the duration, so that his invaluable local knowledge was immediately available to the team. Behind the second van, Steve Macmillan was pulling up in his car, which also held Kelly Smith and Rosa Linda Montalbán. The lead van was some two hundred yards from the Carter bungalow. Morgan had chosen the spot. The house was invisible from the vehicle because of a sharp bend in the road to the right just ahead, which meant that the vehicle was also invisible from the bungalow.

Walker-Jones turned towards the rear of his vehicle. 'Ready, Ronnie?'

'All set, sir,' Trooper Ronnie Wardle replied cheerfully. Like most of his fellow troopers, Wardle was a non-commissioned officer in terms of his Army career, but the SAS tradition is that other ranks are simply 'Troopers' for the duration of their SAS service, reverting to their rank only when leaving to take up another assignment. The first part of the plan called for a single member of the team to get as close to the bungalow as possible without attracting attention. DS Morgan's drive-by patrol had kept constant watch throughout the day and had reported only limited activity. Fortuitously, at about 18.00, a young woman believed to be Carter's girlfriend, now identified as Maureen Callaghan, aged 19, and known to all as Mo, left the house driving the white van as a patrol car was passing. The patrol car followed her to a small, family-owned grocery store a mile or so from the house, then handed her off to another car which followed her as she drove back home, bearing quantities of beer, baby food and nappies. The only other events recorded were that the house lights had been switched on by 8 o'clock, and were switched off just after midnight. At 02.45, when DS Morgan called off the drive-by patrols, everything was reported quiet, with the house in darkness.

Wardle was dressed in a dark camouflage uniform and a helmet with night vision goggles. He jumped lightly from the rear of the lead vehicle, and disappeared almost immediately into the field at the side of the road. His radio was switched off. His C8 SFW assault rifle, light and dependable, hung down his left side, ready to be called into action at a moment's notice.

Wardle was an expert in reconnaissance. He kept a good distance from the road, pausing here and there to check his distance from the bungalow and other visual markers he had filed away in his mind, and to be on the lookout for unexpected hazards, such as low fences or barking dogs. In his line of work it was important to notice things like that, and to work quickly without rushing. Methodically, he approached the row of small bushes which marked the perimeter of the Carter bungalow. The house still seemed dark and quiet. There was no moonlight. He noted a street light on the same side of the road, about a hundred yards beyond the bungalow. On the other side of the road, a further hundred yards or so, was a group of three houses, just as DS Morgan had said. They also seemed dark and quiet. No traffic passed by. Swavesey had closed down for the night. He walked quickly past the back of the house on the grass and, avoiding the gravel on the side footpaths and the parking area at the front of the house, made his way unhurriedly back towards the lead vehicle. There was no reason to risk using his radio. It was just as effective, and much safer, to report in person. He approached so deftly that no one in the lead vehicle saw him until he opened the back doors and climbed in.

'Quiet as the grave, sir. Nothing moving,' he said. 'The only real problem is that you've got a gravel parking area in front, but you can get to within four or five feet of the front door on grass and flowerbeds. The near side is the best approach, sir – no street lights this side of the house.'

'Right,' Captain Walker-Jones said. 'Let's pay them a visit.'

He spoke quietly into his radio, and the unit left the two transport vehicles silently. Steve Macmillan was to follow at a safe distance along the road with Kelly and Rosa, and approach the house only when informed that the entry had been completed successfully. DS Morgan was assigned to wait with the vehicles. Following Trooper Wardle, the team made its way quickly and quietly across the grass to within striking distance of the front door. Each team member then trod the gravel with infinite care, led by Trooper Raymond Banks, whose expertise lay in gaining access to buildings, and the second in command, Staff Sergeant Hendricks.

Banks examined the door. Then, having done so, he put his hands over his ears and shook his head, meaning, no burglar alarm detected. Hendricks nodded. That was a welcome piece of news, but there were always concerns about booby traps and other less formal but equally effective alarms It was never wise to underestimate the sheer cunning of the bad guys. Trooper Sandy Vincent joined them quietly. Now they were close enough for thermal imaging, and she had been taking readings around the house. Sandy pointed left, held up two fingers, then gave the universal sleep sign, her hands together under her right jaw and ear. Next she pointed right, held up one finger, then made the universal baby rocking in the cradle sign, holding her hands loosely in front of her, moving them to right and left alternately. Her facial expression conveyed that the age of the third person was informed speculation. Hendricks nodded again, and gave the thumbs-up sign to Captain Walker-Jones, who returned it. Walker-Jones nodded to Banks, who inserted a device into the lock of the front door, and turned it once or twice. Banks smiled happily to himself. They didn't come any easier than this. His eight-year-old son could have done it with a screwdriver, he thought, as he stood aside to allow the first members of the team to enter.

The door creaked a little as it sprung open in response to Trooper Banks' expert touch, but whatever noise it made was academic. The entry team, led by Captain Walker-Jones, found its way easily to the bedroom with the aid of their night vision goggles. When they pushed open the door and switched on the light, the only two occupants of the room were in the double bed against the far wall, fast asleep. The team pointed their assault rifles directly at the bed. Staff Sergeant Hendricks had been appointed to do the shouting. He was a former drill-sergeant and had a stentorian voice which could terrify new recruits at a range of a hundred yards.

'Get out of the bed now!' he thundered. 'Let me see your hands! Come on, let's have you! Get out of the fucking bed, now!'

As they heard the shout, Steve Macmillan, Kelly, and Rosa broke into a run and made directly for the front door. No one stopped them from entering, and they made their way to the bedroom at full speed. Walker-Jones and Hendricks, with three troopers, two male and one female, were covering two figures, who stood with raised hands against the wall, completely naked.

'The man has identified himself as Wayne Carter, sir,' Sergeant Hendricks said to Steve Macmillan. 'I can't get any response from the woman.'

She was petrified, Kelly saw at once. She was ashen and shaking; she had urinated on the floor.

'It's all right,' Kelly said, walking over to her. 'We're not going to harm you. What's your name?'

She began sobbing violently. 'Don't kill my baby. Oh, please don't kill my baby. Please.'

'No one is going to harm your baby,' Kelly said. 'Are you Mo Callaghan?'

It took her some time to calm herself and stifle the sobs. She nodded slowly.

'Where is the baby? In the other room?'

Mo nodded again.

'All right,' Kelly said. She turned to the female Trooper, Jo Johnson. 'Find her something to wear and take her to see the baby.' The sound of a baby crying could now be heard from the living room. Trooper Johnson escorted Mo hurriedly out of the room.

Steve Macmillan had already cuffed Wayne Carter's hands in the rear stack position. Like Mo Callaghan, Carter had literally leapt from the bed in terror when he heard Sergeant Hendricks shout. But now he was beginning to recover his composure.

'Who the fuck are you?' he demanded. 'You're the Old Bill, aren't you? You can't just burst in here all tooled up like this to arrest me for selling a few drugs, not when my old lady's in bed with nothing on. It's a violation of my human rights. I'll fucking have you, the lot of you.'

Steve Macmillan put a hand under Carter's chin and forced his head against the wall.

'Take a look around you, Wayne. You're in no position to have anybody.'

He tightened his grip on the chin.

'Let me ask you something. Does this look like a drugs raid to you? No? That's what I thought. So let me explain who we are, and what we want. I'm DI Steve Macmillan of Special Branch. This lady is Kelly Smith, the Director of the American FBI. These gentlemen are members of the SAS. We want the answer to one very simple question. If you cooperate, no harm will come to you. If not, believe me, I'm going to violate a lot more than your human rights. So, here's the question, Wayne. Think carefully before you answer. Where is Dani Ryan?'

Carter's eyes opened wide. He tried desperately to cover up his reaction to the question, but he was taken aback and unable to conceal his fear.

'Never heard of her. I don't know nothing about that.'

'Well, which is it?' Macmillan asked. 'You never heard of her, or you know nothing about it?'

'It's got nothing to do with me,' Carter blustered. 'You can't prove I had anything to do with that. I'll have supplying Class A, all right? I heard you nicked Carl Gibson, yeah? I did a few jobs for Carl, all right, so I'll put my hands up to that. But that's it. You ain't got nothing on me on that other thing.'

Macmillan shook his head. He pushed Carter's head back into the wall.

'Wake up, Wayne. We wouldn't be here if we didn't know all about it, would we? Someone's grassed you up, mate, that's your problem.'

Macmillan registered the startled movement of Carter's eyes, a look bordering on panic.

'We know that you were the driver when Dani Ryan was kidnapped. We're going to take away your van, and our forensic people are going to go over it with a fine-toothed comb. These people are really good, Wayne. If there's any evidence at all to connect you to Dani Ryan, even the smallest trace, they will find it. And I'm betting you haven't even cleaned it out, have you? Would you like to guess what you'll get for the kidnap and murder of the US President's step-daughter? Do you want to say goodbye to Mo and the baby now, while you have the chance?'

Carter swallowed hard. He looked wildly around the room.

'I haven't murdered anyone,' he blurted out, a little too quickly.

'Maybe not yet,' Macmillan agreed. 'But if we don't find Dani soon, that's what's going to happen, isn't it? And we will nail you for it as an aider and abettor, no problem. They'll throw away the fucking key, mate, take it from me.'

'Actually,' Kelly said, stepping forward to stand alongside Steve Macmillan, 'I can do better than that.'

Steve caught her eye. 'Really?'

Kelly nodded. 'My instructions are to have everyone involved in this crime extradited to the United States to stand trial in Federal court. We're not thinking prison here. This is a Federal death penalty case. You're going to end up with a needle in your arm, Wayne. Then they'll bury you in the prison grounds. There won't even be a gravestone for your son to look at.'

Carter squirmed.

'You can't do that,' he protested.

'Watch me,' Kelly replied. 'I'm the Director of the FBI. You have no idea what I can do. Do you really think you can kidnap the President's daughter and be tried in this country and get away with a few years in prison? I answer directly to the President of the United States. Do you have any idea of how powerful the President of the United States is? I'll have you on a plane to Washington DC in a couple of weeks.'

'Fuck off. You're bluffing,' Carter responded, but his voice was losing its confidence.

Steve and Kelly simply continued to look at him from a distance of a few inches. Carter suddenly became very agitated, shaking his head rapidly from side to side. His breath became very rapid.

'What if he tells us where Dani is?' Steve asked Kelly.

'The President would be very grateful,' Kelly replied. 'If he does that, and if he was only the driver, we might just leave him here and let you guys deal with him.'

Carter did not reply at once.

Steve shrugged. 'Apparently, he doesn't care,' he said.

He turned towards Simon Walker-Jones.

'Captain, I think you should bring Mo and the baby in so that Wayne can say goodbye before we haul him off.'

Walker-Jones turned, as if to leave.

'No,' Carter said. 'No. Wait a minute … fuck…'

He seemed to make a supreme effort to control himself. He focused his gaze on Kelly and took a deep breath.

'Do you have something to say?' Steve asked.

'I don't know the address,' Carter said. 'But I can take you there. For fuck's sake, don't tell them I grassed them up.'

* * *

'Best actress in a leading role,' Steve Macmillan commented, as they walked to the car. 'But I assume you know that the British Government would not extradite anyone to the United States unless the death penalty is off the table. We have treaty obligations.'

Kelly looked up at him innocently, her lips showing the faintest suggestion of a smile.

'Oh, my God. Really? Thanks, Steve. I'll bear that in mind in future.'

55

AT JUST AFTER 08.00, Doug Morgan stopped his car at the side of the narrow country road and switched off the engine. In the front passenger seat Steve Macmillan turned to face the rear of the vehicle. In the rear seat sat Wayne Carter, in handcuffs, between two members of the SAS unit dressed in civilian clothes. The team had taken Wayne Carter back to Cambridge Police Station in double quick time. At greater leisure, two plain-clothes officers escorted Mo Callaghan and her baby to temporary accommodation, where a female police officer was assigned to stay with her until further notice. Forensic officers quietly removed Carter's van for a detailed examination. Steve Macmillan allowed the team only a short respite for rest and refreshment while he and Doug Morgan debriefed Wayne Carter further. Carter drew them a map showing how to get from Cambridge to West Fen Road, a rural road leading into some quiet fen country just outside, and to the west-north-west, of the historic cathedral city of Ely. He marked with an X the location of the house in which he claimed they would find Dani Ryan. Steve Macmillan and Simon Walker-Jones agreed that no time should be lost in taking Carter to West Fen Road for reconnaissance, to identify the house beyond doubt.

'Is that it? That house in the field?' Macmillan asked.

'Yeah,' Carter replied. 'That's it.'

'You'd better not be playing me. Think carefully, Wayne.'

'That's it,' Carter repeated.

Macmillan nodded. Beside him, Morgan placed a call on his mobile phone to the situation room at Cambridge Police Station.

'John, is that you?'

'Go ahead, Sarge.' The voice belonged to DC John

Birmingham, the Cambridgeshire Constabulary's resident technology guru, who had been drafted into the situation room to lend his expertise.

'We're about a quarter of a mile south to south-east of the venue. Do you have us on GPS? Does it give you our coordinates?'

'Yes, I see you. I'm bringing you up on Google Earth now... give me a moment. Right, got you, Sarge. I'm seeing the building, and I am bringing it up on the big screen now. I'll have all the details for you by the time you get back.'

'We're on our way,' Morgan replied.

* * *

Over sandwiches and coffee the entire team sat and looked in detail at images of The Rambles, West Fen Road, an early nineteenth-century house situated between two and three miles from Ely in the direction of the village of Coveney, and set back about a hundred yards from the road. According to land registry records, The Rambles was owned by Frank and Betty Mayfield, a local couple in their late 60s. DC Birmingham had also made copies of a five-year old grant of planning permission for the Mayfields to add a shower room to their basement.

'They've got to be holding her in the basement,' Captain Walker-Jones said. 'John, can you bring up those outbuildings again.'

John Birmingham made them appear, centered them on the screen, and enlarged them. The two outbuildings appeared to be garden sheds about thirty feet apart and about fifty feet from the main house at the rear.

'They are too small, for one thing, and they would be worried about the risk of someone hearing something.'

'Besides,' Steve Macmillan added, 'they would have to be constantly on the move between the main house and the out-buildings. That would expose them too much. There aren't going to be too many Indian residents in that area. The local people are bound to know the Mayfields. They would attract attention immediately. Far too dangerous.'

DC Birmingham brought the main house up again and rotated it slowly through 360 degrees. There was silence for some time.

'Assumptions about numbers and arms?' Walker-Jones asked.

'Carter said there were two of them,' Steve Macmillan replied, 'one man and one woman, carrying automatic side-arms He didn't see anything else.'

'Then we will assume three or four with assault rifles,' Walker-Jones said. 'No disrespect to our friend Wayne, but I doubt they took him into their confidence to the extent of showing him everything. Suggestions about entry strategy?'

'It's a tricky one, sir,' Staff Sergeant Hendricks said after some time. 'Not the entry itself, or overcoming resistance, but the approach. Look how far the house is from the road. It's flat and open, no trees to speak of, no cover at all, really.'

'I don't like it at all,' Walker-Jones said. 'John, can you give me a 360 on the basement level?'

'Coning right up' DC Birmingham replied. The team watched the slow revolution together.

'It looks like the basement has two windows,' Walker-Jones said. 'We're calling it a basement, but actually, it's not entirely subterranean, is it? The top is above ground. Those two windows must be set high in the walls. One of them seems to be in the new shower room. The other must be in the main room.' He turned and looked over his shoulder. 'Ray, could you take one of those windows out?'

Raymond Banks got as close as he could as DC Birmingham rotated between the two windows.

'It's difficult to be sure, sir,' he said. 'But they are probably standard-size modern jobs. I don't think anyone does custom-made wooden windows any more. So they probably don't fit too well into that old wall. If I'm right about that, they would come away pretty easily.'

He paused and turned towards the team.

'Of course, I would have to make enough noise to wake people up in Cambridge.'

'You would have to blow them out?'

'It's the only practical way, sir. Theoretically I might be able to saw and chip them out, but it would take hours, and still make too much noise.'

Staff Sergeant Hendricks got to his feet and stood next to Banks.

'Those are fairly big windows,' he said. 'We could climb through once the window is gone, couldn't we?'

Banks nodded. 'Yes, you could, Sarge, one at a time. But I'd have to blow a bloody big hole in the wall, to make sure of giving you the space.'

Hendricks turned towards Walker-Jones.

'We would be putting all our eggs in one basket, sir. And it's probably a bit of a drop to the floor of the basement from the window. God knows what the floor is like. If it's really uneven, someone could turn an ankle, dead easy. But it would be a great entry point, and number two or three could fire from the window without entering.'

Walker-Jones stood decisively.

'All right, what about this? We improve the odds by using multiple points of entry. We take out both windows, three troopers to each. At the same time, the rest enter through the front door. There's no way they can cope with all of us. We will still need a little luck, but the odds are much better that way.'

'The only thing is, sir,' Banks said, after a pause, 'there's no guarantee that the whole window would come away cleanly. Those metal frames can be stubborn buggers. You might have to pull the debris away before you could enter. The windows might even be stronger than that old wall. If I blow a section of wall away, the window might just shift without coming loose, and leave no way in at all.'

Kelly stood. 'Suggestion?'

'Go ahead,' Walker-Jones said.

'We don't know for sure where they are holding Dani. I agree, it's probably the basement. But what if we are wrong? If you enter making that much noise, they will be alerted immediately, and if they are close to Dani they have every chance to kill her before we can confront them. John, can you bring up the floor plan again?'

She walked forward to the screen.

'It looks like the only entry to the basement is via that staircase in the living room,' Kelly pointed out. 'If you enter through the front door, you've got to cross the living room and then trust to the staircase. It's probably old, and God knows what condition it's in. It doesn't look very wide. There may only be room for one at a time to go down, and if we've woken them up, they could pick us off one by one – after they shoot Dani. So you'd better hope Ray is wrong about the windows, otherwise the front door team is exposed with no back-up.'

Steve Macmillan could not suppress a smile. He watched Simon Walker-Jones grit his teeth as he listened diplomatically to an American civilian commenting on his proposed entry plan.

'I'm sure you've made entries a few times, Kelly,' Steve said. 'How would you do it?'

'I wouldn't go in using shock and awe unless I had no choice,' she replied. 'Ray, what's your take on the front door? John, can you bring it up, as big as you can?'

Raymond Banks smiled happily. 'It looks like an original period wooden door, doesn't it? It shouldn't be a problem, barring alarms and booby traps, but that's always a risk, however you go in. I'd prefer to have Ronnie take a few long-distance shots with a zoom lens beforehand, in daylight, if that's all right.'

Kelly nodded. 'If you can get us in without making any noise, the team can split up and cover the whole house – upstairs, downstairs, basement – in a matter of seconds. We have a much better chance of getting to Dani without alerting them.'

She turned to look at Walker-Jones.

'You said it yourself, Simon, there are no guarantees, it's a matter of improving the odds in our favor.'

Walker-Jones nodded. 'Thank you all for your input. I need time to think this through, and I need some time with the unit to make some detailed plans, whatever I decide. Let's meet again at about 15.00.'

The team began to disperse, tired but on edge and keen. Kelly took Simon Walker-Jones's arm and led him to one side.

'Don't take this personally, Simon. I had to say what was on my mind. I know how good you guys are. I trust you, and it's your decision. But it's my hostage in there.'

'As I said, I'll think about it,' he replied stiffly.

She walked away. He looked after her as she went, shaking his head. Staff Sergeant Hendricks approached to join him.

'The lady's got a point about the entry sir,' he said quietly.

'Fuck off,' Walker-Jones said.

'Yes, sir, very good, sir,' Staff Sergeant Hendricks replied cheerfully.

56

THE TEAM GATHERED in the situation room for the last time at 23.00. Steve Macmillan had been only too glad to give the SAS unit whatever time and space they wanted to plan the coming campaign. But he wanted everyone on the same page now that the time was approaching. Ronnie Wardle had earlier been driven to within a mile of the site by a plain-clothes officer in a nondescript car, looking like a rambler or a bird-watcher, but with some well-concealed observation and photographic equipment to which even the keenest bird-watcher would not have access. The unit would bring his operational kit with them when they joined him. He had already called in his report to Captain Walker-Jones and had now settled down to keep watch on the house, so that he could alert the team to any unexpected development.

Simon Walker-Jones used a baton to point to the image behind him on the screen.

'A decision has been taken to enter quietly via the front door,' he began, with a glance towards Kelly.

'Ronnie Wardle was able to get some decent shots of the door, and it appears to present no real difficulty. We must be alert for unseen problems when we enter. No lights. We rely on night-vision and we move through the house as quietly as possible. Kelly and I will lead the first team which makes directly for the staircase to the basement. I will go down first, relying on Kelly to cover me. The other members of that team do the same for Kelly and each other. The second team makes its way upstairs and covers both rooms up there. The third team clears the living room and kitchen as quickly as possible and, once those areas are cleared, that team is on standby to render assistance wherever needed. Complete silence is to be maintained unless and until shooting starts. We will have medical, ambulance, and other assistance behind us. They will remain on the edge of West Fen Road until the scene is secured, but they can be with us in a matter of minutes. Rosa, I would like you to be available with them. I want Dani to have someone she knows there when we bring her out. Planned time of entry is 02.15. Any questions?'

'What about the approach to the house?' Steve Macmillan asked. 'It's set back a long way from the road.'

'Slow and methodical,' Walker-Jones replied. 'Ronnie has scouted the best routes. Fortunately, we can do it over grass. It shouldn't be a huge problem approaching the house. It's once we are inside the house that it gets tricky.'

'Kelly, what about Kay?' Rosa asked, as the meeting was breaking up. 'Do we bring her with us?'

Kelly shook her head. 'No. But have a car ready to bring her from Cambridge as soon as we give the word.'

* * *

For ten of the longest minutes of her life, Kelly debated what, if anything, to tell Ted Lazenby. Simon Walker-Jones had ended the meeting by repeating his demand for total radio silence. No risks could be taken at such a sensitive moment. No one in the United States was to be told that Carl Gibson had given up the name of Wayne Carter, or of any developments since then. Kay Ryan was not to be told anything. Any leak could be fatal to the success of the operation. If Carter had been lying, or if Dani had been moved since being seized – a hazardous, but not illogical course for the kidnappers to take – any wind of the operation might tip them off. She knew he was right. On the other hand, during her daily calls she was increasingly aware that the mood in the White House was turning rapidly to despair, even to resignation. Ellen was going through hell. If she could offer a glimmer of hope, it would mean so much.

* * *

Lazenby hung up and turned to look at Ellen. He shook his head.

'Nothing new. She said they have one or two good leads, but nothing concrete. I'm sorry, Ellen.'

They were in the residence. The crisis committee was still meeting at least once a day, Jeff was putting out increasingly desperate stories to the press, but they were going through the motions. Time was ebbing away, and there was nothing they could do. Ted Lazenby had, in theory, one thing he could do. Pendulum had passed safely through Islamabad, had made his way up country with his guide, and was now scouting positions around camp site four. Soon he would be awaiting a coded order. But Lazenby was almost sure he would not do it. Ellen looked tired and drawn.

'I heard the same from Kay,' she said.

She looked up at Lazenby.

'Ted, if this doesn't work out – if Dani doesn't make it back safely – I'm going to resign,' she said.

He walked over to the sofa and sat next to her.

'Ellen, that's not necessary. There was nothing you could have done. Everyone would understand that. The only people who would want you to resign are those damned religious bigots, and they want you to resign anyway. Don't give them that satisfaction.'

She smiled.

'That's not the reason,' she replied. 'It's just that if Dani dies, I need to be with Kay. I can't make it right for her, but I would need to give her all the time and all the energy I have for the rest of our time together. She has to be my priority. I can't give that to her and be President at the same time.'

She saw that he was about to renew his protest. She stood.

'I've made up my mind, Ted. You will serve out my remaining term of office. I'll talk to people in the party. I'm sure they would arrange things so that you don't have an opponent in the primaries. You would have a straight shot in the election. You would win. I know you would be a great President.'

57

BY ABOUT 02.00, the unit's transport vehicles had parked quietly on West Fen Road, about two hundred yards short of The Rambles, on a slight bend in the road. As the van's lights were switched off, Captain Walker-Jones saw Staff Sergeant Hendricks give him a broad grin. He nodded across the field in the direction of the house.

'Look at that, sir. That's a bit of luck, and no mistake.'

Walker-Jones followed the direction of the nod, and smiled.

'It is indeed. Bugger me. I wonder if Dougie Morgan ordered that up for us. Nothing like having a local boy with you, is there?'

'Can't beat it, sir,' Hendricks replied. 'The bad guys are definitely not seeing us now, are they? Not through that lot.'

The day had been a warm and humid one, but the temperature had fallen during the night. Because of the resulting dew point, a classic Fen country ground mist, gray, wispy and slow-moving, hung over much of the field that separated them from the house. Nature had provided the unit with its own, perfect, cover.

Ronnie Wardle had recommended two approaches to the house, one from either side. Without discussion, the members of the unit vanished silently into the mist to take up their positions. Doug Morgan and Rosa Linda Montalbán sat together in silence in the gathering gray shroud in the front seat of Morgan's car. They exchanged glances with each other and with Steve Macmillan, who sat in the rear. The glances said it all. 'Nothing we can do now, except wait. And pray.'

Raymond Banks inspected the front door carefully and, when

he was satisfied, turned to give a thumbs-up sign to Simon Walker-Jones and Kelly Smith. Walker-Jones returned the sign. Kelly wore all black civilian clothing with a black bullet-proof vest. She was also wearing the high-quality night-vision goggles which the unit had provided for her. Staff Sergeant Hendricks had spent an hour working with her during the afternoon to help her grow accustomed to them, and it was beginning to feel natural. But she still had to make a conscious effort to trust what she saw, and resist the impulse to tear the goggles off and let her eyes adjust to the dark on their own. There might not be time for that.

In perfect silence, Banks worked his magic on the old wooden door, which opened for him almost immediately and without resistance. He stood back. The first entry team exchanged glances and thumbs-up signs, and Captain Walker-Jones led the way in. The house was absolutely quiet. There was no one in the living room. It was sparsely furnished. Kelly, following close behind Walker-Jones, saw him point towards the far left corner, where a stair post and the top of a bannister indicated the staircase leading down to the basement. Troopers Alan Harding, Jo Johnson and Raymond Banks followed immediately behind Kelly. As soon as they were safely inside, Staff Sergeant Hendricks led teams two and three into the house. They dispersed noiselessly.

Walker-Jones paused at the top of the stairs. There was no sound. The staircase was wooden, narrow and steep. It was not carpeted. The bottom few steps curved around to the left, so he could see nothing of what awaited him in the basement. His assault rifle lay across his chest. He had both hands on the weapon. It was ready for immediate action. Gingerly, he placed one foot on the first stair. It seemed secure and made no sound. He placed his other foot on the same stair. Again, secure with his full weight on it, and no sound. He repeated the procedure with equal care on the second stair, then the third, then the fourth, then the fifth. By now, he could see that there were another three steps straight ahead, then three or four to the left. One more and he would have some visual on the main room of the basement. Kelly followed a step behind, equally careful and deliberate in her movements, pointing her Glock nine millimeter automatic down through the stairwell into the basement. Team two must have cleared the downstairs area by now. There had been no sound from them. Dani must be either upstairs or in the basement.

When Walker-Jones placed his first foot on the sixth step, it creaked loudly. He froze. He allowed several seconds to elapse, and was about to try his other foot, treading more towards the edge of the stair, when the light came on. Instantly, Kelly tore off her night-vision goggles and peered round him into the basement. In the far right corner she saw Dani Ryan, sitting bolt upright against the wall, clutching a blanket. In front of her to the left, a young Indian man was getting slowly to his feet. She recognized Bev Prasad from his photograph. To Bev's right was a young Indian woman. She was moving away from the bottom of the staircase, and must have been the one who switched on the light. She was dressed in a gray top and black trousers, her feet bare. She was pointing an automatic pistol in Dani's direction, but had only half turned away from the staircase. She must have been sleeping in the basement with Dani for security. She had been taken by surprise. Kelly breathed a silent prayer of gratitude that the team had made no noise when entering the building. She trained her own weapon on the young woman.

'Drop your weapon, and put your hands in the air,' she shouted. 'It's over. You have no place to go. We have armed troops all over the house.'

'I will kill her,' Kali shouted. 'Get out. Get out now. If you don't leave, she's dead.'

'Don't be stupid,' Kelly replied. 'Don't make things worse than they already are. We can talk about this. No one has to die. Just put down your weapon. What's your name?'

Kali did not answer.

'Her name is Kali,' Bev replied.

Kelly looked into Kali's eyes, and felt her stomach churn. Every professional instinct told her that she was not dealing with an average kidnapper. Kali was not afraid of death. There was a hardness, an intensity, about her that told Kelly she was dealing with a fanatic. There would be no negotiation with her, no compromise. Desperately, Kelly went through her options. Simon

Walker-Jones was poised but had not tried to aim his weapon. Kelly realized at once that his angle was wrong. Any shot he fired at Kali would pose some risk to Dani. Kelly had a better angle. She could bring Kali down easily enough. But she could not control the probability that Kali would kill Dani first. The only guaranteed method would be a clean head shot. But that would involve adjusting her aim, and a head shot taken so quickly was a low-percentage shot. She felt sweat trickle down her neck to her back.

'This is your last warning,' Kali was screaming. 'You have five seconds to get out. She dies in five seconds. Get out now. One …'

'Drop your weapon, Kali,' Kelly insisted. 'There is no way out.'

The options were narrowing now. She began to raise the sights of her pistol towards Kali's head. She must not be too obvious. By bending both knees slightly she could reduce the distance by which the weapon had to be raised and she could give herself a more comfortable stance. The tension had made her legs and feet tense up. She deliberately relaxed them.

'Two …'

'It doesn't have to be like this, Kali.'

'Three …'

Kelly was almost in position. Her weapon was almost at Kali's head. Then she saw that Kali was moving slightly to her right, ready to turn and fire.

'Four … last chance …'

In moving to her right, Kali had brought herself closer to Bev. He had been standing perfectly still, his hands in the air. Suddenly, he turned towards Kali, his face contorted with anger.

'No!' he screamed. 'No! Not like this.'

Kali was momentarily caught off guard, and turned her eyes in his direction. Bev lowered his arms, and lunged at Kali, enfolding her in a high tackle, his arms around her body, pinning her arms to her sides. The force of his lunge was too much even for Kali's perfect balance. They fell together to the floor, wrestling in desperation, screaming at each other. They rolled to Kelly's right, closer to the staircase. For a few seconds the outcome was uncertain. Then Kali's knee went savagely into Bev's groin. He cried out in pain, and had to loosen his grip. Kali burst free. She fired twice from the floor. The two shots echoed, terrifyingly loudly, in the cavernous room. Bev rolled over on to his stomach and lay completely still.

For a second no one moved. Then Kali began to struggle to her feet, and Kelly saw her weapon move in her hand.

'Svatantra Kashmir!' Kali screamed.

Kelly had followed her every move with her Glock. There was no need to risk a head shot now. Before Kali could turn any further towards Dani, she fired six bullets into Kali's body in quick succession. Kali fell back to the floor, the gun falling harmlessly from her dying hand.

58

SIMON WALKER-JONES LED the way downstairs and kicked Kali's weapon away. Kelly ran over to Dani Ryan, who was sitting up against the wall, clutching her blanket, her eyes and mouth wide open, shivering in abject terror.

Kelly knelt by her side and held her. 'You're safe now, Dani,' she said softly. 'It's over. You're going home.'

Having cleared the remaining area of the basement, Simon Walker-Jones was checking Bev Prasad for a pulse. He looked up towards Kelly and shook his head.

Within a minute, to Kelly's amazement, the versatile Ronnie Wardle appeared on the staircase, carrying an enormous metal cutting tool, which resembled a giant shears. In a second or two he had cut Dani free from her chain. She turned her eyes towards Bev.

'No. No,' she wailed. She began to sob uncontrollably.

'Come on,' Kelly said. 'Let's get you out of here.'

Dani was unsteady on her feet after being confined during her captivity. Kelly and Ronnie Wardle helped her slowly up the staircase, across the living room, and out into the cool night air. Lights were on all over the house now and, in passing through the living room, Kelly noticed a young Indian man seated on the sofa between two troopers. He was naked apart from a pair of underpants and his hands were handcuffed behind his back.

'That's the other one,' Staff Sergeant Hendricks said quietly as she passed. 'He gave us the name of Samir. He was sleeping like a baby upstairs. There's no one else here.'

Once outside, Kelly paused to allow Dani to lean against the front wall of the house by the front door. By now uniformed police officers were arriving, and she saw Rosa approaching at a jog, holding a phone to her ear. Kelly took out her own phone and switched it on. She called a number on the speed-dial, which was answered immediately by a familiar voice.

'Kelly?'

'We've got her, sir,' she said. 'Dani's safe and well.'

There was silence for a moment or two, then an ear-piercing roar.

'Ellen, they've found her,' she heard him shout. 'They've found Dani. She's safe and well.'

She heard the scream on the other end of the line, raw and visceral.

'Oh, thank God,' Ted Lazenby said, more quietly, after some seconds. When he spoke again, his voice was breaking.

'I'm with the President. She had to sit down for a moment. She will call in a couple of minutes. My God, I'm feeling a bit faint myself. This has come out of the blue. We had no idea. We ...'

'Yes, I'm sorry about that,' Kelly said. 'There were some things I couldn't tell you about in advance. I wanted to, but ... I'm sorry.'

'Kelly, what happened?'

'It's a long story, sir,' Kelly replied. 'I can't talk now. I've got some things I have to do at the scene. But I will make a full report as soon as I can. I promise. Could you tell Jeff I'm fine, and I will call him too, as soon as I get the chance?'

'I will, Kelly. Well done. My God, well done.'

By the time Kelly had disconnected the call, Rosa had reached Dani. Dani pushed herself off the wall and practically fell into Rosa's arms. They embraced, both in tears. Rosa kissed her and pushed her phone into Dani's hand.

'I have someone on my phone who wants to say "hi",' she said, smiling through her tears. 'She's on her way from Cambridge. She will be here in a few minutes.'

A doctor and a nurse were also moving purposefully towards Dani. Kelly held up a hand.

'She's OK,' Kelly said. 'Give her a moment.'

She walked a few paces in front of the house, gratefully inhaling the cool night air. Steve Macmillan came towards her from the side of the house.

'We made a search of the entire property,' he said. 'We found two bodies in one of the out-buildings. An elderly couple, executed, bullets to the back of the head, arms tied behind their backs.'

Kelly shook her head. 'The Mayfields?'

'I assume so. We are making inquiries about next of kin. Forensic will be here within the hour.'

'I wonder how much the Mayfields knew about Kashmir,' Kelly mused aloud.

'Not enough to die for it, that's for sure,' Steve said.

He walked away to join a uniformed officer who was calling to him.

* * *

Ted Lazenby stayed with Ellen Trevathan only long enough to ensure that she could compose herself sufficiently to call Dale Harrison and then Kelly. She had hugged him and wept hysterically. He had to stay for some minutes. But he excused himself as soon as he could. He walked quickly to the situation room and activated the large mobile.

'Pendulum, this is Moderator,' he said. 'Come in. Over.'

Seconds passed. Lazenby felt the tension rising throughout his body. He didn't need anything to go wrong now. He was so close to being able to close the book on the worst few days of his life. His mind started to make a list of all the things that could go wrong. The site had become insecure. A Pakistani patrol had stumbled on Pendulum. Something had gone wrong with his radio. He couldn't charge it up. He had had an accident of some kind.

'Come on, for God's sake,' he muttered to himself. 'What are you doing?'

Eventually there was a crackle, then a voice, not very loud, but quite clear.

'This is Pendulum. Go ahead, Moderator. Over.'

'Moderator is activating Code Alpha. Repeat, activating Code Alpha. Please acknowledge. Over.'

Another long silence. Then …

'This is Pendulum. Code Alpha is acknowledged. Thank you, Moderator. Over and out.'

Ted Lazenby switched off the radio and placed it on the table. He sat down, held his head in his hands and wept aloud.

59

BY THE TIME Kelly arrived back in her room at the Universtity Arms Hotel, it was after 11 o'clock and the city of Cambridge had begun another working day. Before leaving the police station she had spoken in turn to Jeff, Ted Lazenby, and Ellen Trevathan. Full reports would have to wait until she returned to Washington, but she gave them the basic story of the past forty-eight hours. They bombarded her with questions, and it was some time before she could return her attention to what was going on at the police station.

She immediately passed on thanks to the team from Ellen Trevathan. But there was work to do and there were formalities to observe. Steve Macmillan and Doug Morgan had arrested Samir on suspicion of kidnapping, blackmail and murder, and were arranging for him to receive legal representation before being interviewed. DC Birmingham had been assigned to coordinate the forensic reports and other evidence, as and when they made their way in from the Rambles. Kelly was asked to make a witness statement dealing with her role during the previous two days, including the circumstances under which she had discharged her firearm.

The media knew by now that Dani Ryan was safe, and were laying siege to the police station, demanding details, and seeking interviews with everyone involved. Steve Macmillan, who had too many other things to do to worry about the press, had neatly passed the ball. He had asked the Home Secretary to coordinate the necessary press conferences, and sent a message to reporters that the matter was out of his hands for reasons of national security; a press conference would be held as soon as possible, later in the day. Meanwhile, a senior uniformed superintendent appeared, and made a brief statement confirming that Dani had been rescued, without taking questions. While all this was going on Kelly was able to leave, unnoticed, by a side door.

By rights Kelly should have been exhausted, but she was wide awake. There was no question of sleeping. She was wound up and still running on adrenaline. She switched on the TV. The BBC was running an extended morning news show to cover the dramatic rescue of Dani Ryan. Word was already out that the events had unfolded at a house just outside Ely, and questions were being asked about the involvement of Indians, rather than a middle-eastern group as had previously been supposed. But most of what was being said was, of necessity, no more than speculation.

Kelly gratefully stripped off her clothes and took a long, warm shower. Emerging from the shower, she threw on a T-shirt and jeans. She opened a closet and found the bottle of Bushmills Irish whiskey she had bought on her first day in Cambridge. She had kept it sealed, to await either celebration or despair. She opened the bottle now, poured herself a generous measure and settled down to watch the BBC. She smiled as she saw the reporters standing in frustration outside the police station.

'Just be patient,' she said to herself. 'You'll have one hell of a story before too long.'

'We will bring you continuing coverage of the Dani Ryan rescue story throughout the day,' the anchor said, as the image of the reports faded away.

'Meanwhile, in the United States, it was alleged yesterday that a leading conservative religious figure who has repeatedly called for President Ellen Trevathan to resign sexually abused at least one teenage girl during his earlier career. According to the *Washington Post*, Tommy Lanier, a popular Dallas talk show host who uses the nick-name "Bubba", had a long sexual relationship with a fourteen-year-old girl in Baton Rouge, Louisiana, as a result of which the girl became pregnant. The *Post* quotes the girl as saying that she believes she was not the only girl Lanier abused, and has demanded that he give a sample of his DNA so that she can establish paternity. The girl, who is black, also told the *Post* that

Lanier had repeatedly threatened that harm would come to her family if she told anyone about their relationship. Lanier has been calling for President Trevathan to resign ever since she came out as a lesbian and moved her long-term partner, Kay Ryan, to live in the White House. He had begun circulating an electronic petition which, he claimed, had been signed by more than two million Americans, although sources close to the company overseeing the petition have refused to confirm that number. Within the last few days Lanier outraged public opinion, not only in America, but in much of the world, by claiming that the kidnapping of Dani Ryan was God's judgment on the two women, and was no more than they deserved.'

The BBC's file picture of Bubba Lanier gave way to that of Hank Betancourt.

'The incident has caused considerable embarrassment in political circles. Hank Betancourt, the conservative Governor of Texas, who had been widely tipped as his party's next presidential nominee, had appeared to endorse Lanier's comments. And in further bad news for Governor Betancourt, it emerged today that a substantial sum of money, perhaps as much as half a million dollars, which should have been in his re-election fund, may have found its way into a personal bank account held in the Cayman Islands. A Justice Department source, who asked not to be identified, has told the BBC that an investigation will be opened within the next few days, and that the Governor is a person of interest to the investigation. Many senior legislators in his party are saying today that Betancourt will not be their choice to run against President Trevathan.'

Film rolled with the caption 'courtesy of CNN', which showed Senator Joe O'Brien being interviewed by a CNN reporter.

'My party has no truck with Bubba Lanier,' the Senator said. 'We deplore this personal attack on the President while she is struggling with, not only a personal crisis, but a serious national crisis. No politician who identifies himself with such tactics can rely on the support of this party, whoever he may be.'

'Neither Mr Lanier nor Governor Betancourt was available for comment yesterday,' the anchor concluded. 'The President's press secretary, Jeff Morris, said that the White House welcomed Senator O'Brien's remarks, and thanked everyone who had supported the President throughout the crisis, regardless of party affiliation. "The President has always maintained that basic human decency is not the sole preserve of any political party or group," Morris told reporters at the daily White House press conference.'

Kelly smiled as Jeff's image flashed up on the screen.

The anchor placed her notes about Bubba Lanier and Hank Betancourt on her desk, and turned to a new topic.

'And now to other news,' she said. 'The Prime Minister of India, Anand Mehra, has arrived back in New Delhi after his three-day visit to Kashmir along the disputed border with Pakistan…'

Film rolled showing the Prime Minister disembarking from his official aircraft and being welcomed by officials. The scene switched to a military outpost, where an Indian sentry stood guard against the backdrop of a snow-topped mountain and tall fir trees.

'The official purpose of the Prime Minister's visit was to inspect military installations along the troubled border,' the anchor continued. 'But it is being reported today that he may also have met behind closed doors with senior Pakistani officials, with a view to arranging further talks between India and Pakistan about the long-term future of Kashmir. To general surprise, the Pakistani Government, which usually condemns visits to the border by Indian politicians as acts of provocation, has welcomed the Prime Minister's visit, saying that it welcomes any serious approach to solving Kashmir's problems, and is open to the possibility of resuming talks in the near future.'

There was a soft knock on the door. Kelly walked quickly across the room and opened it.

60

'CAN I COME in for a minute?' Rosa asked.

'Sure,' Kelly smiled. 'How about a drink? I know it's not exactly the right time of day, but ...'

'I don't think anyone's worrying about that today,' Rosa replied. 'Certainly not me.'

Kelly waved Rosa into a chair, poured her a generous glass of whiskey, and refilled her own.

'How is Dani doing?' Kelly asked, switching the TV off. 'I lost track of her once we got back to the police station. There was so much going on.'

'She's doing great,' Rosa replied. 'She is very anxious to thank you, Kelly. She knows you saved her life.'

'Me, and a lot of other people,' Kelly replied. 'There will be lots of time for that when we get back to the States. I'm going to be here for a few days dealing with formalities. When is Dani going back?'

'They are keeping her at Addenbrooke's hospital today and overnight for observation,' Rosa said. 'She's absolutely fine, but you know what doctors are like. They want to run a few tests. But by the time I handed her over to the nurses she was almost back to her old self. I didn't ask her any questions. I wanted to let her talk about it in her own time. But she said she wasn't badly treated. She said that, in some ways, Kali and Samir seemed very opposed to violence and causing harm.'

'They have quite a way of showing it!' Kelly commented.

'Kali told her they were selected by their group only if they understood that violence was to be abhorred and practiced only when unavoidable,' Rosa replied. 'Don't ask me to explain that.'

She raised her glass towards Kelly as a toast, and took a long drink.

'The thing which seems to have upset her most was Bev being shot.'

Kelly snorted. 'Bev was up to his neck in it, wasn't he?' she asked.

'She didn't see it like that,' Rosa replied. 'Dani says he was very conflicted. She really liked him. And he did try to save her, Kelly.'

'That's true,' Kelly admitted.

They were silent for a time.

'I will be traveling back to the States with her,' Rosa continued. 'The President has arranged for a private jet out of Mildenhall Air Force base. We will leave as soon as Addenbrooke's signs off on her.'

She paused.

'I will hand her back to the President with my letter of resignation.'

Kelly put her glass down on the small table beside her chair.

'There's really no need for that, Rosa.'

Immediately tears appeared in Rosa's eyes.

'She went missing on my watch, Kelly.'

'No one blames you. You followed the protocol everyone agreed to. There was no way you could have prevented it.'

Rosa's head sank.

'It doesn't matter, does it? Every time some newspaper, or magazine, or TV show mentions the Dani Ryan kidnapping, every time some student Googles the story to research an assignment, my name will come up as the agent on duty. There is no place for me to hide. At least, if I resign, I will be taking responsibility. I may get some credit for that.'

Kelly left her seat and knelt by Rosa's chair. She took her hand.

'Rosa, some agent is always on duty when things happen,' she said. 'Agents were on duty when Kennedy was shot, when Reagan was shot. Sometimes, there is nothing you can do. In this case, you did everything you could. It wasn't predictable. And the good news is, we got her back. And you were part of that, too.'

'I appreciate your saying that, Kelly,' Rosa said. She had taken a handkerchief from her sleeve and was wiping away tears.

'You're going to hear the same thing from your Director,' Kelly said, 'and from the President.'

'It's what I'm telling myself that matters most,' Rosa replied.

Kelly squeezed her hand.

'I'd like to tell you about something that happened to me. May I?'

Rosa looked up and nodded.

'Before I became Ted Lazenby's Personal Assistant at the Bureau, I was a field agent in the New York office. I volunteered for an undercover assignment in a factory in the Bronx. The place was outwardly respectable, but in fact it was a front for two Mafia families who were using it to run all kinds of contraband. My assignment was to find evidence of what was really going on, and then get out. I got the evidence, but I got greedy. I just knew there was more I could find, evidence that could implicate some more senior mob figures. I stayed in when I should have got out. My cover was blown. I had to shoot my way out. I called for back-up, and two agents, Joe and Tina, who were good friends of mine, came to my aid. They both died in the fire fight. I got out.'

'My God,' Rosa whispered.

'I blame myself to this day,' Kelly said. 'Lazenby told me, everyone told me, that it wasn't my fault, that I was just doing my job. They sent me on leave for four months, but it wasn't helping. Then, Lazenby brought me back and offered me the job as his Personal Assistant. I was all ready to quit. But something told me I had to keep going. I know it's never going to go away entirely, Rosa. I still get nightmares about it. But ultimately, there's nothing I can do. I have to move on. You have to do your job, and when you do your job, sometimes things go wrong, and you have to live with it. That's how it will be for you, too. I know it seems like the end of the world right now. But I promise you, in time you will have a different perspective on it. Take some time. Go away for a while.'

Rosa returned the squeeze of the hand.

'Thank you,' she said.

'Will you think about it, at least?'

Rosa stood.

'Yes, I will,' she replied. 'I will think about it.'

'And you will take some time? Frankly, I don't think Director Solari will give you much choice about that anyway.'

Rosa smiled.

'No. I'm sure you're right about that. I'd already decided, anyway. I'm going back to New Mexico for a while. That's where I'm from. And that's another complication.'

'Oh?'

'Yes. Steve Macmillan said he has always wanted to see Santa Fe and Taos. He said he might drop in.'

Kelly laughed out loud.

'No kidding?'

Rosa smiled weakly. 'As if I needed that in my life right now.'

'Maybe he just wants to see Santa Fe and Taos,' Kelly said.

'Yeah, maybe.'

'So, give him the guided tour,' Kelly said. 'It might be fun, and you look like you could use a little fun. What do you have to lose?'

61

July 2

DANI RAN HAPPILY into the kitchen. She kissed Ellen, who was seated at the table with a glass of wine, then Kay, who was tossing a salad at the worktop. She picked up a small spoon Kay had left by the salad bowl, reached in and took a little of the salad dressing to taste.

'Mmm,' she said. 'Delicious. You would not believe how good it feels to taste something as simple as salad dressing again. Dad says "hi", by the way.'

A doctor had been checking on Dani each day since her return home, and Kay had been watching her every move. A counsellor had called, and Dani had willingly taken the opportunity to talk to her, but she was well physically, and mentally, she seemed calm and composed. Mostly, she was glad to be home and to have put the nightmare behind her. Ellen and Kay had not questioned her in detail about her experience. There were plans for the Secret Service to debrief her, but Abe Solari had indicated that he would do so personally, and he had left the timing up to Kay. They had decided simply to keep the conversation at home as close to normal as possible. But if Dani raised the subject, they would try to respond naturally.

Ellen smiled. 'Was your diet a bit monotonous?' she asked.

Dani smiled back. 'No,' she replied. 'It wasn't monotonous. That's what surprised me, because it was mostly Indian food. They gave me eggs and coffee for breakfast, but for the rest of the day it was all Indian. I haven't had much experience with Indian food, but before, I always had the impression that it was all covered with the same spicy brown sauce and tasted the same.'

She seized a piece of lettuce and devoured it.

'But it's not. Kali cooked for us, and she made something different every day. It always tasted fresh. Sometimes it was really spicy and sometimes it was quite mild. Sometimes we had Indian bread, sometimes rice.'

'She looked after you,' Kay said thoughtfully. 'At least as far as food was concerned.'

'Yes,' Dani replied. 'She did. She seemed to enjoy cooking. She would eat with me quite often, instead of going back up to eat with Samir. I don't think she and Samir got on very well. She would tell me what the dishes were, and how they were prepared. She even told me about how she learned to cook. Her grandmother taught her in India. She showed her how to grind the spices, how to mix the herbs and spices, how to prepare the dough for the bread. She talked a lot about her grandmother. Never about her parents, though. I got the impression that something bad had happened there. I asked her once, but she shut down. She wouldn't talk about them at all. Only her grandmother.'

'It sounds like she was trying to get to know you,' Ellen said. 'Did she ask you questions about your life?'

'About my childhood, yes,' Dani replied. 'About you guys; how you met; what you were like; what it was like living in the White House; what it was like to go to college in America; why I was studying law; why I had an interest in international criminal law. That was a big thing. What is a war crime? Is there any difference between combatants and civilians in today's wars? Is there a difference between oppressors and freedom fighters? Do international courts take into account your motivation, what you are trying to achieve? But the questions always seemed personal. She seemed genuinely interested in what I thought, and the strange thing was, I never detected any hostility. And it wasn't all one-way. She told me some things about herself. She told me she had studied Indian music and classical dance. She would have liked to teach it.'

Dani looked down towards Ellen.

'I know this is going to sound really weird. But in other

circumstances, I think we could have been friends; maybe good friends.'

'Don't forget that she had every intention of killing you,' Kay said.

'That's another weird thing,' Dani replied. 'I know she would have. But I felt that she didn't want to harm me; that she was hoping it wouldn't be necessary.'

Dani shook her head.

'I'm not sure why I feel that way. It wasn't really anything she said. She had a gun trained on me every time she unchained me so I could take a shower. I have no doubt that she would have used it if I had tried to escape. But there was just something about the way she dealt with me. I don't know.'

She paused.

'Ellen, what's going to happen to Samir?'

Ellen smiled. 'Is he your friend, too?'

Dani shuddered. 'No. He gave me the creeps. But I think he had the same effect on Kali.'

'The British will try him for the offences he committed there,' Ellen said. 'So far, that amounts to two murders and a kidnapping. When they are through with him they will probably extradite him back to India. I think that ought to take care of him. I told Justice I didn't see any point in bringing him over here. But you may be needed to give evidence against him.'

'I am fine with that.'

Kay served the salad and poured more wine. They started dinner.

'The Indian boy, the student – Bev Prasad. What did you make of him?' Ellen asked. 'The Secret Service vetted him before you left for Cambridge and found nothing. But after you disappeared, the FBI in Houston interviewed his family and his girlfriend. They concluded, and it seems clear now, that he was a sleeper, that his family had been planted in Houston years ago by SK. What impression did he give you?'

Dani put down her knife and fork and thought for some time.

'It's OK,' Ellen said. 'If you don't want to talk about him ...'

'No. It's not that,' Dani replied. 'I've thought about him a lot. I liked him, and I think he liked me. I feel sad for him, because the only way I can make sense of it is that he was totally messed up in the head. He didn't know who he was. He didn't know whether he was American or Kashmiri; whether he was a law student or an agent of SK. He was one person out in the world with his friends, and was suddenly told that the role he was expected to play was another person entirely. If they had come to him in five years' time, if he could have moved away from home, maybe got married to his girlfriend, I think it might have been different. But what disturbs me, Ellen, is that I don't know that for sure. On one level he was horrified by what was going on, but on another level he had some sympathy for what they were doing, or at least for their reason for doing it.'

She paused.

'But I do believe that underneath it all, he was a thoroughly decent guy. And I can't help feeling that if he could just have got out from under all the crap, he would have been OK.'

Kay cleared away the salad plates. She already had water on the boil for the pasta. She threw the pasta in, gave it two minutes, drained it and added a cream sauce with smoked salmon and black pepper. She took bread out of the oven. Ellen refilled the wine glasses.

'This is wonderful,' Dani smiled appreciatively.

'No Indian food for a while,' Kay returned the smile. 'I promise. Not that I know how to cook Indian, anyway.'

She put down her fork for a moment, her eyes filling.

'You have no idea how good it is to have you back, Dani.'

'And it is so good to be back,' Dani replied. 'I know it must have been terrible for you, not knowing how I was. I know they sent you those two videos but, even so, I know it was tough.'

Kay paused in the act of picking up her fork.

'Two videos?' she asked. 'I only saw one video.'

She looked across the table at Ellen. Ellen felt her stomach tighten. The feelings of nausea had largely subsided after Kay had left for England, and since Dani's return she had been free of them. Now they threatened to return.

'I made two recordings,' Dani was saying. 'I don't know how many they sent. Maybe they only used the one.'

'They did send a second one,' Ellen replied quietly. 'I couldn't show it to you, Kay. It confirmed that Dani was alive and had not been harmed. But I couldn't show it to you.'

Kay put the fork down.

'What? Why not?'

Ellen exhaled heavily and set down her own fork. She took a sip of water before replying.

'The text they gave Dani to read said something I couldn't share with you.'

Kay was silent for some time.

'Something you couldn't share with me, with her mother? I don't understand.'

'Please try to understand, Kay. We were trying to manage a very complicated situation. There were certain things we dared not let out of the crisis committee. We were ...'

'No,' Kay said. 'I'm Dani's mother. I was right here in the White House. I wasn't going to talk about anything to anyone. Didn't you trust me? Is that it?'

'Mom...' Dani said quietly.

'No, I want an answer, Ellen. Is it that you didn't trust me? You couldn't tell me that Dani was alive and well because you didn't trust me?'

'No,' Ellen protested.

'Well, what then? What made it so secret that I couldn't even see a video of Dani? You showed me the first one, and it was just as well you did, wasn't it?'

'Mom, leave it, please.' Dani's voice was anxious. 'I'm sure Ellen had a good reason for doing whatever she did. And it worked. I'm back home, safe.'

'The second video was sent together with the second ransom demand,' Ellen said quietly. 'The real ransom demand.'

Kay and Dani sat back in their chairs, silent.

'What real demand?' Kay asked eventually. 'They were asking for ... Are you telling me that the demand for the plans for the drone was ...?'

'It was a cover,' Ellen said. 'SK didn't want to draw attention to what they really wanted. They told us to run with the drone as a cover story. They made it clear that they would kill Dani if there was any publicity about the real demand. And it was a demand which we couldn't have made public anyway.'

Ellen stopped.

'Well, are you going to tell us?' Kay asked.

'Yes,' Ellen replied. 'I was always going to tell you. I thought it best to allow some time to go by before doing so, so that we could all get some distance on it. But now that it has come up …

She paused and drank some wine.

'SK asked the United States to assassinate the Prime Minister of India while he was on a tour of military installations in Kashmir, and to make it look as though the Pakistanis had done it. Their intention was to ignite a new conflict in the region between India and Pakistan.'

'My God,' Dani breathed, aghast. Ellen watched some of the color drain from her face, as the implications of what she had said became clear.

'But you wouldn't … you couldn't do that…'

Ellen nodded.

'No, Dani, I couldn't have done it.'

The silence was total.

'So, you wouldn't even have thought about it?' Kay asked. 'Not even to save Dani?'

'Kay, there was no real guarantee that it would have saved Dani,' Ellen replied. 'And even if there were, I couldn't do it. I mean that personally. But also, as President, I could not order the assassination of the prime minister of a friendly state, especially when it might have provoked a nuclear war.'

She paused.

'It wasn't that I didn't think about it. I did. I thought about it a lot. I forced my mind to contemplate it. I summoned up all my demons, believe me, Kay, I searched the very depths of my soul. If I could have given my own life for Dani I wouldn't have hesitated. But to take another innocent life in exchange for hers was different. I couldn't do it. I'm sorry, Dani.'

Dani stood slowly, walked around the table to Ellen, and embraced her.

'You were right,' she said. 'You couldn't have done it. I wouldn't have asked you to do it.'

'That's why I didn't tell you, Kay,' Ellen said. 'As things stood, you believed that we were negotiating our way out of the situation. You had hope. I couldn't take that hope away. It would have crushed you. You weren't strong enough. I wasn't strong enough.'

Kay stood.

'I'm sure I will come to terms with this, Ellen,' she said. 'But right now, I'm angry. I trusted you to do the right thing. I knew there was no guarantee that you could get Dani back. But I trusted you to do your best, and I believed that you would. I know it's wrong of me to be angry. I will get over it. But not tonight. If you will excuse me, I need to be alone for a while.'

Dani was kneeling on the floor, holding Ellen's hands.

'Sit down for a moment, Kay,' Ellen said quietly. 'There's something else I have to tell you.'

Kay sat, slowly, reluctantly.

'I'm telling you this because I have to, for my own peace of mind. You would never have found out, because there are very few people who know, and they would never talk about it. But, now that we are having this all out in the open, I would prefer that you hear the whole truth.'

She closed her eyes.

'It appeared that I remained in charge of the situation throughout. It had to appear that way. One of the demands SK made was that I must not hand over power to Ted Lazenby or anyone else. But I couldn't remain in charge, Kay. I felt I had no choice. That was clear even before we received the real demand. I had a conflict of interest a mile wide. Getting Dani back might have compromised a vital national interest. As President, it was my duty not to let that happen. I couldn't hand over formally. But I gave an undertaking that Ted would make the decisions and that I would not countermand any decisions he took. I could have as much input as I wished. But I would not countermand them, and I would announce and defend them in public as if they were my own decisions. It was the only thing we could do.'

Kay recoiled as if she had been hit in the face.

'We discussed that,' she shouted angrily. 'You explained the conflict of interest to me. Then you promised me you would remain in charge.'

'I know.'

'You lied to me.'

'The President lied to you.'

'You deceived me.'

'Kay, you know me. You know that I am an honest person by nature. I myself have never lied to you. But as President ...'

'No, Ellen, this was not about the presidency. You lied to me.'

'The President had to lie to you. I felt sick about it. I still do.'

Kay paused.

'You handed Dani's life over to Ted Lazenby without telling me. My daughter ...'

'It made no difference, Kay,' Ellen said. 'When the real demand came, Ted and I sat down and talked about it. He took exactly the same view as I did. He wouldn't have done it. I wouldn't have done it. It made no difference at all.'

Dani stood, walked to her mother and put her arms around her.

'Mom, please. I'm here. I'm safe. I haven't been harmed. All I need now is to be with my family. Please don't be mad at Ellen. I understand what she did. And I understand why she couldn't do any more. She was right. Let it drop, OK? Please?'

'It has made a difference, Ellen,' Kay said. 'I trusted you. I knew you didn't have a magic wand to wave to bring Dani back. But I trusted you to at least tell me the truth. I feel betrayed. And I don't know how to deal with it. Honesty has always been what we are about. Even before we came out, we always agreed we would tell the truth – to each other and to Dani. I don't know how to deal with this.'

'Mom...' Dani said quietly.

But Kay was making her way out of the kitchen.

62

WHEN ELLEN ENTERED the bedroom a few minutes later, Dani having volunteered to clear away after dinner, Kay was packing a few personal things into a small carrying case.

Ellen put a hand over hers as she was placing a nightgown on top of the other items

'Come on, Kay. What are you doing? We are going to get past this. After all we've been through together?'

Kay looked up.

'I need some time, Ellen, and I need some space. It would be best for me to be alone for a while.'

'Kay, Dani needs us to be together right now. She's still recovering. If not for me, for her, stay, please. I promise I will give you space and time, and I will be here to talk when you are ready to talk. If you need to use another bedroom, that's fine. But don't leave. Please.'

Kay withdrew the nightdress. She sat on the bed and thought for some time.

'All right. I'll try to work it out here,' she said. 'I don't know whether I can. But I will try.'

'Thank you,' Ellen said.

Kay looked up at her.

'I'm not ending it, Ellen.' she said. 'Not tonight. Maybe not at all. But it can't be the same any more. I need to think about that. So do you.'

* * *

Later, in the early hours, Ellen went alone to the Oval Office and sat silently at her desk in the dim light. There was another press conference to deal with the next morning, and the daily business of being President to resume. She could do nothing about her relationship with Kay for now. One of the endless waiting periods of her life had ended, and another was beginning – waiting for resolution; for certainty; for liberation. Alone. Another test of resolve.

'As with Kashmir,' she thought, 'so with all of us.'